Corrupt CROWN

Copyright © 2024 Pamela O'Rourke

All rights reserved. No part of this book may be reproduced in any form or by any electronic or mechanical means, including information storage and retrieval systems, without written permission from the author, except for the use of brief quotations in a book review.

This book is a work of fiction. All names, characters, locations, and incidents are products of the author's imagination or used in a fictitious manner. Any resemblance to actual persons, living or dead, or actual events is purely coincidental.

Cover Design: Coffin Print Designs
Editing: Mackenzie Letson

"Behind every strong woman is a story that gave her no other choice."

- Nakeia Homer

DEDICATION

*For everyone who's come out stronger
on the other side.*

May the fire within you continue to burn brighter than any that may surround you.

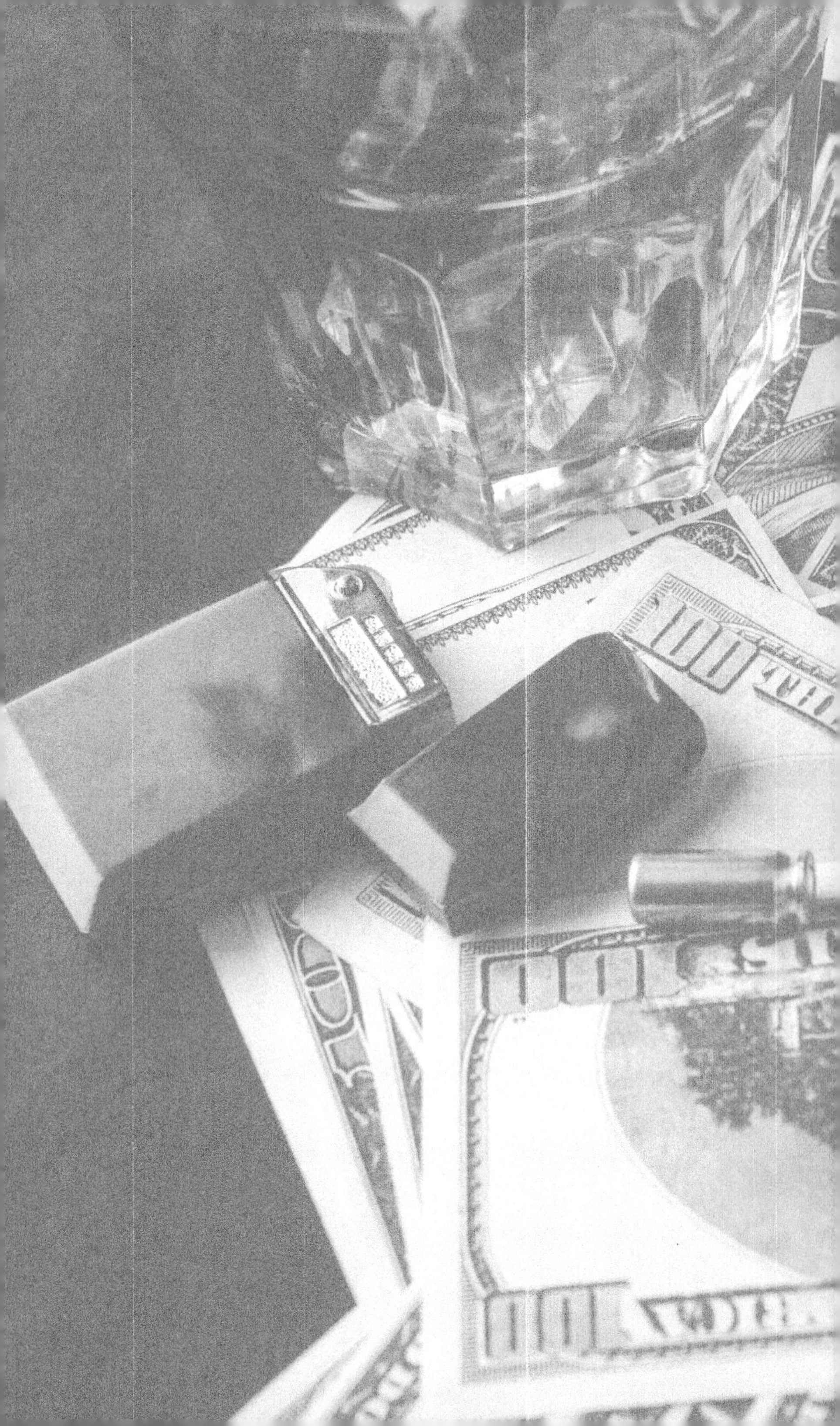

CONTENT WARNING

Violence
Graphic Sex Scenes
Graphic Rape
Physical Assault/Abuse
On-Page Death
Murder
Gun Violence
Profanities
Kidnapping
Torture
Mention of Human Trafficking
Blood/Gore
Branding
Emotional Abuse
PTSD

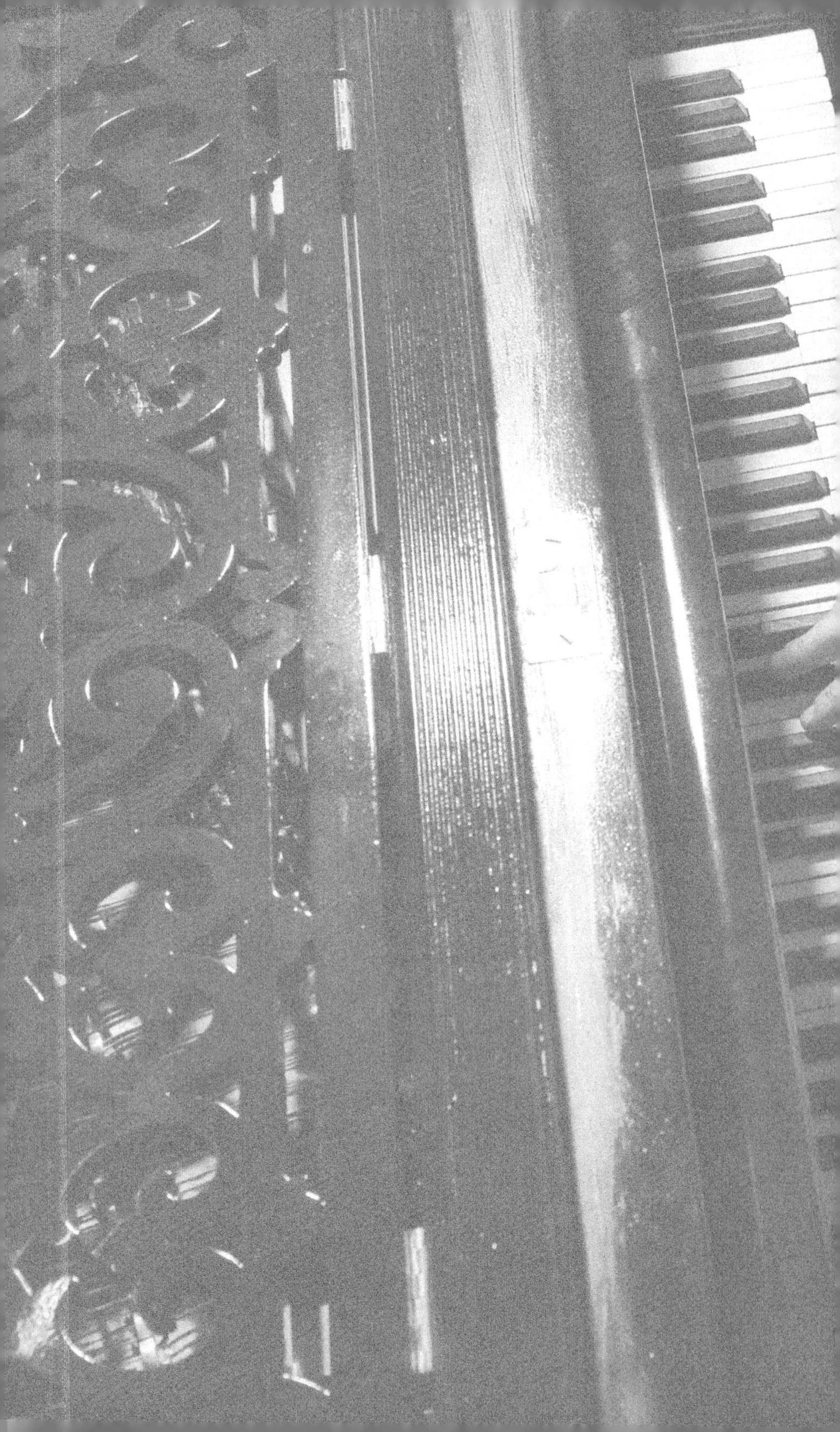

PLAYLIST

You Say – Lauren Daigle
Middle of the Night – Elley Duhé
Tattoo – Loreen
Daylight – David Kushner
Rescue – Lauren Daigle
Infinity – Jaymes Young
Make Me Feel – Elvis Drew
Cosmic Love – Florence & The Machine
Moonlight Sonata – Beethoven

BECKY & VITO'S SICILIAN DICTIONARY

As this book, and the series as a whole, takes place primarily in Sicily, I wanted to be as authentic as possible in my translations. Thanks to my beautiful friend, Becky, and her amazing husband, Vito, this dictionary provides an accurate translation of all the Sicilian used by the characters throughout Corrupt Crown.

TITLES/NAMES:
Zio – Uncle
Fratello – Brother
Principessa – Princess
Signor – Mister
Signore – Sir
Signorina – Miss
Matrigna – Stepmother
Stellina – Little Star
Coniglietta – Bunny
Signor Alto, Scuro, e Bello – Mr. Tall, Dark and Handsome
Tesoro – Sweetheart/darling

EXPLETITIVES/INSULTS

Minchia – Shit/For fuck's sake/Balls etc
Mia piccola puttana – My little whore
Bastardo – Bastard
Santo Cristo! – Jesus Christ!
Stronzo – Asshole
Puttana – Whore
Figlio di puttana – Son of a bitch
Cacare! – Shit!
Muovi il culo – Move your ass

TALK DIRTY TO ME

"*Mia brava ragazza.*" – My good girl
"*Baciami.*" – Kiss me.
"*Bedda mia.*" – My beautiful one.
"*Fai l'amore con me.*" – Make love to me.
"*Così stretta.*" – So tight.
"*Così fottutamente bagnata.*" – So fucking wet.

SENTENCES/STATEMENTS

"*Nessune.*" – None.
"*Grazie, amico mio.*" – Thank you, my friend.
"*Vieni ca.*" – Come here.
"*Ci vediamo domani.*" – See you tomorrow.
"*Capisti?*" – You understand?
"*Ti capisco.*" – I understand you.
"*Il diavolo incarnato.*" – The devil incarnate.
"*Ti amo.*" – I love you.
"*Ti amerò per sempre.*" – I will love you forever.
"*Ti amo così tanto.*" – I love you so much
"*Perfetta.*" – Perfect.
"*Sempre e per sempre.*" – Always and forever.
"*Velocemente.*" – Quickly.
"*Benvenuti a...*" – Welcome to...

"Benvenuto a casa mia." – Welcome to my home.
"Mi scusi." – Excuse me.
"Sei seduto al mio posto." – You're sitting in my seat.
"Non parlo Italiano." – I don't speak Italian.
"Moviti!" – Move!
"Lasciaci." – Leave us.
"Ti salvero." – I will save you.
"Non moviti!" – Don't move.
"Posso prendere il suo ordine?" – May I take your order?
Prendiamo uno di tutto." – Let's have one of everything.
"Uno di tutto sul menu?" – One of everything on the menu?
"Si. E non mi piace aspettare." – Yes. And I don't like waiting.
"Cosa succede quando esprimi un desiderio su una stella?" – What happens when you wish on a star?
"Possa riposare in pace." – May she rest in peace.
"Mangia." – Eat.
"Ti richiamero tra cinque minuti, va bene?" – I'll call you back in five minutes, okay?
"Corretto?" – Correct?
"Te lo prometto." – I promise you.
"Un momento, per favore." – One moment please.
"Va bene." – Okay.
"Aspetta un momento." – Wait a moment.
"Lo giuro sulla mia vita." – I swear on my life.

THE FIVE FAMILIES

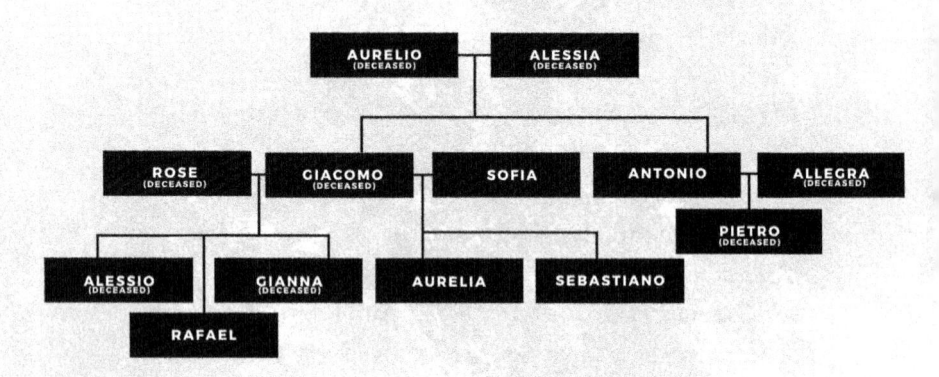

Caruso

- **AURELIO** (DECEASED) — **ALESSIA** (DECEASED)
  - **ROSE** (DECEASED) — **GIACOMO** (DECEASED)
    - **ALESSIO** (DECEASED)
    - **GIANNA** (DECEASED)
      - **RAFAEL**
  - **SOFIA**
    - **AURELIA**
    - **SEBASTIANO**
  - **ANTONIO**
    - **PIETRO** (DECEASED)
  - **ALLEGRA** (DECEASED)

Salvatore

- **LEONARDO** (DECEASED) — **GIOVANNA** (DECEASED)
  - **BENITO** — **LUCIANA**
    - **CATALINA** — **VINCENZO**
      - **SIENNA**
    - **GABRIELA**
    - **LILIANA**

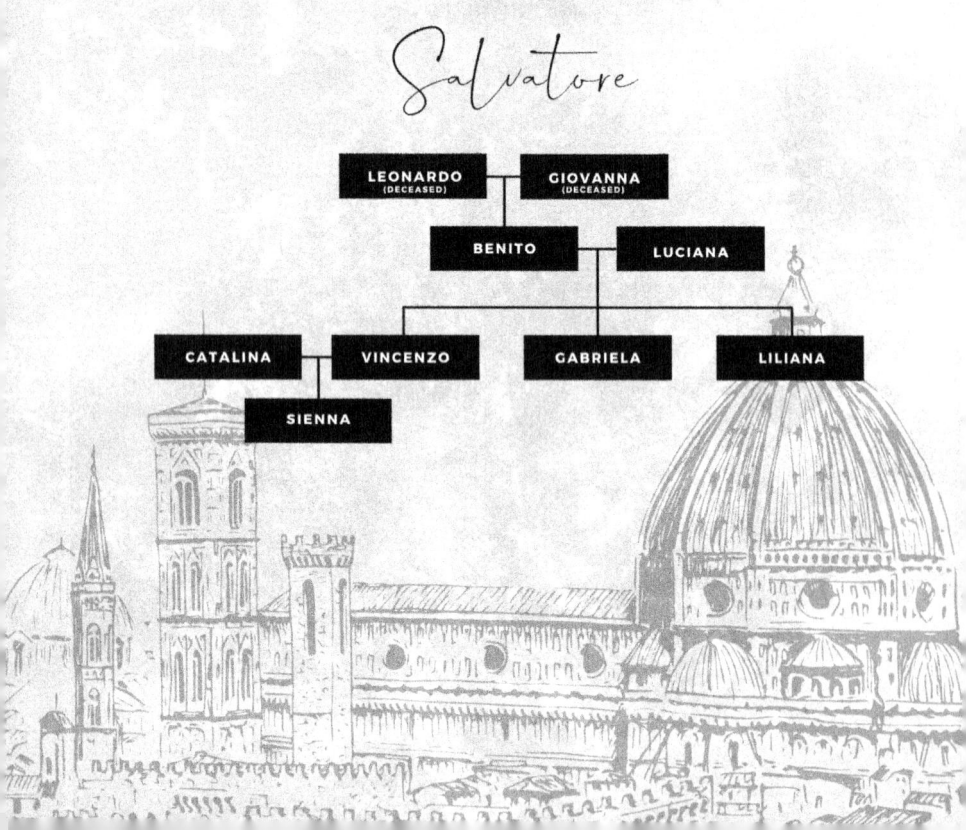

De Marco

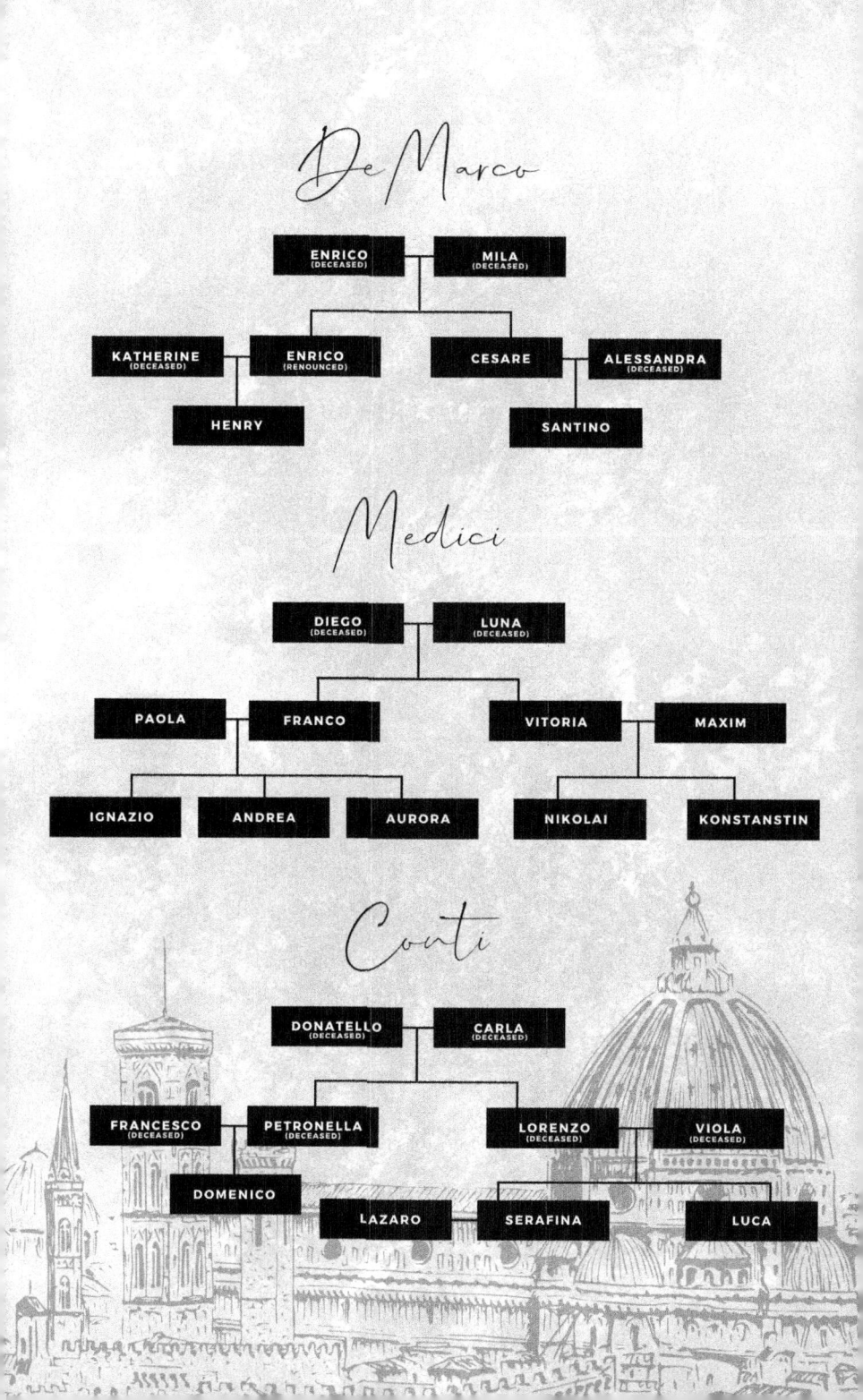

- **Enrico** (Deceased) — **Mila** (Deceased)
  - **Katherine** (Deceased) — **Enrico** (Renounced)
    - Henry
  - **Cesare** — **Alessandra** (Deceased)
    - Santino

Medici

- **Diego** (Deceased) — **Luna** (Deceased)
  - **Paola** — **Franco**
    - Ignazio
    - Andrea
    - Aurora
  - **Vitoria** — **Maxim**
    - Nikolai
    - Konstanstin

Conti

- **Donatello** (Deceased) — **Carla** (Deceased)
  - **Francesco** (Deceased) — **Petronella** (Deceased)
    - Domenico
  - **Lorenzo** — **Viola** (Deceased)
    - Lazaro
    - Serafina
    - Luca

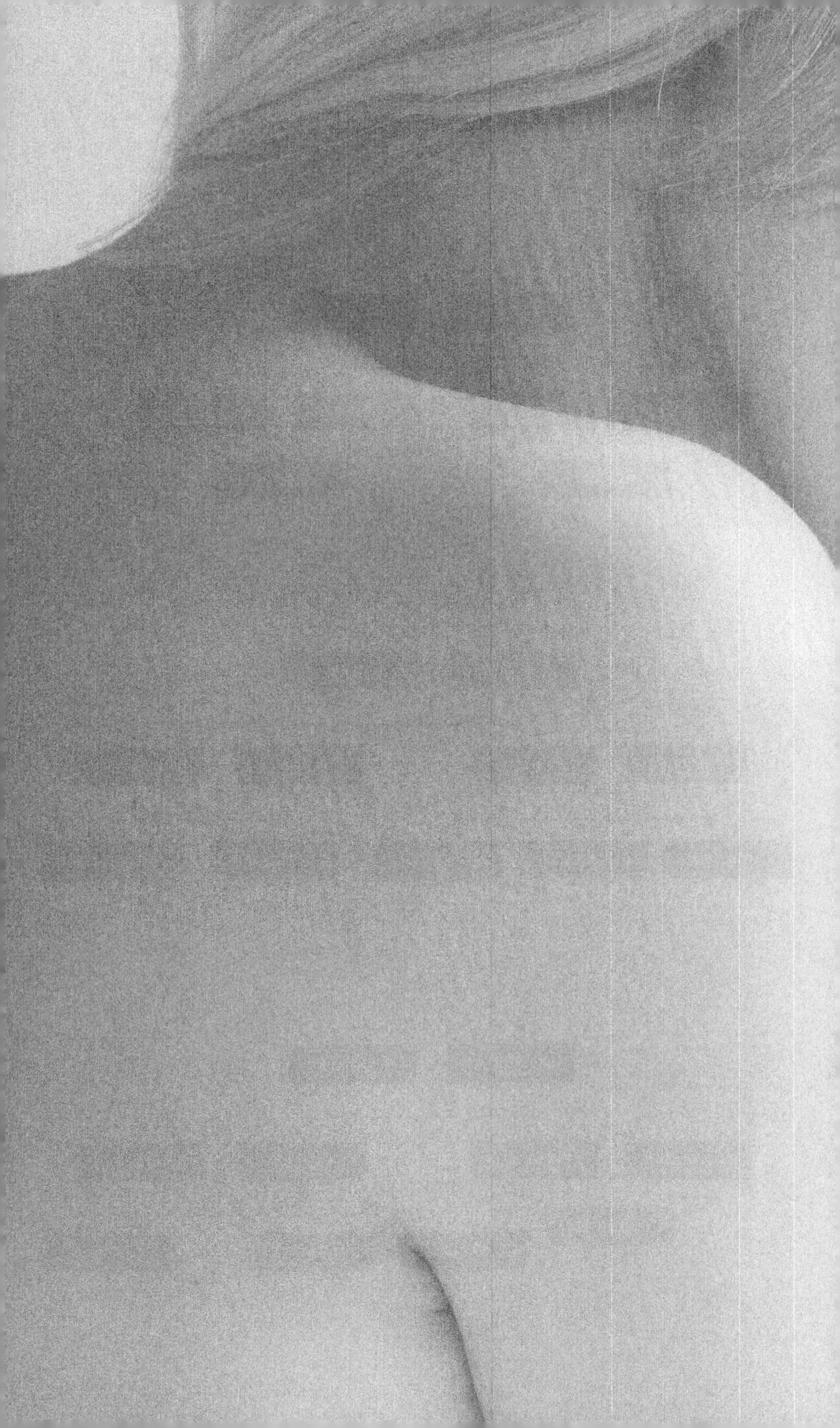

PROLOGUE
ELODIE

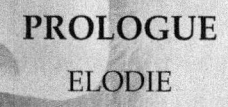

Four Years Ago – Age 20
South Brook, New York

I press my palm against my stomach in an attempt to subdue the rising nausea.

Do what he says, or you know who'll pay the price, Elodie.

My mother's words reverberate inside my mind on a near-constant loop while the severity of her features as she uttered them fills my vision. Her icy-blue eyes held nothing but disdain, a sentiment I am exceptionally familiar with inside these walls.

Walls that have seen too much hate and known too little love.

Walls that have taught me there's nothing to gain by being bitter. After all, if life gives you lemons, you can always make some fucking lemonade.

An embittered laugh tumbles from my mouth, and I swallow as I recall the calculated malice that had oozed from every syllable that left my mother's carefully glossed lips.

You know who'll pay the price, Elodie.

At that, I blow out a steadying breath because I know *precisely* who'll pay.

With that thought at the forefront of my mind, I square my shoulders, tossing my long blonde locks back right as there's a soft knock on my bedroom door.

"Come in." My words sound hollow even to my own ears, and I huff in exasperation, knowing I can do much better than that.

Cleo, the household manager, pokes her more-salt-than-pepper head around the door frame with an easy smile.

"Miss Elodie, the guests are arriving. Your mother has requested your presence in the foyer."

I smile brightly, forcing a lightness I don't feel. I'm getting better at it as the years have passed. Most people don't see the lies behind the smiles.

My goal is that *no one* sees.

So, I inject my tone with enthusiasm. "Thank you, Cleo. I'll be right down."

She nods once, leaving the door slightly ajar as she departs. Keeping my smile plastered to my face, I carefully adjust my jewelry and check my soft nude lips in the mirror before following her.

"Ellie! Come play with me."

An exaggerated whisper from behind makes me chuckle as I glance back to see three-year-old Skye watching through the banister spindles.

"Later, Curly Fry."

I blow her a kiss, making her laugh uproariously, and witnessing her blissful innocence makes my heart feel lighter in my chest.

Shoulders back. Head up. Smile on. You got this, Rivers.

Skye's nanny plucks her from the floor to cart her back to the nursery, as I face forward once more. I steel myself for whatever my father has planned for tonight, locking a smile in place as I begin my ascent to the ground floor.

An early celebration of my twenty-first birthday. I can barely stifle an eye roll at the sheer absurdity.

My family only cares about the aesthetics. How things look. How the Rivers family is perceived.

A birthday party isn't a way to show they care. It's an excuse to show off how seemingly perfect our lives are.

To cover the rot that permeates the core of our family.

As I reach the ground floor, I falter, noticing Father's business partner, Jeremy Danvers, cutting through the crowd, clearly intent on monopolizing my time.

No, no, no, no.

I glance across the gathering, gaze searching, until I spot my mother by the front door, kissing cheeks and welcoming the crème de la crème of New York society to our not-so-humble abode.

Sporting thirteen bedrooms and fifteen bathrooms, a five-car garage, a pool house, an Olympic-sized swimming pool, and a home theatre, our house in South Brook is excessive, even by Hamptons standards.

I'm about to make my way closer, intent on avoiding Jeremy but also well aware that my place is by her side, greeting our guests, when my father's voice cuts through the room like a whip.

"Elodie-Claire. My office. *Immediately.*"

My father, Warren Rivers, financial advisor to the disgustingly wealthy, isn't one to mince words, something that just about every person present is aware of, hence why his bark is met with not so much as a glance in his general direction.

I follow him slowly as my thoughts race, wondering what I'm about to face until I arrive outside the wide teak door of his home office. Before I can lift my hand to knock, the door is ripped open by a tall man in an impeccably tailored navy-blue suit.

He's almost a full head taller than me, and I need to strain my neck to look up at him.

The first thing I note are the intricate circular tattoos covering the backs of both his hands and peeking up the side of his starched white shirt collar.

My eyes travel to his chiseled, clean-shaven face, and my stomach dips when a hint of a smirk plays at the corners of his full lips. Appreciation fills his deep blue eyes as he takes a long moment to peruse my face.

I take a beat to do the same, focusing on eyes that betray nothing as he watches me watching him.

Suddenly, he glances over his shoulder, and my eyes follow his line of vision as I step over the threshold, right into the lion's den, closing the door firmly behind me.

"You never said your daughter was…"

The stranger trails off, facing me with a decidedly predatorial look this time. He brings his hand up between us, brushing the back of his knuckles over my cheek before sighing exaggeratedly. "She's…fucking *exquisite*, Warren."

His eyes darken and quicken my pulse. "The face that launched a thousand ships."

Then he leans closer until his mouth rests by my ear. "You'll be the Conti family's very own Helen of Troy, baby girl."

My cheeks heat, and my breaths come in short bursts as he steps back to hold my gaze for long moments. Without warning, he severs the connection between us to pivot on his heel and march right up to my father's desk. His hand shoots out, gripping Father's jowly neck in his large palm, and I barely stifle a gasp of shock.

"You're one lucky motherfucker, Rivers," he hisses in my father's face, his once handsome features now a monstrous parody of moments before. "If you and your piece-of-shit son weren't so good at cleaning my family's money, you'd both be paying a far steeper price, let me assure you."

Then he shoves my father away, leaving him coughing and spluttering as he glances back in my direction to give me the once-over. "Virgin?"

I can only blink as I swallow nervously, opting to shake my head lest my voice wobble and betray me.

He shrugs. "Pity." Though a slow smile blooms on his face, lending a lightness to his impenetrable gaze. "I'll have fun breaking you in, all the same, baby girl."

I barely manage to suppress a shudder when fear trickles down my spine, but I keep my face impassive as I hold his eyes. Whatever he sees in my face seems to please him, and he nods in silent satisfaction.

Opening the door that leads onto the terrace outside, he pins my panting father with a stare.

"The paperwork will be delivered later today. I'll expect my demands to be followed to the goddamn letter, Warren. No fucking funny business."

And then he's gone, silence following in his wake for long moments.

My heart is racing as I try to make sense of what's just happened when the office door opens to admit my mother.

"I saw him leave, Warren. What happened—"

Having collected himself somewhat, my father cuts her off with a bark. "It's done, Cressida. He's accepted...our *offer*."

My blood runs cold as his eyes flicker to mine for a beat, something like an apology passing across his face before he looks back to my mother.

I follow his line of sight, finding my mother exhaling heavily with relief, her ice-queen features softening in a way they never usually do in my presence.

"And Evan? He's safe? The investments are repaid..."

Father nods once as he expels a breath. "The paperwork is

already en route, I would imagine. He seemed quite taken with Elodie, thank God."

Mother snorts cruelly. "Heavens knows why."

Then she looks me up and down, those piercing blue eyes not holding a hint of warmth when she openly finds me as lacking as she has on every other day of my existence.

Having never been made aware as to *why* she maintains such a strong dislike for me, I've come to accept our relationship as perfunctory at best.

My indifferent gaze moves past her to my father as he types a message on his cell. Though my father tends to ignore my presence for the most part, he's never been cruel.

"I'm afraid I don't understand, Father. Who was that man?"

He glances up mid-text with a small shrug. "His father is the head of the Conti organized crime syndicate in New York City. Domenico was here today to clear up a…slight misunderstanding involving Evan and myself."

His cell rings before he can elaborate. "Evan, my boy…" He holds up a quelling hand when I open my mouth to speak again before he turns to walk out onto the terrace, taking the call with his golden child in privacy.

Evan, my senior by three years, works remotely as he travels the world on our father's money. He's only been given his role at the company because it was expected, not because he was particularly *capable*.

And that same incompetence appears to be the reason this stranger's interest in me is something to be celebrated.

A shiver runs the length and breadth of my body as I face my mother to ask the inevitable question. "And why do you want him to be *interested* in me?"

With a loud tut, she grips my upper arm with force. "Don't be so fucking obtuse, Elodie. All you need to know is that your brother got in over his head, and today—for the first time in your miserable life—you're able to do something worthwhile for this family."

She leans closer, and though internally I plead with the universe to make it stop, I'm no stranger to knowing my place.

After all, despite everything else that's happened, I've been raised to be the perfect little Stepford wife.

"You'll belong to Domenico and the Conti family for as long as they wish. You'll do whatever they demand of you."

My face falls as my heart ricochets beneath my breastbone, and her voice drops to a low snarl, repeating those words from earlier that have now taken on a whole new meaning.

"Do what he says, or you know who'll pay the price, Elodie."

I blink once, then twice, pushing all other thoughts out of my head as I nod slowly, forcing my lips upward in a vacant smile. "Of course, Mother."

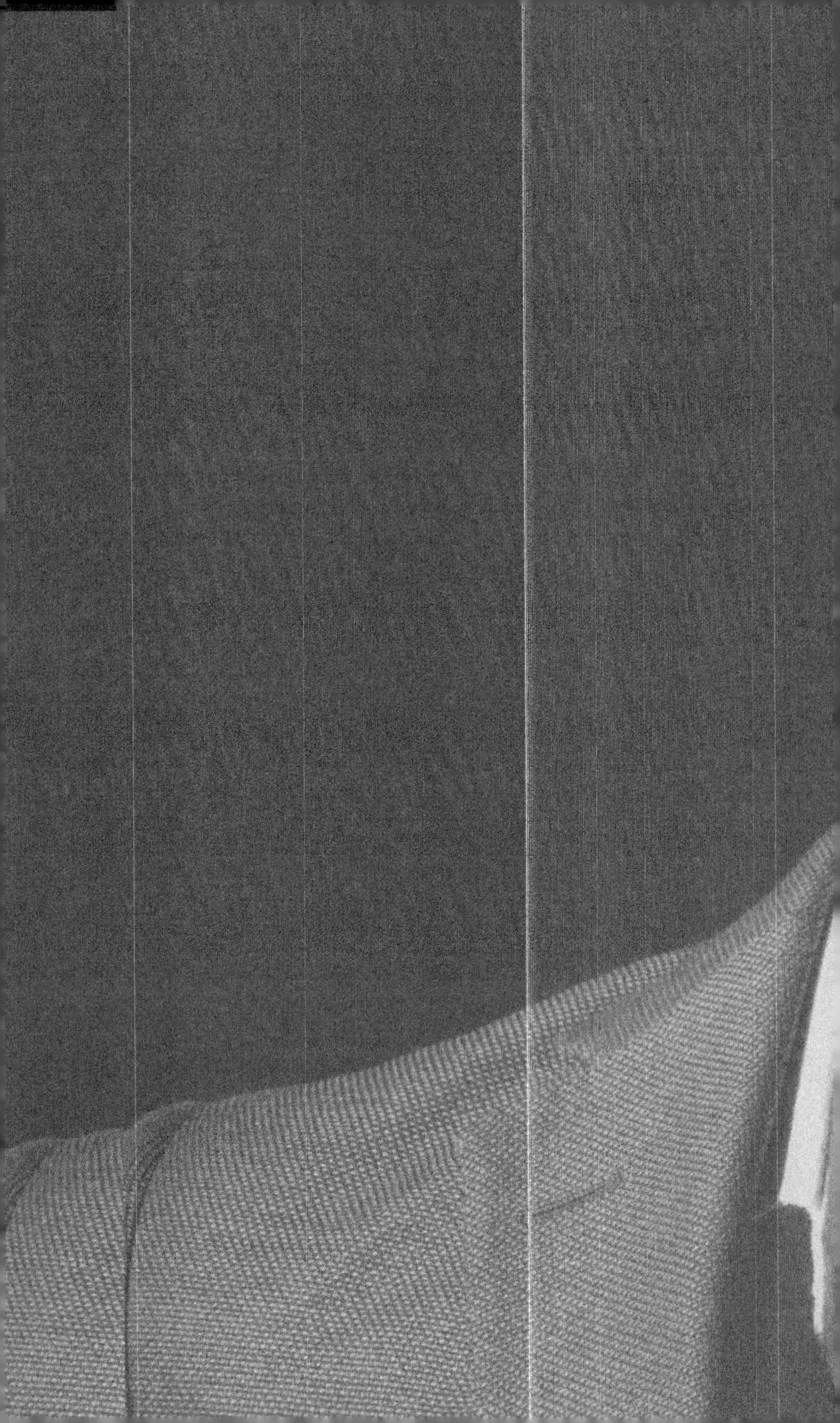

1
RAFAEL

Six Months Ago – Age 31
Sicily, Italy

"The truce with those Conti cunts is over, Rafael. They've *murdered* your father in cold blood. They've *stolen* your sister, *minchia!*"

My consigliere slams down the image that had arrived this morning of my bound and gagged sister, Aurelia, eyes spitting angry mahogany flames, her spirit clearly unbroken.

A sense of twisted pride fills my chest at the venom in her gaze. Strength in the face of adversity.

A true Caruso Queen.

"We don't have confirmation that it was Conti," I say succinctly, my tone even, though my patience has long since run thin.

"We both know it was fucking Conti, Rafael. Stop playing games and step up to the goddamn plate."

Antonio Caruso, consigliere to my father, the late Don Giacomo Caruso, is a shrewd man. A calculated man.

In another life, I trained to become just like him, but all chance of that life is gone now that my older brother, Alessio, was killed in a car accident three short months ago.

This is a side of Antonio that I've never seen, but clearly, his emotions are driving him in the aftermath of my father's funeral earlier today.

"I will do what's best—"

Antonio slams his hand onto the desk between us, spittle flying from his lips when he bellows, "It should have been *you*."

A beat passes as I lazily hold his gaze, guilt rising from the depths of my stomach at the truth in his words. Because he's right. Aurelia went along with our father instead of me.

It *should* have been me.

But even so, I won't abide being spoken to with such disrespect.

Achingly slow, I rise to my full height, towering over my uncle as I round the desk. His eyes widen as my lip twitches on one side before I snake out my left hand to grasp the hair on the back of his neck. He opens his mouth to protest or plead—I'm unsure and uncaring as to which—right as I slam his face down onto the desk at my side.

He groans when I let go abruptly, dusting my palms together as my overwrought uncle slides to the wooden floor at my feet. He cradles his face in his hands when I stride over to the office door, jerking it open to bark, "Emiliano, *vieni ca*."

My childhood best friend and bodyguard rounds the corner at the end of the hall, jamming the remains of a chocolate cupcake into his mouth as he marches closer. I shake my head as he reaches me, but he just shrugs it off.

"You wouldn't be such a fat fuck if you'd stop inhaling that shit."

He flips me the bird and enters my office, closing the door behind him as he waits expectantly for orders.

"I need you to have someone accompany my uncle to his suite." Emiliano glances around me, his eyebrow quirking as I shrug. "He's feeling...a little out of sorts."

Emiliano blinks a handful of times before turning to the nearest soldiers while I shift my gaze to my bleeding consigliere. "Take the rest of the day, *Zio*."

My uncle splays his palm on my desk, pushing himself to a shaky stand before straightening his vest and pushing his grey hair back off his florid face. His chest is rising and falling rapidly when he nods slowly. "*Si*, Rafael. *Ci vediamo domani*."

I incline my head once in acknowledgment. "I don't want to have this conversation again, *capisti*?"

Antonio swallows roughly. His jaw tics as he regards me with cold eyes before he manages to murmur a low assent.

Emiliano quickly escorts my hunched uncle to the two waiting *Soldati* outside my door before closing it as I scrub my palms up and down my face, weary to the depths of my soul.

"He's gone."

Emiliano closes the door behind him, and I nod my thanks as I drop my hands down onto my lap, expelling a heavy sigh. "But he's not wrong, *Fratello*. We need to act. We need to get Aurelia back. Papa must be turning in his damn grave at the thought of his *Principessa* in the hands of Domenico fucking Conti."

"You don't know for sure it was Domenico—"

"This has that smug bastard written all over it, *Fratello*. You know it. I know it. *Zio* knows it. And we'll see it confirmed today, hmm?"

My jaw clenches tightly, remembering the last time I'd seen Domenico Conti at the bi-annual Congress.

The Congress takes place on neutral ground in carefully chosen residences once every two years so the five ruling families of Cosa Nostra can set boundaries, resolve disputes, and arrange marriages. This assures no territories are breached unknowingly. Or attacked wrongfully.

Every Congress is pretty standard, even though, as the second in line up until Alessio's death, I've yet to sit in on a full briefing.

It's an easy way to keep the peace between the five ruling families.

Caruso. DeMarco. Salvatore. Medici.

And Conti.

Francesco Conti is as old as fuck, and as stubborn as a motherfucking mule, but I don't see his hand in any of this.

Clearly, his heir, Domenico, is getting too big for his boots since we last exchanged words.

Stellina.

An image of deep blue eyes and hair like starlight fills my vision before a frown mars my brow at the memories, and I push them away.

"We need to be patient, Rafe. They were painstaking in setting their plan in motion. We must be equally diligent."

I meet my friend's knowing eyes and nod once in silent agreement.

There's a soft knock on the door, and Emiliano slowly opens it to admit the only survivor of the ambush that saw my father gunned down.

My sister's companion, Maria, was left violated and on the brink of death in a burnt-out warehouse that our family had used previously for human trafficking. My father had put an end to that side of the business upon his ascension to power, extending it to the other four families. It was something Francesco Conti had never agreed with.

His son, too.

"You requested my presence, Don."

Don.

Shit! That's going to take some getting used to. That should be Alessio's title, damn him to Hell.

As she slowly steps inside my office, I can see Maria's face is still badly bruised despite the subsequent ten days since the attack.

"Yes, Maria." I gesture toward the chair opposite me. "Take a seat, *per favore*."

She sinks down gratefully into the velvet seat, folding her hands atop her lap before fixing her eyes on mine. Beneath the bruising, I can see she's pale, and it's costing her dearly to be here today.

"You want to know what happened, *si*?"

I steeple my fingers, resting them beneath my chin as I lean forward with a barely perceptible nod. "I'm afraid I've waited as long as I can afford to, Maria. I need to know what happened that day so that I can ensure they pay the price of double-crossing the Caruso family."

She swallows heavily, then nods. "It happened so quickly, Don Rafael. The convoy was taken down in a matter of seconds. Your father threw me and Miss Aurelia to the floor of the SUV, shielding us with his body. Our driver must have taken a hit or something because he suddenly veered away from the fracas, and the vehicle crashed..."

Maria's eyes are dull, her brow furrowed heavily as she relives the horror of my father's last moments.

"Don Giacomo pulled both of us from the wreckage before the attackers got too close, and when he saw where we were, he bade us to run for the warehouse. He said not to look back. Keep running. Keep Miss Aurelia—"

Her voice catches on a sob as tears spill down her cheeks. "He said to keep Miss Aurelia *safe*, no matter the cost."

She slams her eyes closed, and I give her a minute to compose herself, having a rough idea of what comes next but needing her confirmation regardless.

"We reached the warehouse, and I pushed Miss Aurelia inside before I looked back to see if Don Giacomo was still behind us, and that's when I saw…he was kneeling in the dirt. A tall man stood over him with a gun pressed to his temple. They exchanged heated words before your father cursed him loudly, then spat on the man's shoes."

I smile despite myself. My father was his own man, right up until the end, clearly. I can only hope to be half the man he was.

"The tall man spoke one last time before…before pulling the t-t-trigger."

Maria wedges her eyes closed with a low, keening cry. "They came for us then. I hid Miss Aurelia. I kept her safe. I refused to tell them where she was even as they beat me. Even as they took—"

She inhales sharply, her next words escaping on a sob. "*They took turns violating me.*"

Emiliano swears under his breath as he shifts his stance at my side, and I grit my teeth at the depravity this woman has experienced.

Fucking animals.

"The tall one—the one with the obscure hand tattoos—he was American. And he relished the pain he inflicted." Then she swallows roughly. "He did this."

Maria shakily tugs her high-necked blouse to one side, showcasing heavy bruising around her throat. Large fingerprints mar her delicate flesh.

"Right before I passed out, I heard Miss Aurelia scream for them to stop. And—and that's the last thing I remember, Don Rafael."

Long moments of silence pass as Maria smooths her skirt along her legs, and I digest her horrendous story, eventually reaching into the drawer on my left to pull out an image.

"Is this the man who killed my father, Maria? The man who gave you those bruises?"

She lifts her head, and her impassive eyes fill with horror. Her breathing kicks up ten notches, face flaming bright red as the horrors perpetuated upon her play across her features for both me and Emiliano to witness.

"*Si*, Don Rafael. *Il diavolo incarnato.*" She blesses herself three times with shaky hands. "I'm so sorry I let him take Miss Aurelia. I—I didn't—"

I rise from my seat in a fluid motion, stepping around the desk to take her trembling hands in mine when I kneel by her side.

"Maria, you have nothing to be sorry for. *I* am sorry this happened to you."

She looks up from where her eyes have been trained on her hands sitting in her lap. Tears freely streak down both cheeks, and I pour every ounce of promise I can muster into my next statement.

"And you have my word, on my mother's grave, that I will see the bastard pay for his sins."

Once I've walked Maria from my office, with Emiliano for company, I settle at my desk, and open the drawer on my right. I slowly pluck the letter my father had left in his safe in case something exactly like this occurred, intent on re-reading it for the hundredth time.

I slip it from the creased envelope and skim over the words, drawing strength from them as I read.

Rafael, my son.
My heir.
From the moment your beautiful mother brought you into this world, you've viewed it through eyes wiser than your years.

You possess a true gift, Rafe. You know your own mind. You are your own man. No matter what others would say to persuade you otherwise. You know who you are. You always have.

Never lose that.

You may not have been born to lead, my boy, but you've got all the tools you need.

Trust yourself.

I'll be with you every step of the way.

Ti amo, Rafael.

Papa

I fold and refold the paper over and over, mulling over the words of my father and cursing the world that's taken him from us too soon.

The world that took Alessio, and forced me to fill shoes I'm not entirely sure I can fill.

Shoes I don't *want* to fill, but know I must all the same.

I'm not ready.

And in the silence of the office that was once his, I swear I hear his deep voice whisper, "You were born ready."

2

ELODIE

Present Day – Age 24
Lake Garda, Italy

I turn off the vibration on my cell, planting it face down on the table as I ignore the umpteenth text from an exceptionally irate Domenico Conti.

"You know I'm here for you, Ellie."

My best friend, Levi, watches me over the top of his menu. His big brown eyes are brimming with concern that I really don't want to deal with, so I paste a megawatt smile on my face in the signature way I've carefully cultivated throughout my life.

"You really are my favorite condom, Lev."

His face puckers in adorable confusion as I laugh with a flippant shrug. "You're always protecting me when things get hard..."

A gigantic smile breaks across his face, filling me with a lightness that's all Levi James.

"Christ above, Elodie. You really have a unique way with words."

I wink playfully before returning my attention to the slim menu on the table. "This place comes highly recommended courtesy of Trip Advisor. It's the highlight of the *entire* trip, and I fucking *refuse* to allow that prick to ruin our last day. Okay?"

He nods with a lingering grin before returning his gaze to his own menu. "I'll get the bruschetta to start, I think. What about you?"

"Caprese salad, followed by the lasagna." My eyes blow wide with anticipation. "And tiramisu to finish."

Levi chuckles. "I'll be rolling you onto the plane tomorrow."

"That's the goal, my beautiful friend."

We're still laughing when a handsome olive-skinned waiter pops up beside Levi. "*Benvenuti a Melograno.* I'm Adriano, your server this afternoon."

Adriano's eyes stay wholly focused on Levi as he slowly fills our water glasses. "I'll be back in a moment for your order."

Levi, my bisexual bestie, hasn't had sex in over a year, but judging by the eye contact between these two, I have a feeling that the dry spell might be coming to an end.

"You should *absolutely* hit that."

Levi swings wide eyes around to mine, his mouth opening and closing like a fish out of water. The sight makes me snort as I take a sip of my water.

"He's a million miles out of my league, Ellie." Levi shakes his head, making his slightly too-long dark hair swish into his eyes. He pushes it back with a wry grin. "And you *know* I don't do well with rejection."

"The man was practically undressing you with his come-fuck-me eyes, Lev." I shake my head with an exaggerated eye roll. "Live a fucking little. Rock his cock."

Levi chews his bottom lip pensively. "I dunno…"

"If you're ready…" Adriano's wide green eyes train on Levi as his deep intonation fills the area. "May I take an order from you, *signore*?"

His heavily Italian-accented question is filled with innuendo that has me biting my bottom lip to curtail a giggle.

"I'll have a Caprese salad, please." Adriano flicks his eyes in my direction, duly noting my order on his pad, and I grin as an idea takes hold. "Actually...what time do you get off?"

Levi's foot connects with my shin beneath the table as I blink innocently up into the laughing eyes of our server. "This is my last table for the afternoon, *signorina*."

"In that case..." I push my seat back, toss my napkin onto the pristine white tablecloth, and rise to my feet. "I'm not hungry anymore."

"But you said this place is the highlight of the trip..."

Levi stands as I grab my bag from where it's hanging off the back of my chair and hold up a staying palm while making eye contact with the waiter. "My friend Levi here would be happy to do a little sightseeing this afternoon if you're *up* for it."

Levi's groan fills my ears as I lean closer to press a kiss to his cheek before whispering, "And if I see you back at the hotel later, I'll personally castrate you."

In the early evening sunshine, the promenade bustles behind me. Vendors sell their wares to an army of tourists while restaurants along the seafront open their doors to the masses, the scent of authentic Italian cuisine filling my nostrils.

The stone pavement beneath my butt is warm from the rays of the sun as my bare feet dangle over the edge of the pier, the turquoise waters of Lake Garda lapping against the wall lazily.

My eyes linger on a boat far out in the middle of Lake

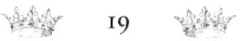

Garda, far removed from the busyness on the pier, and I long to be out there in the calm solitude rather than sitting lakeside with my racing thoughts.

Tomorrow is looming over me. I knew it was coming before I'd even left the States. But there was no way I could miss my childhood best friend Wren's wedding.

Plus, her billionaire husband's private jet was the only way I could leave the US, thanks to Nico's confiscation of my passport.

I tug my cell from my crossbody bag, swiping away two further purposefully missed calls before re-reading today's latest furious text message from my Lord and master.

> NICO: You'll pay dearly for disobeying me, mia piccola puttana.

One of the few Italian phrases I'd been allowed to learn over the years.

My little whore.

And that's exactly what I'd become in the four years since I'd been pretty much sold to the mob to cover the misdemeanors of my family. My father had never again broached the subject with me, and even on the two separate occasions I'd bumped into Evan, he'd just ignored me entirely.

If it hadn't been for Skye, I'd have no family at all.

It cemented the fact that they meant nothing to me, and I meant less to them.

Life with Nico had started out okay, I guess. I got out of South Brook and away from my parents. Away from the life I'd been stifled by.

An elaborate penthouse in the city. All my classes were paid for. My wardrobe was filled with only high-end haute couture fashion. I was at one event or another with Nico every night of the week.

And the sex was liberating. In a way that I'd never thought possible.

Until I realized that it wasn't.

Because I'd exchanged one jailor for another far worse one.

I don't even allow myself to recall the full extent of what happened the first time I did something Nico didn't explicitly approve of. I only remember waking up in the hospital.

My reason for being there is...hazy.

My heart rate kicks up when I press my cell onto the paving beneath me, closing my eyes tight as I mentally slam a lid onto the Pandora's Box deep inside my head where memories I *can't* relive dwell.

When I'd tried visiting a therapist to work through the trauma, she'd told me that my mind had locked that entire weekend away, almost like an ingrained safety mechanism. She'd been more than willing to help me work through it, but I'd not returned to my next session.

Even though I give off the impression of strength, it's all a façade. The simple truth is, I don't know if I'll ever be strong enough to go there.

The physical scars are enough of a reminder that I don't need the mental ones to match.

"*Mi scusi, signorina?*"

A man's voice interrupts my recollections, and I swallow heavily before lifting my eyes.

"*Sei seduto al mio posto, signorina.*"

With an apologetic shrug, I rattle off the only Italian I have. "*Non parlo Italiano.*"

The elderly man scrunches his brow, stepping closer into my personal space and making me scoot back along the seafront.

"*Sei seduto al mio posto. Moviti!*"

"I'm sorry." I press my hands together in a pleading motion, sensing the man's agitation rising. "I don't speak Italian."

Shaking my head helplessly, I raise my voice to enunciate each word as though he's hard of hearing.

"*Non parlo Italiano.*"

I glance over my shoulder, seeking aid as the man begins to spew more Italian at me, looming over me with red, angry splotches on his cheeks as his hands gesticulate wildly.

Another man joins him, and I move to stand but can't, realizing they've boxed me in, and the only place for me to go is down into the waters of the lake.

As panic fills my chest, a tall, imposing shadow blocks the sun, and a voice like warm molasses washes over me. I don't understand a word that the newcomer utters in his lilting Italian, but shortly, both men are chuckling before moving off in the direction they'd come.

"Excuse my compatriots, *signorina.*"

All hint of his Italian accent disappears when he speaks English, though the timbre of his voice is no less intoxicating.

I take the opportunity to stand, holding my hand up to shield the late evening sun from my eyes, only for my breath to desert my lungs because standing before me is *the* most gorgeous man I've ever seen.

He is over a foot taller than me, with black hair that falls forward across his brow, giving him an almost boyish charm. A white shirt and beige pants cover his muscular frame like they've been made to fit his body.

Dark brown eyes brimming with concern hold me their willing captive before he glances down, a slow smile spreading across his handsome face. My lips answer of their own accord.

"Thank you for your assistance, Mr. Tall Dark and Handsome." He dips his head in silent acknowledgment of my gratitude, his grin broadening. "I'm afraid I never learned the language."

What I don't add is that Nico purposefully forbade me from learning Italian to ensure I wouldn't understand anything discussed at the meetings he'd bring me to. It suited him to have me on his arm, parading me past other men in the organization who openly lusted after the woman who warmed his bed.

The woman who was, for all intents, his property. Signed, sealed, and delivered.

And he'd only gotten worse since his father—probably the only person who'd been able to keep him in check—had died almost a year ago.

Mr. Tall Dark and Handsome gestures in the direction the elderly man and his friend have sauntered.

"Lazise is always bustling with tourists. To be honest, it's surprising that man didn't speak English."

"I'm just thankful that you were here to save the day, or else I might have ended up in the lake." His chest rumbles with a deep chuckle as I smile gratefully and extend my right hand.

"I'm Elodie."

His eyes deepen in intensity, the chocolatey brown melting into obsidian as my savior slides his palms alongside mine. The simple touch makes my skin feel electrified. Like he's awakened something deep inside me.

"Rafe."

Our gazes hold for a long moment as his eyes search mine. I can feel my brow pucker as a feeling of déjà vu flows through me, knocking my equilibrium utterly off-kilter.

I sway to the side, perilously close to the edge of the pier, before the hand lightly holding mine increases its grip, drawing me closer until I'm flush against his hard body.

His heady masculine scent fills my senses, grounding me in a way I've never experienced before as he whispers across the top of my head.

"*Ti salvero, Stellina.*"

The Pandora's Box in my head rattles slightly as something

about those words tugs at the edges of my memory. Words I *know* I've heard before, but I just can't place when.

I tilt my head to one side as memories form in my mind's eye of a clear night sky littered with stars. A smile on my lips. A warm hand on my cheek...

But without warning, an image of Nico rises to the forefront, and panic fills my chest, making it hard to breathe.

More than a little shaken at the turn of events, I quickly step back out of Rafe's hold to look up from beneath my lashes, my breath coming in short bursts. "Apologies. I felt a little lightheaded just then. I forgot I skipped lunch earlier."

Dropping down to my haunches, I grab my discarded cell and crossbody bag with shaky hands, somehow managing to upend the contents in my rush.

Rafe crouches beside me, placing his hands over mine. My eyes trace the back of his right hand that's covered entirely in a beautifully detailed rose tattoo. "Take a deep breath, Elodie."

I close my eyes, allowing this stranger's calming voice to soothe me. To chase away my demons. And I do as he instructs, taking several slow breaths until my racing heart has stopped galloping.

Only then do I lift my eyes to his. His forehead creases in concern, but it's the care in his eyes that fills me with a feeling suspiciously like hope.

Something I haven't felt in a long, long time, and I rapidly diffuse it with my signature sarcasm.

"Do you roam the promenade in a bid to rescue damsels in distress often?"

A flash of perfect white teeth paired with a low chuckle encourages me to continue, tucking my hair behind my ear with a wry grin. "You're really well versed, you know. You've undoubtedly perfected your routine because I'm *sold*."

His chuckle becomes a deep laugh that sends a swarm of butterflies rioting in the depths of my stomach, and I forcibly tear my eyes away from him to toss the contents of my bag back inside.

"I'm not actually from around here. And for what it's worth..." He trails off to pinch my chin between his thumb and index finger, lifting my gaze to his. "You don't strike me as the damsel-in-distress type."

My lips lift in a smile, grateful that he's brushing my silly dramatics under the rug.

"You're not wrong, Rafe. Given the choice, I'd much prefer to slay my own dragons."

His eyes narrow as indecision flickers across his face, gone as quickly as it appeared, before he reaches across to brush his thumb across my bottom lip. The move is entirely too intimate, and I revel in it when my heart slams against my rib cage, his eyes dropping down to follow the motion.

"Have dinner with me, Elodie." The request is murmured as his eyes shift back up to mine, and he blinks slowly, the whole world fading into oblivion around us. "Tell me more about these dragons you wish to slay."

3

RAFAEL

I hadn't planned on approaching her. I had intended to keep my distance and let Emiliano do the dirty work.

Following the attempt on my life the day I'd accompanied Sebastiano back to Andros-Baumann, his boarding school in Zurich, the week after Papa's funeral, Emiliano wasn't taking any chances.

So, I've been stuck in Sicily for almost six months. Restructuring *la Famiglia* has taken time now that I've shut down our operations in the US, but it was the right thing to do considering the proximity to Conti. The chance of an all-out war between our families grows every day.

In the days following Maria's confirmation, Conti had reached out, and the arrogant cunt was unmoving on what he wanted in exchange for Aurelia. The only thing I *couldn't* give to him.

Myself.

Six long fucking months of trying to achieve the unachievable. To get my sister back where she belongs.

No matter how many hands I greased, or how many favors I

called in, Aurelia couldn't be located, and Conti had gone underground too.

The goal had felt unreachable.

Until now. Until her.

But I was *strictly* along for the ride. No one outside of my most trusted soldiers was even aware I'd left Sicily.

A day trip. A quick in and out. Job done.

Then, when I laid eyes on her, I couldn't see anything other than her.

And when those men had approached, she'd looked so completely vulnerable. I'd been unable to keep away.

I catch Emiliano's eye from his place at a nearby table and shrug imperceptibly when he stabs me with an annoyed look before I zone in on my menu.

"Everything smells so good here."

I lift my eyes from the menu in my hands to find the object of my thoughts leaning across the table, her long blonde hair cascading down either side of her oval face and her big navy-blue eyes trained on me.

Suddenly, her stomach growls, and her cheeks flush prettily. I can't suppress the smile that wreathes my face as she slaps her palms over hers, mumbling behind them.

"Oh my God, I'm so embarrassed."

"To be expected." I quirk an entertained eyebrow when she snorts a laugh from behind her hands. "You *did* skip lunch, after all, Elodie."

My chuckle is indulgent as my eyes rake over her greedily, taking in everything from the color of her silky hair to the creaminess of her unblemished skin next to the deep blue of her summer dress until the waiter stops at our table.

"*Posso prendere il suo ordine, signore?*"

Elodie drops her hands onto the table, the flush on her cheeks staining the pale skin of her chest as she catches my eye.

Without taking my gaze off her, I smile as I quickly order.

"*Prendiamo uno di tutto, per favore.*"

Then I reach across, plucking the menu from the table in front of her and stacking it with mine to pass it to the wide-eyed server as he stammers, "*Uno di tutto sul menu, signore?*"

"*Si. E non mi piace aspettare.*"

He nods quickly and disappears from sight as Elodie fixes me with a glare. "Most women would find it sexy when a hot Italian man orders for them."

I arch a curious eyebrow as she sits back in her seat, folding her arms with narrowed eyes, her flush deepening in anger. "*However*...I'm not most women, Rafe."

The corner of my lips twitch as I lean across the table, resting my chin on my steepled fingers. "You most assuredly are *not*, Elodie."

Lips pursing in thought, her stomach protests more loudly than before. "I won't eat something I didn't choose for myself."

"You didn't hear what I ordered, hmm?"

"I *told you*." Annoyance fills every word as she grits out, "*I don't speak Italian.*"

Suddenly, with a deep frown, she stands, pushing her chair away from the table with a loud creak along the flagstone beneath us.

"This was a bad idea. I'm just going to..." She jerks her thumb in the direction of the exit as she trails off, her eyes filled with irritation. And something else.

Disappointment?

"I'm just going to leave."

I don't think so.

Before she can finish her sentence, I've rounded the table and taken her hand in mine. She looks around helplessly at the other diners as I lead her to the small dancefloor in the middle of the restaurant, spinning her into my arms.

Her body is tense against mine, and I can practically hear

her brain whirring with ideas on how to extricate herself from the situation.

"I ordered one of everything on the menu."

Her eyes shoot up to mine, confusion dancing across her face as her brow furrows. "What...I—I don't—you said—"

"You're clearly hungry. And I wanted to..." I'm suddenly at a loss for words.

"I wanted to do something nice for you."

Our eyes hold for long moments as the music plays on until she juts her chin out defiantly. "I don't like my choices being taken from me, Rafe."

The hand resting on her hip pulls her closer against me as I gaze at her with an intensity I need her to feel.

"Your choice is yours alone, *Stellina*." My voice drops to a hushed whisper. "I would never take that from you."

Her eyes flicker back and forth between mine like she can't quite figure me out until, without warning, her body slackens in my hold, and she leans closer to press her cheek against my chest.

A sudden jolt of electricity courses through my veins. Her proximity. Her touch. Her delicate scent.

Her fucking trust.

And despite everything else, despite all the outside forces that make anything happening between us an impossibility, I steal this one moment.

I tighten my hold on her waist, and a thrill echoes within my chest when she settles more firmly against me.

We sway softly to the music as plate after plate of steaming hot food is set up along a buffet of sorts at the table we were sitting at.

All too soon, the song comes to an end, and Elodie steps back out of my embrace, finding my eyes with gracious ones of her own. "Thank you."

"What do you want to do, *Fratello*?"

"I don't fucking know. I wasn't expecting…"

I trail off as I pace back and forth along the tiled kitchen floor of *Il Porticciolo*, absolutely torn as to how to proceed.

The plan was simple. Kidnap Domenico Conti's golden-haired lover and trade her for Aurelia.

That *was* the plan.

Except I wasn't expecting to feel this pull to her. This *need* to protect her, to ensure her safety, almost overwhelms me. One glance could bring me to my motherfucking knees.

Just like the first night we met.

I could see in her eyes on the promenade when she had initially tried to place me. I was familiar to her; that much was apparent. But it had cut to know she'd clearly never even given those stolen moments more than a passing thought when I'd relived every second no less than a thousand times.

I couldn't witness a starry sky without remembering…

Emiliano's urgent tone pulls me from my musings as he paces alongside me.

"You should never have approached her. That was the deal. You know DeMarco can only shield our presence in the north for so long, Rafe. You're not safe outside of Sicily. Conti spies are every-fucking-where."

"They're in my own fucking compound, too, if you ask me. So what difference does it make being *here* or being *there*? Answer me that!"

"Don't be an ass, Rafe. This needs to be handled quickly. Efficiently." He gestures toward the restaurant. "None of this flowery shit to soften the blow."

Emiliano growls a low expletive when he levels me with a hard stare.

"You're not here to gain her trust, *Fratello*. She's a pawn that's needed to get Aurelia back. To take Conti down."

"Why doesn't she understand Italian?"

He freezes, looking at me like I've lost my mind, and I'm not entirely sure I haven't. After a beat, he rolls his eyes. "She's assuredly lying. She's Domenico Conti's prized possession. She's treated like a goddamn queen. She *must* have picked up the language in the four years she's been in his life."

Then he throws his hands up in exasperation. "You're overthinking this."

I shake my head slowly, my gut niggling at me. "There's something off about her presence here. She's completely unguarded. Roaming free and alone aside from that friend of hers who's currently railing Adriano. *Why* is that, hmm?"

My friend expels a heavy sigh. "Because she came here safely with her friends. Her filthy *rich* friends who had ample enough security at their wedding that we couldn't touch her. But she left that security because she obviously believed herself to be untouchable—just like the rest of the Conti scum."

We regard one another for a long beat, clearly at an impasse, until he shakes his head. "I've never seen you so taken with some pretty pussy, *Fratello*. What the fuck's gotten into you?"

I grit my teeth hard enough that my jaw aches.

I wish I fucking knew.

Without warning, Emiliano steps around me to move toward the door that leads into the quiet restaurant where we've just enjoyed a feast fit for royalty, taking a syringe from his pocket as he goes.

"Stay here. There's no need to get your hands dirty, Rafe. I'll knock her out. We'll be on the jet within the hour—"

Before my friend can finish his sentence, I've drawn my gun to press the cool steel to the back of his neck. "*Non moviti!*"

Emiliano drops his head, his shoulders sagging when he holds up his hands in defeat. I pluck the syringe from between his fingers, sliding it into my chinos pocket as my friend sighs.

"I'm trying to keep you alive, *Fratello*. I beg you. Stick to the plan. This woman is a means to an end. Nothing more, nothing less. If *Zio* were here, he would give you the same advice as your consigliere."

"I left *Zio* at home because he's a pain in my ass, *minchia*." I push the gun roughly against the back of his neck as I flip on the safety. "But clearly, you two are more alike than I'd have fucking thought."

I shove past him without another word, indecision warring in my chest.

What is it about this woman that can make a man lose his goddamn mind?

Your choice is yours alone, Stellina. *I would never take that from you.*

Except what happens if *I* have no choice?

And even as I deliberate what I'm about to do, I know that my loyalty lies with my family. I'll do whatever it takes to get my sister back and reclaim our family's honor by obliterating the Conti bloodline.

Elodie Rivers is the key to doing that.

Having made peace with my predicament and ready to take action, I slide into the seat opposite her as she takes a small sip of her prosecco. Her big blue eyes smile brightly at me before her lips slowly twitch upward as she tucks her golden hair behind one ear.

"You're a sight for sore eyes, Handsome."

And just like that, I'm fucked. She is my undoing, and despite knowing what I must follow through with, I desperately bargain with myself, needing just a *little* more time. Needing her to keep looking at me like I hung the damn moon.

It's like an addiction, and I physically *need* just one more hit. *A couple of hours can't hurt...*

"My pleasure to be of assistance." Then I tilt my head to one side. "What happened to my full title?"

Her eyes twinkle mischievously. "Handsome just sounds...*right*. Plus, it's more to the point." She shrugs with a chuckle. "And I'm too full to think beyond the blatantly obvious, okay?"

I smirk broadly before glancing at the hand resting on her stomach. "Do you think you have room for gelato?"

Holding up a petite hand, she giggles. "I've made a damn pig of myself." She sobers as I send her an indulgent smile. "It was truly wonderful. Thank you for the highlight of my entire trip..."

Her lashes lower, almost shyly. "I... I truly am sorry for my reaction before."

"No apology required. Witnessing the magnificent claws you slay dragons with was both an honor and a privilege."

She presses her full lips together in a half smile that doesn't quite carry to her eyes.

"I'd forgotten they existed, to be honest."

4

ELODIE

Stars litter the dark sky when we emerge onto a quieter promenade.

Today really had been the highlight of my trip, all thanks to the handsome stranger who'd saved the day. Being with Rafe had shown me a glimpse of the person I could be if my life had taken a different path.

That feeling is entirely too intoxicating, and I soak it up desperately, knowing I'll need it to get through what's coming for me when I go home tomorrow.

What awaits me sends a chill running down my spine, making me shiver despite the warm Italian evening.

"Are you cold?" The concern in Rafe's voice warms me from the inside out, making me smile wistfully.

Without waiting for an answer, he shucks the light beige jacket he's wearing that matches his capris and stands at my rear to drape it over my shoulders. I'm immediately shrouded within his now familiar bergamot scent as he smooths the sides down my arms.

"The night is young." His breath tickles the nape of my neck, and my eyelids flutter closed, allowing myself to have this one carefree moment with a man who—in another lifetime—could have become something more than a tall, dark, handsome stranger.

"Would you like to walk for a little while, *Stellina*?"

"What does that mean? *Stellina*..." His broad chest that's pressed up against my back tenses at my question, and I turn to face him with a creased brow.

Rafe tilts his head to one side as something akin to frustration crosses his features before he brings a hand up between us to tuck a stray lock of hair behind my ear. His hand cups my cheek as the intensity in his deep brown eyes makes my heart hammer in my chest.

"It means 'little star,' Elodie."

"Why?" The single word escapes my lips on a whisper.

He smooths his fingertips along my hair, his eyes leaving mine to follow the movement. "Well...for one...your hair shines like starlight."

Stomach fluttering, my mouth draws up in a bright smile. "*Stellina*..." His gaze deepens even further. "I think that's the nicest thing anyone has ever said to me."

His other hand comes up to cup my face with his warm palms as his eyes flicker back and forth between mine. "*Cosa succede quando esprimi un desiderio su una stella?*"

My forehead creases, knowing I've heard those words spoken before, but completely at a loss as to when, or by whom.

The dull sound of passing pedestrians feels muted in my ears as we stand toe to toe, eyes locked for a long beat until I physically jump when a cyclist rings his bell as he passes. I step back almost guiltily, my eyes watching Rafe's hands drop back to his sides before I blow out a breath.

"Are you flexing a new routine, Handsome, or is this how you roll every day?"

He chuckles as I spin in the direction of my hotel, realizing quickly that I need to put distance between us.

Come tomorrow, this will all be a memory. I shake my head harshly, dispelling the fear that threatens to rise as Rafe catches up to me. "May I walk with you then?"

Not trusting my voice, I nod once, keeping my eyes on my feet as we walk in companionable silence, eventually veering away from the promenade and farther along the darkened lake in the direction of my hotel, *Vista Lago*.

The sound of the lake lapping at the shoreline is soothing as our steps match evenly, and I glance to the side to find Rafe's eyes on me. I open my mouth to speak when a drop of water slashes the tip of my nose, followed rapidly by another on my cheek until, within the space of two breaths, we are standing amid a torrential downpour.

Rafe grips my hand, pulling me after him. "Quick, Elodie. This way."

His jacket slips from my shoulders as we race alongside one another until the lights belonging to *Vista Lago* come into view. Rafe veers toward it, pulling me after him as we rush up the steps onto the veranda that wraps around the front of the building.

"Wow!" Rafe laughs as I tug my hair over one shoulder, wringing it between my hands. "That came out of nowhere."

He pushes his rain-slick black locks back from his dripping face with a smile that can only be described as panty-melting, and my pulse kicks up a beat in response.

"It shouldn't last more than a couple of minutes."

I smooth my dress along my ribs, grimacing slightly when the wet material sticks to my skin. "I'm *literally* soaked to the bone."

"You can say that again!" Rafe snorts, glancing down his torso as he runs his palms along his pectorals before raising his eyes to mine with a self-deprecatory grin.

It's then I realize his white collarless shirt has turned see-through, allowing me to catch a glimpse of several tattoos on his chest and biceps. Mindlessly, my feet step forward until I'm close enough to place the flat of both my palms on his taunt muscles.

"Do they all have meaning?"

"*Si*." The single word fans across my cheek in a murmur as I examine the elaborate ink as best I can.

I trail the index finger of my right hand along the markings, brushing my fingers over the ornate silver cross hanging around his neck. My eyes slowly lift to meet his dark gaze as water trails down his face, streaking through his immaculately groomed facial hair.

His jaw tics ever-so slightly when our eyes meet, unwavering in contact. I inhale shakily, my world feeling as though it's being spun clear upside down as he utterly devastates me with the intent in his gaze before he cups my cheek softly.

Without thinking, I nuzzle against his warm palm as he dusts his thumb across my cheekbone.

"You are so *beautiful* it hurts." He exhales on a sigh, my eyes closing as I soak up the surprisingly easy intimacy flowing between us.

Hearing the fervency in his voice, I blow out a breath, knowing these moments are nothing more than a stolen lie even as I commit this feeling to memory.

My heartbeat roars in my ears as the rain hammers the earth beyond the veranda covering us, and my eyes slowly open to find Rafe's face is closer than before. His slightly accelerated breaths fan across my cheek as he watches me through hooded lids.

My breath catches in my throat, my heart riots in my chest, and I want nothing more than to lean closer to press my lips to his, when suddenly the moment is ripped apart by the sound of my cell ringing from inside the bag draped across my body.

I yank it out, simultaneously disgusted and grateful at the

timing of the disruption, and in my rush to check the caller, I fumble, dropping the damn thing to the wood beneath our feet.

Rafe chuckles as he lowers to his haunches swiftly, scooping it up with ease, but when he stands to pass the device into my palm, his face is devoid of all the tenderness of moments before.

My eyes drop to the cell, noting Nico's name flashing on repeat, and I can feel my cheeks heat as I silence the ringtone.

"Someone important?" Rafe's voice is flat, his jaw tight when I meet his gaze. "You can take the call if you need to."

I shake my head and force a carefree smile. "Nah. It's just my...boss."

Technically speaking.

I inject enthusiasm into my voice as I continue. "Besides, I'm on vacation until tomorrow."

Rafe's eyes flicker between mine, as though searching for answers to questions I'm unaware of.

"In that case..." He trails off when a car pulling into the parking lot grabs his attention. When he looks back at me, he's smiling again, though I'm not quite sure that this one reaches his eyes.

"How about a nightcap before we part ways, hmm?"

RAFE

The bar area of the boutique resort on the shores of Lake Garda is quiet when we enter, and I smile at Elodie when she turns to me with a questioning look.

"How about over there?"

I nod toward a secluded booth in the corner of the room, the hair on the back of my neck bristling when I feel more than hear Emiliano and several others make their way inside after us.

He's my boss.

My gut twists uncomfortably at the lie Elodie had so easily told on the veranda. The moments prior to seeing Domenico's name pop up on her cell phone had been filled with a longing I haven't felt since the last time I laid eyes on her.

A longing that was quashed both then and now by the reminder that she belongs to Domenico Conti.

And *that's* her singular value to me.

Elodie slides into the booth, tucking her silken blonde hair behind her ear with a smile. A waiter fills two water glasses, depositing them on the table as I stand stock still, knowing what comes next as Elodie angles her head to one side in confusion at my inaction. Her eyes caress my face as surely as she's physically touching me before she picks up her water glass, taking a small sip while a frown plays across her brow.

Rather than draw this out any further, I do what I should have done back at the restaurant instead of trying to steal something that isn't mine to take.

I slip into the seat opposite, holding her gaze as I delicately place my gun on the table between us. The light in her blue eyes falters and dies, turning the navy hue to a dull gray and making me grit my jaw in consternation.

Why do you affect me so fucking much?

Sheer terror fills her face as the water glass tumbles from her fingers, the contents splashing onto the table between us.

And as quickly as fear had exploded across her features, it's gone, replaced by a cool disdain and a vacancy I haven't spotted before now.

"Is he with you?"

Her voice is monotone. None of the lilting cadence of before. Cold haughtiness replaces the easy camaraderie we'd shared, transforming her beautiful face.

I tilt my head, pinching my chin between my thumb and

index finger with a thoughtful frown. "Is *who* with me, Miss Rivers?"

She arches a pale eyebrow before crossing her arms over her chest and sitting back deeply into her seat to regard me with unveiled contempt.

"Nico, of course," she fake whispers. "He's not the kind to send a lowdown dog to do his dirty work, so I'm sure he's not far—"

"Your *boss* didn't send me." I cut her off more sharply than I'd intended, her barbed words clearly hitting the mark. "In fact, I reckon he'll be damn pissed when he finds out I've taken you."

Her heavily fringed blue eyes widen almost imperceptibly. "*Taken* me?"

I lean closer, watching as her breathing accelerates. "I'm afraid you're a valuable pawn in a game I can't afford to lose, Elodie."

Having enough of this back-and-forth, I hold up my hand, gesturing for my men dotted throughout the bar to come forward en masse. "And you're coming with me."

5

ELODIE

Despite my racing mind, I'm outwardly calm. Levi—possibly the only person on the planet who I've allowed to *see* me—refers to this as "Swan Mode."

To the naked eye, I'm serene and calm, gliding across the water without a care in the world. But look closely enough, and you'll see my feet frantically paddling to stay afloat. To keep going.

Because, after all, what option do I have?

You know who'll pay the price, Elodie.

Words that have both terrified me and gotten me through the darkest of days drive me forward as I swallow down my fear and meet my demons head-on.

"Well..." I shrug with a nonchalance I don't feel. "If you insist."

Rafe's eyes narrow at the insolence in my tone, and I feel a surge of triumph in the churning depths of my stomach at having elicited a reaction. I hold his stare uncompromisingly until the edge of his mouth lifts ever-so slightly.

"Oh, I *absolutely* insist."

I can feel someone arrive and stand at my side when Rafe's eyes shift from me to them. "Ready the jet, Emiliano."

The same someone disappears as quickly as they'd arrived before Rafe stands, extending his tatted hand, palm facing up. "I know this is unpleasant, Elodie. Let's not make it any harder."

Angry words sit right on the tip of my tongue, ready to unleash a torrent of abuse at the beautiful liar looking down at me, when a memory of running through Central Park with Skye on her seventh birthday flashes through my mind.

"Come on, Ellie. You're so slow."

I purposely gentle my pace, watching with a smile as Skye reaches the Alice in Wonderland *sculpture we always visit on our day trips to the city.*

She spins to face me with a bright smile wreathed across her face. "I win, Ellie! I win!"

As I reach her, a teen in boot skates comes flying out of nowhere, and I run right into him.

"Oh, I'm so sorry." I reach for him to ensure he's okay. "I didn't see you."

He slams to a halt, and I quickly glance around in search of Domenico's men, who are assuredly watching every moment I spend out of his sight.

"Hey! Watch it, lady!"

Skye quickly steps forward with an easy smile, her hand reaching for the boy who clearly has no idea what he's doing.

"You were doing so well. Keep going!"

With a smile, he nods in agreement before taking off in the opposite direction and careening straight into a hotdog vendor who proceeds to tear him a new one.

We both wince as we quickly head toward the Boathouse for our lunch reservation.

"Nice save, Curly Fry."

I loop my arm over her slender shoulder, and she smiles brightly up at me. "Remember when Ollie Stevens was being mean to me at school, and you told me that I'd catch more flies with honey than with vinegar..."

I place my hand in Rafe's, and that now-familiar tingle sends shock waves up along my arm, settling in my chest.
Damn you to Hell, you intoxicating devil.
I ignore it and focus on the plan I'm formulating. "May I at least use the restroom before we leave?"
I blink slowly once, twice, three times, praying to God he takes the bait. His nostrils flare as his forehead creases, but he nods sharply as I force my features to remain indifferent.
"Be quick."
I send him a gracious smile. "Thank you, Rafe."
Then, I turn in the direction of the ladies' restroom at the rear of the bar area.
Once inside, I quickly climb up onto the washbasin, reaching for the small window above it that I knew was there from earlier this week. It gives way easily, and I hoist myself up, panting as I wiggle my way outside.
My palms grasp the moonlit grass surrounding the hotel as I scramble, huffing and puffing heavily until my entire body is free.
Elation fills my chest, and a broad smile breaks across my face just as two impeccably clean Italian leather loafers enter my vision.
I pound my fist against the ground in frustration, barking an expletive. "*Motherfucker!*"
Tipping my head back, I look up along familiar beige chinos, my gaze traveling over the well-fitted, still-damp white collarless shirt up into the dark eyes of Rafe.

"You don't seem pleased to see me so soon." He quirks an eyebrow. "Need a hand?"

I blow out an exasperated breath, rolling over onto my back to stare up into his smug, handsome face with a scowl. "Go fuck yourself."

He just smiles darkly with a deep chuckle. "I'll be thinking of you as I do, *Stellina*."

The laughter drops off his face when I snake out my fist, striking a glancing blow between his muscular thighs before clambering to my feet. I get all of two feet before a powerful forearm wraps around my waist. Rafe's scent envelops my senses, and I struggle aimlessly against his hold.

Before I can loosen a shout for help, a palm covers my mouth as I'm pushed forward against the wall of the hotel I've just escaped from.

"I know I said I'd never take your choice, Miss Rivers, but I'm afraid..."

As he trails off, I feel a pinch on the side of my neck. The world becomes blurry, and Rafe's voice feels strangely far away as darkness consumes me. "I have no choice myself this time."

My eyelids inch open, only to slam closed against the brightness. I try again, slower this time, allowing myself a moment to adjust.

I'm in a large room, face down on a bed that feels like clouds covered in white cotton sheets.

Sunlight pours in through two double doors covered in sheer white gauze, leading to a terrace that houses a table and two chairs. I push down on the nausea that churns in my stomach as my mind races, desperately trying to remember where I am.

A light, sweet floral scent fills my nostrils as the plentiful sunshine warms my aching body.

I lift my head from the wondrously soft pillow beneath my cheek, wincing slightly at the ache in my neck from lying in this position.

It takes me a long moment to remember escaping and being caught by Rafe. The pinch on my neck...

The bastard must have drugged me.

At the realization, a strange concoction of panic and indignation builds within me as I run my fingertips over the spot, checking for evidence of my suspicion but finding none.

"*Signorina?*"

An Italian-accented female voice chimes out, and I twist my head to see a petite young woman standing in the open doorway, holding what appears to be a tray of food.

"I'm Maria." She smiles softly. "Don Rafael sent me."

My eyes blow wide open.

Don Rafael?

"Don..." My voice is scratchy from disuse, so I clear my throat. "You mean...Rafe?"

The woman—Maria—bobs her head with a friendly smile. "*Si.* Though you must refer to him by his title."

My response is to stare stupidly as my brain whirs to life, filled with questions I desperately need answers to, but unable to focus on any.

"Are you feeling hungry?"

Maria steps closer into the room, walking straight out onto the terrace on the other side to deposit the tray on the table before she pivots to face me.

"Come. Eat. You'll feel better."

Just as my face scrunches up in distrust even, my stomach

clenches with hunger pains, and I can't help but wonder how long I've been out of it.

Suddenly, I sit up straight and glance frantically around for my cell. "I need to call my friend. I need to call my—"

Maria glides over and places her palm on my shoulder to squeeze reassuringly. "It's all been taken care of, I assure you." Her smile is genuine and eases some of the trepidation that's swirling in my stomach. "All will be explained in time."

Her kind doe eyes are filled with understanding, and I can't help but feel a sudden kinship with this small Italian woman.

"Now, come." She pats my shoulder, urging me to rise. "Your breakfast is waiting."

I amble after her carefully, and my eyebrows practically hit my hairline as I step outside, noting it's a balcony, not a terrace as I'd initially assumed.

And the view is breathtaking.

Bright Fuschia flowers tumble all around the balcony, flowing down onto the landscaped gardens below. A labyrinth of green leaves and bright red roses sits in the middle of a huge courtyard filled with sprays of white and yellow flowers as several gardeners amble about their business.

But my eyes are drawn to what lies beyond all this, because where the garden ends, the earth drops off into the pristine sea beyond. Several boats bob on the water, and the place is altogether too much like Heaven for me to comprehend.

"Where are we?"

My question releases on a low breath as I gaze out over the beauty before me in awe.

"Sicily." Maria places her hand on my forearm, and I glance at her as she murmurs, "Somewhere safe."

Then she gestures back inside, her eyes swirling with quiet reverence.

"This suite belonged to Don Rafael's mother, *possa riposare in pace.*"

Maria blesses herself before lifting the cloche from the plate on the waiting tray. "*Mangia, Senorina* Elodie."

After sending me a shy smile, Maria departs, leaving me with a bowl of granita and some form of brioche.

I frown as I pick up my spoon and dig in. When my stomach proceeds to complain loudly, I can't help but mumble around a mouthful of brioche, "Would some good ol' bacon and eggs be too much to ask for?"

Despite that, I demolish the lot, feeling fuller than I would have anticipated and ready to tackle whatever the day is about to throw at me.

After taking in the view before me for a long beat, I stand and venture back inside the bedroom, finding my bed dressed and fresh clothes laid out for me.

I narrow my eyes, seeing there are several choices, recalling the words Rafe spoke to me in the restaurant, only to break them within the hour.

Your choice is yours alone, Stellina*. I would never take that from you.*

"Men are such fucking liars." At the reminder, I'm filled with renewed resolve so I grab the clothes nearest to me and spin toward the adjoined ensuite with a scowl.

"All they do is take, take, take."

6

ELODIE

Once I've showered and dressed, I feel a little more like myself, so squaring my shoulders, I tug down on my bedroom door handle, intent on finding someone who can answer the million and one questions zinging through my mind.

But before I've even taken a step into the hallway beyond, a broad chest overtakes my line of sight. I tilt my head up, my eyes widening when they land on the giant in my doorway.

He's easily the biggest man I've ever seen, with a thatch of messy dark brown hair and big green eyes fringed with long, sooty lashes. Eyes that tell me he's not here to play.

But despite his enormous size, sheer girth, and no-nonsense demeanor, I've had *enough* of this shit. I want answers.

"I need to see Rafe right *now*."

The giant narrows his eyes, glowering down at me, fully expecting me to cower, but I'm having none of it.

Not today, fucker.

I step back, planting my hands on my hips to spear him

with a look. "Did you hear me, or do I need to speak slower, Sasquatch?"

"What the hell is a Sasquatch?" His face creases, and I roll my eyes.

"Does Big Foot ring a bell?"

The corner of his mouth twitches once, then twice before his lips curve upwards. I watch his face slowly transform before he throws his head back, howling with laughter. His entire body quakes from the force of it as I stand stock still, my forehead crumpling in confusion.

When he looks back down at me, his eyes are twinkling. "I like it. I think I'm finally figuring out why he went rogue yesterday."

Before I can ask what he means, he continues with a broad grin. "Sasquatch is a new one." Then he gestures to his body as a whole. "When you go around looking like this, nicknames and insults all sound the same. I appreciate the originality, *Coniglietta*."

My stare is blank as he watches my reaction for a beat until I pop an eyebrow, folding my arms across my chest with as much sass as I can muster. "Take me to him."

His smile widens slightly as he leans against the door frame.

"No can do. I'm under strict instructions. You stay *here* until further notice."

"At least tell me why I'm here."

His nonchalant shrug makes my jaw clench.

"Find me someone who can answer my questions then."

"Patience is a virtue."

My voice drops to a dangerous whisper as I step closer until we're toe to toe. "If you expect patience, I'm afraid you're shit out of luck."

I make several attempts to look past him, but the fucker is just too damn big. Letting out a growl of sheer frustration, I step back to look around the space, my brain working overtime to think of a way out of this mess, when my eyes light on the balcony.

"*Fine.*" I smirk at Sasquatch as I stride toward the doors leading outside. "Then I'll just have to *climb* out of here."

He doesn't so much as blink as I call his bluff. I grip the rail and make the mistake of glancing down. My head feels light when I realize we're up much higher than I'd initially thought. Several long minutes pass, and my forehead wrinkles as I weigh my options before my hulking guard calls out behind me.

"Be my guest." I glance over my shoulder, grinding my teeth when I spot his knowing smirk. "But it's a long way down, *Coniglietta.*"

I push away from the rail, storming back inside as my jailor's chest rumbles with a chuckle, and I release a loud huff.

Before I can retort, Maria reappears, looking flushed and slightly out of breath.

"Don Rafael can see you now."

Sasquatch's eyes widen in apparent disbelief, making me smile with triumph.

"He told me to keep her here."

Maria shakes her head, slightly breathless. "Change of plan, I guess." And she disappears back the way she'd come as I watch Sasquatch with a pleased smirk.

"Toodles, then."

I send him a cheeky wink as I slip out past him and into the corridor beyond, taking a right to follow Maria, when she calls out, "This way. Follow me."

I grin despite myself when I hear Sasquatch snort a laugh from behind me as I do as she bids, keeping close as we walk briskly along a long, wide hallway. The plush, deep red carpet muffles the sound of our footsteps until we reach a polished wooden staircase.

As we descend, the sound of a raised voice greets my ears,

getting louder and louder until we emerge into a wide-open space. An elderly man with a shock of silver hair appears to be berating two young men in terse Italian.

He trails off when his eyes land on me, disdain filling his features as he openly looks me up and down, finding me lacking on every level.

I'm familiar with the assessment. I witness it every time I interact with my mother.

But rather than look away, I spear him with a contemptuous look of my own until I follow Maria around a corner and out of his sight. She ducks into an office space, striding through and outside onto a large deck area.

We pass a gigantic pool surrounded by sun loungers before we stroll out onto the manicured lawns beyond. My eyes scan the area, landing on two men in dark sweatpants. Both are shirtless, their similarly tattooed muscular torsos glistening with sweat as they grapple with one another.

One is almost as big as the grinning Sasquatch we'd left inside, except he has fists the size of hams, and I flinch when he makes a solid connection to his opponent's jaw.

My teeth find my bottom lip when I realize the man spitting blood to one side is Rafe.

Despite his bloody mouth, he laughs darkly and beckons the other man closer once more. He's stealthy on his feet, moving swiftly and with ease to avoid the attempted strikes of those enormous fists.

Rafe doesn't even glance our way when I gasp loudly, noticing the other man has drawn a knife. A wicked grin spreads across his face when he lunges forward on his left foot as his attacker charges, the blade glinting dangerously in his hand.

I'm utterly riveted by the scene before me as the knife slashes through the air, coming closer with each thrust. My entire body is on edge, my breath caught in my lungs as I watch helplessly until finally, blessed relief unfurls in my chest when Rafe knocks the weapon from his opponent's grasp.

As fast as lightning, Rafe kicks out, swiping the opposing man's legs out from under him and, in one fluid motion, he plucks the discarded knife from the ground to bring it to the fallen man's throat.

Both men are panting heavily when Rafe extends his hand with a wry grin.

"Nice try, Paolo." Then he drops the knife to the ground as he tugs the other man to stand, half embracing him while they slap each other on the back. "Same time tomorrow, *per favore*."

Paolo nods with a grin of his own before grabbing his discarded shirt and walking back in the direction of the house.

"That will be all, Maria."

At Rafe's words, my companion nods, then she follows Paolo, leaving us alone. My gaze is intent as Rafe wipes his brow and torso with a small towel.

He tosses it over his shoulder, his indifferent eyes finding mine.

"How fucking *dare* you drug me and bring me here—"

Rafe cuts me off coolly. "I have time to answer *three* of your questions." Then he arches a dark eyebrow. "Choose wisely, Miss Rivers. I will *not* afford you the luxury again."

My teeth clench when he refers to me in such a formal manner.

Asshole.

Strolling closer, he plucks a plain white T-shirt from the grass to tug it over his head. The act shields my eyes from the magnificence of his chest, and I don't know whether to be grateful or disappointed.

I grit my teeth at my ridiculous train of thought, suddenly furious at the feelings this man so easily evokes within me.

Damn him to Hell.

My need for answers wars with my need to rip him a new one, but after a beat, the former narrowly wins out.

"Okay, then." I grit the words out through my teeth. "First question." My eyes narrow as they lock onto his. "The obvious one. Why am I here?"

His expression hardens, and he looks out toward the turquoise waters of the sea, bracing his hands on his hips. "Your Conti lover murdered my father in cold blood."

Although I'm not surprised, having witnessed Nico's fiery temper and callous disregard for practically everyone who crosses his path, pain funnels through my heart at the undertone in Rafe's carefully cool countenance.

He drops his head, his dark hair falling over his forehead, almost covering the deep frown that forms there. "Then he took my younger sister hostage and is refusing all *reasonable* negotiations to return her to us."

His next words fill me with nausea and terror in equal measure, as his darkened gaze flicks back to mine.

"But he will undoubtedly trade her in return for his beloved, don't you think?"

RAFAEL

A flood of emotions plays across Elodie's face in rapid succession before she drops her gaze. I wait several beats, silently watching her digest this news until she lifts her head. Her eyes are murky.

Dull. Lifeless. Like they had been when she'd thought I was working with Domenico.

I don't have time to mull it over before she speaks again.

"Second question."

These fucking questions. She'd called my bluff when she'd

threatened to climb off the balcony. I'm feeling grateful that I'd had the foresight to task Enzo with watching the security feed.

This damn woman and her ability to twist me inside fucking out.

I nod for her to continue as she watches me expectantly, her bottom lip tucked between her teeth.

"May I have my cell so that—"

"*No*." My tone is harsh and brooks no argument as I give her my back, striding across the grass to snatch my water bottle from where I'd left it alongside my cell. I take a swig of water before pocketing the cell and turn back to face her, surprised to find her closer than I'd left her.

"I-I need to let my…loved ones know I'm okay." Her eyes are pleading as she steps even closer, almost within touching distance, and I find myself taking a step back, suddenly hyper-aware of how her proximity affects me.

"I've sent word to Conti—"

"My friend is waiting—"

"If you're referring to your friend back in Lazise, you don't need to be concerned. He decided to extend his trip to Verona alongside Adriano when he got your message that Domenico had arrived to escort you home."

Her jaw tenses as I smirk. "I don't think he's the biggest fan of your lover, judging by his response."

"There's no love lost between them if that's what you mean."

We regard one another for a long moment, her eyes filled with something that vaguely resembles hurt. I feel a stab of guilt, having been the one to cause it, but I shove it away as quickly as it appeared.

Fuck it all.

I move past her, intent on reaching the sanctuary of my office, hating the way this conversation is progressing. My bare feet eat the distance, though I can feel her right at my heels until we reach the pool deck.

Without warning, I twist about to face her, to tell her that question time is over.

"Miss Rivers, I—"

She stops abruptly, her sandaled feet slipping on the freshly sprayed tiles, and I snake out a hand to steady her. My palm grips her upper arm as she rights herself to regard me with big blue eyes.

Tilting her head to one side, she reaches up with her free hand to tuck her hair behind her ear. And when she speaks, her words are barely a whisper.

"Third question." She exhales a heavy breath. "*Why?*"

She shrugs as the words leave her lips, and the action sees the thin strap of her navy-blue sundress falling from her shoulder, displaying even more of her creamy smooth skin.

I gravitate closer despite myself, the pull toward this woman almost too much to withstand. "You'll need to be more precise with your question, Elodie."

"Yesterday…on the pier." Her throat works when she swallows as genuine curiosity overtakes her features. "*Why* did you approach me? *Why* did you bring me for dinner and say all those things? *Why* not let one of your men do your dirty work? I *don't*—"

"That's a lot more than three questions." I arch an eyebrow almost playfully, and she tips her chin up in response.

"I need to know *why* you did it, because…"

She trails off, her eyebrows drawing together. "You made me feel safe with you. You made me feel *seen*. Despite myself, I *trusted* you—"

She slams to a halt, sucking in a sharp breath when I ever so gently slide the strap back up her arm, goosebumps arising in the wake of my fingertips.

"You don't remember, do you, *Stellina*."

My voice is low, eyes trained solely on hers.

Her breath catches in her throat when I slide my hand from her shoulder, skimming over the delicate skin below her ear to cup her jaw. I brush the pad of my thumb across her cheekbone, and her eyelashes flutter as she leans slightly closer.

"Remember *what*, Rafe?"

My eyes hungrily absorb her beautiful face, even as frustration eats at me, until my cell ringing renders the tension flowing between us.

I yank it out of my pocket, severing all contact when I step back several paces.

"*Sì?*" I bark down the line, softening slightly when I hear my youngest brother, Sebastiano, on the other end.

"What's up your ass, *Fratello*?"

One corner of my mouth twitches at his signature lack of a fuck to give. "*Ti richiamero tra cinque minuti, va bene?*"

I barely let him murmur his assent before I hang up, continuing to regard Elodie with the same intent she's watching me. Suddenly, I'm overwhelmed by the urge to taunt her. To witness those claws, that fire, that *strength* that I find so magnetic.

"A good house guest doesn't eavesdrop on the homeowner's calls, Miss Rivers."

She huffs. "House guest, my goddamn ass. And for the record, I couldn't understand a word you said anyway, asshole."

Then her eyes narrow to slits before she stalks past me and inside my office. By the time I've caught up, her hand is on the door handle when she pivots to pin me with a dark stare.

"For what it's worth, *nothing* I told you yesterday was a lie, Rafe. *Nothing.*" She juts her chin forward in open defiance, and fuck me if it doesn't make my dick twitch. "I don't know Italian. I wasn't *allowed* to learn, you fucking jackass."

She twists the handle, tugging open the door quickly, but I'm faster. Two long strides put me at her back, and I slam my hand against the door to stall her escape. My breath coasts over the shell of her ear when I lean down over her as rage colors my words.

"You weren't *allowed*?"

I reach up with my free hand to tug her hair off her shoulder, pressing even closer. Her body trembles against me as I inhale her delicate fragrance.

"Tell me, who forbid you?"

The silence between us is broken only by the sound of our breathing, and I close my eyes for a moment. My hands gravitate to her hips of their own free will, and I pull her against me to run the tip of my nose along the skin of her neck.

Her scent is Elodie and Elodie alone. No perfumes. No lotions. Just her with a slight underscore of cinnamon. And the addict that I am feels like I'm soaring higher with each breath I take.

"Who forbid you, *Stellina*?"

I can't help myself from brushing my lips over the back of her neck, and she gasps before I open my mouth over her soft flesh. When I bite down, her moan fills the air, and I press my front against her back, knowing she can feel the hard-on she's caused.

"*Tell me.*"

She stiffens in my hold a split second before I feel an elbow to my gut that makes me double over with a groan. And by the time I've righted myself, all I see is a flash of blonde hair as she makes her escape.

With a shake of my head, as though to banish the spell that she's clearly cast over me, I sink into my desk chair.

I can't knock the feeling that her three questions have left me with a dozen more of my own.

And despite my better judgment, knowing I should keep my distance, I'm determined to get answers.

7

ELODIE

It's past midnight, and I can't fall asleep. I've spent what feels like hours tossing and turning and, at this point, I'm moments away from completely losing my freaking shit.

I flip over onto my back with a huff before sitting up to throw the suddenly too-heavy covers off completely. Then I twist my long hair into a messy knot, securing it with the clip I'd left on the nightstand earlier.

You don't remember, do you, Stellina.

My jaw clenches as I squeeze my eyes closed so tightly it hurts, picturing the look on Rafe's face earlier.

Part disappointment.

Part hope.

It had only succeeded in filling me with *complete* frustration.

I scrub my hands up and down my face before looking around the room as though the answers I'm searching for are lying hidden amongst the shadows.

"Remember *what*?"

My hoarsely spoken words whisper through the warm night air while my mind jumps from one possibility to another, striving desperately to get a hold of my thoughts.

Breath hitching, my heartbeat increases tenfold when my eyelids flicker closed. In my mind's eye, I can make out a hazy vision of myself, wearing a simple white dress. My hair is tied loosely at the nape of my neck, and there's a bright smile on my face that reaches my eyes, making them sparkle.

"*Cosa succede quando esprimi un desiderio su una stella?*"

A deep voice whispers words I *know* I've heard before, and I edge closer to answers I'm desperate to find, until a loud bang from somewhere else in the house splinters the silence of the night.

My eyes fly open, and my feet hit the floor before I'm even conscious of my actions. I poke my head out into the hallway and, despite both Maria and Sasquatch assuring me that I will be treated as a valued guest while I'm here, I freeze in indecision.

The sound of glass shattering followed by a door slamming makes my mind up for me, and my feet swiftly follow the sound, bringing me to the top of the staircase.

A tall, slender woman covered in, what I'm *praying* is red wine is ascending as I begin to make my way down. When her eyes find mine, I realize immediately that she's clearly more than a little drunk. Though she keeps her narrowed, angry eyes on me the whole way, I'm grateful when she moves past me without a word.

I watch after her until she disappears from my line of sight, and then I make a split-second decision to venture toward the kitchen. A glass of warm milk might work.

I'm almost at my destination, when I hear footsteps and two male voices murmuring quietly. Rather than risk being seen—even after the reassurances I'd received—I slip inside the first room I find, lightly closing the door behind me with a soft *snick*.

With my back pressed against the wood, I take a moment to allow my racing heart to slow as my eyes scan the space, widening in sheer delight when I see a pristine grand piano.

She's bathed in moonlight, her ivories bared and beckoning me onward.

My bare feet pad closer, sidestepping a smashed decanter of red wine that confirms my earlier suspicions, until I'm standing right beside her. I reach out my right hand to skim my index and middle fingers over the smooth keys, relishing the familiar feel as though she's an old friend, even though my playing was always subpar.

"Do you play?"

I jolt, slamming my hand onto the piano keys, causing a loud *twang* to reverberate through the room as my eyes search the darkness for the unmistakable owner of that gravelly voice.

With a dark chuckle, Rafe unfolds himself from an armchair in a darkened alcove. The moon paints his features in shadow as he walks closer, having deposited an empty tumbler from his rose-tattooed hand onto a nearby shelf.

He looks disheveled, with his white shirt open at the collar and sleeves rolled up to his elbows to display the sexiest fucking forearms I've ever seen. His hair is messy, as though he's been raking his fingers through it, and my own itch with the desire to touch those locks. To determine if they're as soft as they look.

Instead of acting on the impulse, I step farther away, pressing my palm to my chest in an attempt to calm my racing heart.

"Jesus fucking Christ! You frightened the living *shit* out of me."

I sound breathless even to my own ears as Rafe smiles lazily. If I had expected to find anger on his face following how I'd elbowed him earlier, I'd be disappointed. His face is entirely unreadable aside from the taunting half-smirk dancing on his lips.

He arches a dark eyebrow as his eyes leave my face to skim

down along my body. "Do you often wander through strange houses in the dark dressed like...*this*?"

I'm suddenly self-conscious of the blush pink satin sleep set Maria had supplied me with earlier. I move to fold my arms over my chest, only to pause as anger unravels in my stomach.

The audacity of this motherfucking prick to come into *my* life, turn it completely upside down, and bring me here as some kind of human bargaining chip, only to have the *ignorance* to make me feel as though he finds me offensive...

Not happening, fucker.

Instead, I move my hands to rest on my hips, quirking an eyebrow to match his while I shrug as carelessly as possible.

I can feel my bare nipples brush against the satin, inhaling as they pebble into hard buds at the stimulation. He can clearly see it happen, judging by how his jaw tics before his gaze moves back up to meet mine.

"I couldn't sleep." With a shake of my head, I plaster on an indifferent façade. "Thought a good, hard fuck with one of your men might send me right off."

His nostrils flare, and I feel a surge of twisted delight fill my chest as I tilt my head to one side, widening my eyes in exaggerated innocence. "Know anyone up for the task?"

RAFAEL

"I want my daughter home now, Rafael. *Now!*"

My stepmother, Sofia, dissolves into a flood of drunken tears as I rise from the piano bench, forgetting to close the fall board in my rush.

When I twist about to face her, I'm mildly amused to find she's holding the Sauer P210 hand pistol that my father gave her as a wedding gift. Her hands are shaking as tears stream down her face, the gun leveled right at my brow and, for a moment, I *almost* feel sorry for the cunt.

She was a piece-of-shit wife to my father and an even worse stepmother to both Alessio and me, but Aurelia and Sebastiano are her reason for living. She's made their lives her whole world.

Six months with no updates has clearly driven her off the edge she's teetered on for years.

Without uttering a word, I close the gap between us to knock the gun from her hands. She cries out when it goes off before it slides across the wood and disappears into the shadows of the music room.

The smell of stale wine on her breath makes my stomach churn when I grasp her upper arms, giving her a hard shake. "If it were *anyone* else, Sofia, I'd put a fucking bullet in the back of your head myself, *capisti*?"

In a heartbeat, two *Soldati* appear in the doorway, guns drawn against the threat, but I jerk my head, and bark, "Get the fuck out!"

Once they've vanished, I shove Sofia away with a low hiss. "You can thank your children for my mercy today, *Matrigna*. But be warned..." I trail off, narrowing my eyes to slits as I squeeze her arms even tighter before letting her go. "You will *not* receive it twice."

In her intoxication, she stumbles, falling onto her ass and taking a decanter of wine from the edge of the drinks cabinet as she goes. The rich burgundy liquid ruins the gaudy yellow designer dress she's wearing, but she pays it no heed.

Instead, she rises to stand, dripping wine everywhere as she makes for the door. She rips it open and looks back with hate-filled eyes when she screams out, "It should have been you, *bastardo*! Not my Aurelia."

The heavy door slams behind her, the sound echoing through the space as I pour myself a large tumbler of whisky.

Then I knock it back, gasping even though I relish the burn that kindles a fire in my stomach amidst the churning guilt.

It should *have been me.*

I pour another, some liquid sloshing over the side as I release an angry sigh, hating Sofia even more for the accuracy of her words. Detesting Domenico Conti with everything I possess. Despising myself more and more for my inability to get my sister home safely.

My mind drifts to what she might have endured in her time with Conti.

"*Fuck!*"

I loosen a low expletive before taking a large gulp of my replenished whisky, vowing to make that bastard pay with his worthless life if it's the last thing I do.

My mood has soured too much to continue playing, so I sink down into a wing-backed chair shrouded in shadows and turn my thoughts back to the woman sleeping upstairs. The woman whose very presence has ruined my ability to relax enough to allow for sleep.

Her face is sheer perfection, her body heavenly, but it's more than that. There's something inside of her that calls to me. That has called to me since I first laid eyes on her.

Her quiet inner strength speaks to my own, and it's for that very reason, I *know* I can't allow myself to be drawn closer to her.

Elodie Rivers is a means to an end. The key to getting my sister back.

That's all she can *ever* be. I knew that going into this.

And then, as though my thoughts somehow manifested her into reality, Elodie appears in the darkened doorway.

Her eyes light up when she spots the piano, and as she moves toward it, I take a moment to observe her. To drink her in like an alcoholic, desperate for my next shot.

She's wearing shorts that outline the delectable curve of her ass, and her perky tits sway in a way that tells me she's bra-less. My dick surges to life, flexing painfully against the seam of my suit pants.

I knock back the remaining whisky to distract myself and grit my teeth against the delicious burn.

As I continue to watch, her face lights up when she almost reverently brushes her fingers over the keys, and the words escape before I can stop myself.

"Do you play?"

Then I stand and step out of the shadows, unable to keep my mouth from twitching with a smirk. I plant my empty glass on a nearby shelf as she retorts, having been caught off guard by my presence. My eyes rake across her face, wholly consumed by her, before my gaze drifts downward to flick over her entire form.

The realization that she's been walking around in practically nothing for anyone to see stokes the fire the whisky lit within me moments before.

"Do you often wander through strange houses in the dark dressed like...*this*?"

Her nipples noticeably harden beneath the fabric when she rests her palms on her hips and squares her shoulders. When my eyes move back to her face, she lifts a delicate eyebrow.

"I couldn't sleep." She gives me a nonchalant shake of her head, her stubborn gaze unwavering. "Thought a good, hard fuck with one of your men might send me right off."

Desire snakes through my lower stomach, settling firmly in my growing cock even as I pierce her with an angry glare. The mere *thought* of her fucking anyone else is enough to turn me into a damn caveman, forgetting all else and taking what I want.

My base instinct screams to slam the lid of the piano, bend her over the edge, and fuck her into kingdom come. But I force myself to stand in place, clenching and unclenching my fists as the need to make her mine almost unravels me.

Elodie watches for a reaction, satisfaction filling her eyes for a second before she widens them dramatically. "Know anyone up for the task?"

Her barb hits the mark, like a red flag to a raging bull, and I can feel my face contort as my feet eat the space between us. Elodie gasps loudly as she tries to step backward, but her ass hits the piano keys behind her.

The *twang* is drowned out by the deep growl rumbling in my chest, and the sound of blood coursing through my veins as rage fills me.

Fear lights Elodie's deep blue eyes for a beat, but it's almost instantly replaced by insolence, and I inhale through my nostrils as I strive to keep a lid on my fraying temper.

This woman makes me motherfucking *crazy*.

"You will remain *untouched* while under my care, Miss Rivers."

My gaze holds hers as she juts her chin upward defiantly.

"What difference does it matter to you who I fuck?"

Something like pain flickers across her face so quickly I might have imagined it. "Sex doesn't mean a damn thing anyway."

Her words dial down my ire slightly, but another question is added to the growing list.

Rather than address it, I step backward, holding her stare. "It matters because you're here to serve a purpose. Railing my *Soldati* is not it."

"I'm free to *rail* whoever I fucking want, and you—"

"That's *enough*." I grit the words as I clench and unclench my fists while I glare into her narrowed eyes. Her chest is rising and falling rapidly, making her puckered nipples taunt me from beneath the thin fabric.

The impulse to rip the excuse for night clothes from her sweet body makes my fingers tingle, and I ram my hands into my pants pockets to contain the desire.

Raw want courses through me as I jerk my head toward the door. "Now *go*! Straight back to bed, Miss Rivers."

She pops an eyebrow in challenge. "Make me, asshole."

My hand snakes out between us to lightly grip her throat, and her eyes flare with a blend of fear and intrigue as I tip my head to one side, allowing a wicked grin to part my lips. "Don't fucking tempt me."

We watch one another for a long beat until I step back, putting much-needed distance between us.

"Now be a good girl and do as you're told before I forget my manners and bend you over this fucking piano."

Indecision wars on her face before she tugs her lip between her teeth. My eyes drop to follow the movement, my nostrils flaring dangerously as my self-restraint hangs by a mother-fucking thread.

Whatever she sees on my face makes her stiffen, and she brushes past me, slipping from the music room without once glancing back.

With a heavy sigh, I drop onto the piano bench, willing the hard-on in my pants to fuck off and die.

I slip my cell from my pocket and scroll to Emiliano's number. My thumb hovers over it as I debate what to do. He's at Verità, our main brothel in Palermo, and the pussy there is known to be exceptional.

But, my mood sours at the thought of burying my cock inside any pussy aside from the one I can't have.

Nothing new there, then.

I pocket my damn cell, swearing as I slam the fall board of the piano closed harshly. The sound echoes through the room as I rise and walk to the drinks cabinet.

Clearly, getting shitfaced is the only answer, knowing that although she's currently under my roof, she's as far away as ever.

And it's best for all involved if she remains that way.

8

RAFAEL

"I assure you, Benito," I say with a slow nod, choosing my next words with care, "I am taking your offer under consideration as we speak."

My companion, Don Benito Salvatore, arches a silvery eyebrow as he slowly continues to light his Gurkha cigar, his eyes never leaving mine.

He draws deeply before settling back in his seat.

"I know my Gabriela was to be Alessio's wife, not yours. You don't want to make this decision, but *Rafael*...joining our families now will show the rest of the Cosa Nostra you're more than capable of operating as head of this family, *si*?"

I keep my face neutral when he pauses for a moment to gauge my reaction.

"And obviously, alongside my daughter, you'd have access to my *Soldati* in your fight against Conti. Not to mention, my considerable support, *capisti*?" He shrugs carelessly, even as his shrewd eyes watch me closely. "Domenico has turned even more feral since the passing of his father. It's fair to say that you need me more than I need you, *corretto*?"

My jaw clenches as I nod my assent, just as there's a light

knock on the door. I bark out more harshly than required. "Enter."

Enzo, head of compound security and one of my most trusted soldiers, pokes his head inside. "*Senorina* Gabriela is here, Don Rafael."

I nod sharply as Benito rises from his chair, a proud smile plastered across his face as his daughter enters the library. She glides across the floor toward her father, sending me a shy smile as she reaches him.

"Gabriela, *mio Tesoro.*" Benito flourishes his cigar as though using it to display his daughter. "Rafael was just about to take a walk in the gardens, isn't that right?"

I silently curse the man even though I have known for months that this union is inevitable. Getting my sister back and making Conti pay are the *only* things that matter now.

Salvatore twists about to regard me with a smug gaze before I shift my eyes to a blushing Gabriela.

Heaving an internal sigh, my voice is low when I ask, "Would you care to join me?"

Gabriela, to her credit, doesn't miss a beat, angling herself to face me before dipping her chin. "Of course, Don Rafael. It would be my pleasure."

I force what I hope looks like a pleased smile onto my face as I feel Benito's eyes watching my reaction closely before he bids us farewell, leaving behind Gabriela's chaperone, Phaedra, and the strong scent of his Gurkha.

Our practically silent walk lasts all of five minutes before I escort her back to the main house, desperately needing to get the Salvatores out of my hair.

"Thank you for spending time with me, Don Rafael." Gabriela smiles softly. "I know you are a busy man."

My lips curl upward in a semblance of a smile. "You are welcome, Gabriela. And please, call me Rafael."

Something on her face shifts when her big gray eyes fill

with emotion. "I was so very sorry to hear of Alessio's passing, Rafael."

My heart twists at the mention of my brother, and I nod my thanks as she continues softly.

"I have known for the last twelve years that I was to be the wife of Alessio Caruso, future Don of this family. I've been reared to fulfill my duty to my family, and though we were not intended for one another..." she trails off shyly, her cheeks staining bright pink. "I will do my best to be a good wife for you. A good mother to our children."

We regard one another for a long moment, as I attempt to think of an adequate reply that won't back me into a corner. Thankfully, I'm saved when Emiliano's boisterous laugh from farther inside the house interrupts.

I've kept my distance from Elodie in the two days since the music room incident, ensuring that Enzo watches the security footage while Emiliano babysits her. But there's one thing I'm unused to from my friend, and that's laughter. He's a dour motherfucker at the best of times.

Unable to curb my curiosity, I hold up a single finger, glancing in the direction of the commotion with a deep frown. "One moment, please, Gabriela."

Without waiting for her response, my feet move swiftly through the house, directly to the kitchen. I come to a sudden halt when I take in the sight before me.

Dish after dish of desserts covers every inch of the entire kitchen. And not just any desserts, but stereotypical American desserts. I spot peach cobbler, cheesecake, and key lime pie among trays of assorted cookies.

Emiliano is smack bang in the midst of it. His eyes close in apparent bliss, his cheeks stuffed. As he chews slowly, he moans in pleasure.

"Holy shit, *Coniglietta*." The words are muffled, thanks to his full mouth. "I've died and gone straight to Heaven."

Elodie's head pops up from the other side of the island, and a giggle escapes her plump lips as she drops another tray of steaming cookies onto the surface between them.

"You're lucky I like to stress bake, Sasquatch."

Emiliano booms another laugh, making my jaw practically unhinge as I step farther into the space. Both sets of eyes turn to me, surprise etched on their faces, and I arch an eyebrow in silent question.

Elodie recovers first, tugging off her oven mitts to drop them on the counter. Disdain fills her eyes as she looks me up and down for a beat. Then, without a word, she stacks the cookies into Tupperware, giving me her back in order to ignore me completely.

I spear Emiliano with a glare. "You and that fucking sweet tooth of yours, *Fratello*." Stepping closer, I poke my index finger against the rounded stomach he's amassing. "I've already told you, you'll be as fat as a fool if you keep this up."

Emiliano grins—the sight alone almost disturbing to me—before stuffing another cookie into his mouth.

"Leave him alone."

Elodie glances over her shoulder. "He's *free* to do what makes him happy. Bet he can screw whoever he wants, too." Then she looks back at the task at hand, her words low-pitched when she speaks again. "You're not his damn keeper."

My oldest friend puffs out his chest with a shit-eating smile plastered to his face. I can't help thinking he looks slightly deranged as I step closer.

"Excuse us for a moment, Emiliano."

He's gone in the space of half a heartbeat, and I can see when Elodie's spine stiffens even as she continues to box up the cookies.

"I'm getting the feeling you're pissed off—"

She pivots about, launching a cookie at my head that I

easily dodge. "Whatever would give you that idea, Mr. Tall Dark and Dumbass?"

Another cookie follows as she steps closer.

"Could it be that you've *taken* me against my will? That you've told me practically *nothing* about returning me to my home? That you won't even let me contact the people I care for? People who need me!"

I bristle at that, flames stirring to life within my chest. Clearly, she means Domenico fucking Conti, and the realization doesn't sit well with me. The reminder that she belongs to another man—*that* fucking worthless cunt—makes me see red.

When another cookie flies at my face, I swat it away impatiently, snaking out my hand to grip her wrist. I yank her closer, wrapping my other arm around her to hold her in place even as she struggles against me.

"Let me go, you bastard." She tugs and twists, her voice elevating to a shrill cry. "Take your motherfucking hands off of me right the hell *now*."

I hold firm and, eventually, she stops to pierce me with a look. Her dark blue eyes are like turbulent waves in a stormy sea, and between that and her proximity, I can feel my cock come to life between us despite the handjob I'd resorted to as I'd showered this morning.

Down, fucker.

"If you're *quite* finished, Miss Rivers..."

Her jaw clenches, giving one last unsuccessful attempt to pull out of my hold before she huffs, blowing her now messy hair out of her eyes.

As her body bristles with annoyance, I take half a beat to just appreciate how truly fucking beautiful this woman is.

Every time since the first time I've laid eyes on her, she captivates me mind, body, and soul.

The idea that she's wasted on Conti settles like a lead

weight in my stomach, and I need a minute to shake myself mentally before getting down to brass tax.

"No one seems to know where Conti has holed up, so I wasn't holding my breath regarding contacting him." I give her a pointed look. "Imagine my surprise when he contacted one of our clubs in Palermo, demanding your immediate return."

She blinks owlishly, as though she can hardly believe the words I've just spoken.

"He has suggested opening negotiations for your return to him and Aurelia's return home—" I stop short when something I can't quite identify passes across her face. When she remains silent, I continue. "On the condition that he may speak with you via video call later this evening."

Her gaze is unwavering as we regard one another, close enough that I can feel her breath mingle with mine. She's breathing heavily, her chest rising and falling in time with my own now. Her proximity affects me on an unprecedented level, something I need to remember in the future because when I'm this close to her, it's easy to forget exactly why she's here.

When she finally speaks, it's barely above a whisper.

"Thank God he's open to negotiate."

My jaw tics as my chest tightens. Her apparent desire to return to her lover reignites the anger inside of me. The one she alone seems to hold the match to, and I push away from her.

"You'll be back in his arms in no time, I'm sure."

ELODIE

I've lost count of how many times I've paced the length of my suite. My nerves are shot, and I can barely keep my hands from trembling.

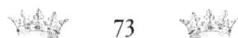

The impending call with Nico looms over me like a storm cloud, and no matter how many laps of my room I complete, I can't outpace it.

My stomach twists, remembering Rafe's words earlier.

You'll be back in his arms in no time, I'm sure.

The tone of his deep voice was neutral, but his eyes told a different story. They were dark pools of barely bridled rage, and I'd spent more than a large chunk of the afternoon thinking about what that could mean.

Why would sending me back to Nico in exchange for his sister make him angry? I'm still none the wiser.

When Rafe told me that Nico had agreed to negotiate terms, it surprised me. Trading Rafe's sister in exchange for me, his glorified whore, doesn't make sense straight off the bat.

But then I realized it's a matter of pride for him. I'm *his*. His plaything to use and abuse at will. And Domenico Conti has never liked the idea of sharing his toys.

Bringing me here was a genius move by Rafe. And I actually feel useful, knowing that I can help get his innocent sister safely home.

And away from Nico Conti. I wouldn't hand my worst enemy over to that monster.

A knock at the door makes me freeze in place. "Enter."

Emiliano—or Sasquatch, as I prefer—sticks his head around the door. "Rafe is waiting for you downstairs."

I nod sharply and give myself a once-over in the mirror before grabbing a container of freshly baked oatmeal and raisin cookies from my nightstand.

When I hold them out in offer, Emiliano grins even as he shakes his head. "You've found the way to my stone-cold heart, *Coniglietta*."

He tucks it underneath his arm, then ambles towards the staircase. He's almost reached it when I catch up to him. "What does that mean?"

He stops at the top of the stairs, surprise clear on his face. "You truly *don't* understand Italian?"

Disbelief colors his voice, but before I can respond, Rafe's voice carries up from downstairs. "We've established that already, *Fratello*."

I look down to find Rafe hasn't graced us with his presence. In fact, the man I'm looking at is nothing like the man I met in Lazise. Miles away from the man who brought me for dinner and laughed in the rain with me.

He's not even like the man who told me he'd bend me over the piano last night.

Wearing a black fitted suit with a black shirt and tie, his ebony hair slicked back off his handsome face, he's Don Rafael now.

And my panties just went up in flames.

"Though her reason remains elusive..."

He slowly ascends the stairs until he's eye to eye with me, and then he extends his hand, palm facing up. His chocolatey eyes are almost midnight, looking into mine as though he can see right down inside of me. "It's show time."

I slip my hand into his, that familiar tingle sending a thrill through me as Rafe shoots Emiliano a look. "And why the fuck are you calling her Bunny? What's that all about?"

Emiliano shoots me an apologetic glance as he shrugs. "Well, *Fratello*...being honest, all that blonde hair, those..." he trails off to a low murmur. "Those big tits, and tiny waist...she reminds me of those Playboy bunnies in the magazines Alessio hid—"

Both Emiliano and I jolt when Rafe barks a genuine laugh before he leads me down the stairs. "Fucking priceless."

When we reach the ground floor, Rafe's laughter cuts off abruptly, all mirth draining from his face as he turns narrowed eyes up at his bewildered friend.

"But if you so much as glance at Miss Rivers's breasts again, our history will mean shit. I'll tie your dick in a knot and wear it as a motherfucking bowtie, *capisti*?"

9

ELODIE

Rafe leads me to an open-plan space with a huge projector screen on one wall. Two chairs are placed before it, with the silvery-haired man from the day of my arrival occupying one of them.

He stands when we arrive, walking closer. "It's almost time. I'll keep her out of view until prompted—"

Rafe cuts him off when he holds up his hand. "Leave us, Zio."

"But Sofia wants me to—"

"*Santo Cristo!*"

Rafe throws up his hands. "You know I could give less of a fuck what my cunt of a stepmother *wants*, Antonio. *Get. Out.*"

The older man presses his lips together for a long beat before he nods and shifts his gaze to mine. That distaste from before is still present, though it's more diluted in Rafe's presence. I raise my chin, holding his stare, until his mouth lifts in a half-smile that doesn't reach his eyes when he glances back at Rafe.

"I won't be far away if you require me, Rafael."

Then he strides briskly toward the door we just entered through, leaving us in silence.

I glance around the room, immediately noting an enormous painting dominating one wall. My feet gravitate toward it. The effect of the picture calling to me is visceral.

As I get closer, I can see it's a photo of a man and woman standing on a clifftop, the sea stretching out at their backs. A tall, tanned man in a dark shirt and pants stands beside a heavily pregnant woman with pale blonde hair wearing a light blue dress. Her smile is bright, and though he isn't returning it, there's a protectiveness in his eyes that shines clear as day.

The love flowing between them pulsates off the canvas and, as I absorb it, I feel Rafe move closer until his chest is almost against my back.

"Who are they?" The question escapes on a whisper.

"My parents."

My forehead puckers as surprise flows through me. "But she's…"

I trail off, unsure of how to phrase the fact that she's clearly not Italian.

"She was British."

I can't keep the surprise off my face, and my eyebrows shoot skyward. Even before Nico had shown me his true colors, I was well aware he'd marry a nice Italian girl as dictated by his father. That meant keeping bloodlines pure. No outsiders.

As though I've spoken the words aloud, Rafe explains softly. "Their marriage was a love match. My father, Giacomo, met his Rose in London while on business. They had a whirlwind affair that resulted in my brother, Alessio."

I twist around to see his face. His eyes remain riveted to the painting as he continues. "When her family found out, they were horrified. The Parkers raised their children to be strict Catholics. That meant no sex before marriage."

His eyes shift to mine, and my forehead creases at the

emotion in his gaze. At the deep respect for his parents shining there.

Seeing him soften, especially following the dark threat to a stunned Sasquatch on the stairs, is truly mesmerizing. I can't tear my eyes away. I don't *want* to.

"Papa married her and brought her back here. I've been told that many members of *la famiglia* took insult from the action, but they didn't remain alive long enough to cause an issue." He shrugs as his lips lift in a wicked smile. "I mean, it's one way to shut the dissenters up."

My mouth twitches, and something tangible passes between us until he steps back. I quickly swallow down the desire to move closer once more.

"You mentioned a stepmother. Does that mean..." I grimace internally, wanting to ask, but fearful of ending our conversation before I'm ready.

He saves me when he answers my unspoken question. "My mother died when I was very young. I only know her through stories. My older brother spoke of her often."

"Your older brother... Alessio, was it?"

His face is unreadable as he murmurs an acknowledgment. "Mm-hmm."

"Have I met him?" I've seen so many men around the compound at this point that I wouldn't be surprised, though I have a feeling I'd know him if I saw him judging by the startling resemblance between Rafe and his father.

"He's dead." My spine stiffens. "Car crash nine months ago."

His eyes are dark as they hold mine while I try to find the right words, but everything falls short. My chest tightens when I'm struck with the knowledge that this man is doing whatever he needs to do in order to get his remaining family back in one piece.

Knowing that I'd move Heaven and Earth to keep the one person I love safe from all harm.

"I—"

I freeze when the projector screen lights up. A dark walnut desk is front and center, a chair behind just waiting for Nico to fill it, and my stomach floods with fear at the knowledge. I push it down, as deep as it will go, and tuck my hair behind both ears before we walk closer to the projector.

"I'm sorry," I barely whisper, making him look down in question. "For your loss. For *all* of your losses." His face softens ever-so slightly and he nods his thanks as we stand before the camera that's sending our image to Nico's screen.

Our eyes hold as this tentative connection between us grows stronger before I whisper, "I'll do whatever it takes to get your sister home safely. You have my word."

I shift my gaze back to the screen as Nico comes into view, even as I feel Rafe's eyes focused on my profile. He waits a beat longer, the intensity of his stare sending butterflies swarming in the depths of my stomach, replacing the fear and bolstering my confidence.

Okay, Rivers. You got this.

Nico's expression is impenetrable as he takes a seat behind his desk, staring at me through the camera lens. He looks my body up and down as though he's inspecting me for damage.

After all, the only damage he likes to see on my body is the type he inflicts.

"I told you she's unharmed, Conti." Rafe's voice is harder than I've ever heard it before. "No point in dragging this out—"

Nico cuts him off as though Rafe hasn't even spoken, his eyes still trained solely upon me.

"Hello, hello, hello." The familiar sadist grin I loathe splits his face. "Oh, how I've missed you, *mia piccola puttana.*"

Rafe tenses at my side, and I tip my head higher in silent protest, addressing the smirking menace on the screen with as much cool indifference as I can gather. "Nico."

"How I've missed that mouth, Elodie. Fuck, have I missed

it." He sighs theatrically, making a point of adjusting himself in his suit pants, and I can feel my cheeks heat at his innuendo. "Whatever shall I do with you, hmm? You've been *such* a naughty little girl."

Rafe's presence gives me the nerve to hold Nico's amused stare unwaveringly even as I feel sweat bead my brow. My heart rate elevates when Nico's smirk widens.

"When you disobeyed me to attend that wedding, you had no idea just how much trouble you'd be facing when you inevitably returned."

RAFAEL

It's making sense now. Why Elodie had been alone and unsupervised in Lazise. She'd expressly defied her lover to travel here.

The same lover who's just referred to her as his little whore.

And she'd been completely unfazed by it, meaning he's used the term before.

"I told you, Nico." I can almost hear Elodie's pulse racing as she stands her ground gloriously, and I can't help clenching my fists, wanting nothing so badly as to drive one into the face of the smug cunt on the screen. "You don't understand. I *needed* to be there—"

"It's *you* who doesn't understand." Conti slams his fist down on the desk, his face stained red with the force of his rage. "You *need* to be where I *tell* you to be, or have you conveniently forgotten the rules of the agreement?"

Her chin stays thrust forward in defiance as she regards him evenly. "How could I forget, Nico? You've ensured I witness the reminder of your ownership every day."

The agreement? His ownership?

Elodie's shoulder stiffens beside mine, and her eyes flick to my face as I keep mine trained on the grinning bastard before me.

He sits forward with his elbows planted on the desk before him. "You're showing a lot more sass than I'm used to." His eyes flicker to me and back to Elodie. "You let this *stronzo* between those pretty thighs, hmm? You let him see what's mine?"

"That's enough!" I bark, stepping forward as a red mist of fury descends over my eyes.

"You've seen her. She's whole. And *untouched*." My eyes narrow, having to speak of her like this. "You have my word as a Caruso—"

"The word of a filthy Caruso like you means *shit*."

His glare takes on an almost predatorial look when they move back to Elodie.

"I mean, you're so starved for affection that you'd let anyone inside that warm cunt of yours."

A growl forms deep in my chest as Elodie frowns, shaking her head. She opens her mouth to speak again. "You can think what you want—"

"And I know *exactly* why you came with me willingly four years ago, *mia puttana*." His eyes light up in sick delight. "Let's just say, your secret isn't so secret anymore…"

Elodie's demeanor freezes with terror as he smirks savagely. "You'll remember your place from here on out, or *you know who'll pay the price…*"

He trails off with a grin, his threat hanging in the air between them before he continues.

"Have you given any information on my outfit to the prick on your left?"

Elodie shakes her head emphatically, the back-talk of moments ago disappearing. "I would never. I *could* never, Nico, even if I wanted to. You made sure I couldn't understand your conversations."

Conti is the one who forbade her from learning Italian.

Another piece of the puzzle, and I frown heavily as it all starts to come together.

Forbidding her from learning his language. Calling her his whore. Her reference to his ownership. The ill-concealed anger on his face that night...

She's not his lover. She's a toy, to be displayed. Used and played with on a whim.

That's why she'd referred to him as her boss when he'd called her cell at *Vista Lago* back in Lazise.

Because he owns her.

Elodie's soft voice breaks through my thoughts, cementing what I've just realized as a powerful surge of protectiveness flows through me.

"I know who I belong to, Nico. I know my place now. And I'll never do anything so stupid as disobeying you ever again. Just please don't..."

She trails off and swallows roughly before uttering one final broken word. "*Please.*"

Triumph blooms across his features as his eyes leave Elodie to meet mine. I force everything inside of me to remain calm externally, to not let him see the force of my rage.

"Now, Aurelia, Conti. Show me my sister."

Conti smiles as he regards me for a long beat before he tilts his head to the side. "I haven't seen you since the last Congress, but you look even more like that old bastard than I remembered." His tone is taunting, and I will myself not to take the bait as he grins maliciously. "He told me to go fuck myself before I blew his brains out. Gotta admire that level of fearlessness."

I blink slowly, giving him nothing as he taunts me. "And as for Alessio, talk about going out in a blaze of glory." He whistles through his teeth, before dropping his voice to a stage-whisper. "Heard you didn't even have a body to bury. *Sheesh*, that's gotta *burn.*"

He chuckles at his choice of words, making my teeth hurt from how tightly I'm clenching my jaw, and I barely manage to grit out, "*Where the hell is my sister?*"

He nods at someone behind the camera and, a moment later, my sister comes into view.

She's wearing a knee-length T-shirt and nothing else. Her long, black hair is mussed, and there's a gag in her mouth, the sight of it turning my stomach. But despite that, her shoulders are squared, and when she faces the camera, I can see that familiar fire in her eyes.

Eyes that are surrounded by deep yellow bruises.

"What the fuck happened to her?"

My pulse hammers as I flick my vicious gaze back to Conti. He shrugs as he inspects his fingernails. "When I discovered you'd taken *mia piccola puttana*, someone had to take the brunt of my anger, Caruso."

I stiffen as fury and misery swell and crash inside me. When I open my mouth to retort, Aurelia steps forward, thrusting her chest out as she shakes her head. Her eyes scream at me to stop, softening when they see the change in me, and I'm filled with bone-deep pride as I hold her gaze. "You're coming home, *Principessa*. That I *promise* you."

My sister's nostrils flare as she holds in her emotions until Nico chuckles darkly, drawing our attention once more. "I'll be in touch with the particulars, Caruso, *si*?"

I nod sharply as Aurelia is led off-screen, my eyes hardening as I regard the piece of shit before me. The same piece of shit I *will* decimate one way or another.

He turns his focus to Elodie. "And I'll keep your dirty little secret so long as you keep that mouth, and those pretty legs of yours closed, *capisti*?" He shoots her a wink. "See you really soon. And this time, I won't just break you *in*, baby girl. I'll break you in *every* way."

The screen goes blank at the same time Elodie falls to the

floor beside me, her palms covering her face as she murmurs over and over again, "Oh God, oh God, oh God."

I sink to the floor beside her, pulling her into my arms, even though I know I shouldn't be letting myself get close. She's too dangerous to me.

But even as that thought enters my mind once again, I know it's too late. I'm already in too deep. It's as though she's somehow gotten underneath my skin. Into my very bloodstream.

She's been seeping into my very being since the first time we met.

Her body trembles beneath the force of her emotions before she raises scared eyes to mine. "I need to get home *now*. Take me home, *please*, Rafe. *Please*. I'll do anything. I need to...I need to see—"

She stops suddenly, and her nostrils flare as she fights for control.

"I can't send you back yet, *Stellina*." My voice is low as I tuck her hair behind her ears, cupping her cheeks in my palms. "He's not your lover, is he?"

She shakes her head slowly, her breaths stuttering as she tries to calm them. Her eyes seem hazy, as though she's remembering when she speaks softly. "My father gave me to Nico to settle a disagreement of sorts. I had no choice in the matter."

My jaw clenches as I mentally add her piece-of-shit father to my hit list.

"Tell me why."

Her eyebrows draw together, and she reaches between us to loosely grip my wrists. "Why what?"

"Why do Domenico Conti and your father hold such power over you?" Her bottom lip wobbles, and she draws it between her teeth to stop it. "Where are those magnificent claws I witnessed in Lazise? The ones from the music room, and the kitchen earlier today, hmm?"

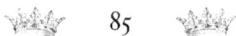

Indecision flickers on her face before her eyes fill with tears. One crests her lashes and streaks down her face, splashing onto my thumb. I gently brush away the moisture, my eyes shifting back and forth between hers as she wages an internal war. I can see it play out behind those beautiful navy-blue eyes.

After a long beat, she parts her lips to whisper, "Everything I've done is for her. I *need* to keep her safe. But now he knows about her…" Her breath hitches on another sob. "Oh God, how do I keep her safe now?"

I frown, not understanding what she means as her eyes beg me to help her. "Keep *who* safe?"

She inhales shakily, her eyes falling closed as another tear falls. I have to strain to hear her barely audible admission. One that shocks me to my core.

"My daughter."

10

ELODIE

My head thumps, my eyes sting, and my body aches as I slowly sit up in my bed.

How did I get here?

I glance around the darkened suite, my eyebrows lifting when I see I'm not alone.

With his long legs stretched out before him, and his head lolled back, the light of the moon allows me to see Rafe sleeping quietly in a bedside chair. My chest aches as I take a moment to let myself look at him unobserved.

A slightly longer-than-usual dark beard covers his jaw. He's changed out of his suit and replaced it with a casual white T-shirt and navy chinos. His feet are bare, crossed at the ankles, looking utterly relaxed if it wasn't for the deep frown marring his brow.

Long lashes brush his olive-skinned cheekbones as his chin rests on one hand. My heart skips a beat when those lashes flutter open, and his midnight gaze finds mine.

"There you are, *Stellina*."

Disuse roughens his voice, and he clears his throat as he sits up, stretching his arms over his head with a low groan. His gaze is impenetrable as he regards me, the silence extending until I drop my gaze.

"How did I get here?"

"I carried you." My eyes shoot back to his as his brow furrows. "You sobbed until you passed out…"

I sit forward suddenly, everything that transpired rushing to the forefront of my mind.

"Oh my God." My breathing accelerates, pulse pounding in time with the steady thump in my temples. "I need to go—I need to…"

As I move to swing my legs over the side of the bed, Rafe swiftly unfurls his long length from the chair with the agility of a cat and kneels beside me. His hands wrap around my upper arms to firmly but gently hold me in place.

"Elodie."

One word. My name. And it centers me enough to hold his concerned gaze.

"I can keep her safe."

I swallow the lump in my throat. My eyes fill with tears at the thought of what could happen to the one person I love as a result of my stupidity.

I should never have come here.

"How?" comes out on a hopeless whisper as regret barrels through me.

"Tell me where she is."

Rafe's hands move from my arms to cup my cheeks. The soft pads of his thumbs brush away tears I didn't even know were falling as he leans his forehead against mine. I can almost *feel* him lending me his strength, sending it through his body and into mine, and my soul aches, fortified by this man.

"I don't want her involved… I want her to have a normal life. A *safe* life," I tell him, my voice scratchy from crying so hard. "Her safety is the very reason I willingly went with Nico in the first place. My parents—"

I halt suddenly, sucking in a breath as those hated words fill my head.

You know who'll pay the price.

Words they've lorded over me from the moment of her birth.

I exhale shakily as Rafe holds my gaze. I've known this man for merely days, yet I feel a strong, unexplainable connection. Almost like we've met before, and I know I can trust him.

"I will keep her safe. *Te lo prometto, Stellina.* I promise you."

I find myself opening up in a way I never have before as I search his eyes filled with sincerity. "You need to promise that she will remain cared for when...when I return to Nico. I need to know she'll have a good life. Away from harm."

Rafe's jaw clenches even as he nods once. "You have my word. For what it's worth."

I lift my hand between us to brush the backs of my fingers across his cheek. "Thank you."

His expression shows his gratitude before he straightens, and my hand drops from his face. "I will personally see to her safety if you tell me where to find her."

"She's in South Brook. At my parents' house." My heart aches as I take a minute to finish my sentence, knowing where this conversation is inevitably going and unsure if I have the strength to go there right now. "She doesn't know I'm her mother. Skye thinks I'm her big sister."

Rafe's forehead puckers in question, his eyes narrowing suspiciously. "Why?"

I scoot my ass back along the bed, resting my back against the frame to hold Rafe's gaze. "On the night of my seventeenth birthday, I'd planned on sleeping with my boyfriend. It was to be my first time—"

I break off as nausea swirls in my stomach.

"You don't need to tell me if it's too—"

"No." Suddenly, I'm overwhelmed with the need to tell my

story. To put my trust in someone who just might be deserving of it. "I *want* to."

Something like approval flashes in Rafe's dark eyes as he nods for me to continue.

"I left the extravagant party my parents had thrown for me. It was still in full swing, so no one would miss us. He went to get something from his car, and I went to wait for him upstairs in my bedroom."

Rafe's entire body bristles as I stop to take a deep breath before continuing.

"I'd stripped down into the negligee I'd bought for the occasion and climbed into bed. But Harrison took so long that I wound up drifting off to sleep."

I groan deeply in my sleep, the sound waking me as I edge closer and closer to orgasm. The only light in the room is coming from the streetlights outside, allowing me to look down along my body. I moan and watch, enraptured when I see Harrison's blonde head between my legs.

He's lapping at me slowly, achingly slowly, until I'm writhing beneath him, and when he slips a long finger into my soaked pussy, I go off like a firecracker.

"Yes, Harrison. Yes. I'm coming!"

He stills as my orgasm plows through me, and it takes me several long moments to come down from the heights he's driven me. My vision clears as I blink once, then twice, and horror immediately replaces my euphoria.

Because the man kneeling naked between my legs is clearly not *Harrison, but his father – and my father's business partner.*

"Mr. Danvers?"

The sound of my heart pounding in my chest fills my ears, as fear and disgust tear through me, but before I can gather myself, he moves over me. "Call me Jeremy."

His palm covers my mouth as his heavy body pins me in place.

"Shush now, baby." *His pupils are blown as I feel his hard length rub against my wetness, and I buck my hips frantically, trying to throw him off.* *"I've seen how you look at me."*

I shake my head desperately, wriggling my hips as best as I can. Trying my hardest to move away from his intrusion.

"I've seen you wearing those slutty clothes for me, baby. Such a fucking tease. Begging for my cock." *He leans right down over me, his lips brushing my ear.* *"Begging me to fuck you."*

I choke on a sob as his palm presses even harder over my mouth, his girth rubbing against me.

"Your mouth says no, sweetheart, but this body is begging to be fucked." *He pumps his hips, and the tip of his cock slips inside the wetness he put there for this exact purpose.* *"See, baby? You're ready for me. Dripping for me."*

Then, even as I buck against him, nausea curdling my stomach, he thrusts fully inside me. Red-hot pain joins the humiliation flowing through my veins as a deep groan leaves his chest.

He pumps once, twice, and on the third time, his whole body jerks as all fight leaves me. I lay there uselessly, tears silently slipping down the sides of my face and onto the pillow beneath my head.

Heavy breathing fills my ears for what feels like a long time until he raises himself onto his elbows and then kisses my forehead ever-so gently. *"Thank you."*

Bile rises up my throat, and I inhale sharply as he finally removes his hand from my mouth. As he slips out of me, I feel his climax leak out of my body, and I swallow a sob, reaching for my comforter to cover myself.

And it's then, as I stare numbly at the ceiling while Jeremy is silently re-dressing, that Harrison finally enters my room. His face falls as he looks from my tear-streaked face to his father's indifferent one.

"Jesus Christ, Elodie. My Dad? *Of all fucking people—"*

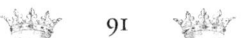

"I didn't—he forced me—" I rush to defend myself, but my voice is hoarse. Fractured, just like my soul.

"That's a lie, son." Jeremy jumps in, spinning to face me. "I didn't force you to come on my tongue, baby. That was all you."

I hesitate, knowing it's a half-truth, if even that, and it's all the evidence Harrison needs.

"You're a lying whore, Elodie Rivers." His eyes are filled with vitriol, and my throat aches from the force of keeping my emotions at bay. There's nothing I could do or say to make him believe me. "Stay the hell away from me and my family."

Jeremy glances over his shoulder as he moves to follow his son. "Even if you won't admit it, I know you wanted it, baby."

With that, he leaves, and I jump up to lock the door, feeling his cum sliding down my inner thighs with each step. I barely make it to my ensuite before I throw up all over the tiles, retching over and over until there's nothing left.

Then I silently clean it up before climbing into the shower to scrub my skin until I'm red from head to toe. As though the water can wash away the stain of the sins committed against me.

11

RAFAEL

"It was a little over a month later, when the morning sickness hit, that I realized I'd missed a period."

Elodie shrugs as she presses her lips together. "I told my parents what had happened, and they..." she trails off, a crease forming between her eyebrows as she brings her fingertips up to brush tears from her left cheek. "My mother slapped me across the face so hard, there was a bruise for weeks. Told me to stop telling lies."

During the entire time she's been speaking, my body has been on edge, humming with ill-concealed fury. My jaw is tightly clenching, my teeth ache, but Elodie is the picture of calm under pressure.

The frown she's wearing is her only physical reaction to reliving her story.

"Harrison stepped up—probably at Jeremy's urging—and *lied*. He told my parents the baby was his..." She continues with a weary sigh. "Mother told everyone I was spending the semester abroad. In reality, I was under house arrest until I delivered Skye three weeks early and—"

It's then she breaks, her voice catching on a low keen as she buries her face in her palms, and as though magnetized, I slide closer to gather her in my embrace.

She sags against me and cries quietly with my face buried in her hair, whispering mindless Italian as my mind races. Visions of torturing the motherfucker who raped her fill my mind's eye, and it eases the burn in my chest, knowing I can make him pay.

That I *will* make him pay.

When Elodie raises her glassy eyes to meet mine, she looks so utterly broken, that I want nothing more than to maim and murder every single person who's ever hurt her.

"Mother told everyone she'd adopted Skye when her estranged sister died in childbirth. The lie was already in effect while I was pregnant... There was nothing I could do..."

Her throat works to swallow before she shrugs once more, at a total loss. "So, I did the only thing I *could*. I stayed."

Her chin juts up slightly in that signature determination I'm becoming more accustomed to than I should.

"I stayed *for her*. Everything that came after was to keep her safe. To ensure she had the best life that I could give her. Even when Jeremy kept finding ways to trap me alone—"

She stops at the low growl deep inside my chest, and whatever she sees on my face makes her cup my cheek in her palm. Her eyes fill with appreciation, and something more, and I know here and now I'd go to war to keep this woman from harm.

"Thank you," she murmurs as her eyes unflinchingly hold mine.

"For what, *Stellina*?"

"For making me feel something I haven't felt in a long time." She smiles softly when my brow furrows.

"What's that?"

Her free hand comes up to cup my other cheek. "Safe."

And despite knowing I shouldn't, I hold her even tighter to

me. Her body is relaxed in my embrace, and I feel a surge of triumph that despite everything she's been through, this woman is choosing to place her trust in me.

And I want nothing so much as to prove myself worthy of it.

I *know* I'm in too deep, but I'm too far gone to care as I press my lips to the top of her head. She snuggles closer with a soft sigh as my mind begins to form a plan, and right at the top of my list is exacting some motherfucking revenge in the name of the woman in my arms.

"Sleep now. You can rest easy knowing you don't need to slay your dragons alone anymore."

I'm awake with the dawn. The thought of setting the wheels in motion to enact revenge in Elodie's name forcibly pulling me from my slumber.

Before I rise, I take a long moment to watch the sleeping woman curled against me. Her face is soft, her brow unmarred as she breathes evenly, and my chest tightens when I marvel at her sheer beauty.

I press a gentle kiss to the top of her head, inhaling her indelible sweet cinnamon fragrance before I ease myself from the bed, and tiptoe from the room.

Without even bothering to freshen up, I march directly to my office and text Enzo to meet me there.

He arrives thirty seconds after I've sat down in my desk chair, closing the door quietly behind him. Then he stands before me with his hands clasped behind his back, awaiting instruction until I gesture for him to take a seat opposite.

Once he has, I give him the names of both Danvers men

and Elodie's parents, his eyes widening when I finish with, "And ready the jet for first thing tomorrow morning."

"You can't mean to do this yourself, *Fratello*. The current situation with Conti is volatile, to say the least, not to mention the repercussions if—"

"I *will* handle this retribution."

My tone brooks no argument, and Enzo rises from the seat with a nod before giving me his back as he exits the room.

My body vibrates with the need to get this motherfucking show on the road, and I rise to my feet to pace my office, needing to do *something*.

Lost in dark, depraved thoughts of vengeance, the sound of a splash rips me from my inner musings. My eyes search beyond the window in the direction of the pool, my breath quickening when a blonde head emerges from beneath the rippling water.

Moving closer to the window, I watch for long moments as Elodie cleanly swims lap after lap until she stops, and remains floating on her back in the center of the pool. A beat passes as I contemplate keeping my distance, but my feet are already out the door before the thought has fully formed.

I shuck my shoes and socks at the edge of the decking and pad closer on silent feet. Her face is serene, her eyes closed as she bathes in the warm morning sunshine, and her long hair floats around her, twisting and curling beneath the water.

Her simple black one-piece suit has slim straps that taper into a squared neckline, showing the smallest hint of cleavage, and even at that, my unruly dick springs to life.

Down, stronzo.

Her eyelids open slowly, and as she blinks up at me, a smile grows on her lips until it shines from her eyes, encompassing her entire beautiful face in a way that electrifies me from head to goddamn toe.

She stops floating and swims closer, coming to a halt in

front of me. Her head tilts to one side, and the light in her eyes dims slightly. "You were gone when I woke."

Clearing my throat, I nod. "I had business that couldn't wait." My eyes rake over her face and a small grin tips my lips at the realization that my absence bothered her. "Did you miss me or something?"

Her cheeks flush a delectable pink that spreads down her body and across her collarbone, and she blinks owlishly before she admits, "Yes."

My grin evolves into a shit-eating smile at her confession, and I just can't help teasing her a little more. "No cookies to toss at me today then, hmm?"

She narrows her eyes, lips pressing together, clearly trying and failing to stifle a smile. A bark of laughter breaks from my chest, and her eyes narrow even further, sending me spiraling. I'm bent double when I hear a splash, and a nanosecond later, I'm soaked.

As I straighten, Elodie's laughter fills the air, and I arch a disbelieving eyebrow as I lift a water-sodden leg. "Really?"

She giggles behind her hand as she nods. "No cookies today, so I'm improvising, Handsome." With a delicate eyebrow quirked, mischief dances in her eyes. "Using what I have at hand. See?"

And then, at the speed of light, she swipes her arm out to send another wave of water all over my bottom half.

"Don't say you didn't ask for it."

Her eyes widen, and the laughter freezes on her face when I peel my white T-shirt over my head. Then I toss it to one side and shoot her a devilish wink before diving into the water.

ELODIE

My jaw unhinges as Rafe disappears beneath the water, still clad in his sodden chinos, and I quickly propel myself toward the edge of the pool.

I loosen a shriek when his hand snakes around my ankle, tugging me back toward him, and I spin about to be met with a wall of water. It fills my mouth as Rafe's deep chuckle fills my ears.

I waste no time splashing him right back, and within seconds, pool water is flying everywhere as our joint laughter surrounds us. My heart feels light, and I embrace the feeling, half afraid it will disappear as quickly as it formed.

Rafe grins wickedly before ducking down beneath the water, and I squeal in protest as his palms enfold my stomach, yanking me beneath the surface. I gasp a deep breath right before I go under.

It takes a second to adjust, and when I do, my inhaled breath stutters in my chest.

Rafe's inky hair surrounds his head, swirling softly on either side of his beautiful face. Jet-black eyes focus solely on me with a depth I feel in my bones, and I feel an almost frightening sense of relief that this man has come into my life.

When I'd woken this morning, finding him gone, I'd been genuinely lost. Last night spent in the safety of his warm embrace was the best night's sleep I can ever recall in my entire life.

Having shared my past with him, and him believing me without question, had lightened a burden I didn't realize I had been carrying.

In the silence beneath the water, he palms my right cheek, eyes fixed on mine as though he can see right down into the deepest parts of me. Down into the fiber of my very being. Into the parts that make up who I am.

And he likes what he sees.

I'm consumed with a warmth that heats me from the inside out, replenishing the parts of me that have been empty for so long. Hope swells within me even as I try to beat it down, afraid to lean into how this man makes me feel, until I kick off the bottom of the pool, and crest the surface to inhale deeply.

Rafe follows, and the laughter from before returns to his eyes as he narrows them playfully. "I'll give you a five-second head start before I dunk you again, *Stellina*."

Maria glances back at me with a small smile as she leads me through the darkened house. I smooth my hands down the silky white slip dress she'd given me to wear as I nibble my bottom lip, anxiously wondering where she's taking me.

Following a gloriously misspent afternoon by the pool with Rafe, he'd been called away on business, and I'd been left to my own devices. Time had passed quickly as I'd wandered through the gardens, and explored the sprawling labyrinth, squealing excitedly when I'd come across a rose-endowed pavilion at the center.

I'd whiled away an hour or more simply soaking in the silence and the sunshine before returning to the house. It was then Maria knocked on the door of my suite, announcing that Rafe had requested my presence at dinner.

My stomach dances with nervous excitement when Maria slips outside and leads me onto a deck-type area that I haven't seen before.

There's a wide-open space, lit up with twinkling lights, as soft classical music plays over a speaker. A round white cloth-covered table is at the center of the space with a chair on either side.

My eyes immediately land on Rafe as he rises from his seat. He watches me as I cross the space, extending a hand when I'm within his reach. I take it instantly, and the touch of his skin on mine sends a now-familiar tingle along my arm, settling firmly in my chest.

One side of his mouth lifts in a smile as he draws me closer until our faces are mere inches apart. I inhale a shuddery breath, my eyelids flickering as his bergamot scent fills my nostrils.

He tilts his head to one side, sliding his stubbled jaw against mine to press a kiss to my left cheek. Then he pulls back, lazily meeting my eyes before leaning closer to kiss my right cheek.

This time, rather than pull back, he rests his mouth by my ear, and when he speaks, his words send that lightning lingering in my chest to race through my veins.

"Since the first time I laid eyes upon you, *Stellina*, you enrapture me."

Then he pulls back enough to find my eyes, palming one cheek in his large hand. "You may be my captive, but you're the one who's taken me prisoner."

12

RAFAEL

"So baking is your stress reliever?"

Elodie nods enthusiastically as she takes a sip of her wine, and I bark an incredulous laugh.

"But you don't eat what you bake..."

It's her turn to laugh as she shakes her head, depositing her almost empty glass back onto the table between us. "Of course I don't." She arches an eyebrow, her gaze filled with mischief. "I have a stressful life, Handsome. I'd be as broad as Sasquatch if I ate even one percent of what I bake."

I throw my head back, laughing long and loud, mostly amused at her ability to poke fun at herself, and when I look back at her, she's still giggling in delight.

"So, no sweet shit for you, then?"

She snorts before bringing her hands up to frame either side of her face. "I'm sweet enough as I am, I'll have you know."

My grin is both entirely shit-eating and a million percent out of character as I incline my head in acknowledgment. "Duly noted."

I'm about to lift a second bottle of Cabernet from the table in a desperate attempt to extend this stolen moment, when Enzo steps into the verandah.

"Apologies for the disruption, *Fratello*…"

Heaving an internal sigh of disappointment, I rise to stand and shoot Enzo a sharp nod. "*Un momento, per favore*, Enzo."

He leaves us discreetly, and as I help Elodie to stand, she barely manages to stifle a yawn.

"Thank you for today, Rafe." Her wide-eyed gaze meets mine as she tucks her hair behind both ears. "And for yesterday, for that matter."

I nod in silent acknowledgment before pressing gentle kisses to her silken cheeks, and as she moves to leave the verandah, I slip my hand into hers, squeezing reassuringly. "I meant everything. I'll keep her safe. I promise."

Hope flickers in her eyes before she lets go of my hand, and makes her way into the main house.

I'll keep you both safe, just mark my words, Stellina.

Having finally worked through all the details for my trip to New York in six hours, I climb the stairs, and in my sleepy haze, find myself outside Elodie's suite.

I blink rapidly, shaking my head as a crazy need overtakes my body, and before I can regain control of myself, I've twisted the handle. Pushing open the door, I stepped over the threshold, my eyes landing on the moonlit bed where Elodie is lying curled up on one side.

Her long blonde hair splays across the pillow at her back, her hands clasped beneath her chin as though in prayer. As I move closer, I realize with a jolt that her eyes are fixed firmly on my actions, and I freeze in place.

"I didn't mean to—"

I slam to a halt when she throws back the light sheet covering her body, extending a silent invitation, and at light speed, I've climbed in beside her fully clothed and uncaring in my need to be close to her.

Wrapping my arm around her waist, I bring her back flush against my chest, burying my nose in her fragrant locks.

"*Grazie.*" I breathe my thanks against the back of her neck as my chest tightens with the force of my long-buried emotions.

She burrows against me as a soft sigh escapes her lips, and the last thing that runs through my mind before sleep claims me is that I'd crawl through the fires of Hell to keep this woman safe.

And mine.

ELODIE

"But I want to see him now."

Sasquatch shakes his head for the hundredth time, appearing even more dour than the first time we'd met. There's no sign of the camaraderie we've built up during my time at the Caruso compound. "Just put on the clothes Maria laid out for you. We have places to be."

I let out a frustrated sigh when I glance back at the dark blue workout clothes Maria had placed on my bed earlier. I'd woken alone yet again, disappointed to find no sign of Rafe.

When I returned to my suite after our dinner, I climbed into bed, but it felt altogether too empty without Rafe's warm body next to mine. As soon as he walked through my door, my entire body relaxed in his presence, and it was the most natural thing in the world to invite him to lie beside me.

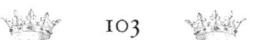

But now, I'm frustrated, and in need of answers, because the question of what the hell is happening between us—or if there could even be such a thing as an *us*—is a burning one, to say the least.

"I just need to ask him something. *Please*—"

"*Santo Cristo, Coniglietta.*" Sasquatch strides past me with a growl, grabbing the clothes from the bed and launching them at me. "He made me stay behind to keep you *safe*. I'm already pissed enough that he's flown to the States without me, don't make it even—"

"The States?" My eyes blow wide as the cogs in my brain turn. "But why..."

"Damned if I know. But he's left instructions that I begin training with you immediately, so get dressed and meet me outside in five."

The room feels empty without the Italian man's enormous presence, and I quickly do as he requested while contemplating why Rafe has gone to the States.

My mind is filled with possibilities, barely daring to hope he's gone to retrieve Skye, when I walk across the lawn less than five minutes later, finding Sasquatch doing some stretches.

"Did he say why he was going? Or when he'll be back?"

His shoulders sag as he deposits his cell and two bottles of water onto the grass. "You're not going to quit, are you?"

Then he twists about to face me, and I shake my head with exaggeratedly innocent eyes as I look up at him.

"Nope. I'm afraid I'm relentless."

He shakes his head with a heavy sigh. "All I know is he's gone to keep the sky safe, whatever the fuck that means."

A sudden lump of emotion forms in my throat as my chest swells with a mixture of relief and gratitude. "Did he say how long he'd be?"

"No more than two or three days. The *stronzo* was adamant on doing it himself, despite the fact it's too fucking dangerous."

My stomach dips uncomfortably. "What do you mean?"

Sasquatch looks at me like I'm a complete moron, and I can feel my cheeks heat. "If Conti finds Rafe in his territory, he *will* kill him."

I nod once, my skin prickling with goosebumps as anxiety unfurls within me. Despite the rising heat of the morning, I shudder at the thought of Nico getting to Rafe. Of Rafe never coming back. Of what Nico will do to Skye if I can't save her.

My breathing quickens as my chest feels like it's about to explode, and I genuinely start to question if I'm about to have a coronary, when suddenly my feet are swept out from under me.

I land on my ass on the grass of the manicured lawn with an *oof* before turning my accusation-filled eyes upward to a smirking Sasquatch. "Hey! What the *hell* was that for?"

He extends his beefy hand palm facing up, and I gingerly accept it, allowing him to tug me to stand. "You looked like you were spiraling, and I thought you could use the distraction."

"So you thought it'd be a good idea to knock me on my ass?"

He grins broadly with a nod, his eyes finally taking on that playfulness I've become accustomed to. "I'll be knocking you on your ass a lot over the coming days, *Coniglietta*."

At my blank look, he chuckles. "I'm just following orders."

"Rafe ordered you to knock me on my ass?" My voice grows high-pitched with incredulity. "I doubt that—"

"He ordered me to teach you how to defend yourself."

Breath hitching, my eyes prickle with tears that threaten to fall as a kaleidoscope of butterflies swarm within my stomach.

How is it possible that this man cares about me more than my own family?

"Now, let's get down to basics."

Three hours pass in a blur of motion, with mostly me ending up on my back, looking up into the smiling face of my instructor. And even though my body is screaming for a break, my insatiable need for knowledge is stronger.

The ability to defend myself, to hit back, to protect the ones

I love – that's invaluable. And something I never thought I'd be given the chance to learn.

"That's enough for today—"

"No. We can keep going." I lower my body into the southpaw position, wincing slightly at the ache in my thighs. "I can go another couple of rounds."

Sasquatch's features soften before he shakes his head. "Tomorrow—"

It's my turn to shake my head. "No. I want to—"

My argument gets cut off when Sasquatch's cell rings, and his face breaks apart in a wide grin as he checks his wristwatch. "Right on time."

He covers the distance in three large strides before he plucks his cell from the grass with one hand and tosses a bottle of water at me with the other. I narrowly catch it as he taps the screen, and I fumble the bottle when Rafe's voice hits my ears.

"I'm too busy to be dropping in for these fucking chats, Emiliano." He sounds frustrated. And breathless.

My feet slowly cross to where Sasquatch is standing. He's grinning as he looks at the video call on his screen. "I need to make sure you stay alive, *Fratello*. Leaving your muscle behind to babysit wasn't your smartest move."

I can barely make out Rafe's form on the screen from my much-too-short vantage point, but his words make my heart race faster than any of the exertion from this afternoon.

"Her safety is the priority." Sasquatch flicks amused eyes to mine as Rafe continues. "Now you've seen me. I'll check in same time tomorrow."

The screen goes dark, and Sasquatch drops the cell into his pocket before bending down to grab his own water bottle from the grass. He chugs half in one go as I take a small sip from mine.

"Thank you." My voice is low but sincere.

He smirks as he screws the top back on his water. "For what? Kicking your ass?"

My lips lift easily in a smile that reaches my eyes. "For keeping me safe."

His face loses all playfulness as he nods once before he nudges my shoulder with his. "Come on. The day's not done yet."

I bounce excitedly, stopping quickly when my legs scream in protest. "More sparring?"

He shakes his head as we start to make our way back inside.

"Nope. For the next two hours, I'll be teaching you Italian. And then I'll be showing you how to use a firearm."

My feet slam to a halt, and I blink several times as my breathing speeds up.

"Why?"

Sasquatch turns to look at me, and he shakes his head with a sad smile. "If the time comes, and he has no other choice but to return you to Conti, he wants to make damn sure you are capable of giving that bastard hell."

He's protecting me as best as he can.

The thought warms me from the inside out, and I jump to action, pushing past Sasquatch to call over my shoulder. "How does peach cobbler for lunch sound to you?"

His hoot of delight makes me run faster, feeling freer than I have in a very long time.

13

RAFAEL

"Please. *Please*. I'll do anything. Plea—"

Jeremy Danvers's entreaties turn into a shrill scream when I ignore them completely and drive the hammer down onto the nail Enzo is holding above the knuckle of his middle finger. One rapid strike bolts it to the table alongside his thumb and index finger.

"Two more to go before we move to your right hand, Jeremy."

My teeth flash in a wicked grin, taking in the sight of the blonde man covered in sweat while I relish the pain that is flowing off him in waves.

"Why are you..." He breaks off with a pant, raising his head to look at me in confusion, sweat dripping down his temple. "Why are you doing this?"

Enzo lines up the next nail over his ring finger, and he tries in vain to pull his hand from his secure restraints. "You have a good, hard think on all the bad shit you've done in your life, Jeremy Danvers. I'm sure you'll soon realize exactly why I'm here..."

I trail off and lift the hammer over the head of the nail,

holding his eyes unflinchingly as I drive it home. His scream sounds like a symphony, and I close my eyes, drinking it in until he whimpers.

"I-I-I never hurt anyone. I never—"

Unbridled fury plows through me as I bring down the hammer on the back of his hand half a dozen times, the sound of my blood coursing through my veins louder than the lying bastard's howls of pain.

Then I drop the hammer back onto the table, and grip his bloodied shirt collar, making him look at me. His eyes are glassy, and he's only half-conscious when I snarl, "For that lie, I'm going to *really* take my time with you."

I drop him with a curse, and his chin falls forward onto his chest as he loses consciousness. Enzo rolls his eyes before he double-checks the restraints, then he slips outside to check on the progress of the second part of my plan.

The alarm Emiliano had set on my cell before I'd boarded the family's jet chimes in my pants pocket, and I lift it out with a heavy eye roll of my own.

I make short work of placing a video call, cutting it off abruptly when Enzo steps back inside with a dangerous grin. "He's just pulled up."

"Bring him to me."

When Enzo slips back outside, I flip the security feed of the compound onto my cell, flicking through cameras until I spot Elodie walking into the kitchen with Emiliano. Her face is flushed with exertion as she grabs a mixing bowl from a shelf.

I smile to myself as I pocket the cell and pluck the cattle prod from the table before stabbing it into Jeremy's gut. He jerks himself awake with a shriek right as his bound and gagged son, Harrison, is forced into the room in Enzo's hold.

Fresh horror paints his face when he looks at me with pleading eyes.

"Please, not my son. I'll do anything—"

I draw back my free hand before propelling it forward to smash it into his face, savoring the sound of my flesh brutalizing his.

"Tie him to this." I kick a chair toward Enzo, who does as I've instructed, and then he stands behind Harrison, arms folded across his chest.

"Now, Jeremy." I inject exaggerated patience into my tone, tipping my head to one side to watch the blonde, sweating man with narrowed eyes. "I'll give you *one* last chance to come clean before you watch Harrison get his just desserts, hmm?"

He shakes his head, and I can clearly see the cogs working as he tries to figure out what I mean. "I-I-I don't...I haven't hurt anyone..."

What little patience I have remaining vanishes and, in one fluid movement, I grab the machete from the instruments lined up beside me to bring it down on the wrist of his decimated hand. The single action severs the hand from his body as his cries of agony fill the room before he slumps forward.

I slowly draw the bloodied blade across the side of my shirt, cleaning one side and then the other before turning to a pasty-faced Harrison.

As soon as I tug the gag from his mouth, he cries out.

"I'll give you anything – *anything*! Please, just let us go."

"Would you consider yourself a good person?"

He regards me with confused eyes before slowly nodding. "Y-yes."

"Then, what's the worst thing you've ever done, Harrison Danvers?"

He shakes his head slowly, opening and closing his mouth before I give him one final chance to give me the answer I'm searching for.

"Do you often tell lies?"

"No." He answers far more quickly than before as he shakes his head. "No, I don't tell li—"

Harrison is cut off when I nod at Enzo, who grips his blonde head roughly before slamming his cheek down onto the table.

I grab a long blade and move closer, the fear in Harrison's eyes mirroring the fear in his father's. "I gave you a chance, you worthless sack of shit. Which was more than you gave to *her* when your father raped her. When you lied to cover his ass. You're as bad as he is."

Harrison's eyes widen in realization, but he's powerless to say a word as Enzo forces his mouth open with his free hand. He fights back, trying to shake his head to no avail while I loom even closer, watching him with hard eyes.

"He's lost *one* of the hands that hurt her." I tip my head toward his passed-out father, whose wrist is steadily leaking blood onto the tiled floor. "He'll lose the other shortly before I sever the dick that stole her innocence."

Harrison inhales sharply through his nose as I bend forward, reaching into his mouth with my thumb and index finger to force his tongue out.

"And for the lies you told, I'll take this."

Then I bring the blade down, taking my time to work through the thick muscle of his tongue. Blood spatters across the wood, covering my hands and his mouth as Harrison loosens a shrill cry from the back of his throat, the sound echoing on and on through the old warehouse.

It takes several attempts before I straighten with a devilish smile, tossing the useless flesh aside with twisted delight barrelling through me.

Harrison has long since passed out, and when I turn to face Jeremy, I find him awake. His eyes are heavy-lidded, and he's pale from blood loss as he tries to shake his head.

"You don't understand. I'm innocent. I did nothing wrong."

I cross the space between us with a snarl, severing the bonds holding him in place to throw him to the floor. "*Nothing wrong?*"

Too weak to do anything but lie there pathetically, Jeremy watches me as I step over him.

"You crawled into the bed of an *innocent* girl and forced yourself on her, and you have the nerve to call yourself innocent?"

I kneel then, unbuckling his pants before I flip him over onto his stomach. Then I lean over until I'm right by his ear.

"Before I take the parts of you that hurt my *Stellina*, first, you'll learn what it feels like to be violated against your will."

His spine stiffens right as Enzo appears at my back, a red-hot poker in his hand and a gleam of dark intent in his eye. I stand, taking the poker as Enzo gets Jeremy in position, his ass facing upward.

"Please don't. *Please*—"

"Cover his mouth, Enzo." My man quickly does as he's told. "After all, he didn't afford her the luxury of begging him to stop. Why should I do the same, hmm?"

And with that, I thrust the poker forward, committing the muted sound of his screams to memory as I take glorious vengeance in the name of the woman who's a danger to all I hold dear.

The same woman I'd move mountains to keep.

14

RAFAEL

It's late evening by the time we've finished with the Danvers, the sun is low in the sky as my SUV arrives at the gates of Elodie's childhood home in South Brook.

A lawn party is in the process of being set up, so getting onto the property goes even more smoothly than anticipated.

Once our SUVs are parked alongside the catering trucks, my small team of *Soldati* and Enzo move quickly to secure the house while I make my way toward Warren Rivers's home office.

On the flight, I'd ensured that all of us were familiar with the layout of the Rivers's family home, so I have no doubt my plan will go off without a hitch.

Just like how I'd made those Danvers bastards pay earlier.

A smile lifts my mouth when I recall how Jeremy had begged at the end. How he'd confessed his sins with tears in his eyes and the barrel of my Glock in his mouth.

How my heart had sung as I'd taken the life of the man who'd hurt my *Stellina* beyond measure.

My smile grows when I think about how I'm about to see more justice done on her part momentarily.

When I open the office door, I'm pleased to find it's empty, so I pour myself a finger of whisky before I take a seat at Warren's desk and sit back to await his arrival. My eyes glance about the space, instantly noting that although photos are dotted throughout the room, not one of them contains Elodie.

My jaw twitches in annoyance before tugging open the desk drawers and checking inside. All are devoid of anything worthwhile, except for one drawer I can't open. It takes me a second to jimmy the lock, and slide it open, freezing when I find a photo of a blonde woman who could be Elodie's doppelganger. They're identical, aside from their eyes. Whereas Elodie's are a deep navy blue, this woman's are icy, almost translucent.

"Are you with the caterers?"

Raising my head, I find an angry-faced Cressida Rivers standing in the doorframe. "You're not supposed to be in here."

I regard her coolly for a long beat before I state, "I'm here for Elodie." Her face pales considerably. "I'm bringing Skye with me."

At that, she lifts her chin to stare down the bridge of her nose. "You can't have her. She's my little girl, and I—"

My whisky tumbler flies across the room, smashing against the door, having narrowly missed Cressida's head. "Don't fucking lie to me. We both know Skye is Elodie's daughter, and you only want her to force Elodie to stay in line, paying the price for your own selfish interests."

I hold her glare with a cold indifference before a frown crosses my brow when I notice her eyes are the *exact* same shade as the woman in the picture.

"Wait a minute..." Holding up the image, I spin it to face her.

"Who's this woman?"

Her eyes flare furiously as she murmurs, "I'll fucking murder that lying bastard." Then she strides closer, reaching out to snatch the image from my hand, but I jerk it away before she can touch it and grip her wrist with my spare hand.

"Let go of me." She tries to pull away. "I don't care who you are—"

"Who. Is. She?" I calmly enunciate each word while spearing her with dark eyes. "You have two seconds to answer me. One. Tw—"

"My younger sister." She drops her gaze for a split second before turning her eyes back to mine. "She's dead."

We regard one another for a long beat, and something like fear flickers through her eyes when I speak again. "Why would Warren keep this picture hidden in his desk?"

She tips her head to one side, arching an eyebrow tauntingly. "You seem to think you know everything else. Surely, you know the answer to that question too…"

I look from her to the photo, conjuring Elodie in my mind's eye, and suddenly, the pieces seem to fit together more easily now. Why her parents never showed her love and affection. Why they didn't believe she'd been raped. Why they gave her to Conti without a care for her wellbeing.

"*She's* Elodie's mother. And Warren is her father."

"*Ding, ding, ding.* We have a winner." I let go of her wrist, and she stumbles backward with a deranged smile. "From the moment Warren met my precious baby sister, Claire, I was second best. I thought if I got pregnant, he'd be forced to marry me, and we could go back to how things were *before*… I thought he'd forget about her."

She laughs then, and the sound is maniacal. "It didn't work. *Nothing* worked. He couldn't stay away from her, or she from him. Then she got pregnant, and we *all* knew who the father was even though no one said it outright."

Warren chooses that moment to walk into the room, and she rounds on him as though I'm not even present.

"You kept her photo in your desk drawer?" Her voice is

high-pitched with incredulity as Warren flicks his gaze between the two of us, and it's then I notice Elodie has the exact same eyes as he does.

His shoulders sag when he nods minutely. "I loved her, Cress. God forgive me; all these years, I could barely look at our daughter because she looks so like her mother—"

He stops when Cressida pushes past him and leaves the office in silence. The manner of Elodie's uncaring upbringing makes perfect sense now.

I'm the one to break the silence. "Giving her to Conti is unforgivable. I'm here to make you pay for your sins, just like I've made Danvers pay for his."

Rather than beg or plead as I'd assumed he would, he just steps closer to the drinks cabinet, fixes himself a whisky, and turns to me with a sad smile. "If I'd been less of a fucking coward. If I'd fought for Claire, we could have been happy…"

He trails off, his eyes turning glassy as he softly murmurs, "I'm more than ready to pay for them. Existing without love isn't truly living."

"You had a chance to love *her*, Rivers." His forehead crinkles when I snarl. "But you were too concerned with yourself to give a fuck about how Elodie might feel. You were too concerned with saving your own ass by handing her over to a goddamn psychopath."

He swallows heavily as I move closer, my blood simmering in my veins with each word I spew. With each moment of witnessing just how self-fucking-centered these people truly are.

"You believed Jeremy Danvers over your own child…" My voice rises as rage roars through me. "You believed the word of a fucking *rapist*—" He flinches, his reaction confirming to me that he'd known Elodie's accusation to be true but hadn't cared enough to do anything about it.

If I'd been conflicted as to how to handle Elodie's parents

before now, this moment right here has made my views crystal clear.

"You're a piece of shit, Rivers. And I'm here to give you exactly what's coming to you—"

The office door flies open, and Cressida storms back inside, the long barrel of a hunting rifle aimed at her husband. His face barely has a millisecond to register before she pulls the trigger, her body jerking with the force of the kickback.

His glass smashes to the floor when the bullet takes off one side of his face completely, and the sound of the single shot echoes through the property as Warren's body falls to the floor. My jaw slackens with disbelief, his wife watching unblinkingly, not wholly cognizant, as I hold up a stalling hand.

"Don't make things worse for yourself..."

I trail off when Cressida drops her rifle beside the dead body of her husband before tugging a small pistol from her pocket. Slipping my hand into my jacket pocket, I slide out my own gun, leveling it at her with an even stare.

"Look what you made me do!" she shouts as she shakes her head exasperatedly. "The scandal will be the end of me. I can't —I *won't* be a laughingstock again."

And with that, she brings the gun to her mouth, pulling the trigger before I can get a word out.

Enzo rushes in the door, taking in the mess between us, and raising questioning eyes to mine.

"Didn't even have to lift a finger this time." I can only shrug with a grimace as I pocket my Glock. "And they say we're bloodthirsty."

Then I step over Cressida's body, heading for the stairs, having let the Rivers take care of their own punishment. "It's surprising Elodie survived with parents like those two."

Enzo grunts his agreement as I take the stairs two at a time, calling after me, "Get the remaining staff evacuated, and tell

Federico he can begin to leak propane from the furnace in five minutes. I want this place burnt to the motherfucking ground."

I speed past several rooms, coming to the door of the one I know is Skye's, but when I enter, she's nowhere to be found. I search inside her wardrobe, and ensuite, checking my wristwatch with a growing paranoia that I won't find her in time.

I walk out into the hall, glancing around to find the white door across from me is slightly ajar. Pushing it open, I grit my teeth when I look around at what can only be Elodie's room.

There are pictures everywhere, plastered across every surface. Several contain the guy she'd been with in Lazise and another brown-haired girl with petite features and striking gray eyes. The edges of some photos appear to be torn, and I wonder if those pictures had featured Harrison.

But the majority of the photos are of a girl ranging from newborn up to recent months when she's blowing out the candles on her seventh birthday cake.

My chest feels much too tight as I focus on the girl who's a mirror image of her mother, except instead of Elodie's poker-straight hair, little Skye has a mass of blonde curls that surround her head like a halo.

Without thinking, I begin to rip everything from the wall, only to stop when a small but determined voice chimes at my back, "Leave Ellie's pictures alone, Mister!"

I pivot on my heel slowly, holding my hands up in surrender. "Ah, you caught me red-handed, Skye."

Her little fists are on her hips, and there's a fire in her eyes that makes her look even more like her mother. Her brow puckers as she takes me in. "How—how do you know my name?"

I lower my hands and return to removing the pictures from the wall. "Your moth—" I swallow quickly and rephrase my statement. "I mean, your *sister* sent me here. My name is Rafe, and we're...friends."

For lack of a more accurate word.

"Are you taking her photos to bring them to her? She wasn't allowed to bring them to her apartment with the other man." Her voice drops with sadness.

Fucking Conti.

"Yeah, I'm making sure she has photos of all her favorite people." I flick a glance over my shoulder and shoot her a wink. "That's mostly just you, kid."

She giggles, and I can't help the smirk that lifts my lips as I return to my work.

"Is that the only reason you're here, Rafe?"

"No."

Having finished collecting as many photos as I can fit in my pockets, I turn back to Skye to find her worrying her bottom lip between her teeth. "I'm here to pick you up. Elodie is sending you to a special school for special kids in Switzerland, and it's *my* job to get you there safely."

Her navy-blue eyes light up when they meet mine. "Is Ellie gonna be there?"

"Not yet." I shake my head, and her shoulders sag. "But she'll come visit as soon as she can."

She blinks up at me with eyes that seem older than her years before she nods and extends her hand trustingly.

"You're nicer than the other man." Her lips tip up in a smile as I enclose her small hand in mine. "I think I like you. And if you're Ellie's friend, then you're mine too."

The innocence of her youth hits me like a sledgehammer, and my mouth lifts in a genuine smile. "I'd like that a lot, Skye."

Clearly having made her decision, she leads me back toward her bedroom, and I stand in the threshold, watching as she packs a small bag.

Her toothbrush. Some hair clips. A change of clothes. A small brown bear plush.

And a photo album filled to bursting with pictures.

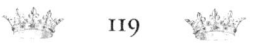

I step closer, glancing over her small shoulder to find that every single image is of Elodie. Sometimes, she's with Skye; other times, she's alone, lost in thought, or smiling brightly.

"She's *super* pretty, right?"

With a nod, my eyes never leave Elodie's perfect face as I whisper, almost unknown to myself. "The most beautiful woman I've ever laid eyes on."

Skye giggles, and I raise my eyes to hers. "When I grow up, I want someone to look at me like that."

Clearing my throat, I shake my head, realizing the girl is as perceptive as her mother – possibly more so. My voice is gravelly when I ask, "Did you want to pack some photos of your parents?"

Then I silently curse myself for mentioning Warren and Cressida, fearful she'll ask to say goodbye to them. But she surprises me.

"Nah. They won't even notice I'm missing. But I'd like to see Sully before I go."

"Who's Sully?"

Her smile is enormous as I take her bag, and she leads me from the room without a backward glance, confirming to me that taking her away from these people was the right call.

"The neighbor's cat." Looking back at me with those familiar blue eyes, she blinks solemnly as her words hit deep. "He's the only one who'll miss me when I'm gone."

I grit my teeth and focus on my breathing as we jog down the stairs, deciding that, although I'd been torn regarding how severe Warren and Cressida's punishment was to be when I'd arrived, right now, I'd happily have ended their pitiful lives.

As I reach the front door, I stop, looking at the house that Elodie grew up in, and I can't help but feel a sense of poetic justice, knowing that these same walls that hid such neglect and horror will soon be smoldering piles of ash.

For you, Stellina.

"Are you coming?"

Skye stands about five paces ahead, her eyebrows raised expectantly, and the resemblance to her mother at this moment puts a huge smile on my face as I close the distance.

"You're impatient, aren't you?"

She nods with eagerness. "I've been home-schooled since Ellie left, and I can't *wait* to make some new friends." I open the door of the waiting SUV, and she steps inside with a grin. "Plus, I've never been on an airplane before. Can I have the window seat, please?"

I chuckle at her enthusiasm, already more attached to this kid than I have any right to be. "It's a private jet." Her eyes widen and so does my grin. "So, you can swap seats as many times as you like."

She chatters excitedly as Enzo climbs into the driver's seat with a small nod. He starts the engine, and we quickly leave the Rivers's family home in our rearview mirror.

And as we make our way closer to the airfield where my jet awaits, the permanent ache that's sat in the middle of my chest since hearing Elodie's story lessens, having seen some unpredicted justice served.

15

ELODIE

The three days that Rafe is gone are the longest of my life, though I'm grateful for the physical and mental exertion with Sasquatch to keep me busy, which means I can fall asleep at night without dwelling too much on my fears.

I've just stepped out of the ice bath Sasquatch had convinced me to take for my aching muscles when Maria calls from my suite.

"I've laid out some really nice clothes today, *Senorina* Elodie."

The pained wince on my face turns into a frown. "What about sparring?"

"Not today."

I narrow my eyes suspiciously as I wrap the towel around myself and throw open the door. "Has he canceled because I'm in a little pain? Because if he has, I swear I'll—"

Sasquatch's voice comes through the door of the suite from the hall beyond. "Just get dressed, *Coniglietta*. Lunch is being served, and I'm famished."

Me and Maria exchange an amused look before she excuses

herself, and I quickly throw on the simple blush pink sundress and matching sandals she'd laid out for me.

I check myself in the bathroom mirror, noting the natural color in my cheeks that wasn't there when I first arrived at the compound. The light tan on my shoulders from my time spent in the glorious sunshine. My smile is wide when I walk into the hall and playfully nudge the waiting Sasquatch with my shoulder.

"You don't need to wait for me every time I plan on leaving my room, you know."

"Just call me your human shield." His green eyes soften when he looks down at me. "Your stress baking was the way to my heart, *Coniglietta*. You're stuck with me now."

As we reach the top of the stairs, he shoots me a wink. "Besides, Rafe would put my nuts in a vise grip if you got so much as a paper cut on my watch."

"Don't you fucking know it, *Fratello*."

My body freezes in place, and white noise fills my ears as my eyes slowly shift down to take in the man at the base of the stairs.

He's dressed like he was that first day in Lazise in a casual collarless white shirt that opens halfway down his chest with dark beige chinos and bare feet. His black hair is messy, falling across his forehead to give him an almost boyish look, and when his lips part in a bright smile that's just for me, my feet jump into action as his name leaves my lips on a breathless whisper.

"*Rafe.*"

I race down the stairs, and before I know what I'm doing, I've launched myself forward into his arms. Rafe enfolds me against his chest, and I close my eyes as a contented sigh leaves my lips, soaking up the security of his embrace.

His signature masculine scent fills my senses, soothing the

ache I've been unable to subdue. The ache of missing his presence.

"She's safe, *Stellina*." The tension I've been carrying suddenly lifts, and I press my cheek even harder against his broad chest. "And my parents let you take her?"

He sighs heavily. "That's a long story. And one I will tell you very soon." His arms tighten around me. "But first, I need to hold you."

His soft admission sees a flicker of hope swelling within my chest, and we stand for long moments, just existing in our own bubble.

"*Grazie, Signor...*" I sigh, pouting as I try to think of the words I've learned for tall, dark, and handsome before pronouncing them very carefully. "*Alto, Scuro, e Bello.*"

A low chuckle rumbles beneath my ear, making me smile as he whispers, "*Brava ragazza.*"

Someone clears their throat at Rafe's back, and I push away, suddenly mindful of how inappropriately I've just behaved. As Rafe turns to face the interruption, he slips his arm across my shoulder and holds me tight to his side.

I look up at him, eyes full of questions, but he keeps his trained straight ahead. "*Zio* Antonio."

His uncle inclines his head slightly, darting a suspicious look at me before refocusing on Rafe. "Rafael. We need to talk—"

"We're not currently at war, *corretto*?"

Antonio shakes his head as he opens his mouth to speak, only for Rafe to cut him off sharply. "And there has been no further correspondence from Conti regarding the exchange, *si*?"

"*Si*, Rafael, but I—"

"*Va bene.* Everything else can wait. There's been a slight change of plan regarding our terms." My eyes shoot up to his face again, but Rafe's hard eyes remain focused straight ahead. "I will confer with you once I have eaten, *si*?"

Then, without waiting for an answer, Rafe moves us both toward the door and away from his seething uncle. I chance a look back over my shoulder as we leave, finding his angry eyes plastered to our departing backs.

I don't have time to dwell as Rafe leads me through the house and up another set of stairs, leading me outside onto a *terrazza* that's set up for lunch.

He escorts me to my seat, helping me get settled before taking his own opposite me. His eyes move across every inch of my face, and I can feel my cheeks heat under the force of his gaze.

Something has shifted between us in the time he's been gone. The dynamics feel different now that I've given him my trust. His eyes are like a physical touch on my skin, and I glow under his silent praise.

"Lessons are going well with Emiliano, *si*?"

I nod almost shyly as Maria appears, bearing a tray of food and a decanter of red wine. She deposits them on the table and leaves without a word.

Rafe takes a slice of the thick-based pizza topped with prosciutto and serves it onto a plate before passing it to me. Then he grabs one for himself, forgoing a plate in favor of sinking his teeth right in and taking a huge bite.

"Hungry much?"

He grins around the mouthful, the sight making my stomach flip-flop as I take a much smaller bite from my own slice.

"It's been a whirlwind trip, Elodie." Leaning forward to pour us both a healthy glass of wine, he continues. "I've been so busy that I've barely had time to eat."

I swallow my food, dropping the rest of the slice back onto my plate to lean closer. "Is... Is she okay?"

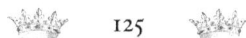

He snorts into his wineglass, putting a confused frown on my face before he answers. "She's better than okay, believe me. And she's safe, I guarantee you that. I took the liberty of enrolling her as Skye Caruso. My brother Sebastiano attends the same school. I thought it would be wise to ensure she had a support system if she needed it. She will visit us regularly during midterm breaks and whatnot."

My breath catches at his thoughtfulness, and I can't help wondering what this means for me moving forward, as his eyes darken when he reaches for my hand.

"No one will lay a finger on her. Or use her as leverage. Never, *ever* again, *Stellina*. *Te lo prometto*."

I squeeze his fingers as he brushes his thumb over the back of my hand, and I watch the action as I force out words that need to be spoken.

"And when...when I go back to Nico, you'll continue to keep her hidden…"

When I raise my eyes to Rafe, his features are tight, with eyes that are almost black and completely unreadable. His hard stare bores through me for long minutes, making me squirm beneath the force of it.

Just when I think I could cut the tension with a knife, Rafe rises smoothly from his seat. His eyes hold mine with an intensity that should scare me. Instead, it enraptures me. I'm wholly focused on the air sizzling between us.

"I brought you some gifts from the States." He gives me his back when he goes to fetch a large wooden box from the edge of the *terrazza*.

When he returns, he kneels before me and opens the lid.

Contained within are photos of Skye, the ones I left in South Brook to keep her existence a secret, and as I skim through them, tears fill my eyes.

Skye's first day at pre-K. Her first and last ballet recital. Ice-cream in Central Park last summer.

My heart fills to bursting, thankful beyond measure for such an invaluable gift.

I look past the precious images and find several newspaper articles, freezing when I note today's date on all of them.

"What..." I raise my eyes to Rafe, but he gives nothing away, so I open the first one, inhaling sharply at the headline.

SUSPICIOUS DEATHS IN SLEEPY HAMPTONS TOWN

My eyes skim the article, my jaw unhinging further with each revelation, until I get to the end and raise wide eyes to Rafe.

"They...they're dead?"

He nods unflinchingly, and I tilt my head to one side, blinking several times as I attempt to process my thoughts.

"By your hand?"

"No." His answer is firm before he heaves a sigh. "To be truthful, I went there with the intention of making them suffer. I didn't know exactly *how*, but I thought perhaps something business related..."

He trails off with a shrug of his broad shoulders. "I couldn't have anticipated the turn things would take."

His jaw tics as he looks at me. "I know they were your family, and I—"

I press a finger over his lips, needing him to understand me. "They were never my family. They hurt me when I needed them the most. Sold me to a truly heinous man. Withheld my daughter from me in order to force me to their will. And they never gave her the love she deserves. We're already better off without them, Rafe."

I shake my head vehemently as he watches me with indiscernible dark eyes. "That's not family. It's the very *opposite*." I jut my chin forward. "In my time here, I've witnessed the true meaning of the word. How you would willingly walk through flames to protect those you love...now *that's* family. And if it makes me a bad person for feeling the relief of being free from them, then..." I trail off with a shrug. "Then I guess I'm a bad person."

I pull my hand away from his mouth, blowing out a breath as I scrunch the article in my hand and drop it back into the box before moving to the next one. My eyes blow wide open as they register the headline.

BUSINESSMAN & SON BRUTALLY MURDERED IN ORGANIZED CRIME HIT

I read the entire article in disbelief, and then re-read it before I look up at Rafe. His mouth is hard set, and his eyes are unfathomable as I lean closer to palm his cheek.

"This one *was* you."

It's a statement, not a question, and his eyes flash with vicious delight when he nods. "*Si*. And I'm only disappointed that I can't do it all over again."

"But why? Why did you do this?" My brow creases and pulse quickens as a twisted joy overtakes me, already knowing the answer to my question.

"He hurt you. They *both* hurt you. And anyone who has ever hurt you will answer to *me*."

I'm no stranger to violence, and given the *choice*, I'd never willingly choose it, but at this moment, my heart swells, knowing the lengths this man has gone to in order to ensure justice was served on my behalf. Knowing that such awful men—men who hurt me immeasurably—got what they deserved.

And, clearly, I *must* be a bad person now because my only wish is that they left this world in the most agonizing way possible.

Rafe brushes the gift box aside, allowing him to edge closer, pulling me onto the floor to hold me close. His lips brush my ear, sending butterflies swarming in my stomach.

"When it comes to your safety, *Stellina,* know that I *am* judge, jury, and executioner. You need to understand that no one will hurt you *ever* again. Not while there's breath in my body."

My breathing quickens as he pulls back enough for his dark eyes to pierce mine. His intense gaze makes my mouth go dry, and I push down on the desperate hope that stirs to life in my belly.

"But the exchange—"

He cuts me off with a growl. "You're *never* going back to that crazy son of a bitch, *Stellina.*" His eyes flick between mine as he wills me to feel the impact of that declaration before his tone softens. "I can't do it. I *won't* do it. You'll stay here. With me."

My heart stutters as he enfolds me in a tight embrace and whispers in my ear. "I've taken lives in your honor. Burned the oppressive walls of your childhood home to the ground. I've given your daughter my name, both of you are under my protection, and once it's safe, she will come to live here with us." His voice deepens. "Make no mistake about where it is that you belong."

I inhale sharply, tears prickling the backs of my eyelids when I slam them shut. A tidal wave of emotion tears through me, swirling with fear, anxiety, trepidation, and that sprinkling of longing for what my life could look like.

It feels crazy to even be having this conversation. The thought that I could finally be free of Nico is surreal, but not as surreal as the feelings this man stirs to life so easily within my jaded soul.

My stomach twists with the knowledge that by doing this, by keeping me here, he's risking so much more than just Nico's displeasure.

"What about Aurelia?"

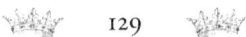

"Enzo stayed behind to follow some new leads." He rubs soothing circles on my back as he murmurs almost more to himself than to me. "We *will* get her back from that bastard."

Then his hand on my back stills as he growls, "And if he's ever laid his hands on you in anger, I will savor every single moment that I spend tearing him apart with my bare fucking hands."

16

RAFAEL

Elodie stiffens in my embrace, and my pulse quickens, instantly on high alert as I pull back to find her gaze.

"He hurt you."

It's a statement, not a question, and her eyes tell me all I need to know.

Following how he'd spoken to her, I'd had a hunch, but now that I *know*, my desire to murder him in cold blood has grown exponentially.

"How many times? How often? Where, when, how, *Stellina*." She shakes her head as her eyes fill with unshed tears, and I grit my teeth, cursing the cunt for the millionth time. "I *need* to know so that I can make him pay in kind."

The tears crest her lashes, tracking down her face, and her gaze closes off as she pulls away from me to stand, walking to the farthest edge of the *terrazza*. She hugs her arms around her middle, and the sight makes my chest ache with the need to comfort her.

Silence surrounds us while I keep my eyes trained on her back until she speaks, barely above a whisper.

"He didn't start out all that bad. In fact, for a time, he was decent to me. Even the..." she trails off and clears her throat, her cheeks heating as she murmurs, "Even the sex was good."

She shrugs with a shake of her head, her blonde hair swishing over her shoulder blades as I painfully ignore the sheer jealousy flowing through my veins.

"Or maybe I was willfully ignorant. Maybe I made myself believe it was as good as I deserved... Who knows."

She expels a heavy sigh, and I let the silence stretch out between us once again, giving her all the time she needs.

"It all soured on a winter weekend two years ago on his family's property." My spine stiffens, my senses on high alert as she continues softly. "All I know is that's when he hurt me for the first time, but I don't remember exactly why. That weekend is missing entirely."

She slowly turns to face me as my heart ricochets within my chest, and she frowns when she sees the look on my face. "What's wrong?"

"The Congress."

Her frown deepens, and she shakes her head. "What's that?"

"You were there. In Vermont two years ago with Conti." I stand in a fluid motion, striding across to cup her cheeks with my palms. "With *me*."

"I don't understand why we both *must attend.*" I heave a sigh of annoyance as my father watches me while a smirk toys at the corner of his mouth. "You're still young, the Five are at peace, and Alessio is ridiculously healthy despite the fact he'd fuck anything in a dress—"

Both me and Papa laugh loudly when Alessio flips me the bird before returning his attention to the screen in his hand.

"I can just wait in the city and meet you two on Monday when it's over, si?"

My intention to join my father and brother in the States was purely for selfish reasons. Beethoven's Sonatas are being performed in Carnegie Hall this weekend, and if I can't follow my passion for music, the least I can do is enjoy a damn show when the opportunity presents itself.

The SUV comes to a slow halt outside the enormous snow-covered house on the Conti's compound in Vermont. It's lit up from the inside with shining white lights, and I can make out both Cesare DeMarco and his son, Santino, arguing heatedly through the large floor-to-ceiling window at the front of the house.

The night sky above is pitch black and littered with stars, and the setting really is stunning, but I have absolutely no desire to be here.

"You're too much of a dreamer for the role you must fill. This weekend will go a long way toward changing that." He levels me with a hard look. "You're attending, and that's final, Rafael."

Shit, shit, shit.

Knowing when the battle has been lost, I follow my father and brother inside, gruffly greeting the other Dons and their eldest sons before being shown to my room upstairs.

As I wasn't meant to be attending, I'm grateful for the room allocated on the second floor among the staff quarters and away from the main players. Their eyes had been both wary and critical as they'd greeted me.

Second sons don't attend Congress. Everyone knows that.

I slide my key into the lock, twisting it open with a sigh. "It's going to be a long-ass weekend."

The suite is larger than I'd have expected, with a super king-size bed in the middle of the floor. There's an open fire on one wall and a decent-sized television taking over the other, with double doors leading out onto a snow-covered balcony.

I step outside, inhaling the crisp, cool air of the night as I look up at the millions of little stars twinkling above us.

"Beautiful, aren't they?"

A soft American voice carries on the breeze from my right, and I look over to find I have a neighboring balcony. And its inhabitant is easily the most gorgeous woman I've ever laid eyes upon.

It takes me a moment to realize I'm staring, and I shake my head like an idiot. "So fucking beautiful."

She giggles, and a shit-eating smile spreads across my face. "I mean, the stars are beautiful, too, but come on. Have you looked in a mirror lately?" I blow a low whistle, making her cheeks flush delicately, and I want nothing more than to see her do that again.

"You outshine every single one of them, Stellina."

She presses her lips together, trying in vain to stifle her smile as she holds me hostage with her eyes. I can't quite make out the color in the artificial light shining out of her room, but they're dark pools that I'd have no qualms about drowning in.

"You're a new hire?"

Rather than go into a long-winded story about the stupid reason I'm really here, I just nod.

"Nice to meet you. I'm Elodie." Her smile is fucking stunning. Perfect white teeth framed by full pink lips.

Lips made to be kissed.

The thought flashes across my mind as her cell rings, and she rolls her eyes good-naturedly. "Duty calls." Then she shoots me a wink. "See you around, Handsome."

"It's Rafe."

She stops just before she goes over the threshold and back into her suite. Her smile is shy when she nods softly.

"Goodnight, Rafe."

Elodie's eyes brim with emotion as they flicker back and forth between mine. I drop my brow to rest against hers, confessing, "I've relived that moment no less than a million times."

She sucks in a breath, and I can feel her forehead pucker beneath mine. I pull back enough to look deeply into her stormy blue gaze, giving her my honest truth. "You've never been far from my thoughts in the two years since."

ELODIE

Rafe's eyes are filled with intent, and I feel the force of his admission like a bolt of lightning.

"I didn't see you again until the next day while the Congress was in full swing. I walked into the compound library, and there you were—"

"Playing chess by myself."

I blink rapidly as memories begin to flow through my mind, falling into place like puzzle pieces. My stomach dips with a strange blend of excitement and anxiety as I whisper, "I taught you how to play chess, didn't I?"

I raise my eyes to Rafe's, drawing strength from his dark gaze as he nods. "I really sucked ass, when all I wanted was to impress you."

My peal of laughter rings out even as tears fill my eyes. "You kept getting the bishop and the rook confused."

His smile is bittersweet. "I haven't played since."

I try to swallow my half-sob, as I slowly allow myself to remember the memories I've kept buried within the scary Pandora's Box in my head.

"What's your favorite pastime?"

Rafe tilts his head to one side and taps his chin in thought as I collect my white chess pieces to reset the board between us.

"I enjoy playing the piano to unwind."

My eyes widen as a smile grows on my face. "I took lessons for years." Then I roll my eyes with a shrug. "I mean, I'm absolutely crap, but who doesn't love a trier."

We laugh easily together, as he throws the question back at me.

"So, how do you unwind, Elodie?"

"I bake when I'm stressed. Or mad. Or sad." I giggle as he shakes his head. "What can I say? I'm an emotional baker."

His eyes twinkle as he watches me closely, placing his chess pieces in the wrong order for the gazillionth time today.

"No, no." I throw my head back, laughing uproariously. "He doesn't go there, silly."

I reach across the board to stop Rafe from placing his rook where his bishop should be, but jerk back my hand when it brushes off his skin. Tingles shoot up my arm, settling in my chest as my eyes meet his midnight gaze.

The look there tells me he felt it, too, and suddenly, despite spending most of the day sequestered in the library with him, I feel very exposed.

I tuck my hair behind both ears, giving my hands something to do aside from reaching over to touch him again.

"I'm too distracted by your beauty to focus on which piece goes where."

My cheeks heat as I shake my head with a small smile.

"Are you telling me I've just wasted an entire afternoon teaching you to play, and you haven't even been paying attention?"

He just arches an eyebrow, his gaze raking over every inch of my face.

"Oh, I've been paying attention alright." Then he sits closer, resting his elbows on his knees with a grin. "When you don't know what to do with your hands, you tuck your hair behind your ears."

"No, I don't—" I break off, realizing I'm in the process of doing just that.

He chuckles indulgently. "You bite your lip when you're nervous—"

"Everyone does that!"

"And your eyes turn into pools of the darkest ocean as you worry that lip between your teeth." He smirks before tossing me a wink, and every cell inside my body vibrates to life.

"In fact, you're doing it right now."

I'm entirely too flustered when the bell signaling the end of Nico's meeting chimes. My eyes blow wide at the thought that we've been *talking and playing chess for close to five hours, so I swiftly rise to my feet, knocking the chess board and all the pieces as I do.*

"Shit."

I drop to the ground, quickly picking everything up as Rafe kneels beside me to help, and as I finish, he places his large hand atop mine. The tingles spread across my entire body this time, and I suck a deep breath in through my nose.

"Can I see you later?"

I can't quite meet his eyes, feeling like I've led him on, and wishing my answer could be anything but what it is. "I'll be working later. And I'm kind of in a...situationship, so I don't think—"

"I only want to talk." When I look up, he shrugs with a wry grin. "And maybe try to suck a little less at this dumb game."

I can't help grinning as I berate him. "You'd suck less if you'd paid more attention."

He holds his hands up in mock surrender. "True, true. All I can say is that I've learned from the error of my mistakes, and I will take it very seriously next time."

Then, he solemnly holds up a three-finger salute. "Scout's honor."

I can't help giggling, so finding myself unable to say no outright, but knowing that I absolutely should, *I murmur a soft, "Okay."*

With a rushed goodbye, I fly from the library, straight to Nico's room on the first floor, where I quickly strip down as I run a bubble bath. I've just climbed in with my hair piled atop my head when Nico breezes through the door.

As he strides straight for his drinks cabinet, I can tell that he's pissed off. My shoulders sag beneath the bubbles, knowing he always takes me much too hard when he's in a mood, and already I'm still sore from this morning.

"My father needs to kick the motherfucking bucket already." Entering the room, he rams the door open with his foot. His face is drawn up in a scowl as he knocks back his glass of bourbon before he spears me with a look.

"And I thought I told you to be naked and ready. The bubbles are a fucking irritation I could do without, Elodie."

I immediately stand, letting the water and white foam flow down my body until I'm bared to his hungry gaze.

He stalks closer with a predatorial look while I try my hardest to keep my smile in place.

"Fuck, baby girl."

He runs his hand down my collarbone, and over the swell of my chest before he cups my breast in hand, squeezing harshly. "I will never tire of fucking this body."

That's what I'm afraid of.

Over two hours later, he's blessedly passed out when I ease my aching body from his bed and tiptoe back to my own room.

I waste no time, changing into my bikini before throwing on a robe and zipping upstairs to the roof jacuzzi. It's open, under the stars, and feels a million miles removed from everything else. Not to mention, the water will soothe my sore muscles.

It's exactly what I need right now.

I've barely sunk into the warm water when I hear someone slip in through the door, and I twist my head about to spot Rafe coming closer in a pair of black trunks. He's looking around and hasn't spotted me yet, so I take a beat to admire the beauty of his body.

Several interesting-looking tattoos decorate his upper arms and pectorals, and a smattering of dark hair continues from his chest right down until it disappears beneath the waistband of the trunks.

When his eyes land on me, his face breaks out in a broad smile that puts an answering one on my own face even as I lower myself deeper beneath the bubbles.

"We have got to stop meeting like this, Elodie."

He slips into the water opposite me, dunking his head beneath the warm bubbles before he emerges. Water drips from his black hair, down his face, off his sooty lashes, and through his closely cropped facial hair.

His eyes are darkly intense as he watches me before a wry grin lifts his lips. "White suits you."

I tilt my head in question, taking a hot minute to realize he only dunked his head under the water to see what color bikini I've worn. I gasp in feigned shock, and he barks a laugh, as I stand, reaching over to swat him on the shoulder playfully.

I miss, and slip, disappearing underneath the bubbles with a squeal. I get slightly turned around, searching for a surface to push myself off of until strong arms encircle my waist, lifting me up.

I inhale the cool night air greedily when my head breaches the water, as Rafe's voice whispers at the shell of my ear.

"Ti salvero, Stellina."

"What does that mean?"

He runs the tip of his nose along the side of my neck. The action makes my knees feel weak, and a shiver rolls up my spine when he inhales deeply before answering.

"I will save you, little star."

My heart slams against my chest, and my head feels light. I'm drunk on him, and the loss of control feels more than a little dangerous.

Sobering, I move out of his hold on shaky legs, turning to face him. "I can't be here. With you." I step back, shaking my head as my forehead creases. "I'm far too attracted to you. And we can't... I'm not free to..."

I pull myself up out of the water, keeping my eyes fixed on him the entire time as he tilts his head to one side in adorable confusion. Bewildered dark eyes spear me, and I rush on before the last of my weakened resolve deserts me.

"I can't see you again. I'm sorry."

As I turn my back to leave, his voice is a harsh growl. "Who the fuck did that to you?"

I turn about, following his line of vision to the fresh bruises on my abdomen and hips. Nico is nothing if not predictable.

He starts to climb out after me, but I turn and grab my robe as I leave the deck, running as fast as I can to the safe confines of my room. One more night, and we'll be heading back to the city, and I can put the Conti's new staff member clearly in my rearview mirror.

17

RAFAEL

Elodie stops mid-sentence when my cell rings in my pants pocket.

"For fuck's sake." I yank it out, cursing the timing of the caller, only to freeze when I see it's Enzo.

I flip the screen around to face Elodie, and her face instantly lights up. "Quickly! Answer it. He might have news."

At her prompt, I slide the answer button and lift it to my ear. "*Aspetta un momento, Fratello.*"

Then I mute the call without waiting for a response, and tug Elodie into my arms to press a soft kiss to her forehead. "I'd rather stay talking with you..."

She sighs contentedly, leaning closer against me as I inhale her essence for a long beat until she pushes back. "Take the call. My head kinda hurts. I think I've buried these memories for so long that recalling them is really taking it out of me."

I help her to gather the box I gifted her with, and shout down the stairs for Emiliano.

"He doesn't need to escort me everywhere, Rafe."

As Emiliano ascends the stairs, I lean closer to whisper in her ear, "Believe it or not, he *wants* to do it."

She turns to me with a bright smile before Emiliano takes the box with a grin. "Can we take a detour, *Coniglietta*? I wound up missing lunch, and I—"

"You *definitely* don't look like you've skipped a meal, *Fratello*." I slap his arm as I pass him, moving down the stairs to make my way to the privacy of my office.

My oldest friend glares at me as I leave before Elodie takes his arm in hers, rubbing it placatingly. "Now, Sasquatch. When would I *ever* let you go hungry?"

His laughter follows me down the stairs and into the foyer. "If you don't keep her, I will."

I plan to.

Having reached the office, I unmute the call, and hold the cell to my ear. "Have you tracked a lead?"

"I have it on good authority that Salvatore is playing both sides."

That double-crossing motherfucker.

"How do you know this?"

"I have a man in each household, Rafe. You know that."

In the aftermath of Conti's attack, Enzo had doubled down on all security measures, including finding the weak links in each family. Paired with the right incentive, it's amazing what you can uncover.

"Do we have further details?"

"All I know is that there have been calls made from Salvatore to Conti discussing a match between Conti and Salvatore's daughter."

I clench my jaw, barely gritting out an expletive as Enzo continues. "But I didn't get to the best part yet. My inside man told me that he overheard Gabriela complaining how she didn't want to marry outside of Italy, and Salvatore told her that Conti was forming a permanent base in Italy."

"That's why we haven't found him. Because he's not Stateside. He's right here, under our fucking noses."

Once I've told Enzo to get on the next flight home, I flop into my desk chair and remove Conti's picture from my drawer. I stare at his face as I recall the bruises he'd left on Elodie, the scars he'd left on Maria, the two black eyes I'd witnessed on my sister.

My hatred grows as I ball up the image and toss it in the trash can. "You'll pay with your worthless life, Conti. Mark my fucking words."

ELODIE

Having received my orders in no uncertain terms, I present myself at dinner on the last night of this Congress that was so important for me to attend – despite the fact I've mostly kept to the shadows until now.

I walk into the dining room with slow steps, smoothing my white knee-length dress over my legs before ensuring that the low chignon I've pinned my hair into remains in place.

Nico greets me with a kiss on the cheek, proceeding to haul me from one man to another, all while palming my ass. It appears that I'm the only woman in attendance, and as such, Nico is in high demand.

Most of the men find any excuse to touch my knee or brush my hair back from my face, and Nico watches on, almost daring one of them to take things too far.

It's like he wants *the peace between these families to come crashing down.*

I'm beyond grateful when they decide to unwind with cigars and bourbon in the Den.

Once they've left, and there's only cleaning staff remaining, I grab a blanket from the pile by the door and slip outside to the firepit.

My Louboutins crunch the snow as I cross the deck, tossing the blanket over my shoulders as I look up at the infinite stars that decorate the night sky.

A shooting star streaks across the sky, and I stare at it longingly, pretending I might one day be as free as that star.

"Cosa succede quando esprimi un desiderio su una stella?"

Rafe's deep voice fills the night, and I look down from the starry sky, finding him doing precisely what I'd planned on doing.

A large white woolly blanket covers his shoulders while his hands extend before him, held toward the flicking orange flames of the firepit. His eyes are like coal, fixed firmly on me as I falter in my heels.

"What did you say?" I swallow roughly before taking a smaller step closer despite myself.

"It translates to 'what happens when you wish on a star.'"

My heart is beating so fast, he can surely hear it. "Did you make a wish?"

He nods slowly, a smile tipping his lips. "I wished for you. To see you tonight."

"Why?" I can't help my wobbling voice as he regards me unblinkingly before standing and moving closer. My feet are stuck to the ground, I couldn't move even if I wanted to.

"Why do you think we keep finding one another, Stellina?"

He's close enough to reach out a hand to cup my cheek with his warm palm. I can feel the tension evaporate from my entire body at the single touch, and I turn my face toward the warmth.

"I think it's because fate put you in my path." With his eyes fixed on mine, he holds me his willing prisoner. "You see, I wasn't supposed to be here this weekend. In fact, I wanted to be anywhere but here. And now..."

He trails off, seemingly in awe as he searches my face before meeting my gaze once more.

"Now, I can't shake the feeling that meeting you has always been written in the stars."

My entire body feels electrified, having soared to life from the sincerity in his eyes, and he moves closer, his cool breath skating across my lips as he closes the gap between us.

"Baciami, Stellina."

My eyes hold his as our mouths inch closer together until Nico's booming voice splinters the moment into pieces.

"There you are, baby girl." I immediately move away from Rafe, confusion covering his face as I plaster a fake smile onto my lips before turning to Nico.

His eyes tell me nothing, but his jaw clenches just like his fists as he moves closer, nodding to Rafe. "Caruso. Glad you could make it, even if it's mostly pointless as the spare."

Without waiting for a reply, he bends down and scoops me up bridal style before shooting a wink at Rafe. "You'll need to excuse us. Seeing my baby girl all prettied up makes me harder than a steel fucking pipe."

Embarrassment rises in my cheeks while a soul-deep sadness permeates my bones as Nico's words remind me, in no uncertain terms, of exactly what my station is.

And precisely who has autonomy over my body, because that person isn't me.

Knowing what's expected of me, I loop my arms around Nico's neck, chancing a look back at Rafe just before Nico steps over the threshold and back inside the house. My chest feels tight when he's nowhere to be seen, and I glance up at the sky full of stars, fleetingly wishing things could be different.

Nico takes the stairs two at a time, whispering in my ear all the ways he's going to make me come until we get to his room. Then he dumps me onto the bed and pins me down with his knees on either side of my body.

"Have I been too lenient with you, baby girl?

Uneasy nerves tingle along my veins as I open my mouth to answer, but he presses his palm over it, silencing me. I'm instantly transported back to the last time another man did the same thing.

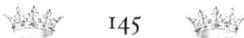

My body freezes when he leans closer, rage slashed across his hard features. "I think you've had a little too much freedom. I think you forget that your family's wealth, position – hell, their damn lives hinge on you making me a very fucking happy man."

His hand presses harder over my mouth, and I whimper at the back of my throat. "And seeing *mia piccola puttana* throwing herself at a filthy Caruso doesn't make me happy in the least. In fact, I'm downright unhappy here, Elodie."

My breathing comes faster and faster when Nico's face transforms. His rage-filled features of moments before morph into a crazed grin that makes his eyes look wild, and more than a little deranged.

Suddenly, he lets me go, stepping off the bed to walk into the ensuite. He starts running a bath while I lie in the middle of his bed, utterly torn as to what to do.

If I try to leave, he'll hurt Skye. If I stay, he'll hurt me.

Well, there's your answer, Rivers.

I take thirty seconds to compose myself as best as I can before following him to the bathroom. His fist meets my face as I reach the doorframe, and I stumble back, holding my bloodied cheek as the pain ricochets.

The momentum of the blow puts me on my back, as Nico descends on me, his face mottled with a fury like I've never seen before. I flip over and desperately attempt to scramble away, but he grips my ankle, yanking me closer.

I cry out for him to stop, tears blurring my eyes, panic filling my chest as he spins me onto my back. His face is contorted when he climbs over me to straddle my waist, and his depraved smile fills my vision as he wraps his hands around my neck, squeezing tight.

So tight.

My mouth is wide open in a silent scream while tears stream unchecked down along my face, and I can't breathe.

I can't breathe.

I can't breathe.

"Elodie, *please*, wake up."

I stir into awareness as Rafe's arms wrap around me, and my scream dies in my throat. His familiar bergamot scent envelops me, letting me know that I'm safe.

It takes long minutes for my heart to slow to a normal rate while perspiration cools on my brow, making me shiver despite the heat of the Sicilian evening.

Rafe rocks me soothingly within his embrace, whispering over and over, "It was just a dream. Just a bad dream, *Stellina*. You're safe now."

I blink heavily before angling my face to his. "I know now why I didn't remember."

His forehead creases with concern and anguish before I reach for his hand and hold it in mine. "When he took me away from you that night, he broke my cheekbone."

Rafe winces as I continue in a completely detached tone, as though I can see what happened, but I didn't really live through it.

"The hospital chart said I'd suffered two broken ribs, and a ruptured eardrum. Bruises and cuts he'd inflicted using a small penknife." A shudder runs up my spine at that, knowing precisely which cuts healed and which ones he'd ensured would scar me for the rest of my life.

My eyes find and hold Rafe's, and I can see he's already thinking through ways to make Nico suffer the most, just like he did with Jeremy.

I move onto my knees and throw one over his body so my legs are straddling him. Leaning closer to palm his face, my eyes showing him everything he needs to know.

"I want him to die begging for his worthless life on his hands and motherfucking knees." Rafe's eyes fill with pride before he nods slowly. "I want him to scream. To cry. To plead. I want him to know truly *excruciating* pain before you send him straight to Hell. Promise me, Rafe. Promise me this."

He sits forward, his gaze intent with dark promises. "I swear to it. On my life. *Lo giuro. Lo giuro sulla mia vita.*"

My racing heart quietens as Rafe's words soothe the ache for vengeance that's steadily burning within me, and he reaches a hand up to cup my cheek so tenderly, I feel I might shatter.

His eyes rake over my face, deepening in an intensity that makes my cheeks flush, and I nibble my bottom lip between my teeth, almost squirming beneath his fervent attention.

When his eyes drop to the action, his jaw tics and the thought that he might close the distance to press his lips to mine sends a thrill of anticipation careening through me. Indecision wars on his handsome face before he neatly flips us so that I'm nestled in the crook of his arm.

"You're far safer there than where you were."

There's a self-deprecation in his tone that makes me look up at him questioningly, and his lips part in a broad smile as he chuckles.

"I would lay down my life to keep you safe, *Stellina*, but I won't deny it…" The humor leaves his face as his eyes deepen in intensity, his voice dropping an octave. "I want you. *Badly.*"

Tension crackles between us as my breathing quickens, my stomach flooding with desire as he brushes the pad of his thumb across my bottom lip. "I'm a patient man. I've carried the longing to claim these lips for two years. And I will claim them *soon*, but only when old wounds have healed, and the memories of what you have relived this day have faded."

He pinches my chin between his thumb and index finger, giving me wide-eyed honesty that only feeds the yearning he's stirred to life within me. "I'll do a lot more than kiss you, Elodie Rivers, but only when you're ready to truly *be mine* in every sense of the word. Because what's between us is so much more than physical, you understand me?"

I nod slowly, even as every molecule of my body screams for

him to kiss me. Eyes as dark as midnight hold me prisoner as I whisper, "*Si. Ti capisco.*"

Then he leans closer, pressing a soft, lingering kiss to my brow. A kiss filled with a tentative promise of so much more, and a contented smile warms my lips at the knowledge as I nuzzle closer into his embrace.

Safe.

Happy.

Home.

18

RAFAEL

Elodie loosens three shots in quick succession, hitting each target Emiliano had set up for her during an earlier practice session with ease. She lowers her arms, glancing over her shoulder at me as delight plays across her face.

The revelations from three days ago seem to be a distant memory, and I relish watching her settle into life here at the compound. If I could manage to get Aurelia back home and Conti six feet under, life would be pretty fucking perfect right about now.

I'd spent the morning on a call with Salvatore. The double-crossing fuck is now under the impression that he's finally pushed me into announcing a union between Gabriela and myself. What he doesn't know is that I am more than aware of his little charade and ready to call him out on it.

"Your proficiency with a firearm is exceptional." My smile grows as Elodie walks closer. "I must say, I'm very impressed."

She preens under my praise, her smile lighting up her face as we retreat back inside, out of the heat of the scorching afternoon. Once we reach the kitchen, I take the gun from her hand,

and tuck it into the back of my chinos, watching as she bends over to check the oven.

"Ooh, these look *perfect!*"

She straightens and claps her hands before reaching for an oven mitt. As she carefully removes a tray from the oven, the inimitable smell of rich chocolate hits my nostrils.

I move closer, watching her deposit several chocolate-filled ramekins onto the countertop. Glancing up, she grins in delight. "Do you know where Sasquatch is? I made him some chocolate souffles."

My eyes narrow as I stalk closer, pressing my lips together to stifle a smile when her forehead crinkles. "I'll have to roll him around this place if you continue to feed his sugar addiction."

Her tinkling laugh fills my ears, and I smile as I watch her, feeling a lightness I've not experienced since our first meeting. She narrows her eyes even as her smile widens. "You're just sore that I don't bake for you, Handsome."

I close the gap and reach around her to grab a spoon from the drawer before dunking it right into the middle of the nearest souffle. Elodie's gasp of indignation makes me chuckle even as I bring the spoon to my lips, and I arch an eyebrow when I meet her gaze.

"If I want something badly enough, I'll take it."

Elodie's eyes widen, and her breath quickens, confirming my earlier suspicion that she's moved beyond the pain of her memories. My words hang heavy with innuendo as I pop the spoon into my mouth, my eyes physically rolling back in my head when the intensely deep flavor erupts on my tongue.

"Holy *shit!*" My exclamation rings out around the mouthful of deliciousness, and Elodie's eyes fill with pleasure as I swallow, quickly scooping more onto my spoon. "No wonder he's always hanging around you."

She chuckles, watching in delight as I devour the entire

soufflé, though her face turns pensive as I scrape the sides of the still-warm ramekin, attempting to gather another spoonful.

"I often wondered where I got the flare for baking from."

I freeze, knowing instantly this is the moment to bring up her birth mother, and although she needs to know, I'm desperately hoping my news doesn't add to her past trauma. Not when she's come so far.

"No one taught me. I just picked it up as I went along, and everything I tried to bake turned out really well." She pouts with narrowed eyes. "Well, *most* everything." Then she shrugs. "Maybe a great-aunt passed along the gene."

With an internal sigh, I put the empty dish on the counter, and close the gap between us, gathering her in my arms. She looks up at me with wide, trusting eyes, and just like that, the words spill from my lips.

Her father's affair with her supposed aunt. The pregnancy that resulted in her. The answer behind why the people who raised her had treated her so fucking poorly.

She remains silent from start to finish, her face utterly devoid of expression until I get to the end, and she expels a heavy breath.

I palm her cheeks, my brow furrowing in concern. "I don't know if now was the right time to tell you, but I need for there to be full transparency between us, Elodie."

She blinks solemnly before the edge of her lips tips upward ever so slightly on one side.

"It explains so much, Rafe. *So* much." Pressing herself close against my chest, her arms wind around my waist as I hold her close. "Thank you for telling me."

"*Si*, Rafael. I will ensure everything goes off without a hitch."

Antonio nods once before ducking out of my office, and I quickly move to follow him. Having spent the last two hours bringing him up to speed on current events and talking through security measures for tonight's party, I'm late to meet Paolo, and I'm anxious to work off some of the uncertainties I have concerning this party later.

I quickly change into simple grey sweats, leaving my chest and feet bare as I go in search of him. Instead, I find Elodie sparring outside with Emiliano, a light sheen of perspiration covering her newly tanned skin.

Her blonde hair is braided on either side of her head, making her look ridiculously young, and I can't help from smiling when she lands a solid blow to Emiliano's ever-growing gut.

"You'd move faster if you'd quit eating all that sugary shit."

Elodie whirls about, her face lighting up with a smile that shines from her eyes. "Leave him alone." The smile carries in her voice, making me smile even more as my feet eat the distance between us.

"*Lasciaci, Fratello.*"

Emiliano doesn't need any further prompting, gathering his things and moving back toward the house as my eyes drink in the goddess before me like a parched man on a summer's day. The pale pink leggings and crop top show off her body to perfection, and I force my eyes away before my hard-on can become any more obvious.

It's then that I notice a similar appreciation in her gaze as it rakes over my torso. Her pointed pink tongue darts out to wet her lips, the simple action making my chub further tent my pants.

Her eyes shift up to mine, widening in shock as I openly adjust myself. I step closer then, my voice dropping an octave.

"You never need to wonder about how you make me feel, *Stellina*."

I trail off as I reach her, extending my hand to gently hold her chin between my thumb and index finger.

"How I feel for you multiplies by the day. By the hour. By the damn minute. Every time you smile for me, it's a shot of adrenaline through my veins. Each time you look at me, I feel alive in a way I'd never imagined possible. And every time your skin touches mine, I'm electrified right down to my fucking marrow."

My eyes flicker between hers, close enough to count each individual eyelash ringing those beautiful stormy eyes now searing into mine.

"My desire to fuck you, to taste your pussy when you explode on my tongue, to feel you shatter around my cock as you scream my name in desperate pleasure…" Then I lean closer enough until I'm tasting her rapid breaths as they ghost over my lips.

"That's a desire—a need—that I *will* fulfill when the time is right. *Only* when the time is right."

I dust my lips over hers, just the barest touch, and her eyelids flicker closed as she inhales sharply. "So you need to be careful, *Stellina*. I want you more than I need air to breathe, but I'm just a man. A man who's desperate to make you his…" My voice drops to a hoarse whisper that's almost a plea. "And I'm hanging by a motherfucking thread here."

A shiver wracks her lithe body as I step back with a smirk and a rock-hard dick in my pants, forcing myself to behave. She opens eyes that are glazed with arousal, and I force myself to put more distance between us, giving her my back.

I stare out at the turquoise water of the bay as I'm once again struck by how this woman can make a man lose his mind. Because, despite what I've just said, I'm *this close* to making her mine on the grass right here in the middle of broad fucking daylight.

Suddenly, I'm flat on my back, staring at the sky as Elodie's delighted face pops into view above me. "Wow! I did it."

Her smile widens seeing the confusion on my face. "Did you just knock me on my ass?"

She nods with delight. "Mm-hmm. First time I've done it, too. Sasquatch is much too broad." I chuckle at the pout pursing her pretty lips. "Needs to stay off the late-night cookie runs."

I grin as she extends a hand to help me up, and I take it softly before yanking her down on top of me. She yelps as she falls, and I bark a laugh when she lands on my chest. Without missing a beat, I smoothly flip us so that she's beneath me, eyes filled with surprise that soon turns to unmistakable desire.

"If you keep looking at me like that, I'll be forced to take things faster than I think you're ready for."

ELODIE

I swallow mutely as my eyes dip to his full lips, a feeling I've never felt before swarming within my stomach.

And despite that, I recognize it instantly.

It's *want*. It's *consent*. It's the overwhelming desire to have this man take me and remold me as *his*.

In the days since remembering that lost weekend, and everything that came about in the aftermath, I realize now that I was in a constant state of Swan Mode. Desperately working to stay afloat.

But since I've been in Sicily, despite the circumstances of getting here, I've never felt more free. That is *all* down to this man. Because of how he makes me feel.

Because when he looks at me, I feel whole. In a way I don't think I can ever remember feeling in my whole life.

Rafe's lips look obscenely soft, and I can't stop myself from bringing a hand up to track my fingertip along his full bottom lip. I run it over and back before he stops me when he draws the digit inside his mouth to lightly bite the tip.

My gasp is low as my eyes shoot up to his. I'm so close I can see small creases on the corner of each eye. A hazel fleck in his right eye that's missing from his left. Thick, silky lashes ring each eye as he blinks slowly, his eyes never moving from mine.

His mouth sucks my finger deeper inside, and he swirls his tongue around and around, making me tighten my thighs around his hips before he releases it with a low growl.

"Fuck it."

In the next second, his mouth closes over mine, and I reach up, palming both his cheeks to hold him closer. His tongue teases the seam of my lips, and I open to him, inviting him in.

I moan in blissful relief when our tongues collide, and his answering groan of pleasure sends a surge of desire soaring through me.

My senses are on overload as Rafe claims not only my mouth, but my damn soul. The caress of his silken tongue tastes sweet, and his body feels hard pressed firmly against me, while his indelible scent fills my nostrils, taking me even higher.

I release a whimper as his tongue searches the depths of my mouth, alternating in light and rough strokes that flood my whole body with desire.

My body melts into his, becoming one being, one entity, and even so, I pull him desperately closer because it still feels like we're not close enough.

Like we'll *never* be close enough.

With a groan, he rocks his hips against mine, ripping his mouth away when he tugs one of my braids to one side. The move presents my neck to his ravenous mouth, and he runs the flat of his tongue from my collarbone to the shell of my ear, nipping the lobe lightly.

"Kiss me again, Rafe." My plea is a gasp, and he lifts his dark head to capture my eyes. His pupils are blown, and the depth within his gaze knocks the breath from my lungs before he seals his mouth to mine again.

When he pumps his hips against me, I cry out as he continues to devour my mouth. I can feel his hard cock rubbing against my clit through the tight workout leggings, hitting me just right, and I wrap my legs around his ass, tugging him closer as I lock my ankles.

He rocks against me, harder this time, and I move with him, groaning into his mouth as sensations I've never imagined roll through my body.

His hands move down and cup my ass, settling me more firmly against him, and he slows our kiss, his tongue languidly rolling against mine. Our bodies are so closely entangled that I'm not entirely sure where I end and he begins, and I don't ever want to find out.

Both of us jump when a loud gunshot pierces the silence, and Rafe immediately crouches over my body, shielding me from the potential threat.

I lie still beneath him, scarcely breathing, until I hear a chuckle rumble deep inside his chest, and he sits up onto his knees with a self-deprecating smirk.

"What happened? What was that?"

He quirks an eyebrow, jerking his thumb behind his back in the direction of the house. My eyes scan the building, quickly locating Sasquatch. He's grinning as he cleans his firearm—the firearm that clearly broke our make-out session—and he doesn't appear to be the least bit sorry for interrupting us.

I look back at Rafe with a smile of my own as he rises to

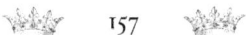

stand, helping me to my feet alongside him before hugging me close to his side.

My arms wrap around his waist as though it's the most natural thing in the world, and another chuckle escapes his kiss-stained lips. "I was right."

As we start back toward the house, I glance up at him, finding him smiling like the cat who got the cream. I lean in closer, unable to get enough of this side of him. The side he gives to me.

Only to me.

"About what?"

Our feet stop as he looks down on me. His eyes are pools of rich, dark chocolate, shining with an emotion that knocks the breath from my body.

I'm unable and unwilling to look away as he tucks a lock of hair behind my ear to cup my cheek and brings our lips together ever-so softly. His words ghost over my mouth, making my heart sing.

"You *do* have lips that were made to be kissed."

19

ELODIE

The twinkling lights of whatever city lies on the other side of the bay twinkle in the distance. The bells of several anchored yachts drift closer in the warm nighttime breeze as I sit silently on the balcony of my suite.

I haven't yet tried to sleep, despite having gotten dressed for bed over two hours ago, because I know it won't come easy tonight. Following the semi-public humping incident on the lawn earlier, my sex has been pulsating all evening.

I'm entirely sure that if I were to brush the pad of my thumb over my clit, I'd come apart instantly. But the thought of self-gratification fills me with nothing but disappointment.

Rafe's confession from this afternoon has been playing on repeat inside my head all day.

"I want you more than I need air to breathe, but I'm just a man. A man who's desperate to make you his..."

My mind can't help reliving that kiss over and over again, and all I know for certain is that it tasted like the promise of so much *more*.

Does he not realize I'm already his?

Before I've even fully allowed the thought to form, I'm on

my bare feet. As I cross the suite, and step out into the hall, I straighten my shoulders, tossing my hair back, intent on my destination. The journey down the stairs takes less than sixty seconds, and before I even reach the bottom, I hear it.

The piano.

I follow the sound, coming to a stop outside the slightly ajar door of the music room to take a moment to listen, instantly recognizing my favorite Beethoven piece, *"Moonlight Sonata."* With a small push, the door opens enough for me to slip inside, and the sight that greets me fills me with raw emotion.

Rafe is sitting at the piano, his hands easily moving across the keys as he tilts his head to one side. Jet-black hair falls across his brow, eyes closed as he absorbs the music. The light of the moon streaks through the room, casting shadows that add to the hauntingly beautiful melancholy of the piece.

I remain hidden, watching as his fingers glide over the keys with ease while the powerful emotion of the piece continues to build. The melancholy. The longing. The *yearning*.

My body feels electrified, each nerve ending standing on edge as I become riveted to the scene before me.

"Come closer, *Stellina*."

Rafe's eyes remain closed, his fingers not missing a single key, when his husky, low command reaches my ears. Of their own volition, my feet pad silently closer until I'm by his side. He shifts over on the bench, and I slip in alongside him, watching his fingers as though mesmerized.

"I played this for you."

My stomach dips as my gaze takes in his side profile. His face is peaceful, his eyes still closed as he stays fully invested in the piece.

"When I returned from Vermont, I played to remember you. Or perhaps it was to forget you, I don't know." He inhales a deep breath, his eyes finally opening and meeting mine. "But since you've arrived here, I've played to keep my distance."

His eyes drop to my mouth, flaring when I automatically draw my lower lip between my teeth. "It's even harder to keep my distance now that I've tasted your kiss."

"I thought we established this earlier." My eyes flicker between his before I gently lay my hand on his bicep. "I don't *want* you to keep your distance, Rafe."

A frown crosses his brow as the music suddenly stops, and he brings his hands up to cup my face between his warm palms. "Fate brought you to me the first time, and it's brought us back together now. And fate won't be denied a second time, *Stellina*. I feel like I've waited forever to have you, and I will continue to wait as long as it takes—"

He breaks off when I stand to throw one leg over his so that I am straddling him. His dark eyes don't leave mine as I loop both my arms around his neck, tugging him closer.

"Don't keep me at arm's length." I tip my head to one side, expelling a soft sigh. "You told me once that you'd never take my choice from me. But you did."

Rafe grimaces, shaking his head as he opens his mouth to speak, but I quickly place my index finger atop his lips.

"Show me now that you meant it. That my choice really and truly *is* my own. That I'm finally *free* to do what I *choose* to do."

I remove my finger from his lips, and he watches me closely for a long moment before his hoarse voice murmurs, "What do you choose, *Stellina*?"

And I answer honestly, freely, and without hesitation.

"I choose you, Rafael Caruso. I choose this life *with* you. I choose everything that comes with it. The good, *and* the bad." I thread my fingers through his soft hair, holding him firmly as I lay myself open to him. "Because you see me. The true me. And within your darkness, you allow me to shine."

RAFAEL

Elodie's eyes glow as though she's lit up from the inside as she bares herself to me. Her confession resounds in my mind, taking a beat to register when my breath catches in my throat.

My heart pounds in my ears, and my vision blurs as I focus solely on the woman before me, laying herself bare for me. And I revel in this moment until the desire to kiss her outweighs everything else.

I loop my hands around her waist, the keys of the piano behind her clanging loudly when I lift her to sit on the lid before I shut the fall board and fit myself between her legs.

My mouth brushes over hers as her tongue snakes out, licking the seam of my lips tentatively, and I open to her. Our tongues meet gently at first, exploring one another as though time is of no consequence.

She tastes of cinnamon sugar, and I groan deep within my chest as I slowly savor her mouth. Her tongue tangles with mine stroke for stroke, and soon, she's panting against me.

I break the kiss and pay homage to the graceful curve of her neck, licking and nipping my way to her ear before swirling the lobe into my hot mouth. She moans breathily, pumping her hips against mine, giving my dick the friction he's so desperately looking for.

As though she's read my mind, she reaches between us to slip her hand inside the waistband of my sweats, gasping when she wraps her delicate fingers around my throbbing cock. She pumps my shaft, and I can feel precum bead the tip already.

I move my hand over hers, easing it out of my pants with a groan. "Next time, *bedda mia*."

Her eyes light up at my use of the endearment. "Your beautiful one?"

I nod before I press a chaste kiss to her mouth, whispering against her lips, "*Si, Stellina*. Now let me make you feel good."

Then I slide my hand up her bare leg and beneath her super short pajama shorts.

"*Shit*," I hiss lowly, my fingers immediately discovering her wet pussy is bare and dripping. "You're fucking soaked."

Her eyes glaze over when I run the pad of my thumb over her clit before pinching it lightly. She gasps as she grips my shoulders, arching against me. "*More.*"

With a growl, I slide my middle finger through her slick folds, before slipping it inside her pussy achingly slowly. My dick protests against my sweats as she chokes my finger with her tightness.

"Holy fuck. You feel so good." I lick up along the side of her neck, making her shiver before I rest my mouth by the shell of her ear. "You're so damn perfect, *Stellina*."

I add a second digit, swirling my thumb over and back across her pulsating clit, as Elodie's face contorts with pleasure.

She's pushing her pelvis against my hand, seeking more as I grab the hem of her top, and lift it over her head. Her tits are as fucking flawless as I'd imagined. Her waist is easily spanned by my large hands, and the feel of her soft, creamy skin drives me fucking wild.

I lower my mouth to a deep pink nipple, sucking the bud and swirling my tongue around the hardened peak. Elodie grips my hair, holding me to her chest with a hoarse cry. "Jesus, don't stop. *Per favore*, don't stop."

A dark chuckle escapes me as I move to her other breast, giving it the same attention, all while slowly thrusting my fingers in and out of her pussy.

The sound of her wetness fills the room alongside her cries of rapture, and when I add a third digit while rubbing tight circles over her clit, she throws her head back.

"I'm going to come. Oh, Christ, you're making me come."

She shatters for me then, her body drawing up tight like a bow as her pussy clenches around my fingers. Her cries escalate, echoing through the music room, and making my cock leak a steady stream of precum into my sweatpants.

As her orgasm begins to recede, Elodie lays back on the lid of the piano while small shudders of delight continue to travel through her body.

While she's still boneless and pliant, I lift her ass and slip her shorts off, tossing them to one side. When I part her legs, I pause for a long beat, my cock thickening when I take in the sight of her climax as it drips from her slit down onto the piano keys.

"Holy shit, the sight of your cum leaking out of your beautiful cunt makes me so damn hard, *bedda mia*."

She whimpers as I lean closer, parting her pussy lips with my thumbs, but then suddenly jerks forward, trying to pull her legs together. "No, please don't look at me there."

Her voice sounds frantic as foreboding fills my chest cavity, and I stop her from hiding herself from me. "Whatever you don't want me to see, *Stellina,* just know that it *won't* make me want you any less."

I can feel her knees wobble with uncertainty, her wide, scared eyes rising to find mine. "Even if I've been *marked* by another? Even if I've been *branded* like a herd animal?"

I grit my teeth as I gently ease her legs open. Her bare pussy is still slick with her orgasm, and I slowly let my eyes travel across her most private parts.

My breath locks in my throat, burning my windpipe and making me feel lightheaded when I see it.

On the inside of her left thigh, no more than four or five inches from the apex is the Conti insignia. And it's been burned into Elodie's delicate flesh, the edges contorted into a nasty scar surrounding the crest.

My vision feels blurry as blood thunders through my ears, and I inhale sharply through my nostrils. The thought of what this beautiful creature before me has endured at the hands of

Domenico Conti makes me see red, and in my mind, I picture *precisely* what I plan on doing to that worthless bastard when I can finally exact revenge.

I lift my head to find Elodie watching me, and I barely manage to rein myself in, knowing instinctively what she needs to hear. I hold her gaze, reaching out my thumb to rub her marked thigh with a gentle brush.

"Nothing will come between us. Especially not something that means *nothing* to either of us." I lean closer, pressing a kiss over the crest, and then another to her other quivering thigh.

My hot breath is right against her pussy when I tip my nose off her clit and murmur, "I don't need to mark you to know that you were made to be mine."

I loop my arms beneath her legs, tugging her ass off the piano to display her wetness to perfection. Then I lavish kisses along the insides of both thighs, making her squirm deliciously until I stop for a moment, my eyes instantly finding hers.

Our gazes hold as I flatten my tongue, gliding it through her wetness before flicking the tip over her throbbing clit. Her back arches, thrusting her pussy farther against my face, and I lay siege to her clit as I slide two thick fingers inside her core.

"Fucking Christ, *Stellina*. Your pussy is sucking me in. *Fuck*! I love how she's taking my fingers. I love how she's begging for *more*."

A moan tears from her chest as I pump faster, swirling my tongue through her arousal as the sound of her wet cunt taking my fingers fills the room. My dick is painfully hard, but I'm too high on this woman to give a fucking shit.

"Fuck, yes. Take my fingers deep." I pump a third digit in alongside the first two, and she cries out as her thighs tighten on either side of my head. "You're fucking magnificent, *Stellina*."

Elodie's eyelids flicker, and her eyes roll back as she threads her fingers through my hair, holding me closer against her.

"Oh my God, Rafe. Oh my God."

"You like that, don't you, *bedda mia*? You like when I fuck you with my fingers, *mia brava ragazza*."

Her deep groan is punctuated by the sound of her head banging against the piano lid when she arches her neck, and I take a beat to admire the perfect view before me.

The woman of my dreams come to life, and the reality easily surpasses everything my mind had conjured before this moment.

Elodie Rivers is perfection personified.

With her chest thrust forward, her nipples poke up like bullets as she moves against my face. She pumps down onto my fingers with jerky movements, and the small sounds she's making in the back of her throat fill me with carnal need as I lave hot, wet kisses along her pussy. The scent of her arousal surrounds me, driving me higher, needing more from her.

Needing *everything*.

"You taste sublime. I could eat you all day and all night, and still, I'd shamelessly beg for more. Cover my tongue with your sweetness. I'm starving for you." With the flat of my tongue, I lick from slit to clit, and back again, my tongue and fingers alternating as I fuck her to the cusp of orgasm.

And when she's right there, her body dangling on the precipice as she frantically tweaks her nipples, I suck her clit sharply into my mouth. Her orgasm barrels through her as I continue to thrust my fingers, her cries of pleasure turning to mewls as she comes all over my tongue.

My hum of satisfaction as I lick her clean makes her whole body tremble before I press a chaste kiss to her quivering clit.

"Watching you shatter for me is breathtaking." Her pleasure-glazed eyes find mine, and I run my flattened palm from her pussy up along her trim stomach to gently cup her breast. "Simply fucking exquisite."

As she comes back down from the heights I've brought her to, I tenderly lift her from the piano lid and gather her into my embrace. Long moments pass before she turns her sleepy eyes toward me, leaning close to press our lips together.

"I've never felt that before, Rafe. That connection, the emotion in your eyes as you watched me unravel. I could *feel* how much you wanted me. How much you wanted me to be yours."

My arms tighten their hold slightly, bringing her closer to rest my brow to hers. Our lips are an inch apart when I reach up to rest my palm on the nape of her neck.

"I want you beyond all reason, *Stellina*. I want this more than I've ever wanted anything in my whole damn life."

Her face lights up with a broad smile, and she moves closer to kiss me. But as our lips brush, she cries out, jerking back suddenly and without warning. Elodie stumbles, falling onto the wooden floor as a very drunken Sofia lashes out at her.

"No whores allowed in the compound. *Get out!*"

I stand from the piano bench, and grip Sofia's hand when she raises it to strike Elodie, pushing her away with a low snarl. "Don't *fucking* touch her."

Elodie manages to grab her nightwear, slipping it on when Antonio bursts into the room. He surveys the scene with disdained eyes, turning to me with an unimpressed murmur.

"Really, Rafael? When you could have *anyone,* you choose her?" He points his index finger toward her, and Elodie cowers into herself ashamedly as Antonio narrows his eyes. "You put your dick inside Conti's *whore*?"

20

ELODIE

My head is aching, and my eyes burn with the force of holding my tears back at the contempt in Antonio's words.

You put your dick inside Conti's whore.

Conti's whore.

Whore. Whore. Whore.

I can see Rafe move to strike him through my suddenly blurry vision, and a large scuffle takes place, but I'm entirely removed from it until Sofia's scream breaks through my barriers.

With a shake of my head, tears crest my lashes, falling down my cheeks, and I move swiftly when I see Rafe holding a small gun to Antonio's temple. Sofia is cowering behind him, her eyes glassy from God knows how much alcohol.

"How fucking *dare* you say those words, *Zio*." He flips off the safety, leaning closer to hiss, "You don't even deserve to breathe the same air as my *Stellina*."

Before he can loosen a shot, I lay my palm on his forearm, stepping closer until my front is pressed to his side. My eyes caress his profile, taking in the harshness of his jaw, the rage contorting his mouth before I whisper softly, "*Enough*. There will be no more bloodshed on my account, Rafael."

My use of his given name for the first time sees him looking down upon me with his eyebrows drawn. "I won't abide the insult—"

I press a little harder. "You've already lost so much of your *famiglia*...I can't be the reason you lose anyone else." My eyes flick to Antonio, narrowing in blatant dislike. "Even when he's a fucking *stronzo*."

Rafe palms my cheek with his free hand, twisting my face around to his. His eyes pierce mine unrelentingly as he brushes the pad of his thumb over my cheekbone, gently wiping away my residual tears.

"You're right, *Stellina*. I have lost many..."

He trails off, the obsidian of his eyes darkening, making my whole body liquify beneath the fervor laid out before me. And when he speaks again, his voice is low, raw with an unchecked emotion that sets my soul aflame.

"But I'd burn the world and everyone in it if the choice was between you and anyone else." Fresh tears fill my eyes as his forehead creases. His tone is guttural when he whispers, "*You are my world now.*"

The whole moment feels utterly surreal as his eyes move back and forth between mine, and I can't stop the desperation that fills my entire body before Rafe drops the arm holding his gun.

When he angles his head to face his *consigliere* and stepmother, his voice is low and nothing short of murderous.

"Let this be a warning to anyone who might consider speaking out against us, *si*?"

Then he shifts back to me, tucking my hair behind my ear with a soft smile as he slips his cell from his pants pocket. He holds my eyes as he hits speed dial, continuing to smooth my hair back oh-so tenderly.

"Emiliano, *vieni ca*."

I hear Sasquatch mumble on the other end, and Rafe rolls his eyes as he answers, "*La sala della musica*." Before I can pin him with a stare for being so rude to my friend, he's already hung up.

"*Zio*, wait for me in my office."

Antonio helps Sofia to her feet, her enraged eyes fixated on Rafe as she's led to the door, and it isn't until they've both left that I can feel my shoulders relax slightly.

Rafe gathers me close to his chest, resting his chin atop my head as he mutters indistinct Italian until Sasquatch knocks at the door, and lets himself in. I can't stop myself from snorting when I take in the sight of his sleeping attire.

He narrows his eyes at me before he yanks his eye mask off his head and rams it into his pants pocket. "I like to sleep in the dark, okay?"

His defensive tone makes both me and Rafe grin, and then I lean up on my tiptoes and press a kiss to Rafe's bearded cheek. "I'll see you tomorrow."

Though his eyes darken, he says nothing as I walk toward Sasquatch, and together we slip into the hall beyond. "A hot pink cupcake covered eye mask. Really?"

He side-eyes me as we reach the foot of the stairs. "It matches my bedsheets."

His wink makes me giggle, and his own self-deprecating snort soon follows. We're still chuckling when we reach the top of the stairs and find Sofia waiting. Wariness snakes down my spine as she holds up a quelling palm before either of us can utter a single word to her.

"This world is ruled by men who follow the old traditions. Rafael and his father both defy the core values of *Cosa Nostra*, and it won't be stood for, let me assure you of that, *puttana*."

My stomach lurches as goosebumps scatter across my skin

at her scarcely veiled threat, but despite that, I'm outwardly in full-on Swan Mode.

"Ouch!" I press my hand to my chest, feigning hurt. "That hurt *almost* as much as looking at your face."

At Sofia's sharp inhalation and Sasquatch's unveiled snort of laughter, I regard her exaggeratedly innocent eyes despite the nervousness flowing through me. "I'd give you a nasty look, but it appears you already have one."

Sofia makes a sound of displeasure before shooting me one last malicious look, and then turning to stumble in the opposite direction from my suite.

"Christ almighty, she's a bundle of joy." I opt for humor to deflect the nerves simmering within my stomach and Sasquatch chuckles.

"She didn't want to marry Don Giacomo, and she made that known to every Made Man in the Cosa Nostra. She's always been a sour bitch. From the day she moved into the compound, she's just *never* been happy."

My chest tightens, and suddenly, despite her venomous words and hurtful actions, I feel the barest shred of sorrow for her. "We all deserve happiness, Emiliano. Even her."

As we reach the threshold of my door, Sasquatch stops me with a hand on my shoulder. His eyes are smiling as he regards me. "You make him happy. Happier than I've ever seen him, and I've known that moody fuck my whole entire life."

My throat fills with emotion, and before I can stop myself, I close the gap to wrap my arms around him. "Thank you. *For everything.*"

Once he's secured my suite, I take my time washing up, then change into fresh pajamas identical to the ones I toss in my laundry hamper.

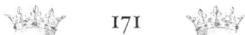

My entire body hums with uneasy energy. The spacious confine of my suite is too small to contain it, so I quickly step out onto my balcony, breathing easier almost instantaneously in the warm Sicilian evening.

The sweet fragrance of flowers fills the air mingling with the soothing scent of the Mediterranean Sea as I look out over the compound gardens, and across the moonlit waters beyond. I slowly blow out a breath, concentrating on moderating my hammering heart, and quieting my racing mind.

It's going to be a long night.

RAFAEL

Antonio regards me with a cool stare from his place opposite my desk. Enzo is at his back, blocking the door, and silence surrounds us following my question.

The same question appears to be going unanswered for the second time, so I repeat myself, except this time, I enunciate it evenly. Calmly, though my inner fury is bubbling just beneath the surface, practically howling to get out.

"How. Should. I. Punish. You. *Zio?*"

His face remains impassive, though his jaw ticks ever-so slightly.

Beneath my desk, I clench and unclench my fists, ensuring my breathing remains even until he eventually speaks.

"I see the error of my ways, Rafael. It's only that I hadn't thought the girl would manage to distort your head as easily as she twisted Conti's—"

"His right hand, Enzo."

My *consigliere* grinds to a halt when Enzo steps forward at my nod, grabbing Antonio's hand and slapping it palm down onto my desk. Antonio quickly glances at Enzo and back to me as I pluck a serrated blade from my drawer.

His nostrils flare, but otherwise, he doesn't react, remaining stock still as I rise and walk to his side with slow steps. I hold his eyes in utter silence, neither of us giving an inch, until I speak.

"Your right index finger. The one you pointed in judgment toward Elodie." I lower the knife as he tries to pull back, but Enzo holds firm. "Yes, this self-righteous pointer finger will pay the price of your sheer fucking ignorance."

My eyes leave Antonio's as I press the knife to the second knuckle, and begin to push down. He flinches as I find purchase, and I look back at his face to witness him suffer for hurting Elodie.

He watches me right back, only reacting when the knife meets bone, and his blood covers the table beneath his hand. Rather than drag it out, I make short work of severing the digit, before nodding at Enzo. "Ensure he's brought directly to the on-call doctor. And make sure he gives me a wide fucking berth for the foreseeable."

As Enzo forces Antonio to rise to leave, I grab his severed finger and ram it into the breast pocket of his suit jacket. His face is screwed up in agony, yet even so, he looks to be on the verge of lashing out before I snarl, *"Don't* think I'm my father, *Zio.* I *won't* allow you to do as you wish with no recourse. And you'd be wise to remember that."

I step back, nodding at Enzo to continue his trip before grabbing my cell and quickly going upstairs. I don't bother making my way to my quarters, knowing Elodie will have gone straight to hers, needing to be with her. To assure myself that she's alright in the aftermath of such hateful words.

Less than sixty seconds later, I crack open the door of her suite, the suite my mama had been given upon her arrival from Britain almost thirty-five years ago.

My eyes travel across the space, finding no sight of Elodie, and I step farther inside, checking the ensuite before moving outside onto the balcony.

I stop as I cross the threshold, taking a moment to just

absorb this woman's sheer magnetism. Her head falls back as she sighs, and my feet move of their own accord until I'm at her back.

As though she'd known I was there, she softens against me before I lift her hair to one side and press a kiss to the curve of her neck.

"I needed to check on you." I kiss the same spot again, praying she's on the same page as me. "I really wanted to hold you while you sleep…"

She glances over her shoulder, looking up into my eyes as a smile blooms on her face. Then she nods, slipping her small hand into mine, and leading me back inside to throw back the bed sheets.

Her navy-blue eyes are soft, hazy with the need for sleep when she lays down and pats the bed in invitation.

"Please hold me, Rafe."

Without hesitation, I shuck off my clothes, leaving only my underwear, and climb in behind her, pulling the sheet up over both of us.

She snuggles back against me and draws my arm around her waist. I instinctively cup her breast through her pajama top and curl my body around hers, reveling in her warmth.

She sighs softly. "Thank you. For tonight."

Her words are a bare breath on the gentle breeze coming through the ajar doors to her balcony, and my arms tighten.

"You're a motherfucking queen. You deserve to be treated accordingly, and it's my job to ensure that."

Her breathing is even, and I can feel that she's right on the edge of slumber when I press a kiss to the back of her neck, inhaling her sweet cinnamon scent deeply before whispering, "Now sleep, *Stellina*. I'll keep the dragons at bay while you rest."

21

ELODIE

My eyes flutter open when I feel the rays of the morning sunshine on my face, and it takes a hot minute to remember why my body is on fire.

I smile as I look down at Rafe's strong forearm wrapped around my side, holding me close with my back against his broad chest. He's impossibly warm, and I know I should probably move away from him to cool down, but I can't bring myself to leave the haven of his embrace.

My stomach flutters as I recall what passed between us in the music room last night. As I remember just how desperate I'd been for his touch. As I recollect his dark eyes piercing me while he'd brought me unprecedented euphoria.

This man touched far more than my body last night. With the way he'd looked at me, he'd seared my goddamn soul.

"Mmm." Rafe's deep grumble makes me smile as he leans over me to kiss my cheek. His longer-than-usual facial hair scratches my skin pleasantly, and I quickly roll over to face him.

His sleepy grin puts an answering one on my own lips.

"Morning." He clears his throat, voice hoarse from disuse. "Sleep well?"

My smile broadens as my cheeks heat. "Even better than the night before."

He shoots me a shit-eating wink, making my thighs press together. "Must have been the orgasms, hmm?"

I cover my red face with my hands, and Rafe's deep chuckle fills my ears as he tugs me closer.

"It's nothing to be embarrassed about." Then he pinches my chin between his thumb and index finger, forcing me to meet his dark gaze. "Bringing you pleasure gives *me* pleasure. And I will be doing it a lot because seeing you come might just be my new favorite pastime."

Leaning closer, he presses a gentle kiss to my brow before sliding his arms around my shoulders to pull me against his chest. I close my eyes, breathing slowly and deeply when my chest feels tight under the force of the emotion he so easily brings to life within me.

The sound of the compound coming to life around us fills my ears. Gardeners and groundsmen outside calling to one another in lilting Italian. A boat's bell chimes in the distance as mumbled voices from downstairs argue over the last brioche.

I'm consumed with such peace and contentment that I could burst until Rafe pulls back to look at me. His eyes are a chocolatey brown today, looking much lighter, and I determine instantly that I want to see this shade more frequently.

"You're to be my guest at a special party tonight. Here, within the compound."

My jaw pretty much unhinges as my eyes widen in shock before Rafe rises from the bed and extends a hand, helping me up alongside him. He presses a kiss to the back of my hand clasped within his, those dark eyes dancing playfully.

"Dress the part, *Stellina*. Let them all see how you shine for me."

"And there will be women there, too?"

My high-pitched, somewhat frantic question is met with a small smile from Maria, and she nods as she collects my dinner tray from the balcony table.

"*Si*. Don Rafael is hosting a special party tonight for Don Salvatore and his family. His wife, Bianca, and their daughters, Gabriela and Eliana, will attend, along with several wives of Don Rafael's highest-ranking Capos."

I begin to spiral slightly at the thought, pacing the length of my balcony as my mind races.

I don't look the part. I have no doubt I can't act the part. And I absolutely don't have a good enough grasp of Italian yet to make small talk with anyone aside from maybe Sasquatch.

"Is Emiliano attending?" I latch onto the thought desperately as I whip around to find Maria extending her hand, a small white envelope pinched between her fingers.

"Don Rafael asked that I give this to you."

I take it with a nod as she shakes her head, answering my question. "No. I believe he's on security detail alongside Enzo."

My shoulders sag at the loss of my singular lifeline, and Maria steps closer, curling her hands lightly around my upper arms. "You will be *perfetta*, *Senorina* Elodie. Don Rafael would not ask it of you if he did not believe you were capable of the task."

She regards me for a long moment until whatever she sees in my eyes satisfies her, and she steps back with a smile. "*Bene*. Now, I've laid out everything you need inside. You will hear the guests arriving, but you won't be escorted downstairs until after 9 p.m., so you have plenty of time to relax and prepare."

Then she takes the food tray and disappears without another word.

I glance at the letter in my hand, smiling to myself when I think about what Rafe could have sent me, so I sink down onto the oval lounger facing the bay and rip it open.

My heart falters in my chest, and tears instantly fill my eyes when I recognize Skye's familiar handwriting.

Sucking in deep breath after deep breath, I read with trembling hands.

Hey Ellie,

Thank you for sending me to the most special school in the world.

I'm studying all sorts of new subjects. My favorite is music. Maestra Clara says I have a beautiful singing voice, but I prefer to play the instruments, especially the piano.

It is so pretty here. It's very sunny and warm right now, but my roommate, Jenna, says that during the winter term, it looks like a blanket of snow has covered the entire campus.

I think you would really like it in Switzerland. When can you visit?

Your friend, Rafe, said that you missed me as much as I miss you. You must miss me an awful lot, then.

I think about you all the time. Please write back to me, and tell me you love me.

All my love,

Skye

When I finish, tears trail down my cheeks, and I clasp the letter to my chest, slamming my eyes closed as gratitude for Rafe and his pre-emptive actions overwhelms me.

I draw in a shuddery breath before re-reading the letter, but this time, I smile at the end and slip the letter into my back pocket, intent on replying after the party.

The sun is almost set on the horizon by the time I stand and pad back inside, noting the beautiful red dress Maria has left hanging from my wardrobe. I run my fingertips along the satin, suddenly excited to wear something other than leggings or shorts for the first time in weeks.

I make short work of showering and washing my long blonde hair. Once I'm dried off and lotioned up, I dry my hair before styling it into soft curls. I keep my makeup very simple, opting for natural colors on my face with a striking red lip that matches the dress.

I've just slipped my red heels onto my feet and am about to step into the dress, when there's a knock on the door of my suite.

"We will join the party when you are ready, *Stellina*," Rafe's deep voice calls out from the other side, and I quickly tug the dress up over my curves, turning to the mirror to find my response dies in my throat.

"I-I-I'll be just a minute."

I blink my eyes in sheer disbelief as I take in my reflection. "*Wow!*"

The dress fits as though it were made for me. The deep red satin molds to every curve with a deep V at the front that hints at my cleavage without being distasteful.

It's a full length gown, entirely backless, with a small train of material that's designed to look like red roses trailing behind me, and it's easily the most beautiful piece of clothing I've ever laid eyes upon.

Once I've double-checked my makeup, I gently push open the door into the hall, finding Rafe leaning against the wall as he scrolls his cell. He's transformed into Don Rafael again for the party, and I take a minute to drink in how goddamn handsome he is.

Hearing me emerge, he lifts his head, and when his eyes find me, they nearly bulge out of his sockets.

He quickly recovers himself, pushing off the wall to wrap his arms around my waist, and pull me close. "You are absolutely fucking radiant, *Stellina*." Then he leans down to press a soft kiss to my cheek. "I cannot wait for all of our guests to see the most beautiful woman in the world on my arm tonight."

My cheeks heat, and I bite my lip as I tuck a strand of hair behind one ear. Rafe watches me with knowing eyes, chuckling as he presents his forearm like some kind of fairytale prince, and I take it with a smile.

"*Grazie*, Handsome."

With shaky legs and a stomach full of churning anxiety, I grip Rafe's arm as he leads me to the top of the stairs, where I can see a party below that's currently in full swing.

I suck in a trembling breath when we begin our descent, and Rafe croons softly beneath his breath, "*Mia brava ragazza*."

The words make my shoulders straighten, and I lift my head just as heads turn our way. By the time our feet hit the third last step, there's silence as Rafe comes to a stop, regarding the sea of faces.

"*Benvenuto a casa mia*. And a special warm welcome to Don Salvatore—"

He cuts off, flourishing his free arm toward a tall silver-haired man with a hard-set jaw. He's flanked on either side by an older woman—seemingly his wife—and two daughters, one of whom is watching me with a deep frown on her pretty face. A tall, slender teenage boy, who could be Salvatore's doppelganger, stands at his back, undoubtedly his son.

"Now, everyone. I invite you to relax, enjoy my hospitality, and please remember to keep the politics for another day." His lips lift in a devilish smile as a chuckle runs through the crowd. "I envision a fun night ahead."

22

ELODIE

Rafe was as good as his word, indulging me with his time for far longer than was probably appropriate until he introduced me to Chiara, the wife of Davide, one of his Capos.

If she knew who I was, and my reason for being here, she made no mention of it, and it wasn't long before we were chatting together like old friends.

"Do you know if Rafe – err, I mean, Rafael, hosts this kind of thing very often?"

Chiara's eyes widen as she shakes her head. "Obviously, with everything with Aurelia..." she trails off, and my stomach twists uncomfortably, recalling the beautiful spitfire on the video call.

"But there's a good reason for this one, Elodie. It's been an announcement that's a long time coming. So, it's not distasteful to enjoy ourselves." She drains her champagne flute, before beckoning a passing server for another.

"What's the reason?"

Chiara plucks a fresh flute from the server's tray, tilting her head to one side in question. "Hmm?"

"The reason for the party." She brings the glass to her lips as her eyes widen, and I repeat myself. "What's the reason?"

"You don't know?" Chiara tilts her head to one side, a frown marring her pretty features as I shake my head.

She freezes mid-sip, her gaze flitting from side to side before she stands suddenly, and excuses herself without even waiting for my response.

Though her reaction was more than a little strange, I quickly deposit my empty champagne flute onto the table before me and stand, intent on using the restroom.

I almost give up, and just go to my suite, when I manage to find an unoccupied one on my third attempt. I quickly slip inside and relieve myself before freshening up to return to the party.

As I leave, I feel a hand on my forearm, and I jerk back, preparing to defend myself until I note it's the girl from before, one of Salvatore's daughters. The one who'd been looking at me with curiosity in her gaze.

"Excuse me, *Senorina*." She smiles pleasantly, and I answer with one of my own. "May I talk with you for a moment?"

I look left and right, then left again, settling on the kitchen door at the far end of the hallway before I turn to her with a nod. "Of course. We can speak in the kitchen."

She follows quickly as I lead the way, holding the door open for her to enter first, then I slip in after her.

Once I've closed the door behind me, she regards me with serious gray eyes and tilts her head to one side before she extends her hand. "I'm Gabriela."

The warmth from the hallway has dimmed when I take her hand in mine with a slight frown. "Elodie." Once I've given her hand a firm shake, I drop it and step back, tucking my hair behind my ears as I hold her inquisitive eyes. "How can I help you, Gabriela?"

She blows out a breath, then huffs sarcastically. "Well, you could start by keeping your hands off *my* fiancé."

There's buzzing in my ears, and my vision seems to blur when my stomach lurches with nausea. All I can do is stand there, blinking owlishly before I finally manage to stammer, "Wh-wh-what did you j-j-just say?"

"Oh, you poor fool. You didn't think he intended to remain heirless, did you?" She winces at whatever she sees on my face. "Of course, Rafael will marry to his family's advantage. A union between ours is expected."

And now Chiara's words from before make sense.

Gabriela tips her chin up as she looks down her nose at me, and the action makes the diamonds in her ears sparkle in the low light of the kitchen. Her dark hair is swept up in a low chignon, paired with a demure pastel pink gown. She's the epitome of the perfect Italian wife, and I'm once again reminded that although Rafe may claim me as his, I'll never be more to him than a mistress.

His glorified whore.

And my heart shreds in my chest because I'd allowed myself to *hope* for something more.

Stupid, stupid, stupid *girl, Rivers.*

"Tonight is the night our engagement will finally be announced." Gabriela examines her pastel pink nails as she guts me with her words before she raises her eyes to mine. "I just thought someone ought to let you know before you make a *complete* fool of yourself."

Chest tightening, I slap my palm over it, rubbing harshly to ease the burn as I nod to Gabriela. "I-I apologize...I didn't know—"

My words cut off as I try to inhale, suddenly feeling like I haven't got enough oxygen in my lungs. As my breaths come short and labored, it feels like my heart is about to explode when I move past Gabriela toward one of the doors that lead onto the decking outside.

Cool night air fills my lungs when I stumble past several sun loungers, kicking off my heels as I go. The dewy grass of the lawn grounds me, and I continue to walk, zeroing in on the labyrinth of roses.

The quiet solitude of the rose-covered pavilion that I'd discovered at the center calls to me, and I quicken my step.

My blood is humming in my ears as I enter the tall hedgerows, and I slam my eyes closed against the onslaught of tears.

"*Ciao, Tesoro.*"

I grind to a halt when I hear a rough masculine voice at my back, and I hold my breath as I pivot, instantly recognizing the man behind me as one of Rafe's *Soldati*.

Time seems to stand still for a moment until he smirks.

"It would be such a shame to end your life without sampling the blonde pussy that's got everyone so worked up."

My spine stiffens as he rushes forward, lunging for me, but I throw an elbow into his cheek. The move disorients him enough that I can run blindly into the labyrinth as he laughs sadistically.

"I love it when they fight."

RAFAEL

Benito sits tall in the wing-backed armchair opposite mine as he slowly blows out the smoke of his Gurkha. His eyes are narrowed, and fury flows off him in waves when he speaks.

"You disrespect me and my family when you flaunt your mistress throughout your engagement party, Rafael. I'm not altogether sure that I can overlook the slight…"

He trails off pointedly, clicking his fingers at his only son, Vincenzo. "Find Gabriela and bring her to me."

Vincenzo looks at me with a curled lip, disgust apparent in his hard stare before he slips from the room, leaving just me and his father in the mostly unused library.

We regard one another for a long beat until I rise and walk to the drinks cabinet. I hold up a tumbler in silent question, and Salvatore nods sharply in answer.

Having quickly made up our drinks, I pass him a glass, sitting back down and taking a sip. I swirl the amber liquid around the glass, watching it coat the sides before I raise my eyes to his and casually murmur.

"There will be no engagement, Benito."

The other man flies to his feet, the whisky from his tumbler splashing over the sides and onto the wooden library floor beneath his feet.

"How fucking *dare* you dishonor me and my family this way." He strides closer, face florid. "There *will* be an announcement tonight, or so help me—"

"There will be no announcement tonight...or *ever*. Of that, I can assure you."

Cheeks mottled, his body hums with rage as he bellows, "You pathetic excuse for a man, I'll see you pay for this—"

"Did you think I wouldn't find out, Benito?"

My voice is low and deadly dangerous as I place my glass gently on the side table, but Benito is too far gone in his rage to hear it.

"Are you listening to me, Rafael—"

I stand suddenly, and the action has Benito taking a jarring step backward as I tower over him. My hand snakes out to grip his shirt collar and yank him forward as his Gurkha and tumbler fall to the floor.

"You're playing both sides, you cock-sucking son of a bitch." His face drains of all color, as I jerk him higher, toes barely touching the floor now. "You've been in league with Conti all this time—"

"No, no, Rafael." His sheer desperation almost makes me laugh. "That's not—"

I cut him off when I shove him away, and he stumbles backward, landing on his ass.

"You have ten seconds." I slip my 9mm out from the inside pocket of my suit jacket, flip off the safety, and aim it at Benito's face. "Ten seconds to tell me why I shouldn't put a bullet between your eyes."

He swallows harshly, and I arch an eyebrow. "Ten...nine..."

"You were my first choice for Gabriela—"

"Eight...seven..."

"I never *seriously* considered Conti's proposal—"

My feet close the distance between us.

"Six...five..."

He holds up his hands in a pleading motion. "I can tell you everything he said. All the plans he—"

"Four...three..."

"He has spies. Here. In your household—"

"Tell me something I don't know." Then I press the barrel of the gun against his perspiration-soaked forehead as he squeezes his eyes shut. "Two..."

"I know where he is!"

Bingo!

A smile lifts my lips as I flip on the safety and pocket the gun once more, taking a step back from the trembling man at my feet. "Now, *that's* actually useful, Benito."

I sink back down into my armchair and pick up my whisky. "Take a seat. And tell me *everything*."

"He's in Tuscany. I can give you the calls." As he looks at me in earnest, his words all but gallop out of his mouth. "I have records of every single interaction. It's *all* at your disposal—"

He cuts off when the door to the library opens to admit

Stefano and Gabriela. Shooting me a demure smile, she moves to her father's side. "You requested my presence, Papa."

Salvatore takes her hand in his without meeting her eyes. "There will be no announcement tonight, *Tesoro*."

Gabriela's brow creases as she looks up to find my eyes. "I-I don't understand…" She shakes her head, blinking in obvious bewilderment before tugging her hand from her father's grasp. The action makes him look up, and she meets his gaze with accusation morphing her face.

"You *promised* me, Papa. You promised I would be the wife of Don Caruso—"

"That was not his promise to make, Gabriela." I stand as she swings furious eyes to mine, having had enough of the entire Salvatore family to last a damn lifetime.

I walk past the three of them, shooting over my shoulder, "Don't forget to send that material to my security detail, Benito, *si?*"

He murmurs an agreement as I leave, closing the door firmly behind me as I hear Gabriela's high-pitched shriek of rage as she rounds on her father.

As I return to the party, I immediately notice that Elodie is no longer sitting where I left her with Chiara. A deep frown crosses my brow when my eyes dart around the space, noting that she's nowhere to be found.

I fish out my cell, and flip on the security feed, flicking through it in search of her blonde head, freezing when I see her leave the main party. I juggle between cameras, tracking her steps as she uses the restroom.

My mouth sets in a hard line when I see her interact with Gabriela, following them as they continue to speak in the kitchen. Elodie freezes as Gabriela speaks before she turns and rushes outside, then the feed goes dead.

I flick through several more cameras, finding the screens are black, and I quickly dial Emiliano to find out what the fuck has happened. When the call doesn't connect, I try Enzo, and my pulse races when the same thing happens.

Over the crowd, I catch Davide's eye and nod in the direction of the security bay at the entrance to the compound. He catches my meaning immediately and excuses himself from his frowning wife to do my bidding.

I turn toward the kitchen, intent on following Elodie outside, when Gabriela appears in my path. Her jaw is set as she mumbles a very clearly forced apology before attempting to slip past me, but I stop her when I grip her upper arm.

"What did you say to upset Elodie?" I hiss my demand from between my teeth. Gabriela narrows her eyes as she meets my hardened stare, and her lips lift in a malicious smile. "I told her tonight was to be our engagement announcement." She shrugs indifferently. "I think she was just a *little* put out by the news—"

I push away from her with a low expletive, and my strides eat the floor as I march outside.

Once I've crossed the pool decking, my eyes catch on a pair of red heels and my senses are instantly on high alert. I glance around as a boat chimes in the distance, and my stomach dips when I think of what might happen if she were to stray too close to the cliffside with only the light of the moon to guide her.

My feet strike out to walk toward the edge of the property where the land meets the sea, only for a shrill scream to fracture the stillness of the night and chill me to my core.

I pivot in the direction the sound came from, my eyes landing on my mother's rose-covered labyrinth right as another scream pierces the air.

"*Please stop—*"

Before my brain has even registered the owner of the voice, I've kicked off my shoes and I'm running toward her as my blood pounds in my ears.

Ti salvero, Stellina.

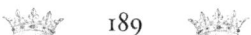

23

ELODIE

My feet slip on the damp grass as I rush headlong into the labyrinth. My only hope is to make it to the center and in front of the security cameras surrounding the pavilion.

Maybe I can buy enough time for Sasquatch to see me on the feed...

I hike my dress higher, cursing the weight of the fabric even as I push my body to move faster.

"You can run all you like, *Tesoro*," the voice behind me calls out, and I stumble forward, my palms hitting the grass as I barely manage to save myself from face-planting.

My foot catches on my dress, and the rose-ruffled hem tears with a loud rip.

I scramble away from the serrated fabric, glancing over my shoulder as my heart pounds frantically against my breastbone. He's still not in my line of sight, and a spark of hope ignites at the thought that I *might* just make it.

I race on, pushing my body to the very limits until I crash into the circular space housing the white wooden pavilion. My eyes immediately scour the area for the cameras I *know* are here, having seen them on previous visits.

When I spot one, I wave frantically as I jump up and down, pinning everything on the idea that *someone* is watching.

My pursuer rushes into the space at my back, and I whirl about to face him, feeling more confident now that help is surely on the way. He regards me for a moment with a humorless expression before his lips tilt up in a sadistic smile.

"If you were planning on alerting security, you'll be disappointed to know that the system was hacked just a little while ago..."

Nausea unfurls in my stomach as he trails off, stepping closer as he continues with twisted delight. "So, as was planned, no one knows you're here, *Tesoro*. The party is in full swing. Rafael is otherwise *engaged*... Get it?"

He snorts at his own joke. "Meaning there's *just* enough time for me to sample that pussy before I'll be missed at my post." He advances closer as I retreat until my bare back hits the pavilion wall. "And when one of my comrades finds your ravaged body, Salvatore will get the blame, and the stifling peace among the Five will be broken. Just like he wants."

Then he lunges forward, and I land a solid right hook, connecting directly with his chin. Even through my fear, I feel a flicker of pride as he spits blood. Swearing loudly, he throws a punch that connects with my abdomen, sending me stumbling backward with a groan.

His smirk is dark, his teeth covered in blood as he comes closer, and his hands reach for me, only to grasp air when I sidestep him, just as Sasquatch has been teaching me, putting me on his left. I strike out my foot, neatly taking his legs out from underneath him, and a surge of elation fills me when he hits the grass with a thud.

I turn and rush toward the safety of the darkened labyrinth, but he snakes out a hand that fists the torn hem of my dress, sending me careening onto the dew-damp grass. As I fall, I cry out helplessly, knowing that I've lost the little advantage I had.

My nails dig into the grass, desperately trying to flee, but he crawls over my body, raising the hem of my dress higher until I feel the cool night air on my exposed ass. I jerk against him, screaming in utter despair as hopelessness crashes into me like a freight train.

"Please stop—"

My plea is hindered when he slaps his hand over my mouth before leaning over my back to rest his mouth by my ear. "The fight just makes my cock harder, *Tesoro*."

I can hear him fidgeting with his belt and zipper, and I thrash harder as I desperately try to bite the hand covering my mouth. My breathing grows harsh, and the burn in my chest puts tears in my eyes as I fight him with everything I have. But the position he's caught me in makes it an impossible feat.

Tears stream down my face as I scream behind his hand. Knowing he has the upper hand sends a shiver of absolute fear clean through me, but I still buck against him, refusing to let anything else be taken from me.

My head throbs, and my body trembles, but I continue to fight when he snorts a wicked laugh. "This might hurt."

RAFAEL

I push my body as fast as I can when I plunge into the darkened labyrinth, my bare feet flying across the grass, taking me farther and farther from the house. The silence surrounding me fills me with dread, and when I spot shredded red ruffles of Elodie's dress, I sprint faster, my worst fears driving my body to its limits.

When I burst out into the open space surrounding the pavilion, my chest fills with an overwhelming rage as I see a dark figure holding Elodie down. Her blonde head is thrashing from side to side as her body bucks frantically in an attempt to dislodge him.

Using his body to hold her down while his hand covers her mouth, Elodie's attacker—who I'm surprised to recognize as Fabiano, one of my security *Soldati*—chuckles to himself as he frees his hard cock from his pants, and I charge forward, bellowing at the top of my lungs.

I plow into his side, knocking him to the ground, and rolling with him so that I'm straddling his hips. Fabiano strikes out, landing a tidy blow to my torso that I don't even register in my rage.

My clenched fist rises above my head, slamming down to grind into his face. The crunch of his nose shattering fills my ears as I drive my fist into his face again.

Blood thunders in my ears as he groans, and I rise, jerking him to stand alongside me before I drag him toward Elodie.

Her eyes are wide, watching everything closely when I push Fabiano to his knees. His body sags as though to fall forward, and I yank his hair harshly, forcing him to remain upright.

"You asked that there be no more bloodshed in your name, *Stellina*." I'm panting as I hold Elodie's impossibly dark blue eyes. Eyes that strengthen in resolve with each word I speak. "So, I am giving you the *choice*. Say the word, and I will end his worthless life. I am yours to command."

She regards Fabiano's blood-drenched face as she wipes her hands off the dirtied front of her tattered dress before lifting her chin in pure, unfiltered condescension. When she raises her eyes to mine, she extends her hand, palm facing up, and demands in an even tone, "Give me your gun, Rafe."

My nostrils flare as I reach into the inside pocket of my jacket and pull out my 9mm Glock. Once I've flipped off the safety, and tugged back the slide, I pass it into her waiting hand.

Her fingers close around the grip, holding the gun with unexpected confidence as she aims it toward Fabiano.

I step slightly back and to the side, watching the scene unfold with depraved pleasure.

He sobs loudly, pleading in rapid Italian before she forces the muzzle between his lips as she quirks a taunting eyebrow. "This might hurt."

Then she pulls the trigger without hesitation, and the bullet tears through Fabiano, exiting the back of his skull before he crumples to the grass at Elodie's feet.

She stares at his dead body for several moments before raising her eyes to mine. "He deserved it."

I nod as I move toward her, sliding the 9mm out of her now trembling hands, and dropping it to the grass before cupping her cheeks in my palms. My chest is tight, and the thought of what could have happened makes my stomach bottom out.

And, as though she can hear my thoughts, Elodie softly murmurs, "Thank God, you found me in time…"

We stand in one another's embrace as I rub soothing circles along the bare skin of her back, feeling her breaths calm. Once my heart rate has evened out, I bend and scoop her into my arms. She settles against me, looping her arms around my neck and resting her head on my shoulder as I walk us back through the labyrinth.

As I get closer to the exit, I hear shouting in the distance, and by the time the house comes back into view, I see Davide, Emiliano, and Enzo among at least a dozen *Soldati* racing toward the labyrinth with their guns drawn.

"Stand down."

My voice is firm as I step closer to the light, and every single one of them freezes in their tracks.

"The threat has been neutralized." I tip my head in the direction of Fabiano and growl, "I want that shit disposed of and every shred of evidence removed within the hour, *capisti*?"

Enzo nods succinctly before moving off and barking orders at the surrounding *Soldati* as Emiliano approaches, swearing to the heavens. "The bastard put an EMP jammer in the damn security bay. We thought it was an internal fault until Davide came barrelling inside, and..."

He trails off, swallowing roughly, shifting his gaze from mine to Elodie, and then back again. "I should have been with her. This is my fault—"

Elodie lifts her head then, and my old friend grinds to a halt. She reaches out to pat his broad shoulder. "I'm okay. Truly." Her lips lift slightly. "I knocked the son of a bitch on his ass with a roundhouse kick you'd have been proud of, Sasquatch."

I huff a dark laugh, my eyes raking over her beautiful face with pride bursting inside my chest. "Then she made him eat a bullet."

Emiliano's eyebrows practically hit his hairline, and he glances around us toward the *Soldati*-filled labyrinth at my back. "Now this, I have got to see."

24

RAFAEL

Having drawn her a bath, I press a kiss to Elodie's temple and leave her in privacy. Once I've ensured that Emiliano and his nephew, Romeo, are stationed at her door, I venture back downstairs to confer with Enzo. The compound has been emptied of all guests, with Salvatore the very first to leave, an exceptionally irate Gabriela at his side.

I find him in my office, wading through security footage on an iPad from earlier in the day. He lifts his dark head, his jaw clenched tightly before he snarls in frustration. "I can find fucking nothing. *Less* than nothing. *Figlio di puttana.*"

Then he bangs his fist against the desk in frustration. "There's nothing to indicate Fabiano was anything other than loyal to this family, damn it all to hell." He scrubs his hands up and down his face, muttering angrily, "I vetted him myself, for fuck's sake."

I cross the space, sitting down in my desk chair with a heavy sigh. "We've thought there's a traitor in our midst for a while now, *Fratello*. Let's just be grateful we discovered him before he could carry out whatever he had planned."

A shudder wracks my body at the thought of what Fabiano had planned for Elodie, and just how close he had gotten to executing. "Elodie mentioned that Fabiano said something that made her think of Conti."

Enzo's head perks up immediately, and I continue. "He said that once she was found…" I trail off, inhaling sharply through my nostrils at the thought of that cocksucking son of a bitch, and what he'd intended to do to my woman.

I blow out the breath and grit out the rest of the story. "He said that the peace among the Five would be broken. Just like *he* wants."

"And you think he was referring to Conti?"

I shrug with a weary sigh. "I don't fucking know at this point. But Elodie said she often thought Conti only did the shit he did to provoke. It's a possibility."

Then I push myself out of the chair and reach into my desk drawer for the details Salvatore had left behind before I pass them to Enzo. "If we can deduce where he's holed up, we can ask him that question ourselves, hmm?"

Enzo accepts the documents with a nod, and with a tersely murmured farewell, he leaves through the door leading onto the decking, apparently making his way toward the security bay to get started.

I grab the iPad that he left behind, dragging today's footage to the bottom of the screen to flick over to a real-time view. Enzo had been able to get it back up and running almost immediately once he'd deactivated the EMP jammer.

I do a quick run through the compound, noting the labyrinth appears to be devoid of all memory of what occurred there barely two hours past.

Satisfied that we're safe from the most recent threat, I shut off the device, and make my way back up to Elodie's suite.

My chest constricts when I find Emiliano sleeping across the threshold of the door into the suite, and I tug his blanket up around his shoulders before stepping past him with a wry smirk.

Fine guard dog you'd make, Fratello.

I close the door with a soft *snick* and quietly make my way to the open ensuite door. The tension I didn't realize I was holding in my shoulders lessens when I see Elodie, still in the tub, washing the evidence of the evening from her creamy skin.

For long minutes, I watch her in silence until she glances over her shoulder. "Are you going to just stand there all night?"

One side of my mouth lifts in a shit-eating grin as I walk closer and step around the side of the tub. She looks up at me with a sweet smile, holding up two very wrinkled palms. "I think I'm all pruned out for now."

I grasp her outstretched hands and help her to stand before leaning closer to gather her against me. She stiffens suddenly, her eyebrows shooting skyward. "You'll get all foamy."

"Then I guess I'll get all foamy." I chuckle and bury my nose in her bubble-covered neck, holding her even closer as she shrieks in surprised delight. When my eyes find hers once more, she closes the gap between our faces to drop a light kiss on the tip of my suds-covered nose as I carry her across to the bathroom counter.

Once her ass hits the marble top, I grab a towel from the heated wall panel and drape it over her shoulders before pressing our brows together. Cupping her cheeks, I stroke my thumbs lightly across her cheekbones.

"I thought I wouldn't get to you in time. The thought of losing you...*fuck*—" I stop suddenly, pulling her roughly into my embrace, and she shivers before nuzzling closer.

"You have me, Rafe. I'm yours." She lifts her face to mine, and I frown when I see those navy-blue eyes brimming with pain. "I don't care if you're marrying that girl. I'll take you however I can have you—"

My heart ricochets around my chest as I cut her off. "You want me so much, you're willing to share me?"

She openly flinches before nodding. "I told you, Rafe. I'm *yours*."

My palm creeps around to the nape of her neck as I stare intently into her eyes, and when I finally speak, it's low and dangerous. "You *are* mine, *Stellina*. I want you more than I need air to fucking breathe. And I would *never* share you with another soul..."

I trail off, my eyes flitting between hers and over the contours of her face before I close the gap to press a chaste kiss to her lips.

"But I'm not marrying her. You can believe me when I say, I've been *yours* since the moment our eyes met."

She gasps as her fingertips skim along my jawline, touching me as though she can't really believe what she's hearing.

"I've known from the first time I saw you on that balcony in Vermont. The stars aligned, and our worlds collided. It doesn't matter what came before tonight, because *this*...you and me, *us*, right here and now, was as inevitable as the changing from night to day."

ELODIE

My breath catches in my throat, and blood rushes through my veins as Rafe murmurs against my lips. "I am yours and yours alone, Elodie Rivers. And someday, when the time is right, I will make you my motherfucking queen, for all the world to see."

Euphoria overtakes my entire body when I wrap my arms around Rafe's neck, pulling him close to cover his lips with mine. He stiffens, his hands moving from the nape of my neck to rest lightly on my shoulders, keeping me at a distance.

He groans huskily when I run the tip of my tongue along

the seam of his lips, over and back teasingly, until he opens his mouth, giving me what I so desperately need.

What I *need* in order to wash away the stain of this night. What I *need* to reaffirm he still feels the same about me. That he still wants me as badly as I want him.

Our tongues dance together, slowly and sensually, until I'm squirming on the countertop.

Rafe pushes back suddenly, gasping for air as though he's run a marathon. "We need to stop, *bedda mia*."

I reach up, palming his cheek as my forehead creases in confusion. "I don't understand."

He sighs when he tips my chin up with his index finger, his thumb brushing across my lower lip as his eyes watch the action. "Tonight was traumatic, but I don't think I can hold myself back if we—"

"I don't *want* you to hold back any longer." I tilt my head to one side, shaking it once. "Tonight could have ended very differently. At one point, I thought I'd never see you again, let alone feel your skin against mine."

He swallows roughly, his eyes flicking between mine. "I don't—"

I silence him when I press my index and middle finger to his lips. His forehead creases as he regards me with concerned eyes, and I worship him all the more for it, even as his restraint frustrates me to no end.

"I need you to touch me. To take away the memory of this wretched night. To negate the feel of another man's hands on my body." His body bristles as I continue, my words pouring out of me like water from a broken dam.

"I need you to show me that I'm yours, Rafe. That despite everything that's happened, or could have happened, you still need me as much as I need you. Words aren't enough this time. I need…I *need*…"

I trail off as frustrated tears fill my eyes before he pushes my fingers from his lips. His jaw tics as his eyes darken so much that I can't tell where his irises end and his pupils begin.

His voice is low and hoarse with raw emotion. "I'm *terrified* of hurting you, Elodie."

My heart stutters as I swallow harshly, his words almost knocking the breath from my body. Rafe steps closer, his hips fitting between my legs when he grips my hair to tip my head back to meet his stormy gaze.

"I need you, Elodie. So *fucking* badly. I don't know if I can be gentle..."

He groans, his eyes flickering between mine as his tone takes on a desperation I feel in my bones.

"My body *craves* to be part of yours so intensely, my soul *aches* to be one with its other half..." He tips his head closer, his lips brushing over mine as he whispers softly. "My heart feels as though it's finally awoken in the presence of its match, and the sheer force of how I feel for you scares the *shit* out of me."

Having spoken words that are a direct line to my heart, my arms reach up practically of their own volition to wrap around his neck and pull his mouth to meet mine. We kiss frantically, tongues warring for dominance until Rafe's hands drop from my face to rest on my thighs.

Strong thumbs move in languid circles that search higher and higher with each pass, and I press myself closer, my nipples brushing off his shirt deliciously. I moan into his mouth, and he pulls back slightly.

His eyes are dark pools that I would willingly drown inside when he brings his index finger to my wet pussy, slipping between the folds with a husky groan that makes me even wetter.

And when he speaks against my lips, his words *should* scare me. "I want to break you to remake you so that you can see yourself the way I see you, *Stellina*."

Instead, they turn my blood to molten lava, and I stroke my

tongue along his top lip before nipping his bottom one between my teeth. He gasps at the sting before I suck it into my mouth, swirling my tongue over the irritated flesh.

My eyes meet his, and I whisper, "Then remake me, Rafael Caruso." His gaze sears me to the spot as his nostrils flare, and I palm the nape of his neck, pulling him even closer.

"You turned my life upside down and inside out when you brought me here, yet I'm more myself now than I've ever been in my whole life. And that's because of *you*. Because you found beauty in my broken pieces."

I shake my head, giving him everything and holding back nothing.

"So, *take* me, Rafe. *Break* me. *Remake* me. *Mold* me to your will. I'm not above begging you…" I dust my lips over his, my focus fixed on those midnight eyes that see deep down into my soul. "Just make me yours. *Fai l'amore con me.*"

25

RAFAEL

At her declaration, my self-control snaps. I cover her mouth with mine, devouring the whimper she loosens and relishing the relief I sense within that sound. Holding her close, her perfect tits press against me as I feed her with an answering growl of my own.

She wraps her legs around my waist as I palm the curve of her ass, taking her into my arms and, without breaking the kiss, I walk us into the bedroom until my knees hit the edge of the bed.

When I toss her onto the bed, she quickly scrambles onto her knees, looking up at me with a naughty-as-fuck grin. She plants her palms on my thigh and slowly brings her hands up to my belt buckle, running the tip of her tongue along her upper lip in anticipation.

Within seconds, the belt, button, and zipper have been opened, and she pushes my pants down my legs until they puddle on the floor. I step out, kicking them to one side before inhaling sharply when she palms my rock-hard cock through the material of my boxers with a low murmur of appreciation.

Then she slips them down my legs, letting my dick spring

free, and into her waiting hands. Her eyes widen, taking in the size and girth, and I smirk devilishly as I pinch her chin between my thumb and index finger, lifting her unblinking eyes to mine.

"We'll make it fit, *bedda mia*." My voice is deep, hoarse with unfiltered, raw need.

Then I press the precum-soaked tip against her soft, plump lips, spreading the wetness along her bottom lip. "Now, open for me."

Her eyes flare with unmistakable desire as she presses a kiss to the slit before swirling her tongue around the head of my dick, and my groan of pleasure fills the room. She moans in response, opening her mouth to take me all the way into the back of her throat, and my balls draw up tight, desperate to fill her sweet cunt.

"Fuck, yes. *Mia brava ragazza*. My good fucking girl." My hips pump forward, and she gags, tears filling her eyes as she continues to work my dick eagerly. "*So* fucking good."

Her moans of pleasure fill the room as she takes me deep into the back of her throat, all the way to the root, and my head falls back as my hips move of their own will.

"That's it, *bedda mia*. *Fuck*, take all of me. Take my cock like you were made to suck it."

She groans deeply around my length, and when I look back down at her, I almost come on the motherfucking spot when I see her free hand has disappeared between her legs.

What little control I've managed to retain slips further from my reach when I piston my hips, driving my cock deeper into her warm, wet mouth on each thrust until her mewls of pleasure center me, stopping me from ending this before it's properly begun.

Gathering myself together, I pull my cock out of Elodie's mouth and bend to pluck her up into my arms. She giggles as I twist about before falling backward onto the bed and tugging her smoothly on top of me.

Her hips straddle my thighs as her wet cunt lines up perfectly with my saliva-soaked dick, and I palm her hips, grinding up into her, hitting her clit perfectly.

"Holy shit, you look so fucking perfect right now." She grinds harder, her body shivering as a rush of wetness coats my cock. Leaning over me, she brushes her lips off mine, trailing them down my neck and back again as my cock twitches.

Her eyes are glazed with want when her bullet-like nipples slice into my pecs, turning me on impossibly more.

"Kiss me, Rafe. Kiss me, *please.*"

I smirk broadly. "With pleasure."

At the speed of light, I've gripped her slim waist and hoisted her up my body, placing her legs on either side of my head. She looks down with wide blue eyes, and I can feel her legs tremble, whether in anticipation or apprehension, I'm not sure.

"Now, I'm going to kiss this perfect pussy until you feed me that sweetness, *bedda mia*. Until you come all over my damn tongue while you scream my name until your voice breaks."

Then I draw my tongue through her wet folds, swirling the tip around her clit as she cries out. "Oh, Jesus. *Fuck.*"

"Ride my face. Take what you need," I growl against her slick heat, and my tongue is flooded with more of her delicious arousal. "Mmm, yeah, that's it. Fuck my mouth, Elodie. *Own me.*"

Another shiver runs through her body as she moves her hips almost experimentally, and I bring my arms around her smooth thighs, using the pads of my thumbs to part her glistening pussy lips.

I suck her swollen clit into the heat of my mouth, softly at first, but increasing the pressure as her hips buck against my face.

"Shit, shit, shit, yes. Keep doing that." Her cries of pleasure fill my ears as my cock leaks a steady stream of precum onto my stomach, desperately wanting to get inside her.

As Elodie's hips undulate and circle, I worship her clit, groaning heavily as I lap at her pussy before I push one thick finger inside her pulsating core.

Her answering groan sees her body falter in its rhythm, and I know she's close to the edge. I add a second finger, pumping faster now while flattening my tongue against her engorged clit, feeling just as needy for her release as she is.

Tits swaying, eyes closed in utter abandon, she rides my face, and it's when I add a third finger, thrusting deep into her tight cunt that she goes off like an atom bomb.

"*Fuck*, Rafe! I'm coming. You're making me come."

I roll my tongue along her convulsing pussy as she repeats my name like a prayer, devouring every single drop of her sweetness. Tremors rock her body as she cries out, and I continue to lap at her, moaning my own pleasure from witnessing her shatter for me.

Her head falls forward moments before her eyelids flutter open, her passion-glazed orbs hooded and intense as they look down at me. Filled with the desire for *more*.

Her lips twitch upward. "That wasn't the kiss I had in mind."

I press a soft kiss to the scar on her inner thigh, and she brushes her thumb gratefully against my cheekbone. Then I palm her waist and lift her so that she's lying flat on top of my body. Gathering her close, I press our mouths together as I tweak a hard nipple between my fingers.

At her gasp of surprised pleasure, I thrust my tongue inside, and she moans as I deepen the kiss, clearly enjoying the taste of her arousal on my lips.

Within moments, the kiss turns explosive, and I greedily grip the back of her neck, holding her to me with a desperation that flows between the two of us. A desperation to be as close to one another as two people can be.

"Fuck me, Rafe. Fuck my pussy," Elodie breathes against my lips. "Fill me with your cock. I *need* you."

Her pleading stirs something crazy to life within me, and in the space of half a heartbeat, I've flipped us to fit myself between her legs. My throbbing dick is surrounded by her wetness as I rub myself through her slick lips, moaning deep inside my chest.

I continue to grind myself along her opening before slipping down her body to take a pointed nipple into my mouth, my eyes never leaving hers. The navy-blue irises have all but disappeared, while she hooks her legs around my waist, anchoring me against her as she rubs her dripping core against my lower abdomen.

Our bodies move together as I suck first one perfect tit, and then the other, our gazes never once straying.

When she's writhing and whimpering desperately beneath me, I slide up her body, notching my cock at her entrance as I take her lips with mine in a hungry kiss.

My tongue ravages her mouth, and she meets me stroke for stroke until we're both panting frantically, needing more when I finally ease the first inch of my dick into her pussy.

"Tell me we don't need to have anything between us, *bedda mia*. Tell me I can fill your sweet cunt with everything I have when I *claim* you as my own."

I push forward slightly, and she gasps against my mouth as I whisper, "I need for there to be no barriers when I *give* myself to you."

ELODIE

Tears prickle my eyes, and I nod as his eyes hold me in their thrall.

"I'm clean, I swear. I've been meticulous—"

He silences me with a sweet, chaste kiss to my brow, before drawing back to meet my gaze once more. "I'm clean, too."

His eyes deepen in their intensity before he brushes the tip of his nose against mine. "In fact, I haven't been with anyone since I met you in Vermont."

I inhale sharply as a lump of emotion lodges in my throat. "Oh my God."

"I told you, *Stellina*. Since the moment our eyes met, there's been no one for me but you."

He rests his brow against mine, his breathing labored as his eyes devour me with an intensity I feel in my soul. "*Ti amo, Elodie. Ti amo così tanto.*"

He loves me?

He loves me!

My heart races wildly as I rock against him, feeding more of his hardness into my core, and he tenses, his body trembling as he clearly tries to retain control.

I pull his head closer, resting my lips by his ear to whisper, "Then make love to me, Rafael Caruso."

His sharp intake of breath is all I hear before he loses control entirely. Raising up onto his knees, he grips my ankles and places them on either side of his head before pulling his cock out of my pussy.

And when he speaks, his voice is rough and trembling. "I'll try to be gentle."

I meet his gaze, raising my hips to brush my wetness over his dick. "I don't want gentle, Rafe. I just want *you*."

His eyes darken for a split second before he pushes his thick cock inside me, and I cry out half in pleasure, half in pain.

"You can take it, *bedda mia*." A flood of arousal soaks my pussy, coating his enormous length as he slides another inch into me. "You were made to take this dick. Made for *me*."

He brings a hand between us, strumming his thumb over my throbbing clit as he continues to rock into me. I strain against him as he presses inside, still needing more. Needing to be full of him.

"Almost there, *mia brava ragazza*. I'm almost home."

I rock closer into him, taking those last inches into my pussy with a deep keen. "Oh *fuck*, Rafe. You're so deep. So fucking deep."

His growl sends shivers running up and down my spine as he rocks his hips, opening me up to him. "You feel so fucking amazing. Holy shit, it's taking everything I have not to cream your pretty cunt right now."

Our eyes meet and hold as he circles his hips round and round, continuing to rub my clit and drive me higher until he suddenly freezes. His chest rises and falls so fast that his pupils are blown, and his whole body trembles with the force of holding himself back.

"I—I need...I need..."

I raise my hands above my head, crossing them at the wrists in supplication as my eyes hold his, and I nod. "Give me everything."

Rafe expels a feral groan before he slams forward, and I cry out when his dick hits impossibly deeper. He continues to move, faster and faster as he circles my clit with the pad of his thumb, driving us both higher with each thrust.

"Look at you. So fucking beautiful." Rafe's words tear from his chest on a low growl as his eyes pierce mine. "Your pussy is choking my dick so damn good, *Stellina*."

I inhale through my nostrils, his filthy praise sending a surge of pleasure throughout my entire body. As I palm my breasts, Rafe's jaw tics, and he rocks faster, making me whimper when his length hits a hidden spot within me.

His thrusts continue to massage that same spot, over and over, and I feel a powerful orgasm building. "Oh, *shit*. So deep, so fucking deep."

Dark eyes like pools of liquid desire pierce mine, the intensity of Rafe's penetrating gaze holding me captive as our bodies climb higher. Perspiration beads his brow as he pants, "I need you to come with me, *bedda mia*."

His movements turn almost frantic, and I arch against him, needing just a little more. Rafe reaches between us, unerringly finding my throbbing clit to roll his thumb back and forth, driving me higher.

"I'm close, so fucking close." He increases the pressure on my clit, while circling his hips. His teeth are clenched tight, his eyes molten, searing all the way to my soul.

And right now, in this moment, I can *feel* him claim more than just my body.

He pinches my clit between his thumb and index finger, driving his hips forward, slamming home deeper than before, and my throat constricts when, without warning, my climax plows through me.

"*Fuck*, yes. Deeper, harder, Rafe. Come inside me."

I cry out as obscene pleasure like I've never known overtakes my entire body, and I can feel my pussy gripping Rafe's dick, sucking him deeper.

His groan is almost pained, and his eyelids flicker, threatening to sever our connection as his hips still when his cock erupts, shooting a flood of cum deep inside my convulsing pussy before he releases my legs. They fall uselessly on either side of his perspiration-slick body, and he lowers himself over me, taking my mouth with his in a languid kiss, continuing to watch me with all-consuming eyes.

When he draws back, his eyes fill with emotion, and he

leans his forehead on mine. He's breathing is labored as he pants, "Did you feel that, *Stellina*?"

My brow creases and a smile shines from his eyes as his breath ghosts across my lips. "The moment when our souls became one."

My heart fills to bursting when I smile, wrapping my arms around him as I speak my truth. "I feel it every time you look into my eyes."

26

RAFAEL

My eyes trail across each exquisite feature of Elodie's face as she breathes deeply and evenly. Her dark lashes fan over her cheeks, hiding those beautiful blue eyes from my greedy gaze as she sleeps.

As my dick flexes against my abs, I silently curse the fucker. Despite waking Elodie three separate times throughout the night, clearly my need to bury myself inside of her hasn't been satiated.

And honestly, I doubt that I'll ever get enough.

I sit forward, tugging down the white sheet that's covering her tits to expose them, before leaning forward to take a soft nipple into my mouth. Rolling my tongue over and back, I groan when the bud grows firm and then move to the other one, repeating the action as Elodie squirms.

She sighs as her eyelids slowly open. "Mmm. That feels so good." Her fingers tangle in my hair, smiling into my eyes when she holds me close.

I move my hand to slide between her legs, when suddenly there's a frantic pounding on the bedroom door, and Emiliano calls out, "*Fratello*. You need to come quickly."

Before he's finished speaking, I'm out of bed, and tugging on my discarded pants. Ensuring Elodie has covered her bare chest, I open the door to find both Emiliano and Enzo.

"What the fuck is wrong now?"

"There's a call for you in the den." Emiliano shuffles his feet before continuing. "It's Conti."

Elodie's sharp inhalation at my back makes me clench my jaw as Enzo steps forward. "He said he is ready to negotiate now."

I run my hand through my hair, cursing the motherfucker's timing. "Have you gotten anywhere with the information Salvatore left?"

"It's going to take some time. A couple of days, at least."

I suck in a breath through my teeth before I shrug. "Do what you can. I'll try to delay him..."

As I trail off, Emiliano winces as he murmurs, "You might want to get to the den. *Zio* is currently occupying Conti..."

Fucking Antonio!

"*Cacare!*" I spin about, looking around for my shirt, when Emiliano continues.

"He said he has Aurelia with him, but he's demanded to see Elodie, too."

Elodie's eyes widen for a split second before she visibly squares her shoulders, her face automatically taking on that air of cool indifference that I've come to associate with Conti.

"Give me two minutes, please."

She shoots Emiliano a reassuring smile as he closes the door before she throws back the sheet and walks closer, sliding her nakedness into my embrace to press a kiss to my lips.

"You think Enzo can find where he's hiding?"

Her eyes are unrelenting, and I tip my chin in quiet assent as my arms around her tighten. "I won't return you to him, *Stellina*." My chest clenches as my gaze caresses her face. "I'll die before I allow him to lay a hand on you *ever* again."

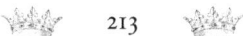

Elodie sets her jaw in determination before nodding once. "Then let's buy you that time you need." Her eyes flicker between mine. "Whatever he says or does, *don't* react. Don't give anything away. Do what needs to be done."

ELODIE

Having made the decision to double down, I quickly throw on a simple cream shirt and matching chino shorts before making my way downstairs with Rafe at my side.

Emiliano shoots me an encouraging smile as I enter the den at Rafe's back with my head held high.

"And we are pleased to be able to get negotiations underway, at last—"

"You may leave now, *Zio*."

The silver-haired man pivots about when Rafe cuts him off unceremoniously. His eyes shoot to me, narrowing slightly as he cradles his bandaged right hand against his chest before he looks back to Rafe with a small nod. "Of course, Rafael."

Then he slips from the room, closing the door firmly behind him.

"Good to see you, baby girl," Nico booms from the speakers, and I narrowly stop myself from flinching at the effect it has on me. "You look good enough to fucking devour."

I fold my arms over my chest almost in an effort to hide from him, and Nico smirks knowingly, leaning closer to the camera as rage bristles from Rafe at my side.

"You can't hide from me, Elodie. I know each dip and curve of your sweet body. I know the exact color of those rosy nipples when you're about to come all over my cock."

My cheeks heat, and my eyes sting as I try to hold back the sudden assault of tears, but Nico just smiles sadistically. "That sweet as fuck sound you make in the back of your throat when I fuck your mouth raw... *Shit*! So fucking hot, baby girl."

Adjusting himself in his pants, he swings his gaze to an outwardly indifferent Rafe, then back to me. "Don't act shy. It's not like he hasn't sampled you himself by now..."

He trails off, watching me closely as I shake my head, my blonde ponytail swishing down my back. "No. I haven't—"

"*Don't* lie to me, *mia piccola puttana*." Nico's voice lashes out like a whip, and he grits his teeth. "Don't you think I know what you look like when you've been freshly fucked?"

My stomach lurches, though I give no outward sign of reaction at his vile words as Rafe steps closer to the camera. His spine is ram-rod stiff even though his hands are raised in entreaty as he shakes his head slowly. "When you get your lover back, you'll see first-hand that she's remained untouched, and has been treated exceptionally well during her time here."

Both men regard one another before Rafe continues. "Now, you've seen her. I've been informed that you have my sister with you."

Nico gestures behind the camera and, a second later, Aurelia steps into view. She's no longer bound and gagged, but there's less fire in her eyes than there was previously, and my heart physically hurts, thinking of what she might be living through while I'm here falling head over heels for her brother.

Her brother who loves me.

And even in the midst of this madness, my chest warms at the knowledge.

"I'm okay, Rafe. I just want to come home."

"I'm working on it, *Principessa*."

Brother and sister watch one another for a beat before Nico claps his hands together, rendering the silence. "Let's get down to it, then. Just me and you, Caruso."

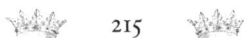

I slip from the office, finding Sasquatch waiting for me. His eyes are filled with keen understanding as he tips his head to one side.

"Come on." He moves off toward the kitchen. "I feel a stress bake is in order."

Even with the myriad of emotions rolling through me, his words make me chuckle, and I move to follow him. My feet freeze once I've taken a handful of steps, and my voice stops him in his tracks.

"I don't need to bake, Sasquatch." He pivots to face me, a blend of disappointment and interest playing across his face as I narrow my eyes. "I need to hit something. Really *fucking* hard."

His mouth lifts in a proud smile as he leads me outside to the sparring ground. He wastes no time, jumping right back in where we'd left off, and before long, my completely inappropriate sparring clothes are stained and damp with perspiration.

"Again. Harder this time, *Coniglietta*."

Sasquatch settles into a standard boxer's stance, and I exhale heavily as I do the same. Sweat is dripping from my brow, and my muscles feel like they've turned to Jell-O, but the physical activity of sparring while Rafe continues his seemingly never-ending call with Nico has proven to be the perfect distraction.

"Now, block with your right, and jab with your left. Like this." He shows me exactly what he means, and I nod before advancing on the giant man. I follow his instructions to the letter, and I'm rewarded with a heavy grunt when my jab connects with his lower back.

"Perfect." He winces, and I can't help the smug smile that lifts my lips. "You're a million miles from when we first began."

"Thank you for teaching me, Sasquatch." I grip his bicep, squeezing it lightly. "If you hadn't taken the time to, last night would have had a very different outcome."

Just as he opens his mouth to reply, Enzo's voice calls out at my back. "Emiliano, *vieni ca*."

Sasquatch rolls his eyes as he sighs exaggeratedly, making me grin, and as I turn to watch him leave, my eyes light on Rafe marching across the lawn.

When he reaches me, he pulls me against his hard body in a tight embrace, and I let out a breath I didn't realize I was holding. "I'm sorry, *Stellina*."

My brow crumples as I mumble against his broad chest. "For what?"

He pulls back enough to look down into my eyes, and I'm immediately shocked at the storminess in his midnight gaze. When he speaks again, his voice is low and laced with dark intent. "I wanted to tear him limb from limb for speaking to you like that. Only the thought of what I plan to do when I get my fucking hands on him kept me from blowing up right there and then."

I tighten my arms around his waist and press my face into the solid warmth of his chest. "All that matters is that he believed you. Did you manage to delay the trade?"

Rafe kisses to the top of my head. "No." My entire body freezes, and time almost seems to come to a stop. "It's scheduled for next weekend. He's claiming he needs time to travel, which I know is bullshit, but it works for us."

He rubs soothing circles on my back, putting some life back into my frozen body before I look up and palm his cheek. "What do we do now?"

Holding my gaze, Rafe breathes a heavy sigh. "Enzo found a paper trail, and he thinks one of our associates in Palermo may be able to help. It's a start."

I close my eyes as hope flows through me, and he drops a kiss to my nose that makes me smile. "And what happens when we do find Nico?"

Then his face changes, his eyes darkening as his jaw tightens. "We'll take back my sister and massacre them all."

RAFAEL

"We'll confer again in the morning."

I rise from my seat, striding around my desk as both Enzo and Emiliano stand too, leaving Antonio alone. As I leave my office, I heave a weary sigh, frustrated beyond measure at the fact that we can't find that Conti motherfucker.

Each time we find something, it leads us directly into a dead end, including the one Enzo had chased earlier, to no avail. The four of us had exhausted every possibility, and following this latest update, I'm not entirely sure what path to take.

All I know is that I need to see Elodie. Three hours apart is three hours too long, and surely by now she's finished with the special video call I'd organized for her.

I take the stairs two at a time, my long strides eating the hall floor until I come to a halt outside the slightly ajar door of her suite.

Elodie's sweet laugh lands on my ears, and I push the door open a little more to find her stretched out on her bed, the cell still in her hands as her pint-sized mini-me chatters excitedly.

"And then Bastian said that the next time he goes home, I'll get to go *with* him! That we're all a *real* family now." Her little voice is filled with such incredulity, it brings a lump to my throat.

I can hear the emotion in Elodie's voice when she tremulously responds. "We are, Curly Fry. And I can't wait until you can come here. There's so much we need to catch up on—"

Skye cuts her off when she squeals, "Rafe!" And I freeze, realizing I'm farther over the threshold than I'd thought, their happiness driving my feet closer.

Elodie spins about on the bed, her long hair whipping

around her before a bright smile appears on her face, and she extends a hand. "We've been waiting for you, Handsome."

Warmth blankets my chest as I edge closer, almost feeling like I'm intruding, until Skye claps her hands. "Ellie said you play piano and that you have a beautiful grand piano in your music room..." she trails off, quirking an eyebrow dramatically. "Do you confirm or deny?"

My lips part with a cheek-aching smile before I nod. "*Si*, Skye. I've played for as long as I can remember."

Elodie tugs me down onto the bed, and I settle beside her. My heart suddenly feels light despite the war I'm waging on all fronts. Skye's eyes are wide and filled with wonder as she whispers, "Can I please play it when I visit?"

As she squeezes my knee, Elodie shoots me an encouraging nod, and it takes a bare moment before I've launched into music talk with Elodie's doppelganger. The conversation flows between the three of us until Skye's dorm monitor swings by, announcing it's time for lights out.

Having reassured Skye that these calls will take place every day or two, depending on her school schedule, she's all smiles as she hangs up the call. Before the screen even turns black, Elodie launches herself into my arms, peppering kisses all over my face as she murmurs repeatedly, "Thank you, thank you, thank you."

I catch her around the waist, neatly spinning us so she's beneath me, and take her mouth in a languid kiss as though we have all the time in the world. When I break the kiss, I remain close, our breaths mingling as I tip my nose against hers.

My eyes are solemn as I stare deeply into her eyes, telling her the absolute truth. "You never need to thank me for giving you the life you deserve, *Stellina*." Her eyes turn glassy when I press a chaste kiss to her lips. "The life you *both* deserve."

27

RAFAEL

"Where are we going?"

"It's a surprise."

Elodie's laughter fills the air around us, putting a grin on my face.

"Are you sure we can't bring a cell, just in case—"

I shake my head sharply and cut her off. "No way. Enzo's on top of everything here, and Sebastiano has promised to keep an extra close eye on Skye. This is an escape for just the two of us."

Clasping Elodie's hand in mine, I lead her along our private dock toward the waiting speedboat.

Her laugh is riotous, face shining with pleasure as I shoot her a wink. "Trust me. You'll like it."

Then I lift my hand in farewell to a watching Emiliano as he glowers, and Elodie giggles sweetly. "He really is sore that you wouldn't let him come along."

Having reached the boat, I jump on board, and reach back to help Elodie follow me as I shake my head. Emiliano hadn't let Elodie out of his sight in the three days that had passed since Fabiano's attack, but I'd be damned if he was intruding on what I had planned for today.

"He'll survive."

I flip him off before I start the engine of the generously sized speedboat that we keep docked for this specific purpose, shooting Elodie a smile over my shoulder. "You might want to take a seat and hold on to something."

Her eyes blow wide as I rev the engine, and I chuckle when she quickly slides into the seat at my side right before I shift the throttle forward. The bow of the Sea Ray slices through the turquoise water, gaining speed quickly, and within less than a minute, we're speeding away from the shores of Sicily.

Elodie's hair whips around her face, and she laughs loudly as she tries, and fails, to hold it out of her eyes. Once we're clear of land, I pull back on the throttle so that we're cruising at a more leisurely pace.

"Where are we going?" Elodie repeats with a smile in her voice, and I turn to her with a smile of my own.

The last couple of days following the call with Nico have been filled with anxiety. The deadline to trade Elodie for Aurelia is looming, and all of Enzo's attempts to find Conti's hiding place have been fruitless.

But I'm determined to take her mind off it all. And what better way to do that than a trip to the island my father bought for my mother.

"There." I raise my hand, pointing into the distance just as the small island comes into view. Elodie focuses on the land with a creased brow as the boat speeds closer, and I can't help but chuckle at her gasp of wonder when she sees where we're going.

"Welcome to *Isola Rosa*."

Her face lights up as she takes in the lush greenery surrounding the island as we pass. She gasps in wonder when I swing the Sea Ray around, passing a small sandy inlet before reaching the long dock.

When she faces me, her eyes are wide with excitement. "Who lives here?"

"It's owned by our family, but technically, no one actually *resides* here. It's more like a getaway *casa*."

Once I've shut off the engine, I stand and tug Elodie to her feet, crushing my mouth to hers. She wraps her arms around my waist as I entwine my hands in her messy blonde locks, slowly tangling our tongues.

I break the kiss with a low chuckle. "And today will consist of lots of that, away from everyone, and everything."

"The *casa* is right at the top of this hill."

I pull Elodie's hand as she groans, wiping the sweat from her brow. "I didn't dress for a walk through the forest, Rafe."

My chuckle earns me an elbow to the ribs as she increases her stride to move past me. "What's the point of building the house in the motherfucking clouds?"

"Trust me, *Stellina*." She glances back at me, her eyes softening at whatever she sees on my face. "It's worth the hike."

Isola Rosa is a privately owned island my father bought shortly before he met my mother. He renamed it when they got married, and it was our primary residence until her passing.

My feet slam to a halt, and Elodie glances back with annoyance painted across her beautiful face. She opens her mouth to speak, but I cut her off when I tug her off the small trail and into the underbrush.

"I want to show you something before we continue to the *casa*."

My feet fly across the ground, and Elodie only complains

once before the trees give way to a grassy knoll where the earth meets the sea and the sky.

Facing out over the vast expanse of endless blue are four white headstones, all lined up neatly side by side.

I gently pull Elodie closer until we're standing in front of them. I watch as her eyes move from one to the other, reading each carefully chiseled inscription.

"We never recovered Alessio's body, so this is all we have to remember him by."

Elodie slides her arms around me, hugging my waist while she nuzzles her face against my chest, and I move on to the next headstone.

"Giacomo was my father. He's buried beside Rose, my mother. And the marker to her right is for my little sister, Gianna."

Elodie stiffens at that, turning her face upward to regard me with sorrowful eyes. "I didn't realize you had another sister."

"I never met her. My mother was coming home after giving birth when the car she was traveling in was involved in a head-on collision. They both died almost instantly, from what I've been told." I swallow heavily, reliving emotions I'd kept buried for decades. "I wasn't quite three when it happened."

Her face crumples in concern, and I hug her close for a moment, relishing the comfort she gives me. The ease with which she soothes my soul.

I feel a sense of rightness in the air around us, almost as though my parents approve of the woman in my arms, and it's with a genuine smile that I pull back. "We're almost there. Come on."

ELODIE

Rafe wasn't lying when he said the hike would be worth it. Because it totally was.

The view from the hilltop is like nothing I've ever witnessed, and I can see clearly now why this island was the family's primary residence when the boys were little.

I could happily live here for the rest of my life.

"Food's ready."

Rafe's deep voice calls from inside the kitchen, which I was surprised to learn had been fully stocked with whatever we might need earlier this morning.

As I enter the open-plan space, my mouth lifts in a smile when I stop to watch Rafe plate up the lunch he's so carefully crafted. He looks up, his eyes lightening in color as he catches me, and he beckons me closer with a tilt of his chin.

The smell of the delicious food hits my nose, and saliva fills my mouth. "Caprese salad and lasagna?" My eyes shoot to Rafe's. "My favorite! How did you know?"

He shrugs with a wide grin. "I have my methods." Then he pulls out a dining chair with a flourish. "Now, eat your carbs. You're going to need them."

I giggle at the innuendo as he slips into the seat opposite mine and serves us both two large helpings of salad. Digging in with gusto, I finish and reach for more before he's even halfway through his portion.

He watches indulgently as I move onto the lasagna, and his eyes flare with unmistakable desire when I moan loudly, chewing my first delicious mouthful. "My *God*, you are good! Where did you learn to cook like this?"

Once he's swallowed his bite of salad, he shrugs nonchalantly. "Alessio was Papa's shadow. Groomed to take over from the day of his conception..." he trails off with a humorless chuckle. "I kept mostly to myself. I was one of those kids who saw everything because no one noticed I was in the room. Until Emiliano."

His face brightens at the mention of his oldest friend, and my heart feels lighter because of it. "His mama, Beatrice, was our cook." He snorts a laugh. "Clearly, that's where he discovered his passion for food. She was an excellent cook. This is her recipe."

"I'm glad you found Sas—I mean, Emiliano."

He chuckles as he plates up some lasagna. "Even if he drives me fucking crazy sometimes."

I shake my head with a wry grin, glancing around at the clock. When I realize the time, I look back at Rafe with wide eyes. "Now that you mention it, we should get back. He'll be worried."

Rafe throws his head back and laughs loudly before his mirth-filled eyes find mine. "I'll send a carrier pigeon to keep him updated."

My lips curve upward in a delighted smile. "Are we going to stay the night here?"

Rafe nods as he chews around a mouthful of lasagna. "Mm-hmm."

I wriggle my butt on the seat in excitement before realizing that following the heat of the day combined with that hike uphill, I really could use a spare change of clothes. "Umm...did you happen to ask the staff who brought the food to stock some fresh clothes?"

His eyes drop down my body, and despite the temperature, goosebumps of anticipation pepper my skin from head to toe. "I'm thinking clothes are entirely optional for the remainder of this trip."

Then he pops a piece of tomato into his mouth with a completely wolfish expression that makes me laugh. "And I know exactly how to play this one."

28

RAFAEL

"You weren't lying when you said you'd take your lesson seriously the next time."

Elodie's tinkling laughter fills the night air around us as I move my queen into position and spear her with a shit-eating grin. "I believe that is check and mate, my love." Then I quirk a devilish eyebrow. "I'll take your panties for that one."

Her chuckle as she slips her simple white panties down her tanned legs is self-deprecatory, and she passes them into my waiting hands with a shake of her head. "You've clearly spent the last two years perfecting your chess strategies, Rafe. How about we change it up a little?"

I narrow my eyes. "What did you have in mind?"

I'm willing to be indulgent, seeing as she's lost both her shoes, her bra, and now her panties, and she's currently only covered by the light dress she'd put on this morning.

My goal of stealing her only clothes is almost complete, and I give myself a mental pat on the back.

"Hold on a sec." She turns and moves off down the hall, and I hear rummaging coming from one of the bedrooms.

The light of the setting sun paints the living space that

we've been sequestered in for the last several hours, and I quickly make my way outside onto the deck to watch as the landscape changes colors in the dusk of the evening.

Suddenly, I'm gripped by an idea, and I push down my pants, stepping out of them to dive headfirst into the still water of the twenty-five-foot infinity pool at the back of the property. My head resurfaces as Elodie steps out through the double doors leading from the living room onto the deck with a pack of cards in her hand.

She bursts out laughing when she sees my discarded chinos and boxers at the poolside. "Come on in. The water's perfect."

"I thought we were playing games."

Even as she speaks, she places the cards onto a sun lounger before she pushes the straps of her dress off her shoulders.

"We can play a different kind of game if you like..."

She shakes her head as she steps out of the dress before tossing it onto the same lounger as the cards. Then she walks closer, her pert breasts swaying temptingly as her eyes never leave mine.

"What did you have in mind?"

She sits on the tiles before lowering herself into the water, biting her lip. "Ooh, that's cold."

I swim closer with a smirk. "Perfect temperature for a hot summer's night of skinny dipping, *bedda mia*."

Having reached her, I stand and encircle her waist with my hands to lift her into my arms. Her legs wrap around me as I pull her close, and her nakedness presses against me in all the right places.

"So, what about this different game..."

Her grin is chockful of innuendo before I lean closer to whisper against her ear. "Have you ever heard of Hide the Salami?"

Elodie bursts out into hysterical laughter as I chuckle to

myself before pressing a kiss to the curve of her neck. "Come on. I've heard it's fun."

She continues to snigger as I palm her ass, pulling her firmly against me, and her laughter turns into a moan when my dick slides through her pussy lips.

Nipples like bullets dig into my chest as her pussy hugs my already rock-hard cock, and I can't hold myself back from leaning closer to cover her mouth with mine. Her arms are wrapped around my neck, pulling me impossibly closer when Elodie rubs against me, and I deepen the kiss as I turn, pinning her back against the pool wall.

When I break the kiss, we're both panting, and despite having had her twice this morning before leaving the compound, I'm fucking ravenous for her again.

Our gazes are locked when I slip my hand between us to slide my middle finger between her wet folds and into her tight pussy. Her eyelids flutter, threatening to close as she rocks her hips forward with a whimper, and I groan when I add a second finger, pumping both slowly into her needy core.

She drops her left hand from my shoulder, down below the water to wrap her palm around my dick, and I increase the pace of my hand.

"You want my dick, *bedda mia*? You want to jack my dick while I finger this hot cunt?"

Her response is to tighten her grip on my cock as she shakes her head.

"Where do you want me to put it then?"

She answers with a filthy smile. "In my pussy." Then she blinks innocently. "*Please.*"

"*Fuck,* yes."

I growl under my breath as my mouth latches onto her neck, sucking and nipping almost desperately until she's squirming against me.

Her head tips back, resting on the side of the pool as she

continues to pump my cock lazily, and I add a third finger, thrusting faster still when my thumb presses down onto her swollen clit.

The water splashes around her undulating tits as a telltale flush covers her chest.

"Come on my fingers, *mia brava ragazza*. Scream for me."

I lean forward, taking a nipple into my mouth and sucking hard when I increase the pressure of my thumb on her clit. She whimpers in urgency before crying out as her pussy clamps down around my fingers. "Harder, harder, Rafe. I'm coming, *fuck!*"

As she rides out her orgasm, my dick pulsates in her hand, needing more than anything to be inside her sweet body. As she descends from her peak, I smoothly rise out of the water, lifting her after me.

She folds her legs around my waist, and our gazes clash and hold as my long strides carry us from the pool to the living space. When my knees hit the couch, our mouths collide, and we kiss hungrily, our tongues undulating together, driving us both higher and higher.

Elodie leans back to look down on me with passion-glazed eyes, and the light of the setting sun frames her from behind in a way that makes drawing a breath difficult.

My forehead creases when I bring my palm up to caress her soft cheek as my eyes greedily drink her in.

"I could live forever and a day, *Stellina*, and I'd never find anyone or anything more beautiful than you right now, here in this moment."

ELODIE

Tears prickle my eyes at the sincerity in Rafe's voice, and I can't hold back the words any longer. The time just feels *right*.

"I love you, Rafe." He tracks the pad of his thumb across my lips, looking into my eyes as though I'm the beginning and the end of his whole world. "I'm *so* in love with you, I can't fucking stand it—"

My words are devoured when he crushes our mouths together, thrusting his tongue forward to spar with mine as a low whimper escapes from my throat. His answering groan sends a surge of desire straight through me as he brands me with a searing kiss I can feel in my soul.

He pulls back to pierce me with his intensely darkened gaze, and time almost stands still when he breathes against my panting mouth. "*Sempre e per sempre, Stellina.*"

His eyes flick between mine as he draws a rough breath. "That's how long I will love you. Forever and ever and always."

Butterflies take flight in my stomach as my body hums to life, and I press a chaste kiss to his soft lips, drawing back enough to whisper gently, "Show me, Rafe. Show me how much you love me."

With a grin, he sets me down on the floor and gently twists me about so that his chest presses against my back. He draws his wet tongue along the sensitive curve of my neck, and I gasp a breath as he nips and sucks the skin. His hand snakes around my hip before he brushes his middle finger across my swollen clit.

I cry out as my knees threaten to go from underneath me, and he bands the forearm of his free hand around my waist to keep me upright. The swell of his cock is notched against the curve of my spine, and I can't help myself from groaning when he rocks against me.

As his finger slips between my folds, he murmurs against my neck in appreciation. "So fucking wet. Your sweet pussy loves to weep for me, doesn't she?"

He sucks my neck then, and I cry out as his finger slips inside of me, my core clenching around the single digit.

"Shit, *bedda mia*. You feel so good. So *fucking* good." He urges me forward, my knees landing on the couch as he drops to his knees behind me.

His mouth closes over my clit, sucking hard as I desperately grip the fabric of the couch. He flattens his tongue then, licking slowly from clit to slit and back again, driving me slowly to the edge of bliss as my hips jerk against his face.

My thighs tremble as he eats me with barely restrained ferocity until he pulls back, and I twist about, watching his blown pupils when he spits onto my exposed ass hole. Using his thumb, he spreads the saliva around in circles, making me push back against him, desperate for more.

I cry out when his thumb slips inside my ass, pumping slowly as his mouth returns to my needy clit, sucking hard. And I suddenly peak, screaming his name as I come harder than ever before.

My cheek is pressed into the fabric of the couch as I come back down to earth when Rafe stands at my back, bending over me to lick my earlobe.

"I need to be inside you. I need to feel your hot pussy ripple around me. I need you to milk my cock until I fill this pretty cunt with everything I've got."

He nips my shoulder blade as he lines his cock up with my slick center before he teasingly pushes the tip inside. I whimper in protest, my body vibrating following the mind-blowing orgasms this man has given me. As he withdraws to push his cock deeper, I cry out helplessly until he taps his hardness against my throbbing clit.

"You're so fucking perfect." His mouth rests by my ear, sending shivers all the way to my toes before he growls, "So fucking *mine*."

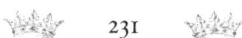

Then he drives himself forward, sliding home in one smooth thrust to fill me entirely. I slam my eyes closed as I cry out, sheer pleasure crashing over me while Rafe begins to move.

And he doesn't hold anything back. Our bodies find a rhythm quickly and easily until he rises, taking me with him.

"Touch yourself, *Stellina*. Play with your clit while I fuck you nice and hard."

My eyes roll back in my head as I do what he commands, sliding my middle finger over and back across my needy clit.

He continues to drive himself home as his hands palm my breasts, tweaking my nipples while he whispers filthy words in my ear.

"*Così stretta. Così fottutamente bagnata,*" he pants heavily, and I can feel his rhythm falter as his orgasm rises. "This tight, wet pussy is mine, *bedda mia*. Only mine."

He pumps harder.

Faster.

Deeper.

And I come apart all over his cock as he groans his own pleasure before filling me with a stream of his hot cum.

We're both still panting, coming back to earth, when he presses a sweet kiss to my shoulder blade before he gently rests his sweat-slick brow on the back of my neck.

His whisper fills the room with words that are instantly embedded inside my racing heart. "Always mine, *Stellina. Per sempre.*"

29

ELODIE

As Rafe steers the speedboat away from *Isola Rosa*, my shoulders sag slightly at the knowledge that we're about to return to reality.

I place my hand over Rafe's on the throttle, and he neatly twists his wrist so that his hand envelops mine. He squeezes lightly, a bittersweet smile on his handsome face before he mouths the words, "*Te amo, Stellina.*"

The weight on my chest lessens minutely as I return his smile, and I turn my gaze to the horizon, watching as the shoreline of Sicily comes into view moments later.

Rafe docks the boat silently before helping me to disembark, and once I'm safe on dry land, he presses a gentle kiss to my brow.

"Thank fuck, you're back."

Sasquatch's voice fractures the silence as he rushes down the dock, holding a cell phone in his hand. My senses are instantly on high alert, noting the severity of his usually calm features.

"It's Sebastiano." Rafe jumps into action, tugging me behind him as his strides cover the ground quickly, and I jog to keep up. He plucks the cell from Sasquatch's outstretched hand and hits the number on the screen before bringing it to his ear.

"*Fratello.* What's wrong?"

He's silent as Sebastiano speaks, his eyes never leaving mine, and though I can't hear the words being spoken, a prickle of foreboding runs up my spine at the sudden shift in his demeanor.

"I'll be there soon."

He hangs up the call and passes the cell back to Sasquatch. "Wheels up in twenty minutes, Emiliano. I need to get to Zurich immediately."

Skye!

Hairs rise on the back of my neck, and I focus on deep, even breathing, as he lowers his voice. "Tell no one aside from Enzo, Gianni, and Romeo. They're with me."

Sasquatch nods once, only stopping to add quickly, "I'm staying behind with Miss Rivers."

My palpitating heart clenches at my friend's thoughtfulness, and I shoot him a grateful smile as Rafe nods. "Yes, that's *exactly* where I need you, *Fratello.*"

Sasquatch rushes ahead to get everything in motion as Rafe turns to me. His eyes are deadly serious, and when he speaks, my world splinters. "It's Skye. She's been admitted to the hospital."

I inhale through my nostrils, sucking deeply, but I can't breathe. There's simply no air getting to my lungs. The dock is spinning when Rafe palms my cheeks, forcing me to look into his deep brown eyes.

"Elodie."

And as he's done before, his tone centers me enough to draw a breath. Several shuddery inhalations later, and the ache in my chest lessens marginally.

Enough so that I can focus on Rafe's words.

"When I enrolled her, I put my name as her next of kin…"

He shrugs almost apologetically. "It seemed the best way to keep her safe. But although Sebastiano is my brother, the hospital staff will only give Skye's medical information to her guardian. And for all intents and purposes, that's *me*."

His eyes flicker between mine as my breathing becomes less labored. "I need to go, *Stellina*. Now."

He grips my hand, pulling me alongside him as my wind whirrs with possibilities. We're entering the house by the time my thoughts have registered enough to form a question.

"Did Sebastiano have *any* information at all? *Anything*?"

Rafe's concerned eyes meet mine. "He said that she came to him from the junior campus earlier this morning, complaining that she didn't feel well. Her face was red and swollen." He shrugs helplessly. "That's all he had. Maybe it's something simple, and all this panic is for nothing, but I need to get there immediately to find out."

Even with my stomach sinking, I send Rafe a grateful smile for trying to keep me from spiraling when we enter his office. He quickly searches through his desk drawer before flourishing the cell I'd used to video call Skye mere days ago.

Days that now feel like years, and I bite down on my lip, desperately trying to keep my rising emotions at bay.

"Keep this with you." I take it from his outstretched hand, my own shaking helplessly. "I'll contact you as soon as I've got news."

RAFAEL

My SUV has barely pulled up outside the University Children's Hospital, when my door is yanked open by my furious younger brother.

"What the fuck took you so long?"

Sebastiano pivots on his heel, barely glancing over his

shoulder as he strides in the direction of the hospital. "Move your ass, *Fratello*."

By the time Enzo has secured the area, and I've moved to follow, he's already entering the hospital.

When I reach him, I swat him across the back of the head, and he flinches with an annoyed, "Hey! What was that for?"

"Watch your mouth."

Then I swat him again, and he grits his jaw in irritation, but before he can question my reason for the second one, I grip his collar, tugging him closer to my face. "And that one was for ducking out on your security detail, *stronzo*."

He shrugs me off with a petulant tut. "I don't need them. They just draw attention anyway."

"You'll do as you're told, Sebastiano. No fucking excuses, *si*?"

He narrows his eyes and neglects to answer me before swinging a left, where we come to a nurse's station. A matronly blonde woman smiles pleasantly when she spots Sebastiano.

"I told you, sir. Next of kin *only*—"

I step forward, and the nurse's eyes widen as I extend a hand with cool indifference. "Rafael Caruso. I'm Skye's guardian. And I need to see her *immediately*."

She accepts my hand before gesturing down the corridor. "She's right over here." Then she leads us to a white door no more than twenty paces from the nurse's station.

"Visiting hours—"

I cut her off as I open the door. "Don't apply to us, *capisti*?"

Without waiting for a response, I step over the threshold, my lips twitching upward when my eyes find Skye, who's sitting up in her bed, singing softly to herself.

The melody trails off when she spots me, and her face lights up. "Rafael!" Then she jumps from the bed to fly across the room and throws her arms around my waist.

I smooth my palm over the top of her curly head with a small chuckle at her exuberance. "How you been, kid?" She pulls back to look up at me, and I grin, noticing she's lost her two front teeth recently. "Did you have a fight with the tooth fairy or something?"

She snorts as she shakes her head. "Don't be silly." Then she purses her lips in distaste. "It was a bee, actually. And the doctors said I was very lucky that Bastian got me here as quickly as he did because I was in ana...ana-fil..."

She trails off, frowning in frustration, as she sighs, "Oh, *what* was the word again!"

The nurse at my back steps inside the room, a genuine smile on her face as she leads Skye back to her bed. "Skye was in anaphylactic shock when she arrived. We've deduced that she's highly allergic to bee stings." She plumps a pillow and slots it in at Skye's back before turning to face me. "It shouldn't be a problem moving forward now that we're aware."

She pulls a slim tube from her pocket and holds it up. "Once she carries at *least* one, preferably two EpiPens at all times, and administers a dose immediately following a sting, then I don't see this becoming a recurrence."

Once she's tucked Skye back into bed, she turns to me with a popped eyebrow. "And as I was saying earlier, visiting hours don't apply to family members of patients under the age of sixteen."

Then she bustles past, leaving me with a chuckling Sebastiano and a grinning Skye. "Can I call Ellie now? *Please?*"

I quickly set up a video call, and Elodie answers on the second ring. "Is she okay? Please, tell me she's okay, Rafe."

My smile is broad as I wink. "Ask her yourself, *Stellina*."

Then I pass the cell into Skye's waiting hands. Her big blue eyes, so like her mother's, fill with happy tears, and I can physically feel myself fall head over heels for this damn kid. This miniature extension of the woman I love.

"Did you still not get my letter? Bastian said he would send it for me." She shoots an accusing look toward my brother. "Did you send it?"

Elodie saves Sebastiano from answering when she laughs, "I got it, and I've replied, but clearly, the postage system is as bad in Europe as it is back home."

"Did you send me any candy?" I snort as Skye continues obliviously. "We're not allowed to buy candy at school, and it's the only thing I miss…well, other than you, Ellie."

"I miss you even more, Curly Fry." Her eyes flick to mine. "Can someone please tell me what happened?"

Once we've relayed what the nurse told me, relief fills Elodie's eyes, and I can see the tension evaporate from her shoulders.

"Thank God for that." Her brow puckers. "Though, an allergy like this is still super serious, but wow—" She cuts off to blow out a heavy sigh as I ease the cell from Skye's hand. "My mind was taking me to Crazy Town since you left, Rafe."

I move to the window for some privacy as Sebastiano entertains Skye quietly in the background. "I'll get all the information on these EpiPens and what that entails. And I've had Enzo add Sebastiano as Skye's next of kin, so that if anything were to happen…"

She picks up where I've trailed off. "Then at least we wouldn't be in the dark like we were today."

I nod slowly, my eyes moving over her slightly less fraught features. "Exactly. I'll return once Skye is safely back at school, and—"

Elodie's face freezes at the same time I hear the unmistakable sound of gunfire.

"What was that?" She rises, taking the cell with her as my chest tightens. Sebastiano walks closer with a heavy frown on his face, and even Skye sits unmoving on her hospital bed.

I can see Elodie move out of her suite, and onto the balcony. She looks all around before her eyes meet mine through the screen when she shakes her head slowly, apparently seeing nothing out of the ordinary.

"Maybe it was Sasquatch cleaning his gun again." She chuckles at the memory, and I force my lips to lift fractionally as niggling anxiety pools in my gut. "I'll go find him, and—"

There's a sudden commotion in the background, and I hear Emiliano's deep, even voice as he addresses Elodie.

"The compound is under assault." Elodie gasps, and she looks at me through the camera lens with wide eyes as Emiliano grits out. "And I'm getting you out of here right now, *Coniglietta*."

Before I can question what the hell is going on, the screen goes black. I frantically redial to no avail before I try Emiliano's cell to find it's also out of service. My damn chest feels like it's going to explode when I rake my palm through my hair and raise wild eyes to my brother.

"I need to—I must..." My thoughts race wildly as my younger brother crosses the room and places his palms on my upper arms.

His brow is clear, and when he speaks, his words are mature beyond his seventeen years.

"Whatever it is that's happening at home, you can't fall apart, Rafe. *La famiglia* needs you now more than ever."

I clench my jaw, blowing a breath out through my nose before shifting my gaze to a concerned Skye. Eyes identical to her mother's immediately center me, and something inside of me snaps into place.

"*Grazie, Fratello.*" I nod gratefully at my brother before closing the distance with Skye, taking her little hand in mine.

"I'll be back to bring you to visit your mo—your sister *real* soon, okay?"

She nods solemnly, and I squeeze her hand. "In the meantime, Sebastiano is at your beck and call for anything you need." I lean closer, stage-whispering, "Just keep away from the bees this time."

I cluck her under her chin, making her lips lift on one side before I nod in encouragement as Sebastiano speaks at my back.

"Go. I've got Skye. Do what you need to do, *Fratello*."

Before he's even finished speaking, I'm halfway out the door, dialing Enzo, ready to rip the world apart with my bare hands in order to keep the woman I love from any further harm.

30

ELODIE

My cell screen goes black, and Rafe's dark eyes disappear from my line of sight as Sasquatch tosses a pair of white sneakers at me.

"Put these on. We need to get out of the main house *now*."

I quickly lace up the trainers, my eyes never leaving Sasquatch's. "I thought we were safe here."

He snorts a dark laugh. "So did I." Then he ducks his head out into the hallway as I stand up, moving to his back. My head is spinning, adrenaline pumping, and I know if I give myself a minute to think, I'll begin to spiral, so I do the only thing I can do.

I rise onto my tiptoes, as close to Sasquatch's ear as possible, and whisper, "What's the plan?"

He glances over his shoulder, and his usually kind face is tight, hard-set in a grimace. "We need to get to the dock. The boat is our only way out of here if they've already gotten inside."

His bushy eyebrows draw closer together as he presses a 9mm Glock into my hand. "Stick to my side, *Coniglietta*. And remember to shoot first, ask questions later, *capisti*?"

I blow out a breath and nod, then he checks the hallway once more before slipping out my door. Following swiftly behind him on silent feet, the sound of my racing heart fills my ears as we make our way to the top of the stairs.

Maria appears at the base, her eyes widening as terror fills her pretty face when she spots us. She gives us an almost infinitesimal shake of her head, and we freeze at her silent warning as she spins back to face whoever is with her.

"I believe he's with *Senorina* Elodie, if you wish to wait here, Senor—"

My blood turns to ice when Maria's words are cut short, and the sound of a single gunshot echoes through the house. I watch in absolute horror as red stains the front of her crisp white shirt, and when her eyes find mine, they're telling me to run.

Pleading with me to go. *Now*.

Sasquatch moves before I do, gripping my wrist and tugging me back toward my suite. He barricades the door as best he can before he moves past me, out onto the balcony.

I watch his actions, not entirely registering anything that he's doing, as Maria's face plays on a loop inside my mind's eye, and I swallow roughly past the enormous ball of guilt wedged in my throat.

"Let's move." Sasquatch pops his head around the corner of the balcony door, frowning when his eyes land on me, and he glances behind him before coming back inside to crouch down. He rests his huge hand on my knee and pats it gently.

And when he speaks, his words are low, reminding me of exactly what's at stake here.

"He's coming for you. *Now*. Don't have Maria's sacrifice meaning nothing, Elodie." His eyes flicker between mine. "So, let's get the fuck out of here, okay?"

I clench my jaw with a sharp nod, renewed determination

filling my body as I stand and walk outside. My feet falter when I realize that as I'd had my mini breakdown inside, Sasquatch had been busy out here.

"Are those my *sheets*?"

"Some towels and a bathrobe, too." Sasquatch appears at my side, jamming a peanut butter cookie into his mouth, and shrugs as he chews. "I've seen it done on TV. No reason it can't work for real."

My eyes blink several times in sheer disbelief, vaguely noting the thorough job he's done of anchoring the sheets to the giant statue on the edge of the space, when I hear voices outside my bedroom door. "Oh, shit. We need to move."

I swing my leg up, intent on climbing down first, but Sasquatch stops me and gives me his back, lowering himself to a crouch. "I'll carry you. You'll need to cover us when they break through."

My stomach lurches, realizing he's right, and I check my gun before hopping onto his broad back. "Hold on tight."

Sasquatch eases himself over the side of the balcony, testing the sheets with his bulk before beginning his descent. He walks his feet down as far as the wall goes, taking a deep breath before he continues to lower us without any foot leverage.

His thick arms move quickly but carefully, carrying both our combined weights down the makeshift rope far easier than I'd have thought possible.

As we reach the end, I glance down and notice that the rope stops a good ten feet from the ground. I'm in the process of psyching myself for the fall when I feel Sasquatch's shoulders stiffen. "I can hear them. They're in your suite."

My heart slams against my chest as we reach the end of the sheets, and Sasquatch whispers underneath his breath, "Quickly, *Coniglietta*. You jump first. *Velocemente*."

Before I can give myself a chance to think, I bend my knees

and let go, barely stifling a squeal as I fall much farther than I had anticipated. My feet hit the ground, and I tuck myself into a roll as my body follows.

"She's here!"

A loud, masculine shout from above makes me push to my feet, ignoring the ache in my legs from my subpar landing as I pull back the slide on the barrel of my 9mm and angle it toward the balcony.

I pop off a shot, the bullet grazing the forehead of the owner of the voice, and he jumps back as Sasquatch drops to the ground somewhere to my left.

Two long rifles and a handgun appear on the balcony in the same place the wounded man disappeared from, and I inhale sharply before Sasquatch bellows for me to run.

"Move, Elodie. *Go, go, go!*"

I take off at a pelt as the sound of gunfire chases me, and I hear Sasquatch's heavy breathing right at my back as we race across the landscaped gardens. Bullets hit the ground all around me, blowing up chunks of soil and grass, and I cry out in pain when one grazes the fleshy part of my upper arm.

My chest burns, but I don't dare stop even though my legs feel like they're about to go from underneath me, when suddenly I'm being hoisted into Sasquatch's arms.

He keeps running, forehead beaded in perspiration as he grunts, "Almost there."

And then, I hear *his* voice.

"Stop shooting, idiots. You could hit *her*!"

Nico sounds furious as the gunfire comes to a sudden stop, and as we put distance between us and the house, I can hear him barking orders at his *Soldati*.

We crest the small dip in the lawns before the ground gives way to the long dock. My stomach does a little jump for joy when my eyes light on the speedboat, gently bobbing on the waves.

"We made it." My exclamation escapes on a breathy sigh as I turn to look up at Sasquatch, and my sigh catches in my throat. Reaching up my hand, I draw the pad of my thumb through a steady stream of blood trailing from one side of his mouth.

I quickly jump down out of his arms, noting how pale his face is as he blinks heavily before I pat his arms and shoulders, checking for injuries. Every muscle in my body freezes when I move around to his back.

"Oh, Emiliano." My soft cry escapes on a sob as I take in the absolute carnage before me. His black cotton T-shirt is riddled with bullet holes. Torn flesh is blended with the black fabric, and all of it is drowned in dark red blood.

So much blood.

Dripping endlessly from his back, now pooling on the earth beneath our feet.

My mind races, wondering how he's still standing.

I extend my hands to cover the wounds, desperate to stem the bleeding, and within seconds, both hands are covered in red. My breathing kicks up a notch when Sasquatch abruptly drops to his knees, and I reach for him, attempting to ease his fall. I barely manage to lower his heaviness to the ground and cradle his head in my lap.

His usually bright green eyes are dull as he watches me, and I swallow back a sob when he brings a bloodied hand up to brush his thumb across my cheek.

"I saved you, d-d-didn't I?" His voice is small. Completely unlike his normal, larger-than-life self.

I nod in answer as tears fill my eyes before I force my lips upward in a tremulous smile. "My human shield."

He snorts a laugh that turns into a cough, and it wracks through his whole body. Once he has it under control, he smiles softly. "You remembered."

The ball of emotion lodged in my throat lends a rough edge to my voice. "I'll never forget."

His lips twitch with the effort, eyes lighting up for a moment as I brush his thick black hair back from his brow.

"T-t-thank you," I whisper as tears stream unheeded down my cheeks. "For *everything*."

His huge chest rattles as he exhales a deep breath, and I watch helplessly when the life slowly fades from the green eyes of my gentle giant. Eyes that stare unseeing at the big blue sky above us.

I bring my palm over his face to close those lids for the last time as a blend of overwhelming grief and hopeless fury flows through me with the force of a tsunami.

My chest aches, my head throbs, and I'm so *fucking* tired of it all that I want to scream.

And even though I want nothing more than to sit and mourn for my friend, I'm jolted back to the here and now when I hear American accents cresting the slope of the lawn.

I ease Sasquatch off my lap, palming his cheek one final time before pushing to stand. Two men dressed from head to toe in black come into view, and I quickly grab the Glock before ducking behind one of the nearby deck chairs.

They spot Sasquatch and amble closer, laughing as they kick his side. I slip out of my hiding spot, blood boiling as I notch the gun, take steady aim, and unerringly pull the trigger.

The bullet goes straight through the neck of one soldier as I line up another round, taking down the second before he can lift his own firearm.

I rush past them, intent on getting to the boat and making both Maria's and Sasquatch's sacrifices mean something, when I feel a sting on my upper arm.

All of a sudden, my legs feel like Jell-O, and I look down to see a long tube protruding from my bicep. I blink several times, feeling as though I can't believe what I'm seeing.

Feeling entirely removed from the situation.

Sounds around me become muffled, and my vision blurs as my knees lose all strength to hold me upright. I fall to the dock, staring up at the sky as my eyelids shutter closed, and the last thing I see is the face of the man who haunts my nightmares before the world turns black.

31

RAFAEL

"I thought you fixed the electronics following the shitshow with Fabiano and the EMP jammer."

Enzo doesn't lift his eyes from the screen as he types furiously, murmuring. "I did, *Fratello*."

I've reached my wit's end. We've been on board for over an hour, and I've yet to see the security footage from the compound.

My patience snaps when I reach for him, grabbing his collar and pulling him to stand as I snarl. "Talk to me here, Enzo. I'm about to lose my motherfucking shit."

He regards me for a moment before nodding slowly. "And I'm trying to help you, Rafe. Just give me another couple of minutes, *si*?"

I swallow harshly, my chest tight with fear as I let go of my friend, and move to the back of the jet in an attempt to calm down. With close to another hour to go before we touch down in Sicily, I feel like I'm about to go out of my goddamn mind.

The look on Elodie's face, as it changed from incomparable joy to absolute terror, replays on a loop in my mind, and I'm moments away from descending into madness when Enzo shouts out, "I'm in."

Fucking finally.

I'm by his side in a heartbeat, and when I look at what he's pulled up on the screen, time seems to stop when I immediately recognize the ransacked living area of my home.

"You have access to the security feed?"

With a nod, he taps away on the keys. "When I said I'd fixed the electronics, I *meant* that I'd installed EMP shielding for the cameras."

He pans through several camera feeds, and rage bubbles in my stomach when I see so many of my loyal *Soldati* brutally murdered at the hands of a fucking lunatic.

As the camera pans across the foyer, my breath catches in my throat when my eyes land on the still form of Maria, and I look closer, praying Elodie's not nearby.

He turns his face up to mine. "This feed is streaming in real-time, *Fratello*..."

As he trails off, I realize what he means, and I look back to the screen to find he's flicked over to Elodie's suite. I inhale sharply when I observe the wreckage. Furniture and clothes are strewn everywhere, and the door is hanging off its hinges.

"Can we rewind the footage? That is possible, *si*?"

Enzo nods, blowing out a heavy breath. "Do you really want to watch? You may not like what you see—"

"Just play the damn footage, Enzo."

Several taps later, and I can see a flurry of movement as Emiliano appears to be barricading the door into the suite. My brow creases in a deep frown when I see Elodie sitting on the bedside chair with a vacant expression, until Emiliano shakes her into awareness.

She spurs to life, both of them disappearing onto the balcony.

"Change the camera, dammit."

Another flick of a button, and when I see them go over the edge of the balcony, I watch on in horror. "Is there another camera facing that balcony?"

I ask the question knowing there's not, and Enzo confirms, "The next time they'll come into view is when they reach the lawn."

He flicks to that feed, speeding the time-lapse slightly, and it's not long until Elodie runs into view. Emiliano follows, and they both run in the direction of the dock.

Hope fills my chest at the knowledge that the Sea Ray would have still been docked since this morning. But that hope dies a swift death when Enzo flips the feed forward and we watch the lawn to spot Conti race after them.

He returns several minutes later, laughing with his men as he carries an unconscious Elodie over his shoulder.

"Mother*fucker*." I spit the word, watching helplessly as Conti quickly tosses her into the backseat of his waiting car, climbs in after her, and peels out of my driveway, taking my *Stellina* with him.

My blood is thundering in my ears as I search my mind, wondering how the *fuck* something like this could have happened, and how the hell I'm going to get her back.

Because I will. I'll move Heaven and Earth to find her. I'll make a deal with the motherfucking devil himself if it means I can keep her safe.

"Thank you, Enzo." He nods his assent as I slip back into my seat. "Please watch through the rest of the footage and try to get an idea of what awaits us, *per favore*."

Feeling like I might be sick, I pinch the bridge of my nose between my thumb and index finger, focusing on keeping myself together. My breathing is coming more smoothly, when Enzo swears loudly.

"*Minchia!*"

I shoot to my feet, and look over Enzo's shoulder, my blood running cold as I watch the scene unfold on the screen.

My mind races frantically as I try to fathom what I'm actually seeing play out before me, even though it's as clear as day.

Domenico Conti strides straight through my goddamn front door and clasps the hand of my smiling *Zio*, the man I'm supposed to trust implicitly.

And at his side stands my worthless stepmother, welcoming the man I've sworn vengeance on with open arms. Into *my* fucking house.

"I've seen enough." I turn my back on the screen, disgust mingling with the sting of betrayal in the pit of my stomach, and I clench my jaw as tightly as I can before I calmly face Enzo again. "Arrange a video call with *Cesare* DeMarco. I have a feeling that I might require some outside assistance cleaning up this mess. He's the lesser of two evils, and fuck knows, I can't trust Salvatore anymore."

The SUV grinds to a halt on the driveway before Enzo jumps out, holding the door open for me to follow. My eyes rake across the property, rage curdling in my stomach as I take in the sight of more than a dozen loyal *Soldati* who were massacred as a result of Antonio's betrayal.

With Gianni and Romeo on either side of us, we climb the front steps of the house and go inside.

As I reach the top step, three *Soldati* exit the house, straining to carry another casualty of this insanity, but it isn't until I step aside to let them past that my stomach lurches. Blood pounds in my ears, and the floor beneath me suddenly feels uneven.

"*Fratello.*" My most trusted friend's name comes out as a whisper, and the *Soldati* carrying him stop in their tracks. I step closer, placing my palm on Emiliano's broad chest, looking down on his peaceful face.

A wave of furious agony tears through me so forcefully that I struggle to breathe, and I lean closer to my fallen brother, whispering in his ear.

"*La vendetta sarà mia,* Emiliano. I swear to you, I *will* have vengeance."

When I rise, Enzo and Romeo step forward, taking Emiliano from the Soldati and bringing him back inside.

I follow after, to find Sofia sitting on the last step of the staircase. My face scrunches when I see mascara streaking down her once-pretty face, and she quickly jumps to her feet when she sees me.

"Oh, Rafael. Thank heavens you're here." Her tone is saccharine-sweet, and she rushes closer. "The compound was attacked while you were away, and—"

"I'm *fully* aware of precisely *everything* that happened in my absence, *Matrigna*." I spear her with a pointed look, and she pales considerably. "And I'm here now to ensure the culprits responsible pay the ultimate price, *hmm*?"

She purses her lips together, glancing around, probably in search of Antonio to tell her how to react, but when she comes up blank, her sense of self-preservation kicks in.

"Forgive me, Rafael. I don't know what I was thinking."

She rushes forward, all signs of sweetness gone as desperation overtakes her features. "It was all Antonio. He said Sebastiano would be Don if I helped him to get rid of you and Alessio—"

I reel back as though I've been physically hit, shaking my head in disbelief. "Alessio died in a car accident…"

She shakes her head, her dark, bedraggled hair swishing

around her shoulders. "No, no. It wasn't an accident. Antonio had the car tampered with—"

"You stupid bitch."

Antonio's voice rings out like a whip, cutting off Sofia, and she shrinks back in fear. "I—I only wanted my daughter returned to me, Antonio." Her eyes fill with tears when she turns to me. "Taking Aurelia was not part of the deal, and now Conti refuses to give her back. Aurelia was never supposed to be there that day. Conti was supposed to end you and Giacomo."

The truth of her words hits me like a sledgehammer as I recall Antonio's angry words from the day of Papa's funeral.

It should have been you.

I swing cold, dead eyes back to regard my treacherous uncle, my feet moving closer to him as I growl dangerously. "You orchestrated the deaths of my father and brother. My sister is lost to us. You tried to kill me. *And* you've handed the woman I love back to the man who will deliver her to a fate worse than death."

I extend my hand, palm facing up, and Gianni immediately passes me a loaded gun. I pull back the slide and aim it directly at Antonio's head. "Fabiano was doing your bidding, wasn't he? *You're* the motherfucking traitor. You've been the one calling the shots all along—"

"You don't *deserve* to lead *la famiglia*," Antonio bellows, his face turning bright red as contempt drips from every word. "You're exactly like your damn father. Thinking with your fucking cock instead of doing your duty to this family."

My jaw tics as he shuffles closer with slitted eyes. "He knocked up your *whore* mother and killed anyone who dared to disapprove, leaving the Caruso family with men who are *unfit* to lead. Men who shy away from the old ways of *Cosa Nostra*. Pathetic, *weak* men like you, your father, Alessio—"

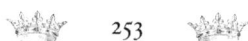

Lip curling in disdain, I pull the trigger, and the bullet rips through Antonio's jowly neck. He cries out, the sound garbled as his windpipe fills with blood. His eyes are wide when he clutches the wound as he falls to the floor, and I slowly walk closer.

His eyes blink rapidly when I reach him and, for the first time, I see genuine fear in his gaze. The sight fills me with renewed energy as I bring the notched gun up to level it at his face.

"*Weak*?" I tilt my head to one side, regarding him with blank eyes. "Was that what you called me?"

He tries to speak, but it sounds like he's drowning in his own blood, and I smile right into his eyes as I pull the trigger. The bullet hits him right between the eyes, and Sofia shrieks as Antonio instantly stops squirming.

No one makes a sound as I flip the safety on the gun, continuing to watch as a pool of blood streams from the forehead of the man at my feet.

"Who's *weak* now, *Zio*?"

My question hangs in the air for a long beat before I turn to face my waiting men right as Santino DeMarco strides through my front door like the motherfucker owns the damn place.

Dark brown hair falls across his forehead as he extends his arms wide with his white shirt unbuttoned almost to his abdomen. His green eyes are filled with their usual flippancy when he slips his shades from his face with a shit-eating grin.

"My father sends his regards. And the location of that asshole Conti." He quirks a dark eyebrow as I stride past him and out the front door.

"You'll hold up your end, DeMarco, *si*?"

I stop on the top step, looking back at my unlikely accomplice.

"Must say, I'm surprised you offered your *Principessa* as my wife in exchange for our muscle, but I won't say I'm sorry about it—"

"It's an *alliance*." My snarl cuts him off, and he holds his hands up at either side of his head. "It seems betrayal has become an epidemic within *Cosa Nostra*, Santino. Alliances like this will keep us all from descending into madness like motherfucking Conti, *capisti*?"

My nostrils flare as I clench my jaw and, without waiting for his response, I strike out toward the waiting SUVs, calling over my shoulder.

"Let's just get this done. Then we'll discuss Aurelia."

I push down on the guilt churning in the pit of my stomach, remembering how Papa had refused every offer for Aurelia's hand that had been brought before him. Knowing this is not what he wanted for her.

But the simple truth is that I need more men than I have available to me in order to take down Conti.

In order to even get Aurelia back to fulfill our side of the bargain.

But right now, I need to focus on what needs to be done. I'll make peace with my guilt once everyone is safe, and Domenico Conti is burning in Hell.

32

ELODIE

My body aches, and my mouth is parched when my lashes flutter open to find pretty brown eyes watching me in concern.

"*Santo Cristo*, I thought you'd never wake up." Despite her words, there's a relieved smile in her voice as she watches me with those wide eyes.

"Aurelia?"

I clear my scratchy throat as she smiles encouragingly. "Here, have some water."

She holds out a bottle, and I accept it with a grateful quirk of my lips before taking a large gulp.

As I re-screw the bottle cap, I scrunch up my face, feeling groggy, and like I've slept for far too long. "Where are we?"

Aurelia shrugs her petite shoulders. "Your guess is as good as mine. I've not seen anything outside of stone walls since they brought me here."

I blink several times, attempting to dispel the wooziness before blowing out a breath. "How long was I out for?"

"You've been here almost two hours, so at least that long."

Then she extends her hand with a tilt of her dark head. "Pleased to finally meet your acquaintance."

I accept her proffered hand, shaking it gently with a small smile. "I'm sorry it's come to this."

She rolls her eyes heavily. "It was never going to come about any other way. I think you'll find that, when Domenico Conti takes something, he has a very hard time parting with it."

Our gazes lock and hold as an understanding flows between us, and instantly, I feel a kinship with the beautiful girl before me.

"Did he hurt you, too?"

She opens her mouth to speak, but before she can answer, the door is thrown wide open.

Luca Conti, Nico's excessively vicious first cousin, steps inside, and I can feel Aurelia shrinking back as he comes closer.

"You're coming with me, *puttana*." He yanks my hair, tugging me to stand as I press my lips firmly together, refusing to give him my pain, and his eyes shift to Aurelia. "And I'll be back to see you *really* soon."

He tosses her a wink before he shoves me out the door, slamming it behind him. Then he marches me forward down a long, winding hallway with no windows. It's narrow and feels entirely claustrophobic, even when we pass by a set of wide stone stairs. It's only once we reach an open space, I can feel my chest expand as I suck in a deep lungful of air.

The walls are all made of stone, and it seems like we're inside some medieval castle or something.

Luca pushes me through a door, where I find a long wooden dining table. It's set as though for a feast, with Nico seated at the head of the table, a roaring fire crackling in a huge open fireplace.

My eyes move past him to take in the narrow window at his back, and I barely stifle a gasp of shock when I see the now-familiar turquoise waters off the coast of Sicily.

He snorts a smug laugh. "Right on that bastard's doorstep this whole time."

Luca pushes past me to jerk a bound and gagged man from a darkened corner of the room. "*Muovi il culo, Alessio.*"

My pulse kicks up a notch at the name, and a chill runs down my spine when the bound man lifts his eyes to mine. Long, matted black hair covers most of his face, but there's *no* mistaking those eyes.

Eyes identical to the man I love.

Alessio Caruso isn't *dead!*

Nico laughs darkly, bidding his 'guest' farewell with a dark, "*Domani alla stessa ora, Fantasma.*"

I give no outward reaction as Nico refocuses on me, rising to stand, before he slowly walks closer. Luca slips back outside with Alessio in tow as he reaches me, his hand coming up between us to grip my chin between his thumb and index finger.

He twists my head from side to side, as though inspecting his property, all while I regard him with a blank stare.

"You look far too well cared for." His eyes lock with mine. "You can't expect me to believe that Caruso filth didn't have a taste of your spectacular cunt, can you?"

I arch an eyebrow, allowing my lips to curve upward in pure malice. I can almost feel Rafe sending me the strength to be the woman I know myself to be now as I shrug nonchalantly.

"I mean, I *was* expecting you to be as dumb as you look—"

He draws back to strike me, the flat of his palm descending toward my cheek when I block with my right arm and bring my left fist up to connect sharply with Nico's side.

Just like Sasquatch taught me.

Sucking in a pained breath, his other hand flies out. I yank my head back just in time so that only the tips of his fingers brush off my cheek.

I take a step back, watching him through slitted eyes as he

stands to his full height, brings his hands up to chest level, and begins to clap slowly.

"Well done, baby girl. Well fucking done."

My forehead creases in a mixture of shock and confusion as Nico turns to pour himself a glass of red wine from the spread on the table. He turns back to me and raises it in salutation.

"I don't know where you got the claws, but the thought of clipping them has given me the biggest fucking hard-on of my damn life."

His eyes flick over me from head to toe before he palms his dick through his pants. "I think I'll fuck your face before passing you around to my *Soldati*."

Pure fear trickles throughout my whole being, though I keep my face impassive as Nico chuckles. "Yes, that's exactly what I'll do. A fitting punishment for giving that *figlio di puttana* a taste of *my* pretty cunt, don't you think, baby girl?"

Judging from the incensed look in his eyes, and despite the fact he's always kept me for himself in the past, I have absolutely *zero* doubt that he means what he says.

My hand darts out, plucking a wineglass from the table, and smashing it off the edge of the hardwood. I brandish the long splintered stem of the glass before me, and lower my knees into a fighter's stance.

"Over my dead body, Domenico Conti." I tip my chin higher as his lip curls in derision. "Touch me, and I *swear*, you're a fucking dead man."

RAFAEL

"This place has been abandoned since my father banned human trafficking."

The caves beneath a centuries old derelict castle had made

the perfect base to move the flesh trade, something that's entirely fitting with Conti being somewhere nearby.

I shoot a questioning look at Santino, who just rolls his eyes. "Well, wouldn't that make it the perfect place to...I dunno. Umm... *Hide*?"

He walks ahead, muttering to himself about working with idiots as I huff an impatient sigh. We've been walking for what feels like hours through dark caves along the Sicilian shoreline. I glance at my wristwatch, realizing it's scarcely been twenty minutes since we left the SUVs on the beach.

While I'd be furious to learn Conti had been under my nose the entire time, I'd had to admit that it made sense.

And Salvatore, that double-crossing motherfucker, feeding me false information about Tuscany, would feel my wrath just as soon as I'd gotten my *Stellina* and my sister back safely.

"There's a door built into the cave wall just ahead. My father was adamant that I wouldn't miss it."

Santino moves more slowly now, leading our combined forces deeper into the caves. He stops abruptly, and I hold up a stalling hand. The entire troupe freezes, and a deathly silence fills the space until Santino raises his leg to kick at the cave wall.

My eyes widen as the cave disappears, giving way to a very basic stone staircase that leads up. Santino twists about with a smug grin.

"Looks like it's game time, Caruso." Bending at the waist, he flourishes his arm out toward the stairs. "Ladies first."

I walk past him, shaking my head before I pivot to face the men at my back when I cross the threshold.

My voice is deep and filled with authority when I speak.

"The goal here is simple. We rescue both women at *any* price."

My eyes rove over the gathered men. All of my uninjured and loyal *Soldati* mingled with DeMarco's men. Every face among them is hard-set and determined. Jaws clenched, fists balled tight at their sides, every one of them vibrating with that intense calm before the storm.

"We move like wraiths once we hit the castle floor. Like a wave of death silently washing this place clean. Take out everyone you meet using hand-to-hand combat *only*. We need the element of surprise, or the bastard will run."

I give them a minute to let that sink in before I lower my voice to a growl, speaking my next words through tightly clenched teeth. "Now...we kill them *all*."

"So much for a silent wave of death."

Santino huffs as he yanks his blade from the chest of one of Conti's *Soldati*, before pivoting to swipe it neatly across the jugular of another. Blood spurts from the deep gash as the second *Soldati* drops to his knees.

I drive my fist into the face of the huge bastard I'm facing off against, momentarily stunning him enough that I can cast my eyes about for a weapon, coming up with nothing. I usually prefer my hands, but this motherfucker just won't hit the deck.

A knife whizzes past me, lodging itself in the skull of my opponent, and I whip my head up to find a grinning Santino.

He tosses me a wink. "You're welcome." Then he disappears through the frenzy surrounding us.

Enzo appears at my side, blood dripping from a gash in his cheek as he pants heavily. "The main rooms are on the next floor, *Fratello*. Will I go ahead and search—"

I cut him off, dark determination filling my voice. "We'll take a handful, and leave the rest to dispatch the majority down here, *si*?"

He nods quickly, snapping his fingers at two nearby *Soldati*. "You're with us. Let's move."

As rapidly as he disappeared, Santino pops up at my side, pushing his messy hair back from his brow before regarding me with devilish green eyes.

"You're not allowed to have all the fun without me."

Enzo jerks his head, indicating a door at the other side of the melee. "Through there, and up the staircase. If they're not there, then they've already gotten out."

The idea that Conti might have escaped with Elodie and Aurelia fills me with horror, and I plow ahead through, using my hands as battering rams to clear the space for the motley crew at my back.

Once I'm through the door, I race up the stairs, my feet freezing when I hear a woman scream out in terror. The sound of a fist meeting flesh, followed by the unmistakable voice of my sister fills my ears.

"*Don't. Per favore*, stop."

My feet move toward her automatically with the others bringing up the rear, until Elodie's voice comes from farther away, through a long, narrow corridor.

Santino glances back and forth. "Divide and conquer?"

I extend a hand, and he clasps it in his with a nod. "*Si*, DeMarco." I tip my head in the direction of Aurelia's voice. "Your bride awaits."

A wide smile slashes his face before he drops my hand and jogs ahead.

"Enzo, stay with him." He nods before rushing after Santino, while the rest of us go in the opposite direction.

A group of Conti *Soldati* crests the top of the staircase as we pass it. "Hold them off."

As my men jump into action, I slip past easily, finding myself running down the stone-walled hallway at full tilt, stopping only when I come upon a single door.

My heart is racing as I swing open the door, only to slam to an immediate halt when my eyes find the sight that greets me.

A long wooden dining table has been flipped on its side with food and drink strewn everywhere. At the very far end of the room, I see a man and woman grappling on the floor, my jaw clenching when I register that it's Elodie and Conti.

He has her pinned down, using the heavy bulk of his body, but she's thrashing against him, fighting back with everything she's got.

"You'll burn in Hell for your crimes, Nico."

He throws back his head and laughs. "I'll send your filthy Caruso lover there first, *mia piccola puttana*. Just you wait, but first..." Managing to pull a gun from the back of his waistband, he brings it to Elodie's temple with a sick smile. "First, you'll let me fuck your throat, or I'll put a bullet in your skull, you understand me?"

33

ELODIE

Hopelessness threatens to overwhelm me, but through the sheer force of my will, I push it back down along with the other useless emotions that Nico brings to life within me.

If I've learned one thing during my time with Rafe, it's that I refuse to be afraid of this man anymore.

Never again.

"I can *guarantee* you, if you put that pencil dick near my mouth, I'll bite it clean off." His eyes flare with anger as he blows out a breath through his nostrils before his eyes fill with wicked malice, but he's stopped from answering when he's thrown from my body by a rapid blur. The gun he'd threatened me with flies out of his hands, landing directly in the middle of the fireplace among the dancing orange flames.

I push myself to sit, my heart soaring to life when I see Rafe grappling with Nico. His face is set in a determined grimace as he rolls them so that he's towering over Nico.

"Take your hands off my *Stellina*, you cock-sucking *figlio di puttana*."

He draws back his fist, driving it into Nico's face hard

enough that I can hear his nose shatter as he shouts. Blood gushes as Rafe draws back with his fist balled again, except as he strikes, Nico produces a small knife he must have hidden on his body.

With the speed of a rattlesnake, he strikes, jabbing Rafe in the side.

I cry out when Rafe falls down, clutching his side as blood seeps from between the fingers covering his wound. My eyes flick around the space, looking for a weapon of some kind, but all the fragments of broken glass and dinnerware seem to be too small to utilize efficiently.

Fear for Rafe outweighs everything as he continues to bleed out while avoiding Nico's ever-advancing knife. Panic sets in when I find nothing useful as I sift through the carnage of the room that I'd destroyed in the process of trying to hold Nico at bay before Rafe arrived.

When my eyes land on the fire, an idea takes root, and I rush toward it, grabbing the long poker from the set propped on the hearth. I thrust the flattened tip of the poker into the dancing flames, glancing toward the men as I impatiently wait for the fire to do its job.

My heart sinks when I see that Nico has gotten the better of Rafe, having pinned him to the floor. Nico brings his blade to Rafe's throat with a sadistic smile, and I yank the poker from the fireplace to rush toward them.

I loosen a shrill cry of attack a bare moment before the red-hot tip of the poker connects with the fleshy part of Nico's cheek, and I push the iron forward as hard as I physically can.

Nico screams as the sizzling smell of his flesh taints the air, and Rafe pushes himself off the floor. Despite the blood trailing from the wound in his side, Rafe wastes no time knocking Nico to the ground and straddling his waist.

He drives his right fist into Nico's face, followed immediately by his left, then his right again. He continues to alternate, a litany of words landing with each solid blow.

"Burn." *Thump.*

"In." *Thump.*

"Hell!" *Thump.*

The same three words on repeat, over and over, until all that's left of Nico's face is a bloodied pulp.

RAFAEL

Burn in Hell. Burn in Hell. Burn in Hell.

The words echo through the stone room even as my voice grows hoarser with each strike of my fists. With every ounce of aggression and frustration I expend.

And still, I don't let up.

I *can't* let up.

My body hums with a rage I've carried inside of me for the last two years. A rage that has only grown over time as my hatred for this man – the same man who's the root of so much pain – has become all-consuming.

For Elodie.

My Papa.

Aurelia.

Emiliano.

Maria.

For every soul that this man has tainted with his mere existence.

Burn in Hell.

As my breathing grows ragged, my vision blurs, and my chest tightens painfully until a delicate hand rests on my shoulder. I immediately still beneath her touch, allowing my head to fall forward as I squeeze my eyes tightly shut.

The sound of my pounding heart fills my ears, drowning

out all else, until I hear Elodie exhale softly, and I lift my head, twisting about to meet her navy-blue gaze. I focus on her, on having freed her from her past, on the fact that we can now have a future.

Together.

And achingly slowly, her understanding gaze quietens the monster within me.

When she drops to her knees with open arms, I heave myself off Conti's lifeless body and crawl to her, laying my head on her lap. Her hand lands on my hair, fingers brushing the sweat-soaked strands back from my brow.

At her touch, my heart slows, filling with an overflowing love for this woman. And a gratefulness that I'm hers. That she's mine.

"Everything I love has always been taken from me."

My hoarse voice renders the silence as my long-buried truth spills unintentionally from my lips, and the hand on my brow stiffens before I look up to meet her tear-filled gaze.

"But you, *Stellina*..." My voice breaks before I whisper, "I'd rather die than lose you."

I push myself upright, the sting from the gash in my side barely registering as I climb to my knees and take Elodie's beautiful face between my palms. "Because, you see, I'm not afraid of dying. There's only one thing I fear now." My eyes flicker between hers, pouring every ounce of emotion into my next words. "The thought of a world without you in it...the thought of living in darkness, of existing without your light. It *terrifies* me."

Tears streak down her dirt-covered cheeks, and I brush them away with the pads of my thumbs before dusting my lips over hers as I whisper, "I know the answer now. I think I've known it all along. *Cosa succede quando esprimi un desiderio su una stella?*"

She inhales sharply, half a gasp, half a sob, as her eyes shine into mine. Her voice trembles when she translates, "What happens when you wish on a star?"

"Us, *Stellina*. And we can finally come true."

She nods before I take her lips in a kiss that sears me to my very soul. She melts into me, and time ceases to exist as our tongues dance together. Everything about her overwhelms my senses, and I hold her even more tightly against me, swearing to whatever God is listening that I'll never come so close to losing anyone I love *ever* again.

A throat being cleared brings us back to reality, and I break the kiss, instantly on high alert, until I spot Enzo loitering at the threshold. He gestures to my side, and I glance down at the blood coating my shirt, shaking my head at the question in his eyes.

"It's a flesh wound." I raise an eyebrow. "Is it done?"

He nods at my sharper-than-necessary question. "The premises are secured. Aurelia is safe, though she's not presently awake. Santino and Davide are having her brought to the SUVs I've called in."

I rise swiftly, taking Elodie alongside me and looping my hand through hers. "Take me to her."

Enzo doesn't move. Instead, his face takes on a peculiar look, and I tilt my head to one side with a frown. "What is it?"

He swallows roughly before shaking his head as though he can't quite believe what he's about to say. "Alessio's alive."

Elodie's hand tightens in mine, and she steps around me, her gaze searching my face as shock careens through my whole body.

"I...I think I've seen him." I can feel my pupils blow wide open as Elodie nods enthusiastically. "When I was brought here, there was a man in chains. They called him Alessio. And his eyes were *exactly* like yours, Rafe..."

My breathing accelerates as I lift my gaze from Elodie's and sternly demand, "I need to see him *now*."

Enzo leads the way downstairs, and Elodie gasps at the sheer number of dead bodies we encounter.

"Losses?"

Enzo glances back at my question, shaking his head firmly. "*Nessune.* Some minor injuries, but no deaths, *Fratello*."

I grit my jaw, my mind instantly returning to the sight of Emiliano's lifeless body. "We've lost enough today."

Elodie squeezes my hand, and I shoot her a grateful look, watching as her eyes fill with renewed tears before I haul her against my uninjured side. I press a kiss atop her head in silent comfort when my feet suddenly slam to a halt, and Elodie stops alongside me.

Romeo is standing beside a bare-footed man in torn, filthy clothes. His face is covered by a long black beard, and his black hair is matted, falling well past his shoulders.

And even so, there's no doubt that my brother is the man standing before me.

He turns his haunted midnight eyes up to mine, and suddenly, my feet move forward right as he does. Our bodies clash as we embrace, and my heart heals and simultaneously breaks all over again at the thought of what my older brother may have endured at Conti's hands.

We draw back, watching one another as small smiles of disbelief lift our lips. So much has happened since we last saw one another, but all I can do now is be grateful for our family's second chance.

I twist about to tug Elodie closer, folding her in against my side as I regard both her and my brother.

"Let's go home."

34

RAFAEL

Two Weeks Later

To look around the compound, you'd never know the devastation that had almost razed the entire place to the ground had ever occurred.

In anticipation for tonight, I'd flown a team in from Milan, and they'd worked literal magic.

Every room has been freshly floored, painted, and adorned in a running theme of classic Italian chic, as per Aurelia's very specific instructions. She'd kept to our father's tastes, and I had to admit, everything looked better than ever.

The only remaining reminder of Conti's attack is the gaping Emiliano-shaped hole that will never be healed. The small burial ceremony we'd had for him on *Isola Rosa* had been intimate, and focused on Elodie's baking, something my best friend would have greatly appreciated.

As for my sister, the only time she'd shown true emotion following her return home had been when she had heard of her mother's hand in the destruction of our home, not to mention her part in Maria's and Emiliano's deaths.

"She allowed *him* inside *our* home?"

Aurelia's voice is high-pitched, her eyes dark with unbridled fury as she glares at me. Elodie's hand lightly squeezes mine when she witnesses my sister's temper for the first time.

And inside, I breathe a sigh of relief, having believed we'd lost the true Aurelia to Conti when she'd first been taken over ten months ago.

At my stoic nod, Aurelia rounds on her mother, and despite her smaller stature, she encompasses the entire room with the force of her fury.

"The man who killed Papa and held me captive. The man who held my brother captive in a lightless dungeon, depriving him of food and water for nine fucking months. You *allowed* that man *inside our home, Mama?*"

Sofia's eyes are wide and pleading when she shakes her head frantically. "I only wanted you home—"

Her head whips to the side when Aurelia snakes out a hand, her palm connecting with her mother's cheek with a resounding slap.

"Placing the life of one above the life of many was your first mistake." Aurelia's voice drips with venom as she coolly regards her mother, who's pressed her hands to her red cheek, eyes filled with shocked hurt. "Your second was thinking I would *ever* forgive you."

My sister turns to me, and I can almost see the rage roll away from her features as she recloaks herself within her shroud of icy indifference. "Ensure she's suitably punished, Rafael."

Sofia's very much unwanted marriage to Maurizio D'Amato, a loyal *Soldati* far beneath her station, had been celebrated two days later, and to say I'd relished in the act would be an understatement.

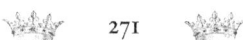

I smirk in remembrance when I walk across the foyer, stepping outside right as the first of three SUVs arrives. Cesare DeMarco disembarks, followed swiftly by an unusually stoic Santino.

His gaze clashes with mine, and I'm simultaneously surprised and intrigued at the tempestuous fire burning within his usually irreverent green eyes.

Both men's eyes shift from me to my right when Aurelia walks out onto the steps beside me, every inch the Caruso queen our father reared her to be.

When I'd confessed to her, detailing the alliance with Santino, she'd handled herself with more dignity than most. Following the trauma she'd just lived through, many women would have crumbled, but not my sister.

I glance to my right, finding her watching both men approach with a cool regality in her mahogany eyes. Her chin tilts upward as she clasps both hands behind her back.

A floor-length black dress with long black sleeves covers her body, hiding several remaining bruises from her time with Conti, but I fear the internal scars may never heal.

I turn my gaze back to the DeMarco men, instantly noting how Santino has shifted his eyes away from Aurelia, focusing instead on the ground as his feet close the distance.

It's the look on Cesare's face that give me pause when I look back at him. Pale brown eyes devour my sister, running the length and breadth of her body unashamedly, and a deep-seated sense of foreboding permeates my body.

"Welcome, Cesare." I nod at the first Don to arrive at our newly formed Conclave, the gathering of the Four Families, replacing the outdated Congress.

Conclave will occur annually moving forward, and will rotate between each household's main compound, alternating alphabetically.

Caruso. DeMarco. Medici. Salvatore.

Even as he nods his thanks and accepts my outstretched hand, Cesare keeps his eyes glued to Aurelia, though to her credit, she remains wholly impassive.

"My most sincere thanks for your help in taking down Conti." He finally meets my gaze with a self-satisfied grin, though it falters as I continue. "Your heir is an exceptional fighter, Cesare. Particularly with a blade."

My eyes flick to a reserved Santino, and I tip my chin in acknowledgment. He nods with a tight smile, his jaw ticking as he grits his teeth. "*Grazie*, Rafael."

Cesare snorts a laugh. "I suppose we're all good at something, *corretto*? And my son has had years to perfect the art of fighting *me* at every damn turn."

His laugh becomes louder as he clearly baits his son, and I can even feel Aurelia stiffen beside me. I'm suddenly grateful that Elodie had thought it wiser to remain upstairs with Alessio while our guests are here.

My oldest brother's ability to control himself following his time in captivity, having suffered God knows what at Conti's maniac hands, has led to some erratic behavior, though Elodie appears to be making headway with him.

I can practically feel the rage bristling from Santino's body, and in an effort to keep the peace before Conclave has even begun, I try another tactic.

"Would you like to wait in the Den, gentlemen? Our companions will be here shortly, and then we can get started on making some long-lasting alliances."

My forehead puckers when I note Santino clench and unclench his fists several times before his father speaks.

"*Si*, Caruso. Marriage alliances are an old tradition, but they work for a reason."

I nod at Cesare's observation, agreeing with him to some extent but not particularly liking the fact. "I suppose you are right. These alliances are a good move on all our parts."

Cesare steps closer, reaching out a hand toward Aurelia. Her brow wavers ever-so slightly, but she accepts his hand with that same indifference I've come to expect since her return.

"You'll see that it's a very good move. And I truly believe Aurelia will be very happy as my wife."

My stomach swoops nauseatingly, and my eyebrows pinch together as I watch Cesare leering at my sister. "Happy with you? I'm afraid I don't... I don't understand." His gaze swings back to me, and I immediately note the gleam of triumph shining in his murky eyes.

"*Of course*, I would never insult your family by offering marriage to my heir apparent." His tone is gleeful, and my chest tightens. "It's only right that Aurelia marries according to her station. Becoming my wife is the *only* option here."

Knowing Conti's whereabouts when it suited him. Demanding an alliance between our families as payment for his help.

The motherfucker played me. Backed me into a corner. And I'd been so focused on getting Elodie and Aurelia back that I'd seen what I'd chosen to see.

But now that Conclave is in motion, he knows I can't backtrack without upsetting the already precarious balance.

And as though the *stronzo* has just heard my thoughts, he steps around me toward the front door of my house, holding my eyes as the second SUV containing Franco and Ignazio Medici grinds to a halt on the gravel.

"After all, we must do everything in our power to prevent the remaining four from succumbing to the same insanity that you've just dispatched by ending the Conti line."

Having bid the other Dons goodnight, leaving them to their Gurkhas and idle chatter, I enfold my sister's ice-cold hand in mine and tug her toward the stairs.

She had sat silently at my side during the entire process, not even batting an eyelid when the arrangement with Cesare had been finalized on her behalf.

I turn to her with a confused frown when she tugs her hand from my grasp. "It's time to retire."

Her eyes flash with mutiny, and she steps back, putting distance between us as she shakes her head swiftly. "I need some fresh air, Rafael."

I have no reservations about allowing her to wander the compound during Conclave. The rules of the alliance merging our families are ironclad.

To fuck with one family, you now fucked with all four. And besides, our home is more secure than ever before in terms of *Soldati*.

But even so, I hesitate until she steps farther back, and a crease forms between her eyebrows. It's the first indication all evening that she's felt a single emotion, and I feel a tentative hope spring inside my chest.

Aurelia's eyes flicker between mine, telling me that she wholly expects me to deny her request. When I nod my assent, the deep brown of her irises sparkles with delight for a brief flash.

"*Grazie.*" A minute smile accompanies her thanks before she turns and walks out the front door. I watch her close the door behind her before ascending the stairs and walking straight to Elodie's suite, stopping outside the ajar door when I hear her conversing softly with Alessio.

Their mutual connection from the cruelty they'd experienced at the hands of Domenico Conti had meant that they'd bonded exceptionally quickly. Not to mention, Elodie seemed to be the only one of us able to get more than two words out of him at a time.

"The memories will fade as time passes, Alessio. Trust me. You *can* have a normal life." I can hear the smile in her voice when she speaks again. "I'm proof."

"Do you move past the physical and psychological torture at some point, or do you just learn to live with it?" There's an edge of desperation in his deep voice. "Starvation. Sensory overload. Sleep deprivation. Isolation. But none of it affected me like the waterboarding."

I hear him take a shuddery breath as my forehead draws together in a deep frown.

"I can't even take a damn shower, Elodie. How fucked up is that?"

ELODIE

Despite the more than ten-year age difference between myself and Rafe's older brother, I'd felt an almost motherly protectiveness over him since the first morning I'd found him sleeping on the pantry floor.

After some gentle probing, he'd told me his own suite was far too big and the bed much too soft, following what he'd grown accustomed to whilst in captivity. And once I'd imparted some of my own Nico-related trauma, a tentative friendship had been struck up between us.

But hearing him say he couldn't even take a basic shower without suffering flashbacks chilled me to the bone, and I quickly cross the space between us to squeeze his shoulder affectionately.

"We'll all help you through this, Alessio. That's what family are for."

I can feel some of the tension drain out of his shoulders,

and when he looks up at me, his eyes have a sprinkle of hope that wasn't there before.

He rises to stand with a small smile. "*Grazie*, Elodie." And as he moves to leave, the door of my suite opens to admit Rafe.

I rush to his side, going up onto my tiptoes to press a soft kiss to his scruffy cheek. "Is it done?"

Rafe nods, tugging me against his side as he addresses Alessio. "All four signed the Conclave Treaty that joins our households through marriage alliances. And it's been decided that you will uphold the original contract Papa arranged with Salvatore."

Alessio shrugs indifferently as I continue. "Aurelia will join with DeMarco...though not Santino as we'd presumed."

My shocked gasp fills the room, and Alessio's jaw grinds together before he hisses, "Cesare DeMarco as her *husband*? The man is old enough to be her father, Rafael. She can't—"

It's the most words Alessio has spoken in anyone else's presence since his return, but even so, Rafe holds up a quelling palm. "It's *done*. There's no going back now."

Both brothers watch each other warily before Alessio nods, straightens his shoulders, and strides from the room without another word.

I close the wooden door behind him and then turn to Rafe, catching his hands in mine. When I lead him to my bed, he sits heavily before I climb up behind him to rub his tense shoulders.

"He was never going to take that well, was he?"

Rafe shakes his head. "The complexities of this fucking arrangement will give me a motherfucking stroke. Trying to keep everyone happy. Ensuring no one feels slighted." His shoulders tighten even further. "And giving my siblings away in loveless marriages while I get to keep you, *Stellina*. How is that fair?"

35

RAFAEL

Guilt gnaws at my insides like a festering sore, and I scrub my palms down my face, blowing out a heavy breath.

Elodie's sweet voice by my ear recentres me, quietening my racing thoughts. "Do you really believe that any of your siblings begrudge you, Rafe? They love you just as much as you love them."

My brow gathers as her words sink in, and I drop my head forward, feeling the burden on my shoulders lessen slightly.

She wraps her arms around me from behind, her palms splayed across my chest as she holds me close. "There you have it, then. They know you're doing what you must to keep everyone safe. To keep the peace between the remaining families. Everyone needs to play their part."

Long moments pass as I'm enveloped in her soothing presence until her cell beeps with a text. Both of us freeze before she gets up and grabs the device from the nightstand.

Her face lifts in a huge smile at what she sees and, interest piqued, I quickly rise and move to stand at her side. My own lips are helpless against the picture Sebastiano has sent Elodie.

It's an image of Skye playing piano onstage at the school talent show. Her face is scrunched up in adorable concentration, several blonde curls falling across her brow, having escaped from her high ponytail.

> SEBASTIANO: Skye placed first. She was so fucking good.

Elodie turns tear-filled eyes to mine. "Is it almost time?" My eyebrows pull together as she swallows harshly. "The n-n-need to see her...to hold her in my arms, Rafe...it's indescribable—"

I cut her off when I spin her in my arms, holding her close against my chest. Palming her cheeks, I turn her face up to mine. "The jet is ready. We fly to pick her up in the morning."

She sucks in a sharp breath, tears falling from her long dark lashes, and I dash them away with my thumbs.

"I'm sorry it's taken so long to ensure her safety here, but the Treaty and this Conclave have secured peace between the four. All I wanted was to guarantee protection for both you and our child before we bring her here."

Elodie freezes, her wide navy-blue eyes blinking once, twice before her lips part on a whisper. "*Our* child?"

She grips the lapels of my jacket when I rest my brow atop hers, and my eyes hold hers with an intensity I feel in my marrow.

"*Si, Stellina. Our* child." She shakes her head as though she can't comprehend what I'm saying before I continue. "Skye is a living, breathing, *perfect* extension of you. And every part of you is *mine*, just as every part of me is *yours*—"

Before I've even finished speaking, Elodie yanks my lapels, pulling me closer to slam her lips against mine. She half sobs, half whimpers in her throat when my tongue slides past her lips to gently caress hers, and I break the kiss, pulling back slightly to find her eyes brimming with emotion.

"I could never have believed a man like you existed, Rafael Caruso."

My eyes flicker between hers as my chest fills with sheer adoration for the woman in my arms.

"I exist for you, *Stellina*. Fate brought me into this world to be yours. And when I leave it, I *will* find you in the next..." I press a kiss to her soft lips, my voice dropping to a whisper as my words ghost over her mouth. "Because soulmates are destined for one another in *every* lifetime."

She brushes her lips across mine, her eyes deepening to the shade of a stormy sea as she breathes, "Make love to me, Rafe. *Please*. I've wanted you so desperately..."

My nostrils flare as my jaw clenches, and my cock roars to life between us, desperate to bury himself within her warmth.

In the two weeks since Conti's takedown, I've had to throw myself into funeral arrangements and Treaty negotiations, not to mention trying to mend the rift in our family while restructuring our hierarchy. Each night, I've been too exhausted to do much more than fall into bed and gather Elodie in my arms. Once I've kissed her brow, and inhaled her sweet fragrance, I've practically passed out.

But even more than that, I've been reluctant to push Elodie to be intimate until she's ready, despite wanting her more than life itself. She's had so much taken from her for so fucking long.

"I've listened to the sound of you breathing at night, praying you'd awaken and kiss me until I'm breathless and begging for you. Pleading for the release only you can give me..."

Her candidness stokes the fire within me, and when she nips my lips between her teeth, a groan tears from my chest forcibly. My hands slip around the back of her neck, and I tug her to me, our lips colliding in a hungry kiss. Her mouth opens beneath mine immediately as she slides her tongue past my lips, dueling against my own with a passion that breathes life into me.

I drop one hand down along her body, and she arches into my touch, meeting my tongue stroke for stroke. My hand skims her breast and down her hip, breaking our kiss to rip her top over her head.

Once my lips are back on hers, I make short work of her bra before I hook my thumb in the waistband of the soft pants she's wearing, pushing them and her panties down over the curve of her ass.

When I feel her step out of them, I bring both hands to her ass and lift her into my arms. She wraps her legs around me, securing her ankles at my back.

Then she leans back to unbutton my shirt, but it's taking too long, so I fist the material in my hands and rip it open as her eyes blow wide with delight. Her arms wind around my neck, pulling my mouth ever closer, and I groan, feeling her bare breasts pressed to my chest.

She wriggles her nakedness against me and, with a growl, I take two steps forward, pinning her to the wall. I pump my hips against her core, and she cries out into my mouth as I suck in a breath.

Her head falls back against the wall, displaying the slender arch of her neck, and my mouth latches on greedily, sucking and nipping as she grinds harder against my pelvis.

"I can't wait any longer... *Per favore*..." Her breathy sigh sends a flood of precum from my raging hard-on into the fabric of my boxers, and I groan against her neck when she whimpers, "I'm begging, Rafe. I *need* to feel you deep inside of me."

Without conscious thought, I reach for my button and zipper, quickly undoing them to yank both my suit pants and boxers down. My thick cock springs free, landing against her leg, precum dripping from me onto her soft skin.

She reaches between us, eyes on mine as she brings me to her arousal-slick pussy. Her jaw slackens and her eyelids flutter as I feed inch after inch of my pulsing hard cock inside her, my balls drawing up tight when I finally bottom out.

"You feel so good, so perfect." I circle my hips, stretching her out, and we groan in unison. "Look at you, *mia brava ragazza*. You're taking my cock *so* well."

I'm panting, sweat beading my brow with the effort to remain still, to allow her to become accustomed to my cock. Her eyes stay fixed on mine, deep, dark pools of wanton desire as she tugs her bottom lip between her teeth and rocks against me.

I pump my hips forward, pushing even farther inside, and she gasps as her face contorts in pleasure. My restraint is hanging by a bare thread when I dust my lips over hers. "As deep as I can fucking go, *Stellina*, and it's still not deep enough."

Then I rock against her, bringing a hand between us to roll my thumb across her clit. She whimpers, her eyes falling shut as I pick up the pace. "I want to bury myself so deep inside you that you'll never not feel me."

Her passion-glazed eyes open to lock onto mine as she flexes around my girth, and I groan deep within my chest before covering her mouth with mine.

We move together, hips in sync with our mouths as the rapture builds, as we inch higher and higher. My hips draw back with each forward thrust until, without warning, Elodie rips her mouth from mine as her pussy clamps down on my dick.

"Come inside me. Come with me, Rafe. *Please*."

Those fucking words are my undoing, and I bite down on her shoulder, making her cry out. Her pussy ripples around me, greedily milking my cock as I follow her over the edge, filling her with thick ropes of cum.

My chest is vibrating, and there's a buzzing in my ears as I come back down to earth, panting heavily against Elodie's neck. I remove my mouth, immediately spotting the teeth marks I've left on her delicate flesh, so I flatten my tongue, licking the expanse of skin.

She mewls as I soothe the pain that I've caused with my cock still buried deep inside her pulsating core.

Eventually, when I lean back enough to find her eyes, they're bright and filled with so much emotion that it almost knocks me off my damn feet.

I carry us to the bed, and gently ease my softening length from her pussy before kicking off my pants and boxers. My eyes drop down between her thighs, and I inhale sharply at the sight of my cum leaking out of her onto the bedsheets.

Without missing a beat, I kneel between her legs and reach between us to slide two fingers through our combined pleasure before slipping it back inside her. Even as she gasps, her pussy clenches my fingers greedily, and despite having just come, I can feel my dick stir against my thigh, already desperate to be back inside of her.

"Lie back, *bedda mia*. Show me what a beautiful mess I've made of you."

ELODIE

I do as I'm told, my eyes watching Rafe's handsome face while he fixates his on my dripping pussy. I can feel his cum leaking out of me, and each time he gathers it to push it back inside, I can't help my body's instinctual reaction to tighten around his thick fingers.

My thighs fall apart as I watch, enthralled, until I gasp when he suddenly leans forward, bringing his mouth to my pussy to trail his tongue from slit to clit. I cry out, my hands tangling in his longer-than-usual dark locks when he sucks my engorged clit inside the heat of his mouth.

"Oh, *Jesus*. I can't... I can't..."

And despite having come damn fucking hard, I can already feel my body begin to climb, helpless under his worship.

He drops back down, flattening his tongue as he draws it through my cum-soaked pussy, his midnight eyes fixed firmly on mine the entire time.

The sound of his fingers fucking my pussy and his moans of bliss as he eats me, combined with the intensity in his eyes, is too much. My breath catches in my throat, and my fingers clutch his silky hair, tugging desperately as pleasure radiates through my whole body.

His fingers continue to plunge in and out of my wetness, and his tongue circles my clit in alternating rough and gentle strokes. The difference in friction is deliciously wicked and driving me wild with desire.

"Oh, fuck, *yes*."

I arch against his mouth, and his eyes become hooded when he groans, "Fuck my face, *bedda mia*. Use me, take what you need."

My eyes roll back as I fist his hair more firmly, and when he plunges a third finger into my soaked core while sucking my clit harshly, my thighs clamp around his head.

"I'm coming, *fuck*, I'm coming."

A fiercely powerful orgasm rips through me, vibrating through every part of my body as fireworks ignite behind my closed eyelids.

I can feel Rafe rise from between my legs and push them apart, and my eyes flutter open, watching as he uses the back of his hand to wipe the evidence of my pleasure from his face.

He fits himself between my thighs, his obsidian gaze piercing me as he takes a shuddery breath. "You're fucking glorious when you come apart for me, *Stellina*." Palming my breast, he kneads the flesh before pinching a pebbled nipple between his thumb and index finger.

I whimper under his attention as he moves to my other

breast while bringing his other hand between my legs to stroke my over-sensitive clit.

"I could watch you shatter all day. Every day for the rest of my life, and it would never be enough. I'll always want *more*."

His strokes get harder, and I gasp when mini tremors shoot through me. His eyes bore into mine, and I feel his dick pulse against my thigh, clearly ready for round two. My eyes widen when he brings himself to my soaked core, and I break eye contact to look down as he notches his throbbing head at my slit.

"Do you have another one in you?" He slides the first couple of inches inside, and despite the two overwhelming orgasms he's given me, my pussy constricts helplessly around his thick length. His desire-laden eyes fill with an erotic delight that only makes my pussy clench more firmly. "Yes, you fucking do, *mia brava ragazza*. Shit, you feel so damn *good*."

He rocks forward sharply, seating himself deep inside my pussy in one thrust, and I arch my neck as I cry out.

"Fuck me deeper, Rafe. Deeper. Harder," I pant as my eyes encompass his gorgeous face, watching as his last vestige of control drains from his features. "Hold nothing back."

With a growl, he grips my wrists, and pins them above my head as he covers my body with his.

I'm tasting his sweet breath when his mouth hovers over mine as he plunges in and out of my pussy, our eyes holding in a connection I couldn't sever even if I wanted to.

"Take me, *Stellina*. All of me. *Take me*, I'm yours." My chest tightens at his words. At the feelings they bring to life within me, and I run my tongue across the seam of his lips, gasping when he covers my mouth with his.

He plunders my mouth, driving my body even higher as I chase the euphoria that's just out of my reach. His grip on my wrists tightens as his forehead creases, and his hips falter when mine rise to meet him, taking him even deeper.

Suddenly, I rip my mouth from his, crying out when he hits that sensitive spot hidden deep inside.

"I love you, Rafe. *Ti amerò per sempre.*"

He takes my mouth in another vicious kiss as my pussy contracts around his dick when a third mind-blowing orgasm tears through me. Rafe follows me over the edge, his pistoning hips stilling when he holds himself as deep as he can reach.

The feeling of his cum painting my insides sends small tremors through my body, extending my orgasm for long moments until both of us are utterly spent.

He leans up to press a gentle kiss to my sweat-sheened brow before pulling back enough to look deep into my eyes.

"Forever and ever, Elodie Rivers." Pressing a hard kiss to my lips, he whispers, "*Per sempre.*"

36

RAFAEL

One Month Later

I press my index finger over my lips, glancing from a grinning Sebastiano to an excitedly bouncing Skye as we round the corner that takes us into the kitchen.

She knows exactly where we're going following her weeklong stay last month before she'd opted to return to Zurich with Sebastiano for the end-of-term festivities.

Elodie hums to herself as she deposits freshly baked cookies onto a wire rack, and I take a moment to absorb that magnetic quality she has that drew me to her from the first.

My sister reaches out a hand to pluck a cookie from the rack, hissing when the heat burns her fingers, and Elodie regards her with a raised eyebrow. "I've told you a million times to *wait*."

Aurelia sinks her teeth into the piping hot treat, blowing air out of her mouth as she mumbles, "Just too good, though."

Sebastiano nudges me with a soft smile, and I nod, assuring

him without words that his older sister is slowly but surely coming back to her old self.

"You can explain to your brother where all the oatmeal raisin cookies went when he gets back—"

"*Surprise!*"

A clearly impatient Skye rushes past me in a blur of pale blonde curls, launching herself at a very shocked Elodie, who wraps her arms around her daughter, eyes blown wide open in delighted surprise.

"Have you missed me, Ellie?"

My chest deflates ever-so slightly when Skye uses her name for Elodie, reminding me how Elodie had decided against telling her daughter the truth of their relationship when she'd first visited last month.

"And do you like it here, Curly Fry?"

Skye turns to Elodie with a bright smile. "Oh, I love it. It's so much better than South Brook."

Her grimace of distaste turns into a frown as she looks at me with fearful eyes. "I don't have to go back there if I don't want to, right?"

I can feel my nostrils flare as absolute hatred for Warren and Cressida Rivers flows through my veins, but I force my lips upward in an indulgent smile. "This is your home now, kid." Her face lights up, easing some of the tension in my chest, and my smile broadens. "We are your family now."

Skye squeals as she claps excitedly, bouncing on the tips of her toes. "Then can I please, please, pretty please with sprinkles on top have the room beside Bastian's?"

All of us share a chuckle as Sebastiano rolls his eyes with a wry grin.

"I'll see what I can do." I shoot Skye a conspiratorial wink, and she curtsies prettily, making everyone laugh out loud.

"But I'll still get to stay in school, right? My friends are so fun, and I don't want to miss the winter semester." Her eyes widen in delight. "There's skiing!"

As I chuckle, my eyes land on a pensive Elodie. She's staring into space with a deep frown on her forehead, and without thought, I'm at her side, urging her to her feet.

"We'll grab some drinks while you guys discuss the winter sports at Andros-Baumann."

Once we make it to the safety of the kitchen, Elodie looks at me with pained eyes. "I can't do it, Rafe. I can't tear her little world apart." Her breath catches on a sob. "Not when she's finally found some stability. I can't..."

I gather my love into my embrace, allowing her to cry in the safe confines of my arms as I try with all my might to take some of her pain away.

It had ultimately been the right decision, and we'll undoubtedly tell her at least some of the truth behind her parentage when the time is right, but for now, Skye's well-being is paramount.

"Curly Fry!" Elodie's eyes fill with tears as she wraps her arms tightly around her little girl. "What a wonderful surprise!"

"I'm home for summer vacation, silly."

Home.

My heart sings as Elodie raises glassy eyes to mine, knowing that a stable home for Skye is something she's longed for since the moment Skye was born.

"And Rafe has a surprise planned—"

I clear my throat, and Skye shoots an apologetic pout my way before she extricates herself from Elodie's hold, coming to take my much larger hand in hers.

Elodie raises a questioning eyebrow as she stands. "A surprise, hmm?"

I exchange a look with Skye, and we both smile before I turn mischievous eyes to Elodie. "You'll find it in our suite."

ELODIE

When I walk down the wide staircase into the foyer, the entire house is devoid of life.

"Hello?"

My single word echoes through the vast space, and I'm left feeling more than a little confused.

When I'd gone to our suite as Rafe instructed, I'd found a beautiful crimson chiffon gown awaiting me. It sat off my shoulders with sheer elbow-length sleeves and hugged my waist before flaring out in layers that fell all the way to the floor.

I'd decided to leave my long hair flowing down my back, and diamond embellished flat sandals completed the look.

"There you are."

Alessio's deep voice from behind me makes me jump, and I twist about, finding him dressed in beige chinos and a white shirt, sleeves rolled up to his forearms, displaying his full-sleeve tattoos. His shoulder-length black hair is tied back at the nape of his neck, and truthfully, he looks the most relaxed he's been in the short time I've known him.

I greet him with a smile before looking around, arms raised in question. "Where *is* everyone?"

Chuckling, he tips his head toward the back of the house. "I'm reasonably sure Rafe is outside. Not sure about everyone else." He tips his head to one side. "I'll search with you if you like."

I nod and fall into step alongside Alessio, keeping up with his brisk pace thanks to the flat sandals Rafe provided.

Our search of the house is fruitless, and when we step out

onto the decking, I begin to walk toward the dock, only to stop short when I notice a wooden arrow jutting up out of the ground. I move closer, finding a note attached, and I read the contents aloud.

"Follow the arrows to find your real surprise."

I look up to a grinning Alessio with an enormous smile of my own before I scan the space for the next arrow, squealing in delight when I spot it almost immediately.

My feet fly across the distance, already searching out the third arrow, which I find easily, and it's the fourth one that brings me to the entrance of the labyrinth. I can hear Alessio chuckling behind me as I race off into the rose-covered hedges, passing three more arrows, but paying no heed, knowing exactly what my destination is.

And when the pavilion comes into sight, my feet grind to a sudden halt as the air is knocked from my lungs. My heart slams against my breastbone as I absorb the wonder before me.

The pavilion is wreathed in sheer white voile and adorned with velvety red roses. Aurelia and Sebastiano are standing on either side of the pavilion steps, and when my eyes travel farther, they light on a grinning Skye sitting prettily in the arms of a shockingly handsome Rafe.

Our gazes meet and hold, and as though magnetized, my feet propel me closer. I vaguely register the sound of *"Moonlight Sonata"* streaming over a nearby speaker as I pass Sebastiano and Aurelia, only stopping when I'm toe to toe with Rafe.

He clucks Skye beneath the chin before setting her onto her feet, and I watch as she dashes off to stand beside Sebastiano, vaguely noting that Alessio finally caught up with me.

When I look back to Rafe, my heart skips a beat when I find him down on one knee, a navy velvet box held out between us.

His heart is in his chocolatey brown eyes, and I can *feel* myself fall even more hopelessly in love with this man.

"I spent two long years in the dark, dreaming of the light that only your star could provide. Holding tight to the hope that *maybe* one day…maybe my wish would come true…"

He trails off, clearing his throat as a ball of emotion lodges itself in mine, making breathing a difficulty.

"And then you did. *We did, Stellina.*"

He pops open the lid of the small navy box, and my eyes fill with tears when I see the exquisite emerald-cut blood-red ruby ring inside.

"The road to get here hasn't been easy." I shift my eyes up to Rafe's intense gaze, and a tear splashes down my cheek, landing on the back of my trembling hand. "And I can't promise that it will be smooth sailing from here on, but I *can* promise you that my heart will beat for you, and *only you* for as long as we both shall live. I *can* promise that I will love you and all of your beautifully broken pieces that make up the other half of my soul throughout eternity. I *can* promise that I will protect you and our family to my dying breath."

He slips the ring out of the box and reaches between us to gently grasp my shaking left hand. His eyes are brimming with one single question as his burning gaze holds mine.

"There could never be another for me, Elodie Rivers. I begin and end with you." I try and fail to stifle a sob of sheer joy when he holds the beautiful ring to the tip of my ring finger on my left hand. "Will you marry me, *Stellina*?"

My answer is a half-gasp, half-sob as I nod frantically, barely managing to whisper, "*Si, si, si. Per sempre*, Rafael. *Sempre e per sempre.*"

He slides the ring home and rises smoothly to capture my lips in a heartfelt kiss, one I feel through my entire body. I'm still dazed when he breaks away, barely registering the cheers from his siblings and Skye until she rushes forward and hugs me around my legs.

Her eyes are shining with happiness when she shifts her gaze from me to Rafe as she bounces up and down. "Can we tell her the surprise now?"

I blink owlishly. "There's *more*?"

My forehead puckers when I look at a grinning Rafe as he calls out, "*Vieni fuori, Padre.*" And my jaw practically unhinges when a smiling priest steps out from the shadows of the pavilion.

A smile grows on my face as my heart sings. He leans closer to press a soft kiss to my smiling lips, and I sigh in absolute contentment as he whispers, "Happy wedding day, almost-wife."

I dust my lips across his. "Happy wedding day, almost-husband."

EPILOGUE
ELODIE

One Year Later

I place the fresh bouquet of red roses on the earth beneath my feet before resting my palm on the gravestone before me.

Emiliano Ribisi.
Beloved Brother. Dear Friend. Human Shield.

As always, when I read that last part, my eyes well with tears, and I brush them away with my free hand, wishing with all my heart that my gentle giant was here to witness the life he selflessly gave to me.

A life I live to the absolute fullest each and every day.

"*Grazie, amico mio.*" I press a kiss to the tips of my fingers and lay them over Sasquatch's name, whispering a prayer beneath my breath before I stand. With one last look at the gravestones of Rafe's family, I turn and leave the small grassy knoll that overlooks the beautiful turquoise waters of the Mediterranean.

As I make my way back toward our house, I turn my face up toward the bright summer sunshine, gratitude filling me from head to toe, and it's when I get within view of the house, my heart fills to overflowing.

In the aftermath of the Conclave and the alliances that were forged, both Rafe and Alessio deemed it was time for Alessio to take his true place at the head of *la famiglia*.

As such, we no longer called the compound our primary residence. That honor belongs to Alessio and his soon-to-be wife, Gabriela Salvatore – a more ill-conceived match I've yet to see, though I pray for Alessio's sake that my intuition is wrong.

Rafe and I had set up home on Isola Rosa a mere month after our wedding, and thanks to his *consigliere* duties being less hands-on, there's rarely been a night I haven't fallen asleep locked in the safety of my husband's warm embrace.

We'd even had a shocked Levi ferried in to visit for close to a month alongside his *boyfriend*, Adriano, shortly after we'd moved here permanently.

An effusive Adriano had thanked me profusely for making it possible for him to find his soulmate. Both men were as infatuated with one another as they had been that first day in Lazise, and my heart sang, knowing my dear friend had also found love in such an unlikely partner.

They visited from time to time, but as Adriano had been assigned to Aurelia's security team, visits were fewer since her wedding.

As I cross the threshold of our *casa*, my heart does a little flip-flop when I hear Rafe's chuckle from farther down the long hallway. I follow the sound, stopping when my eyes light upon my husband leaning over the crib of our three-month-old daughter, Emilia-Rose.

"Who's Papa's best girl, hmm?" he coos down at her enraptured face, her big brown eyes identical to his watching him with a hero-worship akin to my own. "Emilia is, that's who. My Emilia-Rose is Papa's best girl."

RAFAEL

My wife's giggle makes me stand up straight, pinning her with narrowed eyes. "What did you hear?"

She shakes her head, still smiling as she moves closer, sliding an arm around my waist as I tuck her in against my side. "Just how much you love our little girl, Handsome."

I chuckle as I kiss her smooth brow and inhale her sweet fragrance. "I love all three of my girls, *Stellina*. Don't ever doubt that."

Elodie turns wide navy-blue eyes to mine, delight flashing across her perfect features. "Almost summer vacation for Andros-Baumann." Her smile widens. "I can't wait for us all to be under one roof for longer than a handful of nights."

Skye visits often, but her love for her school and friends — not to mention her attachment to Sebastiano — means that she spends most of her time in Zurich. This past spring, Sebastiano turned eighteen, and as such, he'll take over a more prominent role in *la famiglia*, so Elodie is thrilled at the thought of having more precious time with our firstborn.

Emilia starts to whimper, and I immediately scoop her into my arms, ignoring the look on my wife's face when I cradle my little girl against my chest. She quietens instantly, and I shoot Elodie a smug smile.

"You'll spoil her." She arches an eyebrow, and I chuckle, quirking a brow of my own.

"And it's my *choice* to spoil the ones I love."

Elodie sends me a small smile before she saunters from the

room, shooting over her shoulder, "I can't argue with that logic."

Once I've settled Emilia-Rose, I place her back in her crib, press a gentle kiss to her pale blonde head, and follow after my wife, smiling when I find her busying herself in the kitchen.

Wire racks, cake pans, and cupcake tins emerge from cupboards, and I slide up behind her, hugging my arms around her waist with a chuckle. "What's got you stressed out now?"

For a moment, I think she's about to ask me about Aurelia or even Alessio. My wife has formed close bonds with all of my siblings in the months since Conti's death, so I'm not at all expecting the words that come out of Elodie's mouth on a whisper.

"I'm late."

My heart jumps, and I spin her about, the cakepan in her hands clattering to the countertop. Her face is filled with uncertainty as she watches me with stormy eyes, until I palm her cheeks and cover her mouth with mine.

I pour every ounce of love and ardor into the kiss before pulling back with a smile that shines from my eyes. "Another baby?"

She blinks several times before nodding hesitantly. "I—I think so." Then she shakes her head. "But it's too soon. Emilia is still so small, and there's so much going on with *la famiglia*—"

I stop her spiral when I press my index finger over her lips. "And nothing matters aside from the family *we* have made together, *Stellina*."

My eyes flicker between hers as my love for her grows exponentially, and I silently thank whatever divine being brought her into existence before I remove my finger from her lips, dusting mine across them lightly.

"I am yours, and you are mine. And nothing else matters."

Then I close my lips over hers, taking her mouth in a

languid kiss, showing her with actions the truth behind my words.

The truth that has always and will always reside within my heart.

Sempre e per sempre.

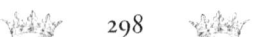

SINFUL SIREN SNEAK PEEK
SANTINO

***unedited and subject to change*ced*

"This alliance has surely worked in your favor, DeMarco."

My fingers tighten around an almost empty tumbler of whisky as Benito Salvatore winks pointedly toward my sire. And despite his nonchalant shrug, I can see the smug gleam of delight in the depths of Cesare's eyes as I toss back the last mouthful, relishing the burn as it goes down.

"It's time to remarry, Salvatore. I've been lonely since Alessandra passed—"

All eyes shift to me when I cut him off with a dark snort. I ignore them, giving them my back when I walk over to the drinks cabinet and lift the decanter of whisky, intent on refilling my tumbler.

Cesare continues like nothing happened, though there's a dangerous edge to his voice that automatically sets me off-kilter. "But even more importantly, Aurelia is young enough to bear me *many* more sons."

There's a buzzing between my ears, and my vision becomes blurred as I unsteadily place the decanter back onto the cabinet. A lump forms in my throat, and I inhale deeply through my nostrils as I clench my jaw so harshly it aches.

Silence reigns supreme until he speaks again. "Not to mention, there's nothing quite like plowing a virgin cunt."

The tumbler in my fist cracks as rage flows through my veins. There's laughter and playful banter at my back, but all I can focus on is the almost overwhelming desire to draw my blade across the throat of the motherfucker who's taken the only thing I've ever wanted.

Before I can act on my thoughts, my feet take me across the room, and I slip out a door that leads me onto a stone-paved *terrazza*. Stars fill the night sky above me, and the only light comes from small lanterns dotting the area, illuminating an enormous pool.

My breathing is as erratic as the heart that pounds against my chest, and I slam my eyes closed, attempting to get ahold of myself.

From the moment Cesare had told me of his deception, I'd known this fucking Conclave bullshit was going to be difficult. But seeing Aurelia Caruso once again, and this time, *knowing* she was to be the wife of Cesare, my despicable father...

"*Minchia!*"

I growl a low expletive and open my eyes, blinking several times in disbelief when I see the same woman step onto the stone paving on the other end of the house.

Aurelia Caruso, the woman who has consumed my thoughts since her formal introduction to *Cosa Nostra* society three years earlier.

Though Cesare had brought me offers of marriage alliance options, I'd always declined despite his ire. I'd refused to let go of the hope that someday Giacomo Caruso would accept the proposal I'd put forward for his daughter's hand.

He never had, and now, she's farther out of reach than ever.

I watch her greedily as she kicks off her heels, picks them

up, and launches them into the pool with a deep frown that mars her beautiful features. Her hands move to her hair, swiftly unpinning it until it flows down her back like a sheet of black satin.

My hands tingle with the urge to run my fingers through those dark locks, and before I realize what I'm doing, I've pushed off the wall and stepped out of the shadows.

My loafers click against the stone, and she pivots to face me, surprise dancing across her face before she replaces it with that aloofness she's displayed all day.

"*Ciao, Principessa.*"

She arches a perfectly arched eyebrow and blinks slowly. "*Ciao.*"

I close the gap between us, my eyes never leaving hers until we're toe to toe, and I tilt my head to one side as I look down on her. Beautiful mahogany eyes framed by long black lashes hold mine as we regard one another in silence for a long beat.

She looks away first, though her eyes return to mine almost instantly. "I never got the chance to th-th-thank you for…"

Her forehead creases when she trails off, and she exhales softly before dropping her chin to her chest. "For saving me from Conti."

My feet close the remaining distance between us as though magnetized, and my hand snakes out between us to gently pinch her chin between my thumb and index finger. She lifts her head, her gaze meeting mine hesitantly, and I nod in silent acknowledgment.

Her sweet scent fills my nostrils, drowning my senses, and I reach out my free hand to run my fingers through her midnight hair.

Eyes like deep pools watch me as she slowly blinks, and my chest physically aches when I finally murmur, "I'd save you every day for the rest of my life for the pleasure of having you look at me the way you are right now."

Her nostrils flare as her eyes fleetingly drop to my lips before meeting mine once more. My gaze deepens intently as I watch her with hungry eyes that eat up every inch of the perfection that she embodies.

"You *need* to stop looking at me that way, Santino."

I blink once, twice, feigning ignorance. "What way is that, *bedda mia*?"

She inhales sharply at the endearment before shaking her head and stepping back. Her chest rises and falls as though she's running a race. When she speaks her words are a bare whisper as her eyes drop to my lips. "Like you want to kiss me."

My jaw tics and her eyes shoot back to mine as I take a step closer. "I want nothing more, Aurelia."

Her breath hitches in her throat, but before she can respond, one of Rafael's *Soldati* rounds the corner.

I slip back into the shadows before he catches sight of me, and when she looks back to where I'd been standing, a frown crosses her brow. I watch for a long beat as she glances about the space before eventually accompanying the *Soldati* back inside.

As I make my way to the quarters I've been given, my thoughts are firmly fixed on Aurelia, and I realize that my obsession with her has become a raging fire with the ability to consume all in its path.

And today…I lit the motherfucking match.

Aurelia and Santino's forbidden mafia romance, Sinful Siren, is releasing this Fall.

ACKNOWLEDGMENTS

Based on word count, Corrupt Crown is the shortest book I've penned to date. However, it's also the one that took me the longest to write. Between researching the subject matter and fleshing out these nuanced characters, I've lived and breathed this story these past five months.

I've had days where I believed writing this book was a complete error in judgment. When I thought everything I'd written was a steaming pile of crap. But now, on the far side of it, I miss the process of telling their story. Of interacting with Rafe and Elodie on the daily.

And I truly hope you can feel my attachment to them (and the side characters) when you read their story!

This story, and everything that I write, wouldn't be possible without the amazing support of my Village.

Adi: There are no words. You know I adore you, and I'll be forever grateful for your support, help, and the beautiful friendship we share!

Aimee, Faith, Katie, and Selena: My amazing Beta readers! Without you, this book would quite possibly be an incoherent mess. You're stuck with me now!!

Danielle and Jen: Your support and encouragement, your feedback and the fact that you put up with me doesn't go unnoticed. Thank you!!

Becky and Vito: My very own Sicilian translating team! Your support, friendship and the time you so generously and selflessly give to me are appreciated more than you know.

Thank you, thank you, thank you!! From the bottom of my heart!!!

<u>Kenzie</u>: My wonderful editor. Working with you is always beautiful, and this time was no exception. I love how you just *got* these guys, and I'm excited for what's to come!!

<u>My Street Team</u>: You guys are amazing. The edits, the tags, the hype – *none* of it goes unnoticed. I truly am so blessed with you guys. Thank you for being in my corner!!

<u>Mom, Dad and Michelle</u>: Thank you for your support and encouragement. Please don't read this one. I love you!

<u>Will, Jamie, Ben, Zach, and Izzy</u>: My five masterpieces. I love you infinity times infinity. *Sempre e per sempre.* You are my world.

<u>James</u>. I love you. It's as simple and as complicated as that. Thank you for helping to make this dream a reality for me. Thank you for always making me laugh until I can't breathe. I couldn't imagine my life without you in it xxx

And finally, to *you*! My reader. Thank you for reading my stories. Without you, this is all just words on paper. I am so grateful to every single person who picks up my books. These stories truly come from my soul.

ALSO BY PAMELA O'ROURKE

SAINTS & SOVEREIGNS

Corrupt Crown

Sinful Siren (coming 2024)

Alessio's Story (coming 2025)

Sebastiano's Story (coming 2025)

THE BROTHERHOOD

Painted Truths

Unwritten Rules

Broken Strings

ROGUES OF MANHATTAN

Rogue Romeo

Rogue Villain

Rogue Knight (coming 2024)

Rogue Angel (coming 2025)

ABOUT THE AUTHOR

Pamela O'Rourke lives in Ireland with her husband, James, and their five young children. Life is hectic, but she wouldn't change a single second of it. She loves sunny days, strong coffee, and daydreaming about her next book boyfriend.

Her books are all available and free to read on Kindle Unlimited.

Come and join my Facebook reader group for a first look at sneak peeks and teasers.
Please note this is a private group, so only other members can see posts and comments.
Pam's Peaches Reader Group